The Tower
of Bones

Frank P. Ryan is a multiple-bestselling author, in the UK and US. His other fiction includes the thrillers *Goodbye Baby Blue* and *Tiger Tiger*. His books have been translated into more than ten different languages. Born in Ireland, he now lives in England. Visit him at www.frankpryan.com

Also by Frank P. Ryan

The Snowmelt River

The Tower
of Bones

Frank P. Ryan

Jo Fletcher
New York • London

JF

Jo Fletcher
New York • London

Copyright © 2012 Frank P. Ryan
First published in the United States by Quercus in 2015

ISBN 978-1-62365-863-2

Library of Congress Control Number: 2015931866

Distributed in the United States and Canada by
Hachette Book Group
1290 Avenue of the Americas
New York, NY 10104

Manufactured in the United States

10 9 8 7 6 5 4 3 2 1

www.quercus.com

For Amy

*Other rumors, equally venerable, tell a different tale—
that long before the age of mortals there was a great
war between the dragons and a brutal race of titans. So
lasting and terrible was this conflict that the bones of the
slain are still scattered over the blighted lands. It is said
that the titans eventually won this war to bring to an end
the Age of Dragons. This ushered in the Age of Tyranny,
when mortals served no purpose other than enslavement,
a tyranny that was ended by the coming of the Arinn.*

If such be true, deliverance surely came with a price.

Ussha De Danaan: last High Architect of Ossierel

Contents

LOST

FROM HER TOWER OF BONES THE WITCH'S SONG
ravished the night. There were no words to the song but
still it managed to convey a terrifying mixture of power
and triumph, flowing far and wide over the blasted
landscape, eliciting echoes here and there among the
wolves attracted to her swamps and marshes. They
howled an answering chorus, gathering about the hill
of the dead, snarling and snapping at one another with
hunger. The Tower was a cyclopean skull, vast as a castle
in its proportions and horned and fanged like some monstrous beast. Within this terrible fastness, in a freezing
dungeon that was only faintly illuminated by a pulsating red light, an emaciated young woman lay face down
against the floor, her hands pressed against her ears, her
auburn hair dank and tangled, mixing with the dust

and spiders' webs. But nothing she did could keep out the dreadful melody.

What was she doing here, in this alien world of continuous nightmare? How long had she been a prisoner of the Witch?

She had no answers to these questions. She had no memory of coming here to the Tower of Bones. She hardly recalled who she was anymore. But now, struggling against the invasion of her mind by the Witch's song, she insisted on remembering her name.

I'm Kate Shaunessy. Kate Shaunessy from the town of Clonmel.

Slowly, through an impassioned effort of will, she recalled snatches of her childhood in the small town in Ireland, with just the Comeragh range of mountains separating it from the Atlantic Ocean. It was a struggle to bring to mind the street names or any clear memory of her home there. Still it comforted her to recall glimpses of the town's meandering streets, the remnants of its ancient walls and the great river that flowed through it, with its three or four limestone bridges . . . and, most precious of all, the names and faces of her friends. Maureen Grimstone . . . Mo . . . Mo and her brother, Mark. And Alan . . . *Alan!*

I couldn't bear it if I lost their names . . .

She recited the small litany again and again. Mo, with her long brown hair and her beautiful hazel eyes. The best friend she had ever had . . . and Mark . . . and Alan . . . Alan, the boy she had fallen in love with, who wasn't from Clonmel, or from England, like Mo and Mark, but from America.

Even now, recalling such things, recalling Alan's name, her heart raced within the half-starved cage of her chest. *Please . . . please! Stop it! Stop stealing my memories. Stop taking everything that matters from me!*

Climbing to her feet, she threw herself bodily against the wall of her cell. She smashed her fists against the hard reverberating surface that looked and felt like bone. She shrieked it aloud: *"I am Kate Shaunessy . . . from . . . from Clonmel!"* She must never forget its name or the . . . the calling. The calling had led them to gather the waters of the three rivers . . . the sisters. *The River!* If she could only clear her mind sufficiently to remember things. The river's name . . . The river that flowed past her garden every day of her life. What was its name?

The Suir—she remembered its name.

She remembered more. All four of them had been seduced into leaving Earth. They had carried the waters of the three sisters to the portal on the mountain of Slievenamon. Through the portal they had arrived, as if by magic, into this alien world of Tír. Their coming here had been for a purpose. They had freed the bear people, the Olhyiu, from slavery in the Arctic wilderness of the Whitestar Mountains. They had sailed the Snowmelt River in the Temple Ship. But that had only been the beginning of why they had been brought here into this alien world . . .

Already her mind was hurting from the effort at remembering. The Witch was invading her being, stealing her mind again. The past seemed so long ago . . . an eternity . . .

With her fingers in her ears to block out the song, she insisted again: *I can't forget . . . I won't forget!*

To memory, unbidden, came a beautiful morning, early, under a summer's sky. Alan was waiting for her. He was astride his bicycle, outside the gates. With a mixture of terror and grief she held tight to that memory, that one brief moment of clarity like an island of wonder in the cloudy seas of her memories.

The memory became overwhelming. The clumsy kiss of the shy, gangly boy—Alan. And how, in that moment, she knew she loved him.

A sound of screaming in the corridor beyond her cell: the clatter of calloused bare feet in the echoing labyrinths of bone. The unmistakable snap of a Garg-tail whip. Faltana was lashing some unfortunate creature. Kate trembled with fright, struggling to recover the precious vision of something so beautiful, but already it had slipped away.

I'm lost, she thought. *I've died and gone to hell—and there's nothing that anybody can do to help me.*

THE NEW KYRA

ACROSS THE THREE-MILE-WIDE ESTUARY OF THE
Snowmelt River, the walled City of Carfon was ghostly
in the half-light of dawn. For Alan Duval the stroll, in
the company of his friend, the dwarf mage Qwenqwo
Cuatzel, offered a brief respite from the despair that
had set, like an iron cage, around his heart. Tall, slim,
almost gaunt in his features, with his thick brown
hair grown a little wild and long, he kept the sea to his
right as he headed in broad sweeping strides toward
the surf.

Carfon! He spoke its name softly, as a man might
speak of a fabled wonder, even when that wonder con-
fronts him in solid stone. Carfon, pearl of the Eastern
Ocean, and the last free city in the entire continent of
Monisle.

No description in words could have prepared him for the reality of this vision. The walls were a vast cliff face of masoned granite, two hundred feet high on their aprons and a quarter as much again atop the towers that studded the battlemented summit, with row upon row of bronze cannons lowering defensively over sea and landscape. Now, leaning on the heavy spear he had been using like a shepherd's staff, its upright blade spirally twisted and warded over its cutting edges with Ogham runes, he stared across the choppy water at this brooding fortification.

Yet for all their impregnable appearance those walls were threatened. There were enemies in this strange and menacing world that would be undaunted by any protection of cannons and stone. Carfon might fall, no matter that such an eventuality was unthinkable. And uppermost in the plans of the enemy, as in his own, was the fact that deep within those ancient walls was the portal to the most powerful force of all, a force so dreadful none dared openly to speak its name.

In his mind Alan whispered that name: the Fáil—a strange and ancient word. Even in whispering it he felt a tingle of its power activate in the ruby triangle embedded in his brow—the Oraculum of the First Power. The tingle spread out, a wave of pins and needles, through his heart and limbs. Such a power could never be allowed to fall into evil hands, or the consequences would be too dreadful to contemplate. Alan knew that much about it although he knew little to nothing of its true nature, or for that matter the dangers it might pose to him and his purpose. But now he was this close to it he had no choice but to confront the Fáil.

He took a deep breath, exhaled it slowly.

He couldn't help but reflect on the fact that he had lost two of the three friends who had been summoned with him to this strange and dangerous world. Thank goodness Mo was safe, sleeping within the protection of the Olhyiu and Shee, whose tents and campfires covered several acres of beach behind him. The very thought was a reminder of the strangeness of this world. The Shee were descended from great cats and the Olhyiu were descended from bears. But as to his friend Mark—heck, he didn't really know where Mark was anymore. Mark had saved their lives during the battle for Ossierel. But he had paid a terrible price for doing so. For all Alan knew his friend might be dead. Mark's body had disappeared from the Rath at the top of the tor. Alan had witnessed the extraordinary change in the statue of the dark Queen, Nantosueta, who now appeared to be locked in an embrace with the figure of Mark. And in his brow Mark bore the same triangle of power as Nantosueta—the Third Power, the Power of Death. The memory caused Alan to hesitate in his stride. He didn't know how to come to terms with what had happened to Mark. It was a problem that wouldn't go away. And yet he had no choice but to put it to one side for the moment, such was his anxiety about Kate. Thoughts of Kate, the girl he loved, had preoccupied every distracted moment of his life since she had been abducted by the repulsive bat-like warriors, the Gargs, during the battle. The Gargs had clearly been in league with the Great Witch. They had carried Kate across the Eastern Ocean to the Tower of Bones. Of the four friends only Alan and Mo had stayed together. Mo had also been terribly injured, an injury to the spirit that she was only slowly recovering from. Meanwhile the abduction of Kate, the thought that he might have lost her altogether, provoked a rising nausea.

Qwenqwo, the dwarf mage of an extinct warrior people, the Fir Bolg, waited patiently while Alan recovered his composure sufficiently to walk on again.

The beach itself was serenely beautiful, an oasis of fine white sand set between sea-worn rocky outcrops. Broad-canopied trees, their foliage as delicate as puffs of olive-green smoke, decorated the undulating sand, the focus of tiny blue-winged birds that hesitated and darted among the branches. Inhaling the briny air, he might be strolling the seashore of some warmer part of his native Earth had it not been for the alien appearance of the two women who watched him from a low headland, perhaps fifty yards away.

A warning, sudden and fierce, cut through his musing.

Halt!

Alan stopped walking, a warning hand on Qwenqwo's shoulder, arrested by the force of the command.

Take not another step!

The command was nonverbal but it invaded his mind with irresistible force through the oraculum. He stood barefoot in the sand, his path, and that of his companion, a wandering trail of prints over the virginal white surface—it had been the inviting prospect of this that had tempted him to remove his seal-skin boots, which he had strung by their leather thongs around his neck. He turned his head to stare at the two women, the taller one in particular. It was she who had issued the warning. But now that he was still, she made no further attempt at communication. *Leaving it to* me, he thought.

Something about the sand.

He gazed ahead at the region immediately in front of him, the place he was about to step into . . .

"What is it, Mage Lord?" Qwenqwo's right hand had crested his shoulder and it rested on the hilt of the double-bladed Fir Bolg battleaxe that straddled his back.

"The Kyra has sent me a warning."

Alan planted the spear in the sand before going down on his haunches and studying the beach in front of him, angling his face to its apparently innocent surface. An offshore breeze played over the surface, blowing sand grains against his cheeks. He saw nothing suspicious, just a few fragments of shell glittering with a mother-of-pearl opalescence. But as he searched harder the ruby triangle in his brow came alive, an inner matrix pulsating with complex whorls and arabesques of light. What his eyes could not see, his enhanced mind quickly detected. There was something there . . . a series of ultra-fine hairs protruding through the smooth white surface. Returning to his feet he retrieved the spear, then poked the blade among the protruding hairs. Four gigantic jaws erupted from the sand. At their center was a maw big enough to swallow his leg, stinking of meaty digestive juices, and with the jaws lined with concentric rows of teeth.

"What demon is this?"

"A hungry one, Qwenqwo—probably detected the vibration of our feet!"

The jaws closed with a violent snap before withdrawing into their den in the sand.

Alan stood back and lifted his gaze to stare at the giantess who still watched him, expressionless, from the headland about forty yards away. He lifted his open hand in a gesture of thanks.

On the headland, which offered a vantage over the entire estuary, the shorter of the two women spoke to her companion.

"You do not respond to his wave?"

The speaker, Milish Essyne Xhosa, Princess of Laàsa and unofficial stateswoman of the Council-in-Exile, was herself a statuesque six feet tall, yet she was dwarfed by her companion.

There was a flattened oval disk? of a pearly smooth material in the center of the giantess's brow, the mark of a Kyra, hereditary leadership of the Shee, and known as the Oraculum of Bree.

The Ambassador placed a tentative hand on the young Kyra's naked shoulder, decorated with a tattoo of naturalistic shapes and forms.

The Kyra shook her tawny head, returning the young man's acknowledgment with a frown. She growled, low in her throat. "There is much I do not understand—or trust—in him."

The giantess's hair was coiled into a braid clasped to her left shoulder. Thick and luxuriant, it would have passed for normal on Earth. But there the comparison ended. No woman on Earth sported those side extensions, which grew down from her temples as ivory-colored sideburns, any more than those symmetrical markings, like large brown freckles, that decorated the downy skin over her face. The Kyra's snow tigress inheritance was all too evident in her size and facial markings, as in the glacial blue of her eyes, the upper lids padded, so they readily closed to slits. The same brown marbling bisected the ash-blond down in two widening tracks, with stripes splaying out to either side and dappling her cheeks. Her oval crystal, like the ruby triangle in Alan's brow, pulsated with an inner matrix of power.

The Ambassador spoke again. "The recent death of your mother-sister has placed you at a disadvantage when it comes to understanding the young Mage Lord."

"My mother-sister departed the Guhttan heartlands without the opportunity to exchange memories. My legacy has not been confirmed."

Milish nodded, understanding what a bitter blow this must have been. The Shee, with their great cat ancestry, did not reproduce in the normal way. There were no males. The mother-sisters gave birth to identical daughter-sisters. And it was essential to the Kyral inheritance that the mother-sister should confer her acquired wisdom and experiences on the daughter-sister with her coming of age. "If he appears distant or distracted it is through grief at the loss of his beloved companion, Kate." Milish continued to watch the young man, her luminous eyes the speckled brown of tortoise-shell. Her voice remained soft, a measured contralto: "In time you will come to understand why your mother-sister trusted him like no other."

"Perhaps."

Ainé was the daughter-sister of the recently dead Kyra in a lineage that stretched back into the mists of history. She was too shocked by the situation she encountered here to be free with gestures of friendship. And none was more puzzling than this youth, Alan Duval, who bore the Oraculum of the First Power of the Holy Trídédana. A callow youth, yet her mother-sister had trusted him like no other? She was obliged to take the word of her companion on that. Milish had been her mother-sister's mentor in perilous times leading to a battle that had already entered legend. And if such legend were to be believed, this youth had stood shoulder to shoulder with the former Kyra in the thick of that battle. Out there, in the estuary, floated the strangest ship she had ever seen. People spoke of it with awe as the Temple Ship. All this the young Kyra knew. But knowing was not understanding. The warrior race of Shee, under her hereditary command, was exclusively female, as was the Council-in-Exile here in Carfon. Theirs was the honor and burden of protecting continental Monisle from the evil that beset it.

She spoke brusquely, a whispered growl: "Nothing in my education by Seers and Aides reveals why such power has been granted to a youth, and an alien youth at that, who has arrived in Tír from another world."

"Appearances are deceptive. The Mage Lord lost his youth at Ossierel. You would be advised to treat him as a man."

The Kyra snorted.

Most disturbing of all, her mother-sister had died without a Seer present, and thus without the opportunity of transferring her memories to her successor. With a sweep of her arm the Kyra drew her cloak about her shoulders. It was loose-fitting over a tough leathery jerkin fastened high about her neck and falling halfway over her pants of pale green, which fastened at midcalf above the cross-lacing over her thin-soled boots. Immediately the enfolding cloak took on the camouflage colors and patterns of the surrounding rocks and sand, so the young Kyra became close to invisible, and yet all the while she continued to watch the young man.

The dwarf mage turned his gaze on the ancient walls, which appeared more substantial and awesome by the minute as the rising sun invaded the estuary from the horizon of the glittering ocean. "I see from your expression that you worry still about the silence from the Council-in-Exile."

"We've already wasted six days here, waiting for these people to agree to a meeting. Meanwhile Kate is suffering at the hands of that terrible creature."

"Mage Lord . . ."

"Alan!"

"Alan—my friend. Though patience is trying in such circumstances, never has it been more necessary. The Councilwoman, Milish, has warned you that Carfon has ever been a city of intrigues."

He shook his head. "You know I find this formality a waste of time. I just don't care about appearances."

"Here, above all, appearances matter. Carfon is a city under threat. Soon it may be under siege. Though the Tyrant's armies have been repulsed from the Vale of Tazan, they may yet attack, in great numbers, from the sea. The Council-in-Exile has its own worries. To them you will appear no more than a distraction."

"Meanwhile we lose another day."

"My friend—when I was a child at my mother's knee, she taught me how to play a board game called 'Strategies'. The aim of play was to win a great prize, a victory of victories. But to obtain that final victory I had to learn not merely the rules of play, but also the importance of planning and patience. From what you have told me of your dreams, Kate is being held in the Tower of Bones. And her gaoler is none other than the Great Witch, also known as Olc."

"I don't know a damned thing about witches."

"It was Olc who sent the succubus that ensnared your friend Mark. It would appear that she understands the need for strategy and patience. Her game set in train the series of events that seduced him and ultimately led him to his present fate. And it is another of her games that torments you through the capture of Kate."

"I'm not afraid of her, Qwenqwo."

"Fear her you should! You fought bravely against the Legun at Ossierel. But the Great Witch is far more powerful than a Legun. She is second in power only to the Tyrant himself. Were you to rush headlong into such a confrontation, you would lose. And what then would become of Kate?"

Alan sighed. "I just can't bear to think of how Kate is suffering."

The dwarf mage shrugged.

"Hey—I know your advice makes sense. But I'm convinced in my own mind that the answer to my problem

lies with the Fáil. We both know that there's a portal to
the Fáil right here in Carfon. I've got to find the portal
and use it to help rescue Kate."

The dwarf mage shook his head. "Even if you persist
in this course you must persuade the Council-in-Exile to
grant you access to the portal. And they have refused
to meet with you, despite Milish's protestations."

The Ambassador, Milish, gazed beyond the estuary to the soaring walls of Carfon, where Prince Ebrit
had offered them quarters in his palace on their
arrival. But courtesy in Carfon was barbed with subtle
obligations—not to mention dangers. The palace, more
than two thousand years old and a labyrinth of hidden
passages and spy holes, offered poor protection. And
so, politely, she had declined the Prince's offer. In the
meantime the new Kyra had arrived to take command
of the encampment of Shee on this side of the estuary.
In the six days since their arrival it had mushroomed to
cover a square mile of hinterland above the beach, with
sentries posted by Bétaald, the dark-skinned spiritual
leader of the Shee, herself not yet fully recovered from
wounds received during the battle in the Vale of Tazan.

Milish was aware of a stiffening in the posture of the
Kyra. In the Oraculum of Bree she observed a heightened flickering. At the same moment a tiny bat-like
creature erupted from the beach below them, close to
the walking figures.

"What is it?"

"A snooper," Milish declared. In a blur of movement, the dwarf mage's arm reached back behind his left shoulder and in a flowing arc of movement the double-headed ax was in his right hand. But Alan reached out to block the dwarf mage's purpose.

"Why does the Mage Lord hold the weapon back?" the Kyra asked.

"To spy, a snooper must need a communicating brain—for it accommodates no more than a tiny mind. My guess is that he wishes to follow where that tiny mind will lead him."

The Kyra followed the flight of the snooper until it passed through a crevice-like window in the city walls. From there, her eyes returned to the youth, whose attention had also followed the flight of the snooper. The movements caused the thick braid of her hair to strain against the silver clasp that tied it down onto her left shoulder.

"The snooper has reported to a spy in the walls opposite. From what you've told me about this city we can anticipate spies aplenty."

A frown creased the Ambassador's patrician face. She couldn't help but be concerned at the thought of somebody spying on them. With her striking beauty and regal manners and posture Milish would have commanded attention in any world. Her hair was a lustrous blue-black, the thick strands parted centrally over her forehead and falling down in careful bundles over her temples, with folds that hid the upper third of her fleshy lobed ears. On Earth, with her hair and coppery complexion, she might have been taken for an Asian noblewoman.

The Kyra pressed her: "Would your instincts suggest that such a spy works for the Council-in-Exile?"

"It's one possibility."

The Ambassador shivered as the offshore breeze blew a tuft of hair loose from her plume of ornamental silver, the liberated hair gamboling over her fine intelligent features.

A Song of Innocence

"OUT—EARTHSPAWN!"

Faltana's figure filled the open door to Kate's cell. The face of the chief succubus was like that of a porcelain doll, but with pallid blue eyes as cold as a snake's. Her rosebud lips were tensed into a purse-string, drawn back over ivory fangs that had turned blue-black and hoary with age.

"Your attendance is commanded!"

Faltana was spare with her flicks of Garg-tail, but cruelly accurate. The scaly whip, as wiry as steel and barbed at its end, raised a bloody welt on Kate's thin neck, just below the angle of her jaw. Pain seared through her, sharp and sickening. She had to clench her fists to keep the scream from her lips. Faltana fed

on such expressions of pain. To scream would provoke
more attention.

"Dung-eating wormchild!"

Faltana gauged the precise moment when the pain had
subsided to bearable levels to lash out again, raising a second welt, after which those doll's eyes studied the effect, as
if relishing Kate's inner struggle to contain her anguish. It
took all of her determination to rein back the tears.

"My mistress is impatient. Do not keep her waiting."

With an occasional crack of her whip Faltana drove
Kate before her, shambling and twisting through the
organic warren of passageways that formed the interior of the Tower of Bones, with its rancid smells and
echoes of pain. In her mind, as always, Kate whispered
the mantra remembered from the school yard of childhood. *Sticks and stones may break my bones! Sticks and
stones may break my bones!* She no longer remembered
what it had meant to her as a child, only that she had
injected it with new meaning here. Let Faltana tear her
skin. Let her humiliate her with words but she would
never break her will. So, driven through the labyrinths
of nightmare, she clung on to tiny comforts, using them
to blot out the terror and pain.

"Soon," Faltana's pointed red tongue licked her fangs
in exultation, "there will be feasting and celebration.
The Ugly Ones have captured a singer."

Kate was overwhelmed with horror: the Ugly Ones
were the horrid bat creatures. And the singer they had
captured must be a Cill child.

"Make haste!"

Faltana had driven her into the great chamber of the skull, opposite the pit that fell away into darkness. The chamber was filled with a choir of succubi who were crooning and writhing their bodies in concert with the Witch's melody of triumph. Faltana brought the Garg-tail whip across the backs of Kate's calves, causing her to pitch forward onto the bleached bone floor. Pain seared through the nerves of both her legs, from her hips right down to her toes. She gasped, feeling her muscles jerk and spasm, with the poisonous sting of the tiny barbs that added venom to the whip.

"On your knees from here!"

Witches! Succubi! It was madness. It was impossible—a nightmare she would wake up from, and, as she had always woken from nightmares, she would go to the barn-like bathroom in her uncle's house and douse her face in cold water over the big old-fashioned white porcelain sink. But Kate saw no hint of normality. And that meant that somehow the nightmare was more real than any memory of the echoing bathroom, with its brass plugs and cast-iron fittings, more real than her memory of her dog, Darkie—friendly, loving Darkie, who must have been really missing her. A nightmare shouldn't go on like this, for day after day. A nightmare shouldn't feel this real. A nightmare wasn't filled with such pain and fear and loneliness . . .

Faltana grabbed hold of Kate's hair and jerked her head around so she had to watch what was happening.

It took all of Kate's faltering reserves of willpower not to shriek in terror.

Gargs! There were seven or eight of them, forming a semicircle in the chamber, their folded wings merging with the deep purple shadows that jerked fitfully over the vault of fossilized bone that made up the ceiling. The Gargs were hugely tall and skeletally thin, their bat-like heads peering down at her and their oily skins reflecting the red glow that permeated the chamber from deeper underground. Faltana had told her that it was Gargs like these that had captured her and flown her here, in some perverted homage to the Witch. And there at the center of the semicircle, bound and venom-dazed on the bone-scattered floor, she saw their captive.

The Cill looked very young, a boy of perhaps seven or eight years, completely naked, and bound into a ball, his body twitching and trembling. Kate was trembling herself, her teeth chattering. She didn't know why Faltana had brought her here. She didn't want to see what they were doing to the boy. It grieved her that she couldn't do anything to help him. But she couldn't just watch and let them do it.

"Let him go, you . . . you monsters!"

Faltana twisted the fistful of Kate's hair so hard it tore at her scalp. She forced Kate's head down and around on her neck until her eyes were only a few feet away from the Cill. "Since you are so interested, you should relish the sight. A Cill so young, it is rarer even than your insolent self. See how its flesh is now diaphanous with fear! Why, it is no more substantial than a puff of smoke. But sever those bonds and it would shift color and form so fast the eye could not follow. It would become part of this chamber, invisible to every watchful sense." Faltana laughed. "Is that what you want to see happen? You would help it to flee?"

"Why do you so delight in hurting him?"

Faltana yanked so hard on Kate's hair that clumps tore from her scalp and a trickle of blood ran down over her face. "Why—but for the pleasure of hearing it sing!"

At this the company of Gargs laughed with their strange throaty gurgles in tune with Faltana.

The Cill were said to be very brave. The older Cill could maintain a stubborn silence even when they were being whipped and tormented to death. But Faltana knew how they could be made to sing. In death a Cill lamented the passing of its soul spirit with the strangest, sweetest song. Kate couldn't bear to think how this child would discover his beautiful voice. He would shrill his death song. All this Kate knew because Faltana had exulted in telling her about it, again and again. The young Cill were prized above all others because they sang so plaintively before they were eaten. Kate had never heard a Cill sing but she had suffered nightmares of imagining those songs of innocence. Of witnessing what she knew would come afterward. The shrieks of glee that would accompany the devouring. The stink of blood and the crunching of bones as the succubi fed like ravens on whatever remained. Faltana had gloated over every detail, how they would lick every last drop of blood from the floor and then gnaw for days on the juicy bones. She took command, addressing the Gargs:

"It must be unbound, in the position of supplication. Take care it does not shape-shift and flee. No shedding of blood—that honor is mine. First take a firm hold of its throat, so tight it can barely breathe. Only then cut its bonds!"

The choir of succubi sang, melodious and vile. At Faltana's demand, a Garg took the Cill by its throat, then a claw extended from the bent wing joint of another, from which a venomed blade, as long as a dagger, slit through the thong that tied the Cill's ankles to his wrists. Kate tried to avert her face. She was gagging from the stink of the Gargs' oily secretions, which grew more copious and rank with their increasing excitement. When their leader spoke, it was through slits in the leathery skin high up in its neck, its voice emerging as a warbling hiss.

"Are we to be honored with the presence of the Great One?"

Faltana rocked from one foot to another, her quivering bulk preening like some love-sick girl: "Yes—*oh, yes*! My mistress is pleased with this gift. She will conduct the sacrifice in person. But first I must prepare the offering."'

High-pitched cattish squeals and cries emerged from the gaping mouths of the succubi, as their singing became distracted by Faltana's tormenting the Cill with precise flicks and lashes of the Garg-tail whip, circling his body with padding twists and turns of her figure on feet that seemed obscenely dainty and delicate, in a parody of a dance of joy. It was a belief amongst the succubi that the fully mature Cill had, through their ability to change form and color, perfected the art of resisting pain. No extreme of torture could make them sing. Only the younger Cill could be made to sing, and the death song of a Cill child was prized as the highest delicacy by their mistress. Olc did not sacrifice children because she was merely hungry for their flesh. She devoured them because she coveted their spirits. This sacrifice would devour the child's very soul, and the strange, sweet death song would adorn her act of spiritual plunder.

Alan paused in his stroll to allow Qwenqwo to reattach the heavy bronze battleaxe with its twin-curved blades to its harness at his back.

"The snooper?" the dwarf mage asked.

"It flew directly to the Prince's adviser, Feltzvan."

"You're sure of this?"

"I'm sure."

A week earlier their arrival into Carfon had been welcomed by a barque of state. On board the barque, Alan's hand had been taken by a short, corpulent man with a deeply pockmarked face and brown eyes as hard as glass. When he spoke his voice had been curiously soft and as high-pitched as a girl's.

"Permit me to introduce myself. I am Feltzvan, emissary of Prince Ebrit, Elector of Carfon. You are most welcome to this beleaguered city. Be comforted that you are now among friends."

Nodding his thanks, there was little opportunity for Alan to speak more than a word or two in reply, since he found himself being greeted by so many dignitaries at once. Within minutes the powerful oars had taken them across the estuary and through the Harbor Gate to enter the docking area, where they were welcomed by a band of musicians, adding a brassy medley to the cheers and general din.

Alan kept his focus clear, scanning the crowds for the bent old woman who had issued a warning, mind-to-mind on their arrival. But there was no sign of her now among these welcoming crowds.

"The Prince Elector," whispered Milish, during a lull in her manifold introductions to people, "is not among them. He's the head of the most duplicitous of noble families, the Ebrits of Werewe. It will be interesting to see who greets you at the Water Palace. Keep alert in your conversations, even the most trivial. Trust no one, least of all those who seem most welcoming."

Alan nodded. "Are you in danger, Milish?"

"The Family of Xhosa have suffered hard times through the prejudicial influence of the Elector, Ebrit, in our affairs." But she would say no more, not wishing to spoil the joy of their welcome.

Alan, Qwenqwo, Mo and Milish had been invited to a civic reception in the Elector's palace, where Alan had been introduced to Prince Ebrit himself. While Milish went down onto one knee before the Prince, Alan had refused to genuflect or bow. Ebrit smiled wanly, but he gripped Alan's proferred hand in a two-handed clasp, his brown eyes gazing with frank curiosity into Alan's own.

"I mean you no disrespect, Sir—but in the country I come from nobody genuflects or bows before anybody else."

"Are there no princes in your world?"

"Not in my country."

"Ah!" The Prince regarded him with a cool amusement for a moment before affecting to bow himself. "Yet, if the rumors are true, you led a motley gathering of forces in the destruction of an entire army of Death Legion in the Vale of Tazan. And you defeated a Legun incarnate!"

"Sir—if I can speak bluntly. Ossierel was just one battle. The war continues. And we desperately need your help."

"As, equally desperately, do we need yours. Come!" The Prince turned to beckon all of the company. "A banquet is waiting, during which I hope to learn all about you and your adventures."

The Prince had shown himself a master of polite conversation all through the dinner—a feast Alan had little stomach for yet felt obliged to partake in—and his obligation continued into the music, dancing and acrobatic entertainment that followed in a gilded hall, under murals of royal hunting scenes. Ebrit had acknowledged the dangers facing his city from the army of the Tyrant, but it was clear that he also thought himself prepared for any siege. Having seen what the Tyrant's armies could do, Alan disagreed with Ebrit.

"Sir—if all you are prepared to do is get ready for a siege, the Tyrant will win. The way I see it, there's only one way to beat him. We have to take him on in his home ground and finish him once and for all."

Prince Ebrit had barked a short laugh. He made no attempt to hide his skepticism. "And how, might I ask, would you go about such a feat?"

"The Tyrant has opened one of the portals to the Fáil. Already he has begun to subvert it to his purpose. That leaves me no choice but to confront the Fáil myself."

Ebrit had stared at Alan, his eyes wide with shock, and he had placed his hand firmly on his shoulder, bringing his lips close to Alan's ear and reducing his voice to the most intimate of whispers. "Be warned, young man! I most earnestly beg you. What you contemplate is foolish even beyond your wildest imagining. As one who would be your friend and ally, I would counsel you to put this perilous course of action out of your mind."

* * *

Recalling that conversation with the Elector, Alan shook his head, staring out into the incoming tide that that broke, thunderously and violently, against the sandstone rocks on the oceanic lip of the estuary.

If only Kate were here beside him. If only he could put his arms around her and hug her to him and take strength from their love for each other. But the Gargs had carried her far from here, to that dreadful place across that glittering ocean.

A sudden sense of despair made his heart falter.

"What is it, Mage Lord?"

"Kate is hurt—in danger."

"How do you know this?"

"I feel it, Qwenqwo!" His voice had fallen to a groan, his hand reaching up almost to touch the flaring oraculum.

Staring out into the sunrise, despair overwhelmed him. He felt her loss as a wound in his heart that would never heal until he had her back or he died in the attempt. He didn't care about the warnings of Milish or the Elector. He would face whatever danger the Fáil would bring if there was a chance it would free Kate into his arms.

In his passion, the oraculum pulsed suddenly, fiercely:

Kate! I'll keep my promise. I'm coming for you!

On the promontory the violent flash of power startled even the young Kyra, causing her eyes to widen and the

Oraculum of Bree burst into flame, even as the rocks beneath her feet appeared to quake.

"By the Holy Trídédana!" muttered Milish, who had to be supported by the left arm of the giantess. "How his power has matured since Ossierel!"

The Kyra stared at the alien youth, who brought the fingers of his right hand to his lips, as if blowing a kiss. The eruption of power condensed to a tiny star of pure energy, emerging from his brow like a bolt of lightning. The Kyra's eyes followed the razor-line trajectory of its flight, from the figure standing before the ocean to cross the horizon in what seemed less than a moment.

"I think," she purred dryly, "the Council-in-Exile will see him now."

FEED THE BEAST

A HESITATION IN THE CHANTING OF THE SUCCUBI raised the hackles on the back of Kate's neck. The Witch was here. Purplish-gray tentacles, like a dense heavy vapor, oozed from the cracks and fissures in the ivory-yellow walls, extending into the chamber from all sides to encircle the tiny trembling figure. Witch's fingers! That was how Kate thought about them. They crept everywhere throughout the Tower of Bones, and far beyond, in deepest night, searching for prey throughout the ravaged landscape beyond.

The succubi choir started up again, though now some of the voices were themselves quavering. Already the sense of malice was overwhelming. The twin scents of blood and terror were attracting more and more of the livid vapor trails. Olc was sniffing . . . feeling . . . tasting . . .

Two great eyes appeared in the whirling vapors, eyes blood-red and multifaceted as a fly's.

Faltana waved away the Garg, who released the Cill's throat. There was no longer any need to stop the Cill escaping. The scored and bleeding figure was surrounded by the Witch's tentacles, the focus of those terrible eyes. Kate gazed, astonished, at the hands of the Cill, which covered his face. The fingers were stubby and nail-less, and between the fingers she saw crescents of flesh—his hands, and his feet, now she looked down at them, were webbed. As those hands were torn from his face, his eyes blinked open and Kate saw their startling turquoise color. The succubi fell to their knees on the chamber floor, beating the ground with their wide-splayed hands and chanting, in awe and rising terror themselves:

"Feed the Beast! Feed the Beast! Feed the Beast!"

Kate had heard them refer to "the Beast" before, without understanding what they really meant. Surely they were not referring disrespectfully to their mistress? The Gargs had stopped whispering among themselves and were standing stiffly erect, their eyes reflecting the blood-red light that permeated the chamber—as if even their relish was now muted by fear, as with liquid hisses of excitement and a flush-like darkening of their naked skins, they awaited the cruel conclusion of the spectacle.

But the boy Cill would not sing easily. Already his waif-like body was changing hues madly, his instincts for the colors and patterns that would offer the camouflage of invisibility. But there was no escape here.

On their perilous journey sailing the Snowmelt River, the Great Witch had sent one of her succubi to seduce Kate's friend, Mark, into betraying them. Brave Mark had fought back against the power of the succubus. But the struggle had injured him, robbing him of his confidence and forcing him to question his loyalty to his friends. Kate hated the Witch for that. And now, in spite of her own terror, she watched for the slightest opportunity to thwart her.

If only she could divert the Witch's attention from the Cill, to free him even for the briefest moment from that horrible focus!

But what could she do? The consequence of provoking the Witch in the act of consummating her hunger terrified Kate.

Yet such was her terror it alerted all her senses. There was something at the back of her mind, a memory prickling through her terror. Alan's power, the ruby triangle in his brow, had been conferred on him by a strange old woman—Granny Dew. And Mo had called Granny Dew the Earth Mother. Granny Dew had given Kate a lesser power in the shape of an egg-shaped crystal.

Kate tried her best to remember the circumstances when Granny Dew had given her the crystal. But no clear memory would come to mind.

34   **Frank P. Ryan**

A feeling of hopelessness invaded Kate's heart. The Cill child was losing its resistance. Faltana's lashing was wearing it down so it was about to sing.

Please—just let me remember!

In the palm of her right hand she felt a throbbing sensation, a familiar distraction—the power given to her by Granny Dew. She recalled the extraordinary experience, it seemed so very long ago now, when, at the center of a labyrinth of caves, Granny Dew had led Kate and her friends into a chamber whose walls shone and glittered. Here, Granny Dew had changed Kate's cell phone into a beautiful egg-shaped crystal, a soft luminescent green in color and alive with shades of gold, like autumn leaves caught up in the whirls and eddies of the wind. Kate had lost her crystal—she didn't recall how. But now she also recalled that there had been some magical union of the crystal with her body and mind. The same patterns of living color had appeared in the palm of her right hand. The crystal had changed her—as the crystals had somehow changed Alan and Mark. They had enabled them to make contact mind-to-mind not only with each other but also with the Olhyiu and anybody else they met in this world.

Falteringly, tremblingly, Kate reached out now through her mind and attempted to make contact, mind-to-mind, with the Cill child. Was she imagining it, or was there a tiny response, a movement of his head toward her, a slow blink of his eyelids, which was followed by a strange contraction and then widening of the turquoise irises?

He had sensed something. But it wasn't enough.

The Cill appeared to have erected some kind of protective mental shield. If only she could penetrate the shield she might be able somehow to make real contact and help him escape. It was a very slight hope, but it was the only hope she could think of, and at least she was determined to try.

On her knees, with her hair still clutched in the fist of Faltana, Kate clenched her eyes shut, and she pressed every ounce of concentration into trying again.

This time she felt a flicker of contact. When she opened her eyes, she saw how his head swiveled to look at her. He was gazing over at her with inquiring eyes.

Yes, she urged, *we can talk, mind-to-mind!*

His eyes beheld hers, imploringly

She pressed the thought to him: *I'm a prisoner too.*

She just knew he understood her. Why—oh why— would he not answer?

She tried again: *You mustn't sing. Don't give in to them. If you sing, the Beast thing will devour you.*

His head fell. She could see that his courage was failing.

Hold on, even a few more moments. I'm trying my best to help you.

His eyes closed, as if at the impossibility of the thought.

I'm going to distract them. If I can distract the Witch, even for a second, you might just have a chance.

Kate shrieked inside, as the agony of Faltana's whip descended onto the back of her neck. The chief succubus had not missed the swivel of the Cill's head, nor the look Kate had received from those tormented eyes as they found a natural ally. But Faltana's attention was distracted by what was emerging from the central pit, where a glow, like molten lava, was creeping over the lip of gnarled and pitted bone.

Kate was cast aside as Faltana flung out her arms to either side of her quivering chest. Her voice shrieked in ecstasy:

"See my Beauty—my beloved Mistress! See how, in homage to your power, the Beast is rising!"

Kate sickened at the sulfurous smell, like burning hair, that was rising out of the pit. She despaired of finding any way of helping the Cill in time. Yet still she implored him to take heed of her advice: *Don't sing— whatever you do, please don't let them make you sing!*

A premonitory keening, high-pitched, like the melodious sigh of a tormented soul, burst upon Kate's eardrums.

No! She implored the child.

But how could he resist any longer, as a lurid furnace of power was rising out of the pit and filling the air with dark energy. Deformed shapes whirled and spiraled within it. Hisses and sighs of expectation filled the chamber as the succubi and Gargs prostrated themselves against the bony floor. The ground trembled in the proximity to such power—a power battening on to terror, pain and blood. Kate shook with fright, dropping her head and squeezing her eyes shut.

Faltana had boasted more than once that it had been the genius of Olc to have discovered the monstrous skeleton entombed in stone that was the remains of Fangorath, a legacy so obdurate and terrible it had survived from a time when darkness and light had fought for dominion over the world. A spark of that malice lingered here still, in the fossilized bones—a legacy of malice that Olc nurtured for her own scheming. She had chosen this blasted wilderness because it was the festering graveyard of a terrible battle that had involved creatures of magic. The witch tentacles that crept out into the landscape were searching for the soul spirits of these inhuman dead. In the residual malice that lay encased within the Tower of Bones, she had fastened on the most terrible of them all, Fangorath, whose soul spirit needed to batten on terror if it was to be resurrected to do the Witch's bidding.

The frail body of the Cill child was outlined, trembling, against the pulsating red glow of the moiling furnace. In his nakedness, Kate saw that his slender body was devoid of breasts, his skin covered in gossamerthin scales that reflected the red light with a curious luminescence. In the extreme of his terror, two fanlike structures opened out on either side of his small rounded head, like petals of lacy fronds three times the circumference of his head, sheening through a kaleido-scope of colors. Kate stared at them in astonishment. But there was no time to wonder what they might be. At the lip of the pit, she glimpsed Olc herself, a gigantic wraith-like face, bowing in homage before the horror that was spilling out into the chamber, the soul spirit of the titan, Fangorath, re-emerging into the fossilized cavity of what had formerly been its skull.

Kate wept with fright.

The chamber warped and crackled with the expand-ing power. As the Witch herself manifested in carnal form, the air was filled with the carrion stench of her monstrous breath. Kate heard the pattering of claws on bone as the Gargs edged backward, panic overcoming curiosity. Even the succubi had stopped their chanting. The silence was invaded by a thunderous clicking and clacking. Retching with horror, Kate realized that it was the sound of Olc's own jaws, mounted sideways, like the gorging mouth of a praying mantis.

The Cill child began to sing; the notes of his terror rose on the air, the beautiful trill of an angel's voice ris-ing out of the cacophony of demons.

The lurid miasma thickened, as if the soul spirit of the Beast and the carnal presence of the Witch took strength from each other, the multifaceted eyes intoxi-cated with glee, clacking jaws closing slowly about the source of its attraction.

Kate stared, mute with shock, unable to breathe.

Something resembling antennae stroked the tiny singer, pausing over the wide open mouth, as if savoring the last morsel of his grief. There was a cawing rasp, like the voice of a jackdaw. The tentacles trembled, as if barely suffused with enough restraint to pause until the death-song faded. The clicking and clacking rose to a thunder, extinguishing all other sound.

At the height of her own terror Kate recalled a similar moment of fear on the summit of Slievenamon, the mountain that guarded her home town of Clonmel. Great danger had also threatened there. And Alan had found safety in a name. Kate's eyed darted behind her. Faltana's closed eyes gave her the opportunity she had been waiting for.

She held her right hand aloft and she opened her palm wide as she screamed that name aloud.

"Mórígán!"

In the palm of her hand the flickering matrix became a tiny source of light illuminating, however palely, the darkness.

The great mouth, between the clacking jaws, roared.

Faltana's eyes sprang open. Her hands clutched at Kate's hair once more. But Kate no longer cared. A moment after she screamed the name a star bright as the sun burst through the bony walls and exploded in the chamber. The pure white light found Kate's upstretched hand, moving in an instant to illuminate her entire body. Kate felt it as if the light of daybreak had suddenly invaded her soul. Alan's voice . . . Alan's love . . . his kiss!

Kate! I'll keep my promise. I'm coming for you!

In the power of the communication, her body rose so she was hovering, embraced by the light, her feet inches above the floor.

"Treachery!" She heard Faltana's scream.

But Kate ignored her. Her senses were lost in the embrace of love. In her ears she heard how pandemonium surrounded her. The Cill had escaped. The succubi were attacking the Gargs and tossing their bodies into the maw of the Beast, in an attempt to assuage its hunger. Over and over again, she felt the blows about her head and body, and she heard the curses and screams of Faltana.

When Kate recovered consciousness, the fury of the Witch was resonating throughout the chamber.

How could such treachery be?

The Witch's voice sounded like the rasping caw of a jackdaw. A claw, curved and sharp as a scimitar, materialized on the end of a tentacle to tear out the right eye of Faltana.

"Eeeeaaaahhhh!"

The succubus screamed, her body trembling with pain, her porcelain face disfigured with the blood-filled orbit. "Oh, my Lovely—my beautiful Mistress. If I have offended you, pluck out my other eye."

Olc's mantis-mouth clacked with rage, her tentacles sweeping about Faltana's faltering shape, poised to begin ripping at the flesh.

You would volunteer your sight?

"Only for you, my Love—my Sacred One! I would volunteer my heart!"

What good would you be to us, blind—or dead?

"I deserve no better. Punish me as you think fit."

A tentacle took Kate by the throat, and the fang, still dripping with Faltana's blood, poised before her eyes. *Succulent little grub. Why have we, with our hunger, kept such meat aside? Soon it will be your turn to feed the Beast. But there is one who has violated our blessed sanctuary with this message of lightning! This one, with its accursed power—we must destroy it, but only after we have sucked the power from its bones. Thus may the grub live only as long as it provides the bait.*

The Witch tossed her acolyte's eye into the pit. *Wretched servant! Because of your carelessness, the Beast must be fed an alternative diet. We will feed it one in ten of your acolytes. In the meantime, we will punish this grub in a manner that pleases us.*

"Mistress—let me lash her to an inch of her life."

Kill it and you will feed the Beast.

"No—Mistress! I am ever careful to inflict pain without lasting wound. Yet even such wounds as I inflict heal too fast. There is a power about this one. I know not what. Yet it is as if some guardian . . ."

Faltana raised her whip, as if to demonstrate, but a sweeping tentacle struck the chief succubus, felling her to the floor.

A guardian, you say?

Another tentacle rose to sniff at Kate's brow, then slid down over her body, sniffing all the while, until it came to her right hand, where the flickering crystal matrix was still faintly visible.

Here is its comfort!

"Then let me cut off its hand."

Stupid servant! Thus is it communicating with the bearer of lightning. We wish this communication to continue.

"But Mighty One—I have sensed such cunning. A plea, perhaps, to some additional source?"

Olc shrieked: *What source?*

"Please do not be angry with me, Mistress. I only wish to serve."

There was a prickling silence, in which the creeping tentacles appeared to pulsate, as if driven by some invisible heart. The clatter of the jaws rose to a rapid crescendo. *We sense a presence! Ach—the Old One! She would not dare to enter here!*

But the Witch fell silent again, as if deeply thoughtful.

Perhaps the Earthspawn is more dangerous than we imagined? Yet we must not kill it immediately. Instead we must discover a way to use it to our advantage.

"Let me teach it a lesson."

A lesson, yes. But not your way. It is a weakly thing, little more than skin and bone. There is another pain, a pain of the spirit, yet one that would provide no escape through death.

"What is your wish, Mistress?"

Put it to silence in the bowels of nowhere—where there is nothing to be heard or seen, or felt—where it will survive long enough to serve our will, yet where there is but hunger and deprivation to torment the senses.

THE COUNCIL-IN-EXILE

As EVENING FELL ON THE FOLLOWING DAY THE clanging of a great bronze bell pealed out from some source deep in the old city, echoing far and wide through the streets of Carfon and carrying over the choppy waters of the estuary. It was the signal Milish had been waiting for, the summons for Alan to appear before a plenary session of the Council-in-Exile. After the tiresome week of waiting Alan now felt that he had had little time to prepare himself. The Council-in-Exile, as he understood it, was drawn exclusively from some kind of nunlike order, sworn to silence when it came to outsiders. In the past they had been ruled by the reigning High Architect, but since the martyrdom of Ussha De Danaan that role had been served by a Pretender-in-Waiting. As such the summons of an outsider to their presence was an extreme rarity, and such a summons to a male—and an alien male at that—was unparalleled.

As the dipping sun inflamed the western horizon a shallow-keeled skiff emerged from the shadow of the Water Gate. Alan watched its progress, illuminated by a single lantern in the prow, and sculled by half a dozen black-cowled figures whose synchronized rhythm dipped and beat the fiery waves. The omnipresent off-shore breeze had strengthened to a squall, making it difficult for the rowers as they skirted the great shadow of the Temple Ship in midestuary to head for where Alan stood, in the company of Milish and the dwarf mage, at the very lap of the tide. Given the nature of their des-tination, Milish had dressed more frugally than was usual for the Ambassador. A simple cape of black wool overhung an ankle-length dress of silver-trimmed gray.

Alan continued to observe the Ambassador, sensing an unusual level of inner tension. "Is something worry-ing you, Milish?"

Milish drew him a few yards aside and whispered urgently: "If I might speak in confidence?"

"Of course!"

"In our haste to discover you, after word began to spread of your arrival in Tír, there was no opportunity for counsel between the Kyra's mother-sister and this daughter-sister. During the maturation of a Kyra, time is put aside for frequent counsel. It allows the trans-fer, from mature to immature, of key experience—the confirmation of leadership and power. With the Kyra's death, far separated from the daughter-sister, the opportunity for such counsel was lost. The young Kyra lacks that peerless matrilineage of memories, of leadership in battles beyond counting, the wisdom and judgment of hundreds of Kyras extending back thousands of years."

Alan considered the implications of what Milish had said as the shallow-keeled boat swept up closer to the beach. When he spoke again, he did so softly, still out of earshot of Qwenqwo. "I hope the young Kyra realizes how lucky she is to have you as her adviser."

Milish turned her gaze riverwards, as if examining the boat's determined progress through the rising dark. With a wave of his hand, Alan bade Qwenqwo to rejoin them. He addressed them both as several cowled and caped figures slid over the gunwales of the boat and, wading to above their knees in the swirling surf, hauled its prow as close to the sand as they could maneuver.

"What strategy should I adopt with the Council?"

Milish spoke urgently. "Discover one high-ranking friend among them, then speak always as if addressing this one friend!"

"If, on the contrary, you would take my advice," Qwenqwo added with equal urgency, "you should trust none of them—least of all the one among them who takes pains to befriend you!"

Alan smiled, then turned to hug his friend, Mo, who was still recovering from the spiritual trauma she had suffered at the Battle of Ossierel. She looked wan and vulnerable, her dark hair blustering about her delicate features in the heightening wind. Mind-to-mind he caught her whisper.

I dreamed about Mark, last night. I sense that he is still here with us.

Alan hesitated, taken aback by the thought. He took Mo's premonitions very seriously. He wanted to know more but now was not the time.

Hey, Mo—I'll be back before you have time to miss me! Take care of yourself, Alan.

His eyes found Siam, Chief of the Olhyiu, whose bravery and leadership had brought them through so many dangers along the course of the Snowmelt River. Siam nodded in understanding. Alan was relieved see that Mo was already cradled by the protective arm of Siam's very capable wife, Kehloke.

The cowled rowers brought the prow around to face the crossing, allowing Alan and Milish to clamber aboard the stern, and they were soon receding from the waving arms of their friends, who were swallowed up by the dark, the squall whipping up a salt-laden mist that soaked the passengers' clothes and faces. Alan had to grab the starboard rail to steady himself against the pitching and tossing, before settling to the rhythm and sway of the boat's movements, all the while attempting to stop himself falling headlong against his seated companion.

* * *

As the boat splashed its way through the deeply recessed arch of the Water Gate, with its intricate carvings set deep into the weathered stones, Alan was unprepared for the maze that now enfolded them. He had expected city streets, roads and squares. Instead he discovered that the Old City was a labyrinth of tunnels carved out of solid rock, honeycombed with openings into still darker tunnels.

In such claustrophobic surroundings he felt increasingly uncomfortable with the silence of the hooded women. At the same time the proximity of great power caused his oraculum to glow so brightly that it cast a rubicund beacon over the skiff, and would have been enough in itself to illuminate the way had there not been torches burning in sconces at regular intervals.

"Wow! How old is this place, Milish?"

"Older, I'm sure, than any other ecclesiastical buildings in all of Monisle. Its written history stretches to more than five millennia, yet the sages believe that it is more ancient still. It guards its secrets well."

After a lengthy and twisting course within the tunnels they arrived at a jetty in a mildewed wall where a solitary figure, gowned in white, stood waiting for their arrival. Unlike the rowers she was uncowled and Alan saw that she was no more than twenty years old and of a dark complexion, with heavy eyelids, a pert nose and wide, full lips. Her eyebrows, like her scalp, were hairless. Her chestnut-colored eyes assessed him curiously, but it was he who broke the silence.

"My name is Alan Duval. My companion you already recognize, the Princess and Ambassador . . ."

"Mage Lord, you need no introduction." The young woman interrupted him, bowing a little awkwardly as if unused to greeting strangers. "I am permitted to speak in order to be your guide."

She indicated where a door stood open onto an ascending spiral of steps. They seemed to climb endlessly, with more tunnels opening off the staircase at many levels, until finally they reached a small and narrow atrium. By now they must be high within the labyrinths of the Old City. With a gesture toward the single stone bench lit by a flickering sconce, their guide made it clear that they should wait for her return.

Alan could barely contain his impatience, pacing around for a few moments before pausing in front of a narrow, unglazed slit window, through which, standing on tiptoes, he could catch a glimpse of the lamp-lit towers of Carfon.

The return of their guide was heralded by the smell of incense. Cowling her head, she led them through a corridor with a worn stone floor, and through a chamber set with wooden benches and kneelers that was lit by candles and proved to be the source of the incense, and still further into a pentagonal room that was the anteroom to the assembly chamber. Here, she stood back, her head bowed before a tall, severe-looking woman garbed in an ankle-length gown of lime green.

"I am Aon."

The woman confronting Alan was perhaps in her early sixties. In assessing Alan, she made no effort to disguise her curiosity. Her gaze focused for several moments on his oraculum before finding his eyes, and once finding them, never leaving them.

"I'm Alan Duval."

"Who, if the rumors be true, has entered this world from another—and who bears the Oraculum of the First Power of the most Holy Trídédana!"

He gazed back at her, eye to eye, in silence.

"I am informed that the Elector, Prince Ebrit, considers you naive, perhaps a dangerous idealist."

"I guess that in his world idealism might be another word for fanaticism. If that's what the Elector thinks of me, I can see how it might make me appear dangerous." He let his words sink in a moment before shrugging.

"It must be difficult in one so young to assume such power without being a little overwhelmed by it. I'm sure that the Princess Laása will also have explained our protocols. It's unprecedented in the history of the High Council to allow a man to attend a plenary meeting of the Half Hundred. We are bound by strict rules. And the Princess Laása will be excluded from the meeting."

"Ma'am—Sister Aon, if that's what I should call you—I'm asking you to let the Ambassador stay with me. This meeting is important for both our sakes, and without her advice I'm likely to offend you without intending to."

"There are those among us who think that the Ambassador, as you call her, should stand before our Court charged with profligate abuse of her role."

"Ma'am! If you want any cooperation from me you're going to have to forget about any such trial. I regard the Ambassador as my friend."

"You speak willfully. Yet greater forces may be at work than you realize."

Alan was rapidly running out of patience with diplomacy. "Sister Aon—I suspect you already know why I'm here."

"You seek the whereabouts of the portal."

"Will you show me where to find it?"

Aon shook her head in vexation. "Perhaps the Ambassador should stay! But be advised that if you choose confrontation you will place your own life, and the lives of all who depend on you, in danger."

"Ma'am, thank you."

Aon turned to Milish. "Have you warned him against such foolishness?"

Alan spoke for Milish. "The Ambassador has repeatedly warned me, much as you have. But I have no choice but to confront the Fáil!"

Sister Aon stared at Alan for several moments, as if questioning his sanity. But the look of determination on his face persuaded her. "Very well! But you will not be allowed to use your power to probe minds in this chamber. And you will both be excluded from our subsequent deliberations."

So saying, she led Alan and Milish into a semicircu-
lar chamber where the remaining forty-nine members,
all wearing gowns of lime green, were seated in tiered
rows. Aon took her place next to a very old woman who
sat on an elevated rostrum at the center of the semicircle, and here the Pretender to High Architect accepted a
small scepter that she tapped just once on the dark oak
bench before her.

"Members of the Half Hundred! The Mage Lord, Alan
Duval, together with the Princess of Essyne Xhosa, beg
audience. Grave times beset us. The Mage Lord wishes
to discover the portal once resident at Ossierel, but
brought here for safe keeping. What are we to make of
such a request?

"None among us, under any normal circumstances,
would sanction a confrontation of the power beyond
that portal. We would assume that it would lead to
the destruction of this ancient sanctuary, even Carfon
itself. Yet these are not ordinary circumstances and
the Mage Lord is no ordinary mortal. In his brow he
bears the Oraculum of the First Power of the Most Holy
Trídédana."

Alan's eyes moved back to the old woman, recogniz-
ing the bent and twisted figure that had warned him from
the assembled crowds as the Temple Ship had arrived
into the harbor. That same figure had warned him that
his quest here might prove to be a poisoned chalice. As
then, a thrill of alarm pulsed in his oraculum.

But what did it mean?

Sister Aon continued to address the council. "We recognize that the golden age of Ossierel is past. A new political reality prevails. The Kyra of the Shee is but across the water. Daily her forces gather. The Elector, Ebrit, supported by the High Families, raises a mighty force of arms in the city's defense. Two armies not altogether allied to each other now ring this chamber, while others more malignant regard our sacred charge with avid eyes.

"And now," she turned to face Alan directly, "this stranger demands audience to demand access to the portal. If I understand him, he offers commonality of purpose to this Council in return for our assistance. Thus do we face the gravest dilemma since the fall of Ossierel. Should we assist him in this seemingly foolish enterprise—or should we refuse? The question is now open to debate."

Several voices called out at once: "Then let him speak."

With a face like stone, Sister Aon waved Alan to the floor in front of her rostrum. "Face the assembly, if you will. No doubt you will speak as frankly to them as you already have to me."

Alan stood erect, forcing himself to relax the fists that had been clenched by his sides. "Sisters—if that is what I'm supposed to call you—you can see I'm no kind of diplomat. I speak my mind. I know what some of you think about the last High Architect, Ussha De Danaan. I understand why you might hate her. She did nothing to save Ossierel. Through the powers of the Mage of Dreams I was taken back to Ossierel and I spoke to Ussha De Danaan as she was dying."

Alan paused to allow the shock of his words to run its course among them. "You must be wondering, just as I did, why she brought me and my friends there to meet her. From what I gathered she didn't do it through madness, despair, or through cowardice or anything like that. She had some kind of a plan."

The chamber was filled with murmuring.

"In the name of the Most Holy—why you?"

"As far as I can see, her bringing us here to your world was part of that plan. Don't expect me to explain because, frankly, I don't understand it myself. All I can tell you is that she called us 'chosen.' Why, or how, we happened to be chosen, I have no idea. But she gave us a clue. The ultimate cause of it all, the evil that's wrecking your world, involves the Fáil. Your enemy, the Tyrant of the Wastelands, has captured a portal and he is actively corrupting its influence."

A stunned silence filled the chamber.

Alan spoke again, his words invading the silence. "I know you doubt her integrity. But I really believe that her heart, and purpose, were true."

A hiss of shock filled the chamber.

"Why then," demanded Aon, "should we believe a stranger when the wisest minds in the land have failed to understand these terrible portents?"

"Ma'am, I don't really know why. As an old woman once said to me, although she used different words, there are times when you have to trust to your heart and instinct. I must ask you also to trust your hearts and instincts."

"You speak eloquently, for all your lack of years, but eloquence is no persuasion. Too much is at stake here."

"Then will you allow the Ambassador to speak?"

Sister Aon tapped the scepter on the bench surface. "Should the Xhosa be allowed to address this meeting? On such a matter of high principle, I would suggest we take the opinion of the oldest and most experienced among us. Sister Hocht will decide."

All eyes turned to the old woman sitting on the rostrum beside Sister Aon, watching in silence as she took to her feet, leaning on an ancient staff of power. Her face, lifting with difficulty on her bent and withered neck, was as dry as parchment, stretched over the angular bones of her skull. Her eyes, deeply set within their shadowed orbits, were gray-ringed with age, yet they clearly held the respect of the entire chamber. The old woman gazed first at Alan and then at Milish. She lifted the staff of power and struck it sharply against the wooden floor of the rostrum. Then in a reedy voice she said: "Let the Princess of Laása speak."

Milish joined Alan on the floor before the rostrum. She hesitated, as if to gather her thoughts, before speaking.

"I thank you, Holy Sisters, for this opportunity to address the High Council. There is much I might say to you, but time is pressing and I will keep it brief. I have had plenty of opportunity to observe this brave young man, witnessing how differently he sees our world. And I cannot help but conclude that, at least in part, we brought downfall upon ourselves. We enjoyed spiritual glory at Ossierel with little thought or care for the peoples of the Wastelands. In our arrogance we dismissed as barbarian much that should have become the focus of our concerns and attention, and in so doing we allowed the greater part of our world to be invaded, and increasingly dominated, by evil. Such were the fruits of our isolationism then. Even today we persist in fighting amongst ourselves and plotting and counterplotting for power in conflict with the Elector and the other city leaders. Meanwhile the forces of darkness encircle us without hindrance or opposition."

A voice exclaimed, "How can we trust these warmongers when we see the example of Isscan, which sued for terms, and still stands, even prospers, despite being ruled by the Death Legion? Prudence dictates that we too should sue for peace—settle on whatever terms we can obtain with the Tyrant's forces."

"Is this the view of many of you?"

A chorus of murmurs indicated that it carried a good deal of approval.

Alan found the source of the voice, a tall woman with bright blue eyes in a florid angry-looking face.

Sister Aon's voice rang out: "How many would disagree with Sister Siebe?"

It seemed, from the rising chorus of voices, that much the same number were in opposition.

Siebe raised her voice in challenge. "What alternative do these warmongers suggest? Are we to risk our lives and the very fabric of this ancient sanctuary in assisting this so-called Mage Lord, who acknowledges that he knows nothing of our world?"

Alan shook his head. "While you bicker among yourselves the life of my friend Kate is in danger. I don't want to offend you. I came here hoping you would help me. But if you refuse, I'll find the portal by myself. But maybe you should think about what's going to happen to you if I fail. What will become of this place, and the city of Carfon, when the Tyrant wins ultimate control over the Fáil? Then you'll find out for yourselves what comes of bargaining with malice."

His words brought consternation, with many voices raised in differing opinions. The voices were silenced by a second tap of the staff of power against the floor of the rostrum.

There was something deeply familiar about the old woman, Sister Hocht. Something more than the memory of her warning on his arrival into the harbor here aboard the Temple Ship.

"Who are you?" he asked her. "Why do you look so familiar to me?"

"Are your wits so confused you cannot remember your guide from the landscape of dreams?"

Vividly, he recalled their spiritual journey back in time to the battle of Ossierel, made possible by Qwenqwo's magic. There had been an old crone who had appeared as a soul spirit herself to guide them through the ravaged streets of the burning citadel. She had led them through an underground labyrinth to stand before the dying High Architect, crucified on the silver gates.

"It was you?"

"Yes!" she cackled. "You remember me now! Was I not Spiritual Rector of Ossierel, and the closest confidante of the De Danaan herself!"

"But then you know I'm telling the truth? You must have heard her words?"

"I heard nothing. She spoke to you, as a mind opens to another, without need of ear or tongue."

"But how did you survive?"

"There are powers, and secrets, even an oraculum-bearer is not privileged to know." She took his arm and leaned on him, while leading him out of the chamber. "Let you, my sisters, argue among yourselves. Let the Xhosa wait here for our return. For this discussion will not come to completion this night, or tomorrow, or this very year, if my instincts are anything to go by. In the meantime, young man, you and I have matters to discuss. It is a discussion I have looked forward to since first I witnessed your triumphant entry into the city—a discussion best conducted between us alone."

THE PROPHECY

ALAN HAD TO SLOW HIS PACE TO WALK BESIDE THE old woman, whose emaciated hand shook as it gripped her staff, and whose words came out slowly and shakily through her blue-black lips.

"Tell me more," she spoke softly, "about your friend."

Alan sensed that this frail, elderly woman, Sister Hocht, would understand things in a way that nobody else he knew might understand. He talked about Kate and what had happened to her on the journey here. He talked about Granny Dew, and how she had conferred crystals on Mark and Kate at the same time she had embedded the ruby triangle of the First Power in Alan's brow. He also told her about Mark's seduction by the succubus, which, as far as he could determine, indicated that the Witch and the Tyrant must have been in league with one another from the beginning. "Kate," he added, "was a target for the Gargs from the very beginning. First they tried to kill her. Then they took her to this Tower of Bones."

"Which means she is the prisoner of the Great Witch, Olc."

"So Qwenqwo Cuatzel believes—yes."

"The question then is—why Olc's interest in Kate?"

"I don't know."

They walked through cloisters of cold gray marble, illuminated by sconces and pitted with age. For a time there was no more than the resonance of their footsteps, hollow and soft, as if muffled by the millennia of secrets that lay cloaked within these walls. Alan pleaded with the old woman. "Sister Hocht—they're tormenting Kate day and night in that horrible place. I sense her pain. And I can't bear it."

"You are brave and good. Of course you care about your friend. And now I see what drives you to such a dangerous course of action. But brave intentions will not suffice. You must not be manipulated into making a fatal mistake."

"Can't you help me? You must know where I can find the portal."

"Ach—you stumble in blind ignorance while appearing foolishly certain of what you imagine your need. Was it not I who was given the honor of moving the portal from doomed Ossierel to these hallowed cloisters? None better than I know how dangerous that portal is. Only the De Danaan had the strength and knowledge to confront it—and we have seen what became of her. Knowing this, will you not heed me now? The Fáil is not merely dangerous to contemplate, it is far more so to confront." She paused a moment to clutch at his arm with fingers so ancient they were little more than tendon-wrapped bones. "My brave young friend, it is dangerous beyond your powers to imagine."

"When I was coming here, I had a strange experience. It was at a very difficult and sad time. I was given advice by what I would guess was some kind of spiritual guide." Alan spoke the strange words that were engraved on his memory:

"All wisdom is contained within the Fáil. Yet such wisdom is perilous beyond your understanding. You must approach your purpose elliptically, not directly."

Hocht's eyes blinked up at him, her neck arched from her stooping shoulders, her skull-like face impassioned but curious. "The message appears vague—it sounds more a warning than an instruction to confront the Fáil."

"The guide told me that the Fáil has become corrupted."

Hocht fell silent, her face haggard with presentiment.

"What's really going on?"

"This we do not know. Only that the De Danaan perceived forces that threatened all we hold dear."

"What happened to the High Architect's oraculum—the Oraculum of the Moon?"

"Fallen, alas, into the hands of evil."

"Does that mean that you, the Council-in-Exile, are no longer able to test the integrity of the Fáil?"

A murmur of despair passed Hocht's lips. "Perhaps," she murmured, "even the Fáil itself cannot last forever. Perhaps even to hope so was the ultimate vanity. Yet belief in its power for salvation was a vanity to good purpose. Through such belief good was venerated over evil. All manner of beauty and harmony prospered under the protection and guidance of the Arinn's creation in beloved Ossierel—alas, what grief that loss still harbors in my heart."

Alan was silent for a moment, thinking about what she had said. "I'm grateful to you, Sister, for your concern and your advice. But there are things I have to ask."

"Ask, then."

"First—the Ambassador, Milish. I don't want her to get into trouble for risking her life to save me."

"The Princess of Laása will suffer no punishment. Even if there were none amongst us who remember what we owe to the family of Xhosa—and in truth there are many—is she not a friend and counselor to the Kyra of the Shee? Her enemies would do well to consider that."

Alan nodded. Ainé would allow no harm to come to Milish.

"You have another question?"

He hesitated. "I need to know as much as I can about the creature that's holding Kate prisoner in that horrible place. This so-called Great Witch, Olc."

"Be warned again. Though it is said that you have led the forces that defeated a Legun in battle, Olc's power is greater than any Legun. And her cunning, as necromancer, is more deadly. Though she may well be working in league with the Tyrant, nevertheless she resents his supremacy and craves to usurp him. In her Tower of Bones, which is set in a desolate plain known as the Bitter Marshes—a place of extraordinary conflict in times past—she seeks to reawaken a force that once resurrected would mean ruin and desolation for all."

"Why would she do this?"

"In her lust for power she seeks to resurrect a soul spirit of truly immense power and evil. If ever she succeeds her Tower of Bones might rival Ghork Mega in power and darkness. More I cannot add since, thanks to the vigilance of her succubi and Gargs, none who has entered her domain has emerged to tell the tale."

"What are these succubi?"

"The succubi are Olc's own offspring, spawned from her corrupted spirit." Hocht hesitated. "Would you, in spite of all I have warned you, be so foolish as to challenge the Witch in that terrible fastness?"

Alan gazed away from the focus of her clouded eyes. Something was wrong. The oraculum in his brow was pulsating.

He said: "Ma'am—I sense danger."

She crashed her staff against the flagstones, causing echoes to crack and reverberate through the cloisters.

"Come then—*quickly*!" She clutched at his arm, blinking away what might have been her own presentiments and fears. "Such talk has reminded me. There is something, a relic of your own world, I need to show you."

The sense of danger was so tangible that Alan probed every alcove and crevice as Sister Hocht led him to a door of black oak that opened off the labyrinth of corridors. The door appeared to be locked, without a handle, not even so much as a keyhole. With a chant, strangely vibrant and reverential from her otherwise dry throat, the old woman performed a spiral with the head of her staff, then lifted her left hand in a simple gesture and the heavy door fell open.

"Welcome, Duval, Mage Lord of Earth," she said, "to the Chamber of Enlightenment!"

Such was the brilliant glow of light that flowed out of the parted door that Alan couldn't help but hurry through to explore the brightly lit chamber. Astonished at the beauty that confronted him, his instincts carried him to the dead center of a floor that was a perfect circle perhaps a hundred feet wide, finding himself at the heart of an exquisite mosaic of multicolored marble inset with semi-precious gemstones. The scenes in the mosaic appeared to represent life in all of its wonder, from intertwining forest trees and brilliantly plumaged birds to the richness of life in the oceans.

But Alan's attention was distracted by the fact that his oraculum was still pulsing strongly with the presentiment of danger.

"Where does the light come from?" He stared about the domed walls and ceiling, carved of a fine ivory-colored marble, and illuminated by a perfectly even glow of light that filled the chamber.

"The walls and ceiling are but a single carved glow-stone."

"Wow!"

"Ach—such beauty as you behold is but a shell of vanity. The real illumination is the blessed light of knowledge."

"I don't understand."

"Behold!"

With another spiral motion of her staff Sister Hocht caused the walls to change. Where there had been a seamless glowing shell Alan now saw a honeycomb of small repositories—pigeonholes. He looked closer and saw that each pigeonhole was annotated, in a script he couldn't read, and filled with parchment scrolls.

"What is it—some kind of a library?"

"A scriptorium. A poor copy of the blessed scriptorium of Ossierel, where the greatest wisdom of our age was gathered. We saved what we could in the weeks before Ossierel was attacked, and brought it here."

Alan gazed about him at hundreds of scrolls filling every shelf and niche. "There's something among these scrolls that might help me?"

Hocht gazed about her, found the niche she was searching for, plucked a single scroll from the many and handed it to him.

A growing impatience caused Alan to snatch at the leather thong that bound it, attempting to tear it open in his hurry to see what was inside.

The old woman's hand enfolded his wrist. It felt surprisingly strong, forcing him to patience. "Hsst! Now I too sense it."

He stared at her, tense with the imminence of danger.

"My young friend—should we not regard each other as friends!" She turned from side to side, as if searching for the source of their common presentiment. "Quickly—*quickly!*" With a sigh of concern she waved her staff at the walls, causing the honeycomb to meld back into its glowing blankness, then spun away from him as if to hurry him back out into the marble cloisters. Once outside she lifted her face and sniffed at the air. "Ach—already it comes! Such little time do I have!"

"What is it? What do you know?"

Scurrying as fast as her tired old bones could carry her she led Alan into a new cloister, with a colonnade to his left that opened directly onto the moonlit estuary. With a wave of her staff she slammed shut all doors opening into the cloister before settling into a small niche, illuminated by torchlight, where she unwrapped the binding thong and then handed him the scroll, which unfurled to a single oblong of yellowed vellum on which he saw five faded lines inscribed with strokes, some perpendicular and some slanted . . .

"It's Ogham?"

"What you see is only a fragment of a greater whole, though scripted in the poet's own hand."

Alan couldn't help recalling, with grief, his grandfather, Padraig, who had known how to read the ancient writing. But it was Mark, and not Alan, who had gone to the trouble of learning Ogham from Padraig.

The oraculum flared.

His eyes lifted from the fragment of parchment to see a growing consternation in the eyes of the old woman. He followed her gaze backward along the corridor to where a wraith of mist had appeared.

"Sister Hocht—I can't read it."

"Well then," her eyes turned from the corridor to confront his gaze, "I shall read it for you. It is but a fragment from the Prophecies of Diarmuid in the *Book of Omens*."

His voice was hushed, as gentle as his anxiety would allow: "Read it to me—please?"

"Hsst!" She silenced him, looking back to where the mist spiraled and turned, as if searching, then grasped the hilt of her staff in both hands and closed her eyes tight in circles of concentric wrinkles. "It comes—*it comes!*"

The oraculum began to pulsate rapidly and powerfully.

"What is it?"

"A deathmaw."

Alan froze, recalling the deathmaw that had threatened the Temple Ship over the river in the Vale of Tazan. The oraculum burst into a lurid red flame in his brow. "Tell me what to do. How do I fight it?"

"Alas, it is too late for that. To fight it will only delay it rather than defeat it. And that might expose you to its master's attention. I must make use of what time yet remains. Ach! I have journeyed far. I have known Dromenon. Let me translate the prophecy in what little time is left to me.

'A dragon is rising
Over the Rath of Bones
Blacker than night his wings
Trailing rainbows
Over the bog of slaughter.'"

Alan shook his head. "What does it mean?"

She whispered urgently. "A fragment of a longer prophecy, the meaning of which is obscure. But my attention was drawn to its mention of the Rath of Bones. Could it be that same Tower in which your friend, Kate, is imprisoned?"

Alan felt the icy mist envelop them. He pressed her: "Is there no way I can stop this—use my powers to heal you?"

Her hand, shrunken as a claw, clasped his own.

"Do not even think to do so. Then it would have you too. Save yourself. In doing so, you will aid what purpose I still serve."

Alan turned the power of the oraculum inwards. His body was flooded with the power spreading throughout his bloodstream. He felt the hairs spring erect on his head. Yet still he returned the fierce clasp of the old woman's hand, seeing blood appear from her nostrils and run, dripping, from the point of her chin. Her gown was smoking, not from the power of his oraculum but from a fouler flame that was consuming her. Her face was turned away from his, upward, as if toward some visions she saw in the heavens. "My death I embrace willingly. My body is weak and easily conquered, but my spirit is strong. My spirit will join the De Danaan in her sacrifice."

Blood issued from the old woman's eyes. Her breath came in gasps. Alan couldn't just stand aside and ignore her torment. He had to help her.

Placing his arm around her shoulders he extended the oracular protection from his own body to hers, allowing her fallen head to rest against his shoulder.

"Foolish! Ach . . . !"

"Please, tell me! You sense something important in the words of the prophecy? Something that connects to Kate?"

"I . . . I cannot be sure. But Diarmuid . . . a great Seer . . . Ach . . . I burn!"

"Diarmuid—what did he mean?"

"Such a spirit . . . omens . . ."

He was losing her. Alan wished he had a little heal-well to ease her suffering. "Hold on—please. Just a moment longer!" He brushed her brow again, cupped it in his pulsating hand. Though it seemed cruel to press the tormented Sister for more information, yet he felt he had to. "What do you mean?"

Her voice gathered a shrill crackling strength from his embrace. "The Great Witch . . . she resurrects the soul spirit of Fangorath. Fangorath . . . the most dread-ful . . . the Dragonbane . . ."

"Fangorath?"

"Half divine . . ." Hocht's voice was the merest whis-per, so he had to listen closely to her dying breath to catch her words. "A god's own son . . . a titan of dark-ness." Her hand flailed, clutched at his face, as if in warning. *"Beware . . ."*

"Beware this Fangorath?"

The old woman's blood was soaking into his shoul-der. His hand was dripping with her blood, yet still he held her to him, infusing what he could of his own life force into her, to keep her alive for mere moments longer.

"What will happen if Olc resurrects Fangorath? She plans to use him—to use Fangorath's soul spirit—to give her the power she craves?"

Hocht clutched at his face with fingers over which the parchment skin and even the very nails had been stripped to bare bone. "Worse!"

"What could be worse? What is it about the Tower of Bones?"

She whispered a few words, so slurred it was almost impossible to make them out. But he saw the shape of them come from her destroyed lips. And he heard them, like a thunderclap, through the oraculum in his brow.

"The Third Portal!"

Alan realized what she must mean. He recalled the advice given to him in Dromenon: *In Carfon is one of the three portals . . .*

"The Tower of Bones—it's a portal? A Third Portal to the Fáil?"

Sister Hocht sighed, a low-pitched guttural croak, and her head fell back, her eyes boiled white.

Slug Beast and Lizard-Dung

Kate knew that Faltana was nearby even though she couldn't see her. She could smell the rancid odor of her and she could hear her labored breathing in the glimmerless dark as she arrived to grasp her arm and check her pulse. Though any sense of contact should have been welcome in this chamber of unfeeling, Kate felt nothing but disgust at the regular visits from her tormentor, knowing that Faltana was terrified of what would happen if Kate died on her before the Witch's purpose was served.

A flare of light: it was no more than the sickly glow of a wyre-stone, its candle-like illumination framing Faltana's hand, but Kate was so accustomed to pitch dark it forced her to clench her eyes tightly shut as if she were staring into the noonday sun.

Faltana's voice hissed so close into Kate's ear she felt the wet of her spittle, "Open your eyes, lizard-dung. I know you hear me."

Through lids swollen with cold and hunger, Kate struggled to see the creature she so hated, etched in sweat by the lurid glow. Seeing Faltana gave her a focus for her loathing, that dark bulk, that slug-beast, a denser evil within the darkness, her empty eye socket rimed where the light glittered over her sweaty countenance.

"Why don't you just kill me?"

"I shall—be assured of it. But not yet. No! In her wisdom my mistress orders that killing is too pleasant an end for you. But pain! Ah, the delicious thoughts of that. I crave your pain as you crave the coming of your savior."

Kate shivered. She couldn't help the trembling that racked her body. But she tried to make her voice stronger than she actually felt. "You don't dare to touch me. I heard what the Witch said."

"Ah, do I not? Is that what you fondly wish for—what you hope for?"

Kate struggled to create a half-laugh, half-cough in her dust-dry throat. "Not if you value the one eye you have left."

The surviving eye of the Chief Succubus glittered back with loathing. It traveled over Kate's shackled limbs in a slow writhe of pleasure. Faltana's spit-flecked whisper crawled into Kate's ear. "He senses it—this savior or yours. He feels what you feel."

"Liar!"

"You know I do not lie. He feels it—every sting. Surely it doubles my delight. But enough of foreplay. Let us engage in earnest."

The first stroke of the Garg-tail gouged Kate's skin, as if it had been brushed with a red-hot poker. Faltana was careful not to lash her—the scourge of the lash would show in ravaged flesh and livid scars. This torment raised a scalding welt of agony, but nothing that would permanently scar her flesh. It was followed by a pause, as precise as the welt, a minute or two to allow the agony to subside, which encouraged the growing dread of the next welt. Kate closed her eyes, shut them tight, again.

"Think you still that he doesn't feel it?" Something sharp—a nail, like a talon—gouged the burning track of the welt, causing her to squirm and writhe. "Yeees— yeees! Upon my poor lost eye, as I feel it still, so also does he. He feels each lick, even more than you do."

Kate sensed how the arm of the slug-beast rose again, that leisurely, almost delicate crescent of contact, the slide of agony gauged to unerring precision behind the pale flat glitter of the single eye. She tried to jerk her body away, but her feet were manacled with irons to the floor. Her heart shrank from the coming pain. But her body was too exhausted to tense anymore.

"Yeees! Let him savor it as we do—mmmmmmmmm!"

As the venomous barb hit a nerve Kate was unable to stop the scream.

"Ahhhhh! It sings!" The liquid sound of her tormentor's lips opening, the slightly rasping sounds of the tongue licking. The barb suspended, waiting for the moment the agony peaked and began to fall, before it repeated the self-same course to elicit another scream. A pause for the scream to fade before the whisper, slobbery now with glee, continued to torment her:

"You hope it will end? I believe you really want it to end. You would welcome death, would you not? Or perhaps you hope that Faltana will tire of her sport? No, no—Faltana will never tire." The arm rose again, the same precise and delicate sketch upon Kate's skin, probing for the same nerve to see if it would work again.

It worked.

Somehow Kate had to find a source of strength, of comfort. She must bear it in the knowledge that it had to stop. Faltana was taking a risk. She was disobeying the Witch's orders. Somehow, she had to find a way to make it stop.

As if Faltana was reading her mind those lips smacked again. "You are praying, perhaps? Praying to some misbegotten god of your world? But it will not work. Believe me, they all pray. But it never works."

"Damn you!" Kate's lips tried to make the sound. Her mind willed her lips to make the words, but no words came.

The barb whispered over her skin, finding precisely the same place, following what must be a livid gouge. Kate shrieked.

Slobbering with the joy of it, drooling spittle onto her chin and neck, Faltana exulted in the fact that she had so easily found her rhythm.

"No respite will come of such wishful praying. No hope lies in your friend coming here to save you. No hope in any direction you wheel and turn. For in this world there is but you and me." She toyed with the welt but fleetingly with the tip of the barb, evoking an exquisite agony merely through toying with her. Kate heard her throaty gurgle of delight. "No hope of Faltana tiring." The barb descended. Another scream. Was it the fifth or sixth time? Kate had lost track of the number. How long could a single nerve be tormented before it died? Then the dreadful thought: just how many such nerves like this were there in the human body?

"No respite—no hope! Faltana will increase your pain, little by little, until you cannot bear it. You will beg your god to let you die. But you will not die. Not until your savior takes the bait and enters the trap."

She was lost in a sea of agony, yet she sensed the barb's descent to score its precise curve of fire through her bewildered consciousness. She would not scream. Not again. She would not scream . . . The scream tore through her clenched teeth, through the fabric of her mind, bringing the darkness she craved, the darkness she hoped would bring a final end to this torment . . .

She rose from darkness to a vague awareness of utter silence. Her eyes were too exhausted to open. As if from a great distance Kate felt Faltana raise her wrist, the probing finger on her pulse. The succubus was ter-rified she had killed her. But the pause would not last. Faltana would merely wait for her to recover from her faint before starting again. But, somehow, Kate was determined that from now on she would not give her the pleasure of hearing her scream. From now on . . .

A hiss in the darkness, a different sound . . . a scary sound, yet it seemed to come from so far, far away . . .

A new voice, much deeper, a cawing . . . It sounded like the scuttling of something dark and evil through caverns of slime and bone:

Did we not give you warning, wretch? If you have killed it . . . !

"No—no! See! I feel her pulse. It is fast but strong. She lives yet. Certainly, she lives. She merely sleeps."

Silence!

The voice alone was more frightening than all of Fal-tana's tormenting.

Fool! You have amused yourself at our expense. You have scourged it perilously close to death.

Kate heard the sound of weeping from very close to where she lay. She cracked open her eyes. Through the slitted lids she saw an enormous claw confront the remaining eye in Faltana's terrified face. The claw made a gouging movement, a pantomime of slowly tearing away the small muscles that held the eye, a painstaking dissection, that would cause the spherical and bloody orb to emerge intact, clutched between the long, sharp talons of the finger and thumb.

"Mercy, beloved Mistress—your faithful servant! Not the other eye—not my dear remaining eye!"

If it dies because of you, much more than an eye shall we extract from you.

A glimpse of the huge multifaceted red eyes and Kate's own eyes clenched shut again. She heard another shriek. Then the screaming even louder than before, followed by the slobbering sound of Faltana's renewed weeping. Kate though that she could detect the smell of blood.

"Muh-Mistress—buh-buh-beloved one! This is a deceiving creature—unlike any I have ever known. Its flesh will not abide with harm."

What foolishness is this?

"I pray thee! I offer blessings, Faltana, your humble servant. Your most obedient servant . . . eternally. Let me show you with a single lash."

The chamber reverberated with the Witch's rage.

Still would you ignore our caution!

"Mistress—beloved . . . !"

Kate cringed from the sudden bellow of pain, then a snapping sound, the breaking of bone, as loud as a blow. Something torn off. Crunching noises as the bone and flesh were eaten. Shrieks, slobbering, the renewed smell of blood . . .

The Witch's presence—Kate was overwhelmed by it. She could feel the raw red heat of it on her face.

One more moan and your entire hand rather than a finger shall it be!

"Blessed, merciful Mistress!"

One more squeal!

Silence then—utter silence, apart from the shudder of breathing. A pregnant silence amid the heavy stink of blood.

Kate could feel the Witch's eyes return to her.

A touch of something sharp and hard on Kate's brow. The lurid glare of blood-red light as her eyelid was raised. Vileness invaded her vision. A sense of shock, as if the talons of the Witch had pierced her chest to feel her very heart inside. Her pulse rose to a frantic flurry.

And yet, though thin, it is not the mere bag of bones we had imagined, knowing the slops you feed it!

Faltana, forbidden to speak, writhed and twisted like a child throwing a temper tantrum on the filthy floor.

A claw-tipped tentacle lifted the Garg-tail, brought it forward for inspection by the insectile eyes, which turned back to inspect Kate's body from head to toe.

Where was the recent scourging—here on its back? Speak quickly, or you will feel our wrath.

"On her back, indeed. Here—precisely six or seven times—this very spot."

We see no mark.

"You see, my beloved Mistress—all is healed, within moments of being inflicted."

A perfidious one, this. More dangerous, perhaps, than we had imagined!

"Dangerous?"

Yet so fertile do we sense in mind and spirit! Perhaps we have been too kind to it?

"Yes—yes. Oh, too kind!"

It is strong—stronger than appearances suggest. There is a power dormant in it, such as we have not seen before. Henceforth no more food—not even slops.

"Such wisdom, beloved Mistress!"

Henceforth only water!

Kate no longer cared. In the enveloping silence, as the Witch and her servant abandoned her to darkness, she hoped that starvation might bring release, even if it was only the release of death. Oh, she hoped so. She so longed for it. She longed for it with every beat of her faltering heart.

THE PORTAL

ALAN WAS BADLY SHAKEN BY THE DEATH OF SISTER Hocht. And there were questions he hadn't had time to ask her. Now there would be no answers. And Kate was suffering again; he sensed the deepening of her pain. But what more could he do? A sense of helplessness overwhelmed him. All he could do was to find his way back to the Council Chamber, where the murder of the venerable old sister threw the Sisterhood into a panic. A furious Sister Siebe descended to the floor and insisted that he should leave the Old City at once. "The murder of our sister is your fault. All these years she has lived here in safety. Not until you come here, with your arrogant demands, does this catastrophe befall us!"

"I'm really sorry about the death of Sister Hocht. But my purpose here remains as vital as ever. My friend, Kate, is in mortal danger."

His oraculum was pulsating powerfully, and Siebe backed away from him.

Sister Aon spoke from the platform. "Mage Lord Duval—I beg of you. Leave this chamber. Please, go at once!"

But Alan refused to budge. "Perhaps Sister Siebe is right and it was my coming here that brought down the Tyrant's rage. But then ask yourself why the deathmaw focused on Sister Hocht? I stood next to her. Why not attack me? Why—unless it was her knowledge of the portal that was important. If the Tyrant can penetrate these walls to kill her, he can strike against any of you here."

Aon rose to her full height in outrage. "In all of history, none but the Great Blasphemer has dared to confront the Portal of Destiny, and the consequence of that blasphemy was the ruin of Ossierel!"

"I'm sorry, Sister Aon, but I can't take no for an answer."

"What you contemplate is as great a blasphemy as that of the De Danaan herself. I speak for all when I say that we cannot help you in this additional blasphemy. Indeed we could not help you even if we wished to do so. There is none left who could assist you—none even who could lead you to the portal."

"Then I'll have to find it without your help."

The oraculum in his brow pulsed once, powerfully, causing the entire council to shrink back in their seats. But Aon stood firm. "The Princess Laása led you here. She knows her way well enough to take you back to the ferry."

Milish came to his side, placing her hand on his shoulder. "Mage Lord—let us go. We will take the counsel of the Kyra and the dwarf mage."

"There's no time for counsel anymore, Milish. Kate's spirit is failing. You'll have to go back on your own. Tell the others what's happening. Wait for me at the camp of the Shee. Look after Mo for me."

With that he stormed out of the Council Chamber, trusting to the oraculum that was pulsating wildly in his brow.

The Fáil was calling him, leading him through a maze of passageways and doors, until it became apparent he was descending deep into the bowels of the ancient city. After some time he found himself in a wide circular chamber, so dark he needed the light of the oraculum to examine it. In that rubicund light the surrounding walls seemed craggy, as if this place had originally been a natural cavern over which the entire ancient city had been built. The oraculum beat even more insistently, as if great power was very close to him here.

A signal from the shadows beckoned him and, to his astonishment, he found it was the young sister who had earlier been his guide. His voice echoed, unnervingly, in the chamber. "How did you know where to find me?"

She placed an anxious hand on his arm. Her voice was soft, full of concern. "I was novice to Sister Hocht and assisted her in negotiating these passages. Now none other than I know the way."

Alan peered about the chamber but he could no longer make out the entrance. It was as if he had come through an opening that had then sealed itself shut.

"Who are you? Earlier you refused to give me your name."

"We have no names, only numbers. But I see your pain and concern for your companion. I know that my teacher trusted you and wished to help you. So I feel it my duty to help you also."

Awkwardly, with bowed head, she pressed something hard and surprisingly heavy into his hand. Alan looked down onto a sphere of perfect crystal, about two and a half inches in diameter. It was chocolate brown in color, semi-transparent, with whorls of silver coursing over its surface like the shapes of continents over the surface of a planet. A tiny pinpoint of light pulsated at its core.

"What is it?"

"My late teacher called it 'the Way.'"

"What's that supposed to mean? Is it some sort of a guide? Aon told me there was no guide. Are you saying that she lied to me?"

"She did not lie." Consternation entered her young face. "Sister Aon knows nothing of this. Only the De Danaan knew of it—and when she feared her coming death, she bequeathed it to Sister Hocht."

"Then this is some sort of guide?"

"Mage Lord, I do not know. We have no time for delay. I have given you the Way. But I warn you also, as my teacher warned me, that the Way forks, each fork leading to one of the two immensities, one to Life as the other to Death." Her young face clouded over, as if panic was close to making her flee. "Time is precious. You stand on the very threshold of the portal."

Alan studied the sphere again, turning it over in his hands so he could search its interior from different angles. There was movement of some sort within it. The movement didn't seem random, more like geometric shapes. As he watched, a line became a square, the square folded to a triangle and the triangle began to multiply until it filled the sphere with a maze of polyhedrons. Immediately, it all cleared and was replaced by the central pulsating pinpoint of light again.

"What are you implying? Is there some kind of a time limit?"

"Time is a forfeit. If your time elapses and you have not chosen, then you will most certainly die."

In the distance he heard the sound of shuffling feet: the Sisterhood were searching for him.

"Please hurry!" Her face lifted, and her eyes, reflecting the sphere in two startling pinpoints of light, looked increasingly panicky. "The Way tests more than you might imagine." She struck the center of her chest with a small clenched fist. "It will search the heart and spirit ... to discover the True Believer. But it will also punish any sign of falsehood or weakness."

"What the heck ... ?"

"I regret that I know no more." Her eyes widened in alarm as the footsteps approaching the chamber grew louder. Alan heard the murmuring of many voices. "You must hurry. I can only tell you what my teacher told me. It discovers the true nature of one who would enter." Her eyes beseeched him. "I must go—before Aon discovers that I have betrayed the Sisterhood."

She turned to flee. "Please, do nothing until I have left the chamber. I am not strong. I would not survive." Her hand lifted briefly, and around her wrist he saw a bracelet of smoothest ebony. Engraved into its surface, in glowing silver, was a symbol, the triple infinity—the Tyrant's emblem.

"You!"

"Goodbye, my sweet!"

Her lips parted to show fanged canines, white as ivory and sharp as a serpent's.

"Remember," she crooned, "there is no going back. The Way now controls you. Release it and you will die. Engage with it and you will be faced with the immensities. In this at least I did not lie."

Too late, Alan recalled the warning of his friend, Qwenqwo: to trust no one, least of all somebody who pretended to be his friend. He had allowed his emotions to lead him. And the succubus was gone, faded into the dark.

The lights of many candles illuminated the hidden doorway, flowing into and filling the chamber. A group of perhaps a dozen cowled figures had formed a circle around him. Traitors, he now guessed, among the Half Hundred of the Sisterhood. There they paused, their hoods concealing their faces, every left hand stretched out against him, with palm upraised. As one they chanted a softly melodic hymn. Alan ignored them, closing his fist about the crystal sphere. He had come here to find the portal—and still, despite the betrayal and the dangers it had to imply, he had no option now but to take his chances. There was something strange about the sphere, its weight and feel, something beyond the crystal shape and substance.

Could he risk hurling the crystal at the stone wall? His instincts told him that would be a mistake. Mark had once dashed a crystal of power against a wall and it had provoked terrible consequences. Instead Alan now pressed it close against his oraculum. Immediately the pinpoint of light became bright as the sun, flooding the chamber through the substance of his fingers. It was pulsating fiercely in synchrony with his heartbeat. The cowled figures continued their chanting.

The sense of power about him escalated. But what did it mean? He recalled the light he had once seen in the forest—the spirit guide that had spoken to him as

Valéra lay dying. Like the succubus it had also talked about the True Believer. He recalled his own voice, filled with anguish and frustration, demanding answers from the spirit guide: "Where is this place?"

It is all places and all times and therefore nowhere and timeless. To some it does not exist while to others it is the only reason for existing. But take care—for those of good heart are not the only True Believers.

Oh, man! He was back among the riddles.

The circle of figures had gathered more closely about him. Their chanting was louder. He sensed their hatred of him, but also their fear of him, or maybe of what it was that he was doing.

He turned his attention back onto the crystal. His oraculum burst into a cataract of bright red flame. Immediately the focus shifted from the sphere to the absolute dead center of the chamber, hovering in midair as a pulsating source of light and power. In its depths he perceived a wonderful motion, complex beyond easy meaning, as if worlds swirled and beckoned. Then it dissolved into an extraordinary kaleidoscope of waves and arabesques filling his senses before condensing once more to become a new focus of light immediately beneath his feet.

Alan stared down to see that he was not standing on a paved floor as he had imagined, but within a pentagon of polished quartz. The light expanded to enclose his body, so he became the dead center.

A sense of panic grew in him, though he did his best to resist it. Through the oraculum he sensed change, powerful and terrifying. The sense of power, of danger, was escalating at a furious rate. He had to assume that this was the portal.

"Shit!"

What had the succubus said? Had any of her words been true?

He had only moments to consider this. She had led him here—and here, he had no doubt, was the test she had talked about. Did she hope that he would die in the act of confrontation? Or did she hope he would pass the test and confront . . . confront what exactly?

He sensed that what she had told him had been at least partially true. There was a safe way—a way of life. And there was another way—a way of death. The portal had registered his presence. The sands were running through the hourglass, only it might not be an hour-glass at all, it might be a minute glass, or a glass that contained the remaining seconds of his life.

While he was thinking, the light condensed once more to a pinpoint, where it paused for an instant before expanding to a glowing line. A perfect line, narrow as a razor-blade, which ran perpendicularly through the center of the pentagon on the floor. Then the line retracted to the pinpoint again before reforming as a horizontal line. Again and again, it traced out lines, fol-lowing the same perfect angles, until the center was connected to five different points in space, all etched in brilliant white light. Then they all retracted in one instant to become the pinpoint focus again. This held, for a heartbeat. Suddenly it expanded into a blinding flare and when this faded he found himself standing at the center of a glowing sphere.

The sense of danger was awesome. This was the confrontation. A question was being asked of him . . .

A riddle?

The muscles of his back were freezing solid, as if ice had congealed deep within their fibers. He dropped the crystal, which was now inert. The confrontation was set: he faced the two immensities. Get it right and he would live; get it wrong and he was dead.

The Riddle of the Way

Mo Grimstone sat in the sand, the tide lapping around her bare feet and her tilted face catching the light of the newly risen moon. Her eyes closed, she was nevertheless aware of the approach of the dwarf mage, who observed her for a moment or two before settling down in the cool damp sand beside her. He embraced her slender shoulders with a burly arm, the warded edges of his bronze battleaxe glimmering in the pallid light, and his aged legs shuffling for a comfortable position, crossed at the ankles.

Mo blinked repeatedly, as if needing time to fully come to. Her brow furrowed, as if deeply troubled, before she spoke:

"Milish has come back without Alan. She's frantic with worry about him."

Qwenqwo's face was equally troubled. "You sense some danger in particular?"

Tears glistened in Mo's eyes. "I sense what Alan senses. That Kate is hurt—and in terrible danger."

The dwarf mage nodded, following Mo's gaze out into the central channel, where the Temple Ship lay unusually still, the great manta ray shape vaguely discernible, holding its position without anchor. In the short time since their arrival in Carfon a great army of Shee had arrived to take up occupation of the hitherto quiet estuary, under the command of the new Kyra. There must be thousands here already, and more arriving by the day. Mo guessed that it would be an uncomfortable place for a lone Fir Bolg to find himself, and his presence had certainly excited curiosity among the arriving warriors.

"I have been meaning to ask you something, though I hesitate to touch upon it. I detect something curious about you, Mo."

"What is it?"

"Four friends come to Tír from another world. Alan is granted the First Power, the power of the land. Your brother, Mark, discovers, at great cost to himself, the Third Power—the power of death. And Kate would have had bestowed on her the Second Power, the power of new life, and healing, had she not been taken from us. You alone are denied such a gift. And yet you are clearly an important member of the company of friends. Is that not curious?"

Mo's gaze turned from the Temple Ship and her tear-filled eyes held those of the dwarf mage, their emerald green transformed to gray by the moonlight amid the dark pools beneath his heavy brows.

It was Qwenqwo who broke the contact, his voice falling to a gentle whisper. "Aye, my young friend! And the more I consider you, the more do I wonder."

"What do you wonder?"

"At Ossierel you confronted a Legun incarnate. That confrontation almost destroyed you, but the hurt was in spirit rather than in the flesh. Even so, Alan could not revive you, not even with the full power of his oraculum. It required the intervention of a goddess to do so, a goddess called down upon you by a communion of powers between Alan and the mystical craft yonder. And now see—have you not walked through soft sand to find this spot, yet where are the marks to prove it? Even in the light of moon and stars, my footprints, as you can see, are clear. Yours, wherever you walked on this sand, reveal no more impression than the alighting of a butterfly."

Mo hesitated, not caring to look at the sand. She knew full well why her body was without weight. It had been the result of one of her wishes when trapped in the Preceptor's pit at the battle zone of the rapids on the Snowmelt River, a wish granted to her by her guardian, Granny Dew. Nevertheless, she was startled by Qwenqwo's words. It was the first time anybody had told her about how she was revived at Ossierel. But she had no more understanding of what happened there than did Qwenqwo.

She sighed. "I'm frightened."

"And I am fearful for you." The Fir Bolg warrior put his arm about her shoulders again. "I couldn't help but notice. You've changed much in the short time we have been here on the shore. I can no longer address you as little Mo. You are fast becoming the young woman."

Mo's eyes turned back to the choppy water. It was true that her menstrual cycle had begun. She was growing very rapidly—inches it seemed in little more than a week. The changes in her body disturbed her, all the more so since she seemed to have no control over them. It was happening so quickly, much faster than she had been led to expect back on Earth. It was as if this world had changed her—was still changing her—as it was changing all four friends. She saw it, felt it, feared it, happening from day to day, even from moment to moment. She had noticed the same in Alan, who was only a few inches off being as tall as his beanpole grandfather, Padraig. He was shaving regularly, with a permanent shadow over his cheeks and chin. Was it possible that time passed more quickly on Tír than on Earth, so much so that a year here might be equivalent to two or even more years on Earth? The thought intrigued her, for it suggested that Alan was now well past sixteen years old and her adoptive brother, Mark, had he been here in the flesh, would have been approaching seventeen. Becoming a man.

She wiped the welling tears away with the back of her right hand. "I—I muh-miss my brother, Mark. I wish he was here with me."

Her fear had brought back a trace of the old stutter, the burden that had been lifted from her shoulders by another of those three wishes granted by Granny Dew. It made her think of the powerful old woman who had helped her so much—was helping her still, like a protective shadow.

Mo reached up to pat the protective hand of the dwarf mage, where it rested lightly on her shoulder. "You are my friend, Qwenqwo."

"It comforts my gnarled old heart to hear you say so."

"You may go ahead and ask your question."

"I do indeed have a particular question. How is it that, although you alone were denied a crystal of power, yet it appears to matter little, for already you appear to possess power enough within you?"

Mo smiled wanly, but she didn't answer his question. How astonished Qwenqwo would be to discover her secret. That her name was not Maureen Grimstone, but Mira. Mira was her secret name, her real name—the name given to her by her birth mother. But there was something dangerous in the evocation of her real name and she was only allowed to speak it when the occasion demanded. She had spoken her true name only once, when Alan's life had been in danger during the battle with the Legun incarnate at Ossierel. Alan had never mentioned it since. Maybe he had forgotten about it in all the confusion and horror? Whatever his reason, it was a good thing he had kept quiet about it, for the only time she had spoken it, it seemed to have changed her in some mysterious and terrifying way. Alan had saved her. He had somehow appealed to the Temple Ship. That much she had already been told by Milish—but what Qwenqwo had just added, that she could not be saved by Alan's oraculum, that between them he and the Temple Ship had . . . It seemed altogether too disturbing to think about.

"Tell me, Qwenqwo, is it true that the Temple Ship is able to think—to feel?"

"The Mage Lord says so. And I believe him."

She forced her reluctant mind to consider it again. When her spirit had been ravaged by the Legun, Alan had called on the help of the Temple Ship to save her. And now, the very thought that the Temple Ship could think and feel! It didn't surprise her as much as it should, perhaps, because she had sensed a presence in the Ship from the time at the frozen lake when they had needed to escape from the Storm Wolves.

Qwenqwo squeezed her shoulder. "Is it the Ship that has called you here? Was it the Ship that directed you here to the water's edge?"

She nodded, a thrill of awe running through her. "Qwenqwo—I need to know. You told us a tale, on the river journey, that the Temple Ship might once have been the Ark of the Arinn. Is this true?"

"I cannot say it is true. Merely that the legends have it so."

"I—I sense it is calling me. I feel that it is trying to tell me something."

"The Ship speaks to you?"

"Not in words, but in feelings."

He followed her gaze to where the Ship, a hundred yards broad from wingtip to wingtip, glowed with some inner, lambent source of energy.

"What does it say to you?"

"I sense foreboding." Mo shuddered. "Qwenqwo, I think—I feel—that it is calling me. I think I should go out to it. Please, will you take me to the Temple Ship?"

Qwenqwo's face grew pensive. "I sense nothing of the kind, though I too am consumed with foreboding."

"Maybe it's calling you too. I see you in my mind, when it calls me. I sense that it is also calling on the Mage of Dreams."

"My friend—recall, I beg of you, what happened when Alan demanded my help—when he insisted I take him back into the landscape of dreams!"

Mo remembered the dying of the High Architect at Ossierel. How Kate had not awoken from the experience.

He added, "The New Kyra will forbid it."

"That's why we cannot tell her." Mo's voice was little above a whisper: "I know how wrong it sounds. But I sense that the Ship is insisting I go out to it. It's calling me, urgently, because Alan is in danger."

The dwarf mage released Mo from the crook of his arm. He confronted her, gazing deeply into her eyes, then shook his head with an almighty frown. "Very well—if you so trust your senses we must do their bidding. Then let us make haste. Before the others realize what we have in mind."

Alan retraced the riddle in his mind. A point had become a vertical line. Then it reverted to a point again. The same point had moved through all of the angles of the pentagon, then reverted to the point. Each line, vertical or horizontal, had exactly measured the radius of a sphere that enclosed the pentagon. He felt a jolt of dread as he realized this could be some kind of mathematical riddle. It made no sense to be faced with a mathematical riddle in this world. It felt jarringly wrong. Had the Way recognized the fact he came from Earth where science, and mathematics, were so important? Did it toy with him in a setting a riddle appropriate to his all-too-scientific world?

He hadn't got a clue.

But it was no good moaning about it. A mathematical riddle, then . . . A point that became a line. To his none-too-mathematical mind it pointed to the most obvious of numerals—one. One measured the vertical and the horizontal of a perfect square. One squared reverted to the point. Even a math dumbo knew that. Did it just emphasize that one squared still equaled one? It seemed so piddlingly mundane, yet he had nothing to lose in speaking it aloud to see what happened. "One squared is one. For that matter, one cubed is one. And the square root of one is also one."

Nothing happened.

Damn! He should have guessed as much. It just wasn't going to be anything as easy as that.

He sensed that a hostile force was beginning to invade his body. He could feel it working against him, weakening his will. The muscles of his neck were turning to ice. He could barely move. There was a sound in his ears, a faint sound, but there was something about it that caused him to break out into a sweat. Was it his imagination, or did he hear the thudding sound of his own heartbeat, slowed to maybe half its normal speed, like some clock inside his head that was slowly ticking?

Try the oraculum!

He tried again; this time rather than speaking his answer he thought it aloud through the oraculum. One squared was one. The square root of one was still one.

Nothing.

He thought he sensed a movement under his feet. A quaver of uncertainty, as if the ground he was standing on was no longer solid. It felt as if his feet were planted on a raft floating in water. *Goddam!* He tried to look beyond the glowing pentagon within the circle, but beyond its glow there was utter darkness.

The ticking was getting louder, like a clockwork mechanism that had come alive inside his brain. The slow, distant rapping sounded distinctly ominous.

He turned his mind back to what little had been given him as a clue. The contraction of the light to a pinpoint in space. The extending of the pinpoint to lines and angles that were, maybe, like the extension of the single focus to the pentagon, drawn not in two dimensions on a floor but in three dimensions within a perfect sphere. Maybe the riddle had nothing to do with the numeral one, but with a three-dimensional pentagon within a sphere?

He felt himself spinning, as if he had become the point, his entire being moved along the many lines and angles, tracing the three-dimensional pentagon within the sphere. A numinous sense of power was all around him, so close it flooded all of his senses, yet he couldn't understand it. It was the proximity to the power that was debilitating him. He felt increasingly weak, his head dizzy. He tried to clear his thoughts to think. *A perfect pentagon inside a sphere . . . and I'm at the dead center of it.*

As in a dream, he recalled his old math teacher at high school. Miss Pemberton was droning on about those ancient Greeks like Euclid, who had discovered how the relationship of a circle to its radius was always the same. The constant was something those ancient Greeks had called pi. She had worked some tired old analogy, with Granny's apple pie, cut into slices, about the importance of pi. He hadn't taken a great deal of notice of Miss Pemberton at the time. He didn't have a clue what pi really meant—and to tell the truth Miss Pemberton hadn't seemed much wiser—but he did recall that you had to use pi as the constant when you were figuring the radius that drew a circle. Maybe it was pi that translated a three-dimensional pentagon into a sphere? How the hell would he know!

But he whispered it anyway.

"The answer is pi."

The force inside him began to expand. He sensed, without needing to have it explained, that if it continued to do that it would end with his death.

He had a vision of an expanding circle. As the circle expanded, a second circle formed at exactly right angles to it, so one expanding circle was within another. Then the inner circle began to rotate within the outer circle, which began to rotate in the opposite direction. And all the time they were expanding—spinning and expanding so very quickly it was becoming a blur.

He himself was at the very core of the inner circle. He was spinning, rapidly, in three dimensions. He had become a third circle, spinning within the two vaster circles.

Then, as if in a final moment of lucidity, he thought about his arch-enemy, the Tyrant of the Wastelands. The Tyrant's symbol resembled a triple infinity. He considered that hated symbol, as he had seen it on the hilt of the Sword of Feimhin, or drawn into Mo's sketchbook, or the swords and shields of the Tyrant's legionary soldiers.

He allowed the symbol to fill his mind: a triple infinity. He tried to find words to describe it, but he didn't possess the vocabulary. He thought of the symbol for infinity, the two interlocking circles, and then he amazed himself by imagining three interlocking infinities all meeting at their centers, opening out into three-dimensional space. With little or no confidence in his jumbled thoughts, he hurled that image into the void. He felt a jarring dislocation. The mathematical symbols were gone. His body was dissolving, just as it had dissolved on that fateful day on the summit of Slievenamon. He felt that same agony as his physical being was being torn apart. Then, abruptly, he was standing on the infinite white plane of Dromenon.

For several moments he felt paralyzed with shock, his mind numbed. It was as if his will no longer belonged to him.

He blinked repeatedly, struggling to regain control. Reaching up, he brushed his fingertips against his brow, as if to reassure himself that the oraculum was still there. He found its smooth inverted triangle, but it felt unresponsive—dead! Abruptly the ticking returned, louder than before, like a measured drumbeat invading his senses. The drumbeat must be important. He tried to locate the source of the rhythmical sound, which was accompanied by a distant tinkling, almost a musical accompaniment—and he glimpsed the distant glint of gold. The gold focused to a figure of sorts, so far away he could barely make it out, a figure that appeared to be striding toward him in a slow-motion majesty of movement. The very landscape looked contrived, like something produced by a computer program. Through this surreal landscape the tiny glinting figure was marching, step by step, in a slow advance in his direction.

"Damn!"

The tinkling was coming from the golden figure and the drumbeat was the rhythm of its march. The whole scene, the gleam of gold moving through the immense white plain, was sublime beyond words, yet horribly mechanical at the same time. And now that he could make it out more clearly, the fantastic intricacies of design that made up the golden, glittering figure, it seemed vaguely familiar to him.

There must be a clue in the familiarity.

Another riddle; he guessed it had to be. Another trial, as if he were not fed up to the back teeth with riddles.

Alan studied it more closely now. He was forced to clench his eyes shut, rubbing at their aching shapes, to get them back into a clearer focus. When he opened them again the figure was significantly closer. The tinkling came from the movements of its clockwork. It was an automaton, a fancy robot. Why was it so maddeningly familiar to him?

He whispered, "This is not the portal!"

A voice, cold as a polar wind, replied: *A True Believer creates his own world through the power of his imagination.*

"I didn't create what I'm seeing."

Yet is it not a world created of and for the imagination of your kind?

A nauseating dizziness caused him to clench his eyes shut again. When he reopened them he found himself in front of an elaborately carved desk. Behind the desk a frail old man was bent over his writing. Gazing about him, Alan saw that he was standing in some kind of library, lined with ancient leather-bound books.

"Is this supposed to tell me something?"

The old man did not look up, but his withered hand reached up, then spun around on its axis, as if dismissively responding to Alan's question. A new complex of sensations invaded Alan's mind. He sensed the waves of the sea. The movements of air on the breeze. The patterns of tissues and organs developing within the eggs or wombs that bore them. It was as if he was being allowed a glimpse of some ultimate truth—like the secrets of creation.

"What's it all supposed to mean?"

I welcome you with an acknowledgment of what is dominant in your world.

Startled, Alan gazed down at the bent head of the old man, a figure with a white beard and long, thinning hair. There was also something very familiar about this figure, something he recalled from a textbook at school. Suddenly he recognized who it was—one of the greatest thinkers and artists in history, the elderly figure of Leonardo da Vinci. Even as he recognized him, the old man raised his head. His eyes were now opened wide, but they were not the rheumy old blue that Alan recalled from the picture in the book, but a malignant all black.

We meet again, oraculum-bearer!

Alan realized at once who the figure really was. He had been hoodwinked into a confrontation not with the Fáil but with his arch enemy, the Tyrant of the Wastelands.

"So it was a trap."

The face, with its black orbits, beheld him in a contemplative silence. Then the claw-like hand spun once more on its axis and pointed, as if to indicate the golden robot, which had continued its march.

Communication

Mo stared overhead at the squealing flocks of seabirds that seemed to be drawn, as if through magnetism, to wheel around the stationary grandeur of the Temple Ship

"Oh, Qwenqwo?"

"Now then—let us face our fears together!"

They hesitated before the smooth flat expanse of ivory that was the blank face of the great horned head. Mo felt a fall in temperature, with the estuary breeze cutting through her clothes to numb her skin. The sound of the waves lapping against the prow beneath her seemed strangely muted in her ears, as if the imminence of change were blunting all of her senses.

"You must promise me, Qwenqwo, that you'll leave me here. As soon as you've helped me find the dream world."

"I can make no such promise."

"I won't be alone, Qwenqwo," she spoke softly. "I have a very powerful friend to keep me company."

Qwenqwo gazed about the Ship with evident skepticism. "I have no intention of abandoning you."

"Please do it for me, Qwenqwo."

"If I left you alone and you came to harm, I would never forgive myself. So I shall not leave you where there is the slightest danger. Accept my presence or there will be no entry into the world of dreams."

Mo reached out and brushed the gnarled right shoulder of her protector. In that instant she knew what she had always instinctively assumed—that the emotion she felt for this man, who owed her nothing yet would surely die to protect her, was the love she might have felt for a father—perhaps even father and grandfather combined—which had been cruelly withheld from her life. Tears came into her eyes with the depth of that realization as she gazed about her at the silent titan that was the Ship, which held itself so utterly still in spite of the movements of waves or weather.

"Then please do it now, Qwenqwo. You must use your talisman to help me communicate with a mind that doesn't think in words."

Qwenqwo sighed, settling himself cross-legged before the blank ivory face on the foredeck, inviting Mo to do the same. "Put both your hands on the runestone I place here on the deck before you. I will put my hands over yours. Think only of your fears—your concern for Alan and Kate."

She did so, closing her eyes. Mo's hands folded around the oval of jade, her fingers numbed by the cold, yet she held it tightly, feeling the intricate carving that covered every inch of the ancient surface, sensing the power and mystery that brooded there. Her nostrils felt congested, as if she couldn't easily breathe through them. When she parted her lips her mouth felt unusually dry, and then the briny taste of the sea arrived onto her tongue, a taste that also reminded her of iron—of blood. With a start she opened her eyes again and saw that Qwenqwo had sliced open his right palm, allowing the blood to flow over her hands.

"I don't have the time to invoke the mysteries in the age-old way, so it must be thus, brutally direct."

Mo watched how the blood ran through her fingers and over the deeply patterned surface of the Soul Eye that had once borne her own image in an urgent message to Alan, at the time she was prisoner of the false Mage of Dreams. She shivered as the blood of the true Mage of Dreams empowered the runestone on the ivory deck, uniting his talisman to the Ship through the living bond of his blood.

She closed her eyes again, waited a minute—two minutes—but nothing happened.

"Why won't it respond?"

Qwenqwo patted her hands, as if to encourage her to be patient. She heard the Mage of Dreams chanting, a whispered incantation, hymnal and powerful.

Still nothing happened.

Against the continuing murmur of the dwarf mage's incantations, she brought pictures into her mind. The moment she, Mark, Alan and Kate had first met at Padraig's sawmill in Clonmel. The summer of sandcastles and adventures that had followed. The growing bond of friendship that had united them then, and forever afterward. Slievenamon . . . That feeling of seduction . . .

She felt the enchantment again, so powerfully her eyes sprang open. In the great blank face, under the twin horns of the great ray, a circle of golden luminescence shimmered, grew stronger, solidified into being.

Once more Mo focused her mind on the forebodings she felt in her heart and spirit, for Alan, and through him, also for Kate.

She stared at the golden circle, observing how shadows invaded its liquid metal shimmer. The shadows swirled and metamorphosed, as if on the verge of becoming the shapes of living things, creatures she might recognize. A single shadow condensed to the figure of a very old man with thinning white hair falling about his shoulders, sitting behind an antique desk, its corners decorated with gargoyles' heads; the figure and desk floated in midair, hovering weightless over a featureless white plain that ran in all directions to infinity. The eyes of the old man were inhuman, all black, as if the absence of light were a tangible property of whatever mind resided there. The figure laughed, an old man's gentle cackle, but it chilled Mo's heart. His voice, when he spoke, was gentle. But Mo could only watch in horror as the words emerging from his mouth changed to a stream of insects, blue flies, wasps, locusts—a buzzing conversation exuding from the jaws and the nostrils of what now appeared little more than flaky skin stretched over a skull. Yet still she heard that dreadful voice inside her mind, and she understood every word:

You struggle to evoke the paltry power of the bauble on your brow. You cannot understand its extinguishing by my power. Even then you seek to find comfort in the fact that it confers a debased immortality, not of the carnal flesh but of the spirit alone. Be warned that the spirit is even more vulnerable than mere flesh. It can be tormented in ways more grievous than any rending of skin and bone. The anguish of the spirit can be extended to eternity . . .

Only then did Mo see Alan. He stood on the strange-patterned ground of lines and curves, unmoving, as if he had been turned to stone. He was staring, his eyes fixed far into the distance, to where something awkward and golden was twinkling against the uniform sea of white.

The horribly buzzing yet incongruously calm voice continued, the words oozing and swarming out of the skull-like face:

A poor adversary, indeed, have you proved to be, your imagination limited to that of a mechanical world. So have I created a fitting execution. A sage of your world, venerated for his wisdom, imagined a machine. For my amusement, I made real his creation. Behold the instrument of your fate.

Mo realized that the golden object was moving closer, however slowly, however jerkily and erratically. The sense of dread was overpowering. Mo felt her mouth open to scream but no sound emerged from her throat. The sound, when it did come, came not from her but from the hateful skull as the twinkling object drew nearer.

Yet still would I save you in both flesh and spirit if only you would go down on your knees and pay homage to me.

Mo heard Alan's determined mutter, "Never!"

Perhaps you should take a little more time to consider.

Mo heard a distracting sound: a loud ticking, as if a thousand clocks had invaded her mind.

"Qwenqwo—that monster is toying with him."

Mo felt the hands of the dwarf mage press upon her own as if urging her to preserve her observation yet keep it hidden. With a shrill anxiety she saw that the object approaching was a clockwork figure, a robot, made out of gold. In less than a minute of her watching it had quadrupled in size, and it was still growing rapidly.

You craved to confront the Fáil. But that council of shaven-headed foppery refused to lead you to it. I will so indulge you. I will allow you a glimpse so that you may be allowed to reconsider your position. But first, a warning!

The ticking grew louder. But throughout all Mo heard a slower, more powerful beat, the implacable footsteps of the robot. By now she could make out every detail of its construction, even at a distance: the glassy unblinking stare of the eyes, the pulleys and wheels, the swiveling mechanical joints, the great feet, rising and falling in the unstoppable mechanical rhythm, and held high above its glittering breastwork, an enormous spiked ball and chain. So ponderous were its footfalls that the white background shuddered with every tread.

Mo's heart faltered as the white landscape turned to utter dark. For a moment she thought she was gazing into a vision of death. But then she saw a speck of trembling at the heart of it, like the faintest star in the first pallid sky of night.

"Kate?" She heard Alan gasp the name. "Kate—is it you?"

Mo wept openly as the speck grew closer. It was hard to believe this scratch in the dark was anything human, yet human it was, curled tight into a ball, the lank hair bedraggled and tangled, the flesh filthy and shrunken, the eyes tightly clenched, lost to a despair as total as the dark that enclosed her.

She heard Alan's anguished roar: *"Kate!"*

Her fate is of the flesh alone. For eternity will your spirit be damned. Even now it is not too late. Yet still would I be merciful. I would save her, as well as you. All I ask is that you yield to me.

Mo heard Alan's answering whisper, trembling, though not she sensed with fear but with utter loathing.

"I'd rather we both died."

Mo screamed: "Temple Ship—if you really are a friend, help him!"

Suddenly the shimmering gold circle in the Temple Ship was invaded by a different darkness: the inky background of the night sky in which pinpoints of starlight flickered and changed, as if constantly remaking themselves. Mo recognized the matrix of Mark's crystal, given to him by Granny Dew. She recalled a game she had played with Mark, a shared secret, when Grimstone had locked them in the cellar all night for punishment. In her mind she heard the rhyme:

> *Take you*
> *Take me*
> *Altogether make three*
> *Who are we?*

Mo whispered, softly: "The Lost Children!"

It was the Peter Pan game—the game they would escape into when their adoptive father had locked them away in the dark. In their imaginations they could travel anywhere they wanted, have the greatest adventures . . .

Only Mark and she knew the game. Mo stared, speechless, as the shimmering circle on the face of the Ship became a screen in which a hand was imprinted, as if pressing toward her from the other side.

Qwenqwo embraced her, then moved forward to place his hand against the impression in the shimmering circle.

"Is it truly you, young Ironheart?" he exclaimed.

Qwenqwo!

"Then it is you!"

I'm here—but I'm not sure I'm real.

"Be assured—you live."

How do you know that?

"I climbed to the top of the Rath of the Dark Queen. The Mage Lord and I, we both observed there was nobody at the summit."

But what does that mean?

"Your destiny you fulfilled, and more. You were subsumed, in the flesh and in the spirit, by the Third Power."

If so—where am I?

"If I judge it right, you have entered Dromenon."

Instinctively Mo ran forward, to place her hand against the impression of that other welcoming hand. The sense of communication was instantaneous.

"Mark—*Mark*! Is it really you?"

Mo—I can sense you!

Was it her imagination or did she feel Mark's hand hold her own, the way he would comfort her when, after Grimstone or Bethel had locked her in the cellar, he would sneak down to keep her company in the dark.

"You're really here?"

I'm one with the Temple Ship.

"I can't bear to think of you so alone."

I'm not alone. But I don't have time for explanations. We're going to have to do something to save Alan. You can't stay here. You and Qwenqwo—you must leave the Ship.'

"I won't leave you. I won't. Not now I've found you again."

Mo—listen to me. It's been so wonderful to be able to talk to you, and to Qwenqwo. But it's too dangerous for you to stay. You really have to get away. There's no more time to explain. You've got to trust me.

"Please, no!"

You must leave the Temple Ship immediately!

The Fáil

THE SENSE OF DOOM WAS LIKE BLOOD FILLING Alan's mouth. The golden robot was about sixty yards away and yet already it appeared as tall as a house. Above its head, held tight in the gauntlets of its two gigantic arms, was the enormous spiked ball and chain, ready to strike. He saw the tension in the cables, the strain increasing as the mechanical wheels turned, the ratchets, cogwheels, cables and hawsers, the gyroscopes that gave it balance, the irredeemable focus of those flat, glassy eyes, the sheer unstoppable ferocity of its purpose.

Thus have you determined your own fate! I have programmed the machine so it will strike, again and again, tirelessly and endlessly. You will no longer have any presence—any physical being—in this exalted place.

With all of his might Alan tried to turn the power of the oraculum against it, but there wasn't even a flicker of a response.

Resist as you will. But it will be to no avail. Your flesh will be scattered to dribbets and flecks, forever to remain rooted in this unforgiving place. Your soul spirit will become one of the ghosts that abide within for eternity, bewailing its fate.

The ground shivered and shook, as if each ponderous step of the monster's approach caused a quake in the fabric of Dromenon.

"You killed my mom and dad. Why—why did you do it?"

Such loyalty is touching. But individual lives are so brief as to be meaningless. What matters if two such candles have burned out prematurely?

"Their deaths matter to me. I know you killed them. And I loathe you for it."

Hate me then—I am no witch goddess that would cherish love. But at least let me open your eyes onto a broader vision. Unshackle your mind to consider what might yet become your destiny. Behold the power you so desperately wished to confront!

Alan was overwhelmed by a shockwave so awesome that even the eye of the oraculum seemed to blink and close before opening again onto a vision that stopped his breath. At the heart of the void an explosion of light came into being and expanded within the same moment, bursting through the darkness in an incandescent swirl of rainbow hues. In the eerie absence of sound, he saw a giant sun come into being from the expanding maelstrom, only to explode again before condensing into what appeared to be a galaxy. The scale of change, of successive being and unbeing, was so gargantuan he could only stare at what was happening in wonder.

"I don't understand."

How could you possibly understand? You can but witness its glory shackled by the mechanical vision of your world.

Alan forced himself to ignore the continuing approach of the robot, which must by now be no more than thirty yards away, the ground underneath his feet heaving as if he were riding a turbulent ocean.

"What does it mean?"

The Tyrant was silent.

It was as if Alan's being had contracted to a mote of dust, against which he beheld a proliferation of galaxies and nebulas that eddied and spiraled about him, gigantic explosions of supernovae, whirling oceans of gaseous energy more brilliant than any rainbow. He was gazing into one of the stellar furnaces where a new universe was coming into being.

"What are you implying? This is some kind of . . . of revelation?"

The witches saw fit to criticize the harnessing of such a wonder. Small minds terrified of the ultimate ambition—infinite power!

Alan's voice fell to a whisper, husky with uncertainty. "You're talking about the Arinn?"

Such power! Of all the beings on all the worlds, the Arinn alone had the knowledge and the courage to harness it. Such was their vision—they discovered how to control the very root of being. They became one with it.

The robot was so close that Alan could feel the radiating heat from its engines. He slithered down onto his knees, his bewildered head dropping.

"But why—why would they do that?"

Can you still fail to see what I am offering you? The choice between life as a short and brutal struggle—or the ultimate control over your own destiny—eternity!

Over the estuary a fleet of ships commanded by Shee had taken to the water, racing toward the boat that was carrying Mo and Qwenqwo back to the shore. Mo was standing in the prow, screaming at them all to stay back. A sound filled the air, a keening so loud it caused widening ripples from around the great shape of the Temple Ship and echoed from the walls across the estuary.

"Row—row! Turn back! Your very lives depend on it!" The dwarf mage shouted to the Kyra, who was standing erect in the prow of the nearest boat.

The great manta ray wings of the Ship glowed, as if aflame with an inner light, its surface becoming incandescent.

It was the young Kyra's turn to roar, a command she transmitted through the oraculum as much as her voice: "Back to shore!"

The Temple Ship began to rise from the water, deluging the sleek craft of the Shee that surrounded it. They were tossed and buffeted by the downdrafts, caught up in a local cauldron of storm winds, as the air was battered down by the beating of the enormous wings.

"See," Qwenqwo marveled, staring upward. "It's changing."

Feathers of the purest white sprang into being over the rising colossus. A raptor's curved beak arose where the blind head of the ray had been, and the eyes above the beak were black, an all-consuming force of determination, in which they glimpsed a fast-pulsating matrix of silver.

"Has your crystal evoked this terror, Fir Bolg?" The young Kyra roared at the dwarf mage with the gaze he well remembered from her sister-mother.

"This is beyond any power of mine," he shouted back.

Holding aloft the runestone, Qwenqwo groaned as he saw it turn black, the silver matrix pulsating so powerfully within it he could barely keep hold of it. Pride glowed in his eyes as he acknowledged the real source and nature of the communication.

"Young Ironheart! Take with you all my hopes and blessing!"

Both Kyra and the dwarf mage paused for a heartbeat then their faces, as one, lifted skywards to behold the leviathan that dwarfed them rising out of the water, with the enormous wings creating a whirlpool in the ocean beneath as it gathered momentum with colossal down-thrusts. The great shape held still for a moment like a hovering eagle, then it spiraled heavenwards, rising at such speed it seemed to gain a mile of loft with a few wing beats, until it had become a mere speck—and then was gone. The Kyra's oraculum pulsated rapidly in her brow.

Across the estuary a host of watchers had joined them—the guard on the walls and the people of Carfon— all eyes staring skywards. A pinpoint of light appeared where the speck had been, expanding in an instant, until it seemed that a star was falling out of the heavens. A moment later they heard the screech of the tormented atmosphere as it fell, the air erupting into fire with its passage. The gasps of awe became screams of terror over the walls of the ancient city as the target of the approaching fireball became clear. There was no time to think, no time even to consider hurling themselves into the sea as the flaming mass engulfed them. But where the Kyra and dwarf mage expected the explosion of its impact into the stony fabric of the ancient city, the fireball vanished, leaving only the incandescent line of its passage still hanging in the air.

The robot towered over Alan. The ground-quaking thud of its feet, that slow booming drumbeat, had stopped.

In its place the vile symphony of buzzing, clicking and ticking had grown deafening, echoing and reverberating inside his skull, as if his head had been invaded by the pestilential hordes of insects. He could smell the oils that lubricated the engine's joints, he could feel the hot exhausts of the engines that powered it, as if he faced the open doors of a gigantic furnace. As the golden arms rose to their highest point, he found himself helpless to prevent his fate, his mind numbed with horror. There was no point in trying the power in his brow—the oraculum was extinguished. He thought instead about his mom and dad, whose deaths the Tyrant had just blamed him for.

He whispered, "I've failed you!"

A hundred feet above his kneeling figure those glassy eye sockets reflected the icy white light of Dromenon.

What was it waiting for? To torment him for a few more seconds?

He raised his voice against the frenzy of buzzing. He brought to mind the last time he had seen his parents, before setting out on the skiing vacation at Aspen. "If I'm going to die, then I'll do it on my feet, like an American."

Struggling back so he was standing, it took all of his will to keep his jerky legs still enough to bear him erect.

Think, foolish child—a final chance?

"I will never obey you. I will never betray my friends for you."

At the top of its reach the enormous spiked ball strained its heavy weight at the end of its chain. Alan's eyes closed, his entire being stiffened, waiting for its ponderous arc to fall. He felt his mind invaded by darkness, as if the Tyrant so coveted his death he had invaded Alan's being to share the experience of it, the annihilation of his body, the complete subjugation of his spirit. Alan did his best to hold onto the image that meant so much to him—that memory of Mom and Dad.

An explosion of light blinded him even through his closed lids. He heard words, mind-to-mind—a voice he recognized:

What's it worth, Alan?

Mark's voice—Mark's sense of humor! It made no sense. Nothing made sense anymore.

Then, abruptly, he sensed something else that felt like a sudden, overwhelming fear. It wasn't his own fear—his own he was familiar with already. But there was no longer time to wonder as his body disintegrated. Alan felt the shockwave pass through him, an explosion so intense it incinerated his being. Yet, strangely, he was still aware, sentient. The universe in which his consciousness remained was a world of silence—nothingness. Then he saw them materialize out of the nothingness, standing immediately in front of him, their arms extended as if to embrace him.

"Mom—Dad?"

He felt his soul spirit materialize as if it had come together again, even if only for a moment, like a single desperate thought lingering in this world of darkness. He felt the impression of tears well into his eyes and run over his cheeks. He saw the same tears fill their eyes. He strained to meet them, moving in a strange slow motion as if under water, yet somehow he closed the distance between them until they could embrace.

He was looking into his father's eyes.

"Hey—I'm sorry."

His father's arm embraced his shoulders as if to reassure him. His mother's two arms were about his waist. They held him, comforted him, for several seconds. Then he saw Mom and Dad each reach out with an arm, their hands opening, fingers splaying, as if to show him something.

Alan stared about himself, unable to comprehend what he was seeing. The darkness had become suffused with stars. He blinked, blinked again, trying to clear his eyes of the bewilderment of tears. He tried to speak, as all three of them embraced, weightless, within a wheeling cylinder made up of the night sky.

But how could he still think like this? How could he think at all? Where was he? How could any of this be happening to him?

It's really beautiful!

The Triangular Shadow

KATE WAS BACK IN THE PLACE OF UTTER DARKNESS; a terrible place, a place designed for torment of the spirit. It wasn't a darkness you could see with your eyes, but a darkness that was the opposite of seeing. Not a darkness you could reach out and feel, but the absence of feeling, a darkness that when you tried to touch it, it swallowed your groping fingers, it swallowed your entire outstretched arm, and then it devoured more of you, your arms and legs, your entire body, even your screaming tongue, until it left nothing of you behind—nothing at all. You couldn't hear it, or smell it, or taste it. The only way you knew it was there was the feeling, the awful, ghastly feeling, of being swallowed whole by it, of being devoured.

The awful thing, the maddening thing, was that she couldn't do anything to help herself. She was utterly powerless. She breathed in and out, deeply, repetitively, just to feel her chest expand. Her voice trembled as she tried to remember the childish incantation: "Sticks and stones may break my bones—but my . . . my memories . . . my poor memories . . ."

She was buried alive.

How could anyone come to terms with that? How could anyone survive manacled to the wall in a coffin-like cell of cold, and darkness and silence? She couldn't help touching herself, putting her fingers into her mouth. She bit determinedly on the knuckles of her right hand, to make herself aware that she was still here. But she couldn't bite on memory, on spirit, on the really important things such as love, or hope, or faith. The silence was leaching those important things out of her. And with their loss her mind was drifting out of her control. She had found a small comfort in constructing dreams. People thought that dreams were random. But in the dark and silence of her coffin-cell she had found a way of guiding her hopes into dreams. She had opened her mind into a dream in which she was lying on her back among the rocky outcrops on the slope above the saw-mill high in the fern-scented field at the foot of the Comeragh Mountains. The sky was drifting overhead—that wonderful summer's sky, a gentle whisper of clouds.

Was there ever a sky as lovely as that? And yet, under that lovely drifting sky, I'm growing excited . . . scared.

The trouble was that the dream was apt to change against her will. And now it morphed into the time when they had discovered they were experiencing the same dream in their sleep. She didn't want the dream to change. It so terrified her that she scurried up the rock-strewn hillside in search of peace . . . and she forced it to change back again, to gaze up once more into the gentle drifting of the clouds. Her mind began to paint the clouds again. How nice to have nothing else to do all day other than to gaze, in perfect tranquillity, at the whispering clouds . . .

Oh, dreaming, let me just escape in dreams . . .

And yet the scary darkness was never far away, the silence all around her, invading her dreams . . .

Oh, God help me!

Desperately, she willed to mind that other sweet, wonderful day. The day she had emerged through the gate in the ivy-clad wall, wheeling her bicycle. And Alan was waiting for her outside the gate . . .

He kissed me. She remembered it. She no longer cared that she was dreaming from the silent confines of her coffin-grave. She willed the memory to mind, caught hold of it and refused to let it go. She breathed it aloud, no matter how much her lips trembled over the words. "He kissed me!"

She clung to that kiss. It was the only hope that remained in the midst of so much darkness. *Alan!* She treasured that memory of him with all of her heart. *Alan loves me.* The memory of that single kiss would keep her alive for another hour. And then there were other kisses she would try her very best to remember. Each kiss had the potential of becoming another dream, another moment of blessed escape . . .

I so love you too. I will always love you. If what must be will be, I will die still loving you.

Kate held onto the dream of that one kiss. She curled her being around it as if she were a minuscule thing, an embryo, snuggling for the comfort it brought her . . .

Wake!

No! She refused to wake up. She squeezed herself even more closed, body and mind, her being ever more tightly curled about her dream.

Hear me, child! The Night Hag is harvesting a library of lost souls. When she extracts their experience from them, all of their hopes and fears, their loves and pains, their spirits are extinguished, like ash. All that they were is lost for eternity. Beware you do not become ash to her gathering.

"I will not wake up!"

She felt strong fingers remove her right hand from her clenched shut eye, her hand pried open. She crabbed her fingers shut again around something hard and rounded and heavy, something cool as marble. Almost immediately she sensed light out there beyond her closed eyelids. Light invading the coffin-cell. And the pain was gone.

The pain is gone!

Wake, now—Kate Shaunessy! Take strength from what, once taken, is now restored to you.

Somebody was calling her out of her dream. A voice, powerful and persistent. But her mind still resisted. Even in the dark silence of the grave, cocooned within her dream, terror could still reach in and clutch at her. She couldn't take the risk. And yet her instincts insisted that something important was happening. Had Alan arrived? She knew—she had always known—that his arrival would herald death for her, her purpose, as far as the Witch was concerned, now spent. But she had consoled her self that at least the torment would end . . .

Wake, child!

It was hardly a voice at all but a rattle inside the walls of her skull. Yet there was a powerful sense of something up close . . . a shadowy being . . . a triangular shadow, looming over her. Perhaps it was Faltana, come to begin another hour of torment? But the voice wasn't that of the succubus. This voice was within her mind rather than in her ears, a voice so deep and full of foreboding it sounded like gravel pouring into an old tin bath.

Wake!

Cracking open her matted eyelids she saw multicolored rays of light splaying out between the fingers of her right hand. She opened her hand a little more to stare at it, seeing something familiar in the green matrix, the soft alluring green of spring, speckled with the metamorphosing, whorling specks of gold.

"It's . . . my beautiful crystal!"

I am here, child! Your time has come.

She gazed at it in wonderment, letting it dazzle her dark-adapted eyes. So brilliant was the light coming from the crystal it was illuminating the entire cell. Then she blinked, slowly, rubbing at her eyes to try to clean them. She licked her lips, which felt fissured and dry as ashes.

"What . . . who are you?"

All she heard was a growling and mumbling, as the figure materialized in the strange half-light within the cell, something dark and substantial, like the pyramidal cap of a mountain. On top of the figure a heavy head swiveled to examine her, revealing an incredible face, wrinkled as a prune, with a tangle of white hair that flowed down like a cataract about the squat triangular body, and a great long nose between two all-black eyes that peered into her own, as fierce as an eagle's. When the broad, purplish lips parted, she glimpsed teeth green as moss.

"Granny Dew," she murmured. "I'm still dreaming!"

Cha-teh-teh-teh!

From her distant memories she recalled that expression—it was hardly a word at all, but something like the underlying meaning of something. With a start, she remembered what it meant. Danger! That was the meaning of the sound still pattering in her mind. Kate blinked her eyes again. The word was like a familiar knock against the shutters of her bewildered mind. She tried to open her eyes wider but she could not. The lids were too swollen, their lashes matted together.

"Danger?"

Daaannngggerrr!

Strong hands brushed her brow. Grimy fingers, moistened with spittle, wiped the caking of pus from her eyelashes, and her eyes now fluttered fully open. At first there was nothing to see. Her cell was very small and bare, nothing in it other than herself and the chains that bound her. She offered no resistance to those grimy hands as they moved down over her body. She could smell them, loamy and moist, like the earthy smell of the mulch that Uncle Fergal cultivated for his insects in the cellars back home.

The hands paused over her heart. They enfolded her right hand, where the crystal, as large as a pullet's egg, throbbed against her palm. A surge of strength rushed through her, tingling when it reached her lips and the tips of her fingers and toes. Then, whether she heard it through her mind or her ears, she didn't know, but the voice was clearer now, like a shovel digging into shards of gravel.

Stand, child!

She did her best, tottering to her feet. The manacles clanked and held her rigidly to the wall. But suddenly she felt different, lighter. Lifting first one foot and then the other, she understood. She was free. The clanking was the manacles falling away onto the echoing floor of her cell.

"Thank you!" she stammered, rubbing at the raw skin where the hard iron had chafed. Tears filled her eyes as if taps had burst open.

A shiver of outrage shook the hands that rubbed at Kate's frozen thighs and calves.

Arrrhhhggh—food and warmth you need. But there is no time even to boil up a pot of gruel!

A crooning chant filled the tiny cell, quavering in rhythm with the rocking of the old woman, as she reached into a fold in her dress and withdrew a purse woven from grasses.

Here!

Into Kate's mouth she pressed a nut-sized tidbit, taken from the purse.

Hold it against your cheek and suck. It will provide sustenance for several hours. The rest you must save to use again, when hunger threatens. There is enough in the purse to sustain you for a day or two—three at the most. If a morsel is but held in the tongue, it will cloak your presence and scent in times of danger.

Kate moved the bitter-tasting food against her cheek and she sucked on it with her tongue. There were hidden flavors beyond the bitterness, perhaps cloves and menthol, and a powerful burning sensation that diffused into her cheeks and palate and made her head throb and spin. She suppressed the urge to gag. There was a peculiar sensation on her tongue and down her throat, as if with each morsel of saliva she swallowed a mouthful of food had entered her stomach.

Arrrhhhggh—time we have not. We are close to malice that even I cannot control. The occasion demands cunning rather than power.

With a crooning gentleness, the old woman hugged Kate's emaciated body to her breast, her hands stroking her matted hair. Then she took Kate's hand, with her fingers still wrapped around the glowing gemstone, and pressed the stone to Kate's dirt-grimed brow. A sparkle of light danced in the center of those all-black eyes, then whirled, like a spinning sycamore seed, as it entered Kate's entranced mind. A lance of pain impaled her forehead and entered her skull like the sharpest auger.

Kate felt the force of the gemstone invade her mind. The magic of it expanded into her blood, invading her heart, which beat powerfully and rapidly, and from there it suffused every nook and cranny of her being. A sense of exhilaration so overwhelmed her that, had Granny Dew not held her steady, Kate would have fainted onto the grimy floor.

Your heart has been weakened, child, through privation and starvation. But the crystal will restore strength of flesh and spirit. In the meantime, remove this dress of rags and let me cover your bones with a cloak of spiders' weave, which will protect you against the chill of this accursed place as well as confusing your scent with that of a scurrying mouse.

Kate allowed the rags to fall from her shoulders to her bare feet, and felt the prickly weave of the spiders close around her limbs. The power of the crystal continued to surge and expand through her bloodstream, until her whole body throbbed so vigorously she felt she would explode.

Granny Dew reached deep into the folds of her dress and removed a second grassy purse, larger than the first, handing it to Kate and instructing her to conceal it within her freshly woven mantle.

"What is it?"

A handful of life—the beginnings of things.

"What am I to do with it?"

Granny Dew ignored Kate's question. There was more rocking and grumbling, then a crooning call; it took Kate a moment or two to understand that the strange figure was beckoning for her to follow. *Let us depart, quickly now, while a bane of sleep still cloaks eyes and senses. You must resist all impulse to draw on your crystal until you are far beyond the eyes and teeth of this accursed place.*

"We can't just walk out of here. The cell is locked."

The door was thrown open and Granny Dew was silhouetted against the open doorway, a triangular shadow against the lurid red glow.

Kate looked with awe at her rescuer in the crimson light—a glimpse of the implacable determination in that doughty face, as weighted with folds and darkness as the dress that trailed across the dirt floor. In the depths of its shadow the tiny pinpoints of spiders' eyes flickered, their spinnerets forever knitting.

About them, as they ascended long tunnels of bone, the succubi lay scattered, deep in sleep . . . seemingly enchanted. Kate could hardly breathe with terror. She prayed that they wouldn't encounter Gargs. She also prayed that whatever power Granny Dew possessed, it would be enough to let them walk out of the Witch's lair without anybody noticing their passing.

After what seemed an eternity of patient progress they arrived at the great portal of the Tower, which comprised the gaping jaws of the gigantic skull. Here Granny Dew hesitated, as if confronted by some invisible danger. Through her bare feet, Kate felt a rising vibration moments before she heard the growl that caused it. She sensed a new shudder of alertness invade the fangs.

Arrrggghhh! The slumberer has awoken!

In her panic, Kate went to bite on a morsel from the first of the two purses. But Granny Dew raised a cautionary finger. Kate trembled within her cowl of spidersweb as the old woman held still, the black eyes pensive, as if gathering her thoughts.

The seed purse, child!

Kate handed back the mysterious second purse and watched the wrinkled face gaze into its contents, then tip something into her palm before returning the purse to her.

Place the purse back in your mantle for safekeeping, then take what I am holding—grasp it firmly in your right hand!

Kate picked it up and saw it was a fresh green acorn. Granny Dew's hand enfolded hers, so between them they held the acorn doubly tight. Her raised finger still cautioned Kate to absolute stillness and silence—not a word was to be spoken. Kate felt a swelling within her palm.

Granny Dew mimicked a movement, as if casting the seed.

With a sweep of her hand, Kate cast the sprouting acorn into the dirt within the jaws of the Beast. The tension had become unbearable. But Granny Dew bade Kate to remain still for a few more moments, as a young oak tree expanded, roots pressing down against the Beast's lower jaw while the trunks and branches strained against the upper.

Kate shrieked as, with a thunderous crash, the jaws of the Beast closed, any escape now blocked by the enormous interlocking fangs.

Cha-teh-teh-teh! So powerful has it become already, though only half awoken from the slumber of eons!

Already the red glare was intensifying about them. Kate saw that the succubi were stirring and stretching, shaking off the enchantment. Faltana's single sleep-swollen eye was blinking, as if struggling to break open.

"Quickly, Granny Dew!"

Grow, mighty oak of the wildwoods, whose roots have caused castle walls to crumble, whose limbs have withstood the storms of ages!

With an almighty creaking and groaning, the oak tree spread and thickened, its roots cracking open bone fossilized to stone, branches thickening until they were feet in diameter, holding the terrible jaws apart, and the great trunk, already thirty feet or more across, forcing apart the clasp of fang on fang.

From deep under her feet Kate heard a roar that rattled the Tower of Bones at its roots. *I sense you, Witch of the Morning. I will break your thrall. Then shall I devour the brat, and possess the trinket you sought to awaken.*

Fire exploded within the foliage. The oak tree was ablaze.

The triangular shadow battled its way deep into the tangle of roots, trunk and boughs, the body of Granny Dew growing and swelling until its base filled the entire floor of the entrance and its brow pressed against the roof.

Quickly now—between my legs!

Kate pressed her body into the entanglement of fangs. She shrieked. "I can't squeeze through. The jaws are closed!"

The triangular shadow expanded further still, provoking fractures in the roof, showering rock and bone over Kate. From the chamber behind her she heard the cries of the awakening succubi. The old woman's spidersweb dress burst asunder. Kate saw an ocean of spiders emerge to fill the space between the jaws, then, like a tidal wave, they deluged into the chamber. The screams of the succubi rose to a new crescendo as the biting mandibles found them.

With a splintering crack the jaws ruptured. Kate tumbled out between the monstrous fangs, falling onto the dirt outside as the first flicker of dawn permeated a leaden sky.

Run!

"Where—where can I run?" Kate had never been beyond the jaws of the Tower. She was terrified of what she would discover outside.

You will discover one both ancient and wise enough to understand your need. In the trial to come, you must trust your heart—let your heart alone guide you!

Kate ran, while about her the dawn sky turned red, like the hinterland of an erupting volcano. She fled, bewildered and directionless, anywhere that took her away from the Tower of Bones and the malignancy that brooded there.

Unwelcome News

In his dream Alan was fighting for his life on the plaza of Ossierel. Green fire and acrid smoke fanned the ruins of the city all around him as he held the Spear of Lug, with its blazing runes, aloft. His mind was filled with foreboding at the imminent approach of the Legun incarnate.

No! Not that!

He was missing something here. Something Milish had said to him—something important. Instinctively he turned to the oraculum, as if to discover what he was looking for through its illumination. The power woke in him, suddenly, explosively—it erupted out from his brow to every cell of his body.

He woke up, tossing and turning inside a circular tent. There was only a single source of light, an oil lamp, somewhere in the background. He had no idea where he was or how he had got here.

"Rest now, Mage Lord! You are safely returned to us!"

It sounded like the voice of an Aides. He tried to sit up but lacked the strength. Judging from the pallid light, he figured it must be night outside but approaching dawn. He lay on a camp bed. The Aides was seated cross-legged by his side, the same woman who had been cooling his brow with the cloth.

He called out: "Milish—are you nearby?"

"I'm here." The bronze-skinned hand of the Ambassador emerged from the background gloom. She took the towel from the Aides to wipe the sweat from his brow.

"Where am I?"

"You are back in the shoreside encampment—protected by Shee."

"How the heck . . . ?"

"Hush now! You need to rest." Milish's voice was low, reassuring. "Aides!" She spoke urgently to the bedside nurse. Murmuring to one another, the two women worked as a team, lifting Alan's head and shoulders from the sweat-soaked pillow. "Now you're awake, we can assist your recovery with a draft of healwell."

"What happened? I need to know."

"If you cannot answer that question, then none other is likely to do so. Contrary to prudence you foraged alone within the labyrinth of the ancient city. We thought you lost. Then . . . Alarm bells everywhere. Bedlam!"

"Bedlam?"

Milish's eyes turned heavenwards, as if appealing to the powers.

"You owe your safe return to the Temple Ship."

"What?"

"It was the Ship that found you. Don't expect me to explain such extraordinary events. Speak to your friend, Mo, and the dwarf mage, who appear to have had something to do with it. It is enough for me to thank the Trídédana that you were returned to us alive and, it appears, without serious injury."

Alan was stunned by what Milish had just said. It was difficult to think clearly with his head spinning with the smallest movement. But some of his more recent memories were returning to him. He recalled the Tyrant, in his guise of Leonardo da Vinci. The golden robot, the great spiked ball . . .

"The Ship, you say? Qwenqwo . . . ? And Mo?"

"Please drink the healwell!"

He accepted two sips of the honey-colored elixir from the turquoise flask. It burned in his mouth. Almost immediately he could feel its reviving properties. It penetrated the tissues of his throat and gut like powerful alcohol, entering his bloodstream and further, discovering his exhausted limbs. A new sweat erupted over his face and body as more snatches of memory returned.

"You're right, Milish. When the Council refused to help me I looked for the portal on my own. A young sister . . . she pretended to help me. But she was a succubus. It was all a conspiracy of the Tyrant's. She led me into his trap."

"Then you are fortunate indeed to be alive!"

Alan shuddered, causing the Ambassador to grasp his hand, hold it reassuringly between her two. "Hey, Milish—something extraordinary happened. I . . . I heard Mark's voice."

She squeezed his hand tighter.

"You're very weak. You've consumed little but water for these two days of tossing and turning. Now you must accept food and rest."

Alan shook his head with disbelief. "Two days? Is that how long I've been out of things? Oh, man!"

"Rest!"

"I don't have time for resting. I need to know more of what happened."

Milish sighed. "We know nothing other than the fact your friend, Mo, sensed you were in danger."

"How?"

"I know not. Only that she had the dwarf mage take her to the Temple Ship. And there . . ." Milish hesitated, shook her head at him. She exclaimed, "Thank goodness!" A second Aides had just entered the tent with a bowl of steaming broth. "Keep him abed, at dagger-point if necessary."

Alan thought it prudent to allow the two Aides to feed him spoonful by spoonful, like an ailing child.

"Hey—there's something else," he murmured, between spoonfuls.

"Always, there is something!"

"I'm serious, Milish. It's important."

"See how, with all of this excitement, the oraculum flares in your brow. It drains what little strength you possess. You must rest or you can be no use to yourself, or to Kate." Milish tried to settle him back on the bier.

But Alan kept hold of her hand. "You're keeping something back from me."

"There, on board the Temple Ship—or so the dwarf mage informs me—Mo spoke with her missing brother."

"Oh, heck!"

"I warn you!"

"Milish—oh, Milish!" Alan hauled himself upright on the bier, his hand squeezing her fingers without realizing he was hurting her.

"Desist!"

He loosened his grip on her hand, but refused to release her. "Not until you tell me more."

Milish recounted what little she knew. Mark, if it was to be believed, had entered into some strange communion with the Ship. He knew that Alan was in danger. Then all had witnessed how the Temple Ship had changed shape to become a raptor of enormous grace and power. Milish described how the raptor had soared into the sky before plummeting earthwards, to disappear above the ancient city, to the terror of everybody who saw it. "The very ground shook, as if struck by a thunderbolt. None saw the Ship return. When we awoke at daybreak it had returned—and you, unconscious but otherwise unharmed, were lying on the shore."

Alan dragged his hands down over his face. He recalled Mark's voice entering his mind at the very moment he had anticipated death. And now he heard that Mark had been somehow been involved with the Ship. This was the most incredible news. There was no way he could lie here in the cot while such amazing things were happening around him. He threw off the light sheet, grimacing at the nausea that swept over him as he slid his legs out onto the sandy floor.

He also recalled what he had been about to explain to Milish.

"I've been thinking about what you said—when you talked about the Kyra as we were getting ready to board the skiff."

She sighed, but met his eyes.

"Milish—I need to talk to the Kyra."

At the water's edge, he stared out at the raptor shape that hovered as if suspended on the inshore winds above the estuary. Its feathers were an opalescent pearly white, the whole being shimmering as if composed of nascent energy that was constantly in a state of flux.

"Wow!"

Still fretful at his being out of bed, Milish inhaled through dilated nostrils.

Alan studied every detail of the enormous being, marveling at the claws adorning the raptor's feet, now curled into sleeping grapnels, each claw large enough to carry an entire boat. He assumed that one of those claws had deposited him on the shore. Across the harbor thousands of the Carfonese seemed to share his awe. They were setting out in all manner of boats to get a closer look at it, the most intrepid of them being kept from touching it by a defensive ring of Shee.

Milish pressed him. "Now you've seen it, you must return to your rest."

He lifted his gaze to stare into the raptor's eyes, which were all-black, glimmering with a matrix of silvery motes and arabesques.

"Then it's true! That's Mark's crystal matrix."

There was so much he still didn't understand, far too much to absorb at once. Alan had to tear his gaze away to look at the flotilla of warships that had gathered in the estuary since he had been ferried across it by the boat of nuns.

"The fleet of the Shee?"

"They're getting ready for war," Milish confirmed. "Their army already numbers tens of thousands. The fleet includes transports so they can sail eastward, to accompany your reckless adventure."

He marveled: "All this hustle and bustle in two days—while I've been out of it, contributing nothing! It's unbelievable—like I'd been gone for a month!"

A deep and growling voice sounded from behind them. "My friend—Mage Lord—it is good to see you on your feet!"

Alan embraced Qwenqwo, though the powerful hug of his friend caused him to totter on his unsteady legs.

"I am, naturally, impatient to hear everything you discovered—though the Ambassador will kill me if I do not wait for a week."

Alan laughed. "Tonight I promise a full explanation. All that I saw and heard. We'll knock heads together— see what we can make of things."

"You look so gaunt—maybe the Ambassador is right. Perhaps a few days rest might be prudent?"

"I'll have plenty of time to rest during the journey. We can't afford to wait any longer. We must call together a council of war."

Alan turned back to Milish. "I'm also going to need your help. I must speak to Ainé—and Bétaald . . ."

"Speak then."

Alan span around, startled, to find himself gazing up into the eyes of the young Kyra.

He hesitated, his voice falling to a murmur. "I do need to talk with you—and Bétaald. But not now—not here."

"If it is to insist we travel immediately, we are not yet ready. We must make preparations, discuss objectives and tactics. You called for a council and a council you will have."

"It isn't that." Alan found it difficult to put into words what he wanted to say, particularly in the absence of Bétaald. "I really need to talk to you, on your own."

Milish tensed, a plea for caution in her eyes, then turned on her heel and strode a short distance away in the company of Qwenqwo. When satisfied that he and the Kyra were alone, Alan spoke softly:

"Milish has explained to me that there may have been a problem with the transfer of experience from your mother-sister. She has also told me that this is very important to you."

She gazed back evenly at him, but there was a blanking of expression in those pellucid blue eyes.

"I respect your privacy and apologize if I am trespassing on what may be deeply personal. But I really have to tell you this: I think it's possible that I may be carrying the memories of your mother-sister."

The shock of his words was plain in her posture and in her face. He saw the reaction in the oraculum in her brow—the sudden precipitous increase in her heartbeat. She didn't need to speak for him to know her thoughts. He read it in the shudder that passed through the frame of the young giantess, even as she averted her face.

Blasphemy!

CAT AND MOUSE

LIKE THE MOUSE WHOSE SCENT THE SPIDERSWEB was said to mimic, Kate darted from shadow to shadow, scurrying barefoot through a frightening landscape of ancient warfare, with colossal ruins poking like tombstones out of the mists of the false dawn. Sometimes, all too mouselike, she had to force herself to pass through labyrinths of caves and hidden passageways underground. Panting for breath, unable to suppress the rising terror in her throat, she skulked in crevices and wept as the memories rose, unwanted, into her mind. The memories of another time she had felt similarly hunted, on that murderous day when Sister Marie Thérèse had saved her by hiding her in a pit in the vegetable garden—the day when Mammy and Daddy and Billy . . .

Dear God, preserve me! She screwed up her eyes and pressed her hands tight over her temples. She just didn't want to think about that. She just didn't want the bad memories to come back.

Granny Dew had done something to her. With trembling fingers she reached up and touched her brow.

"Owww!"

A bolt of pain racked her skull and she had to jerk her fingers away, cradling her hand as it went into a crablike spasm. It felt as if she had suffered a tremendous electric shock.

What did you do to me, Granny Dew?

She couldn't help but recall Alan, how confused he had felt when Granny Dew had put that ruby triangle into his brow. *What on Earth has she done to me?*

The trouble was, as she now curled her body into a frightened ball, it had absolutely nothing to do with Earth. What it had to do with was . . . was magic. Magic at a really powerful level, a dangerous level, that went beyond any human understanding.

Why me? What am I really doing here?

The mountain, Slievenamon—that had something to do with it. All her life she had known that Slievenamon was a magic mountain. But that had only been the local legend. Nobody thought it was truly magical. For that matter, what did she really know about magic, even if she had lived in its shadow all her life? Alan had experienced this bewilderment too. She had seen the reaction in him. But Alan was different from her. He had a darkness all of his own. She had seen that darkness in him the day they had first met, when he had refused to back down before the fury of the swans. Something in Alan had welcomed the danger. Something that was desperately keen to fight back. And Mark too—there had been another kind of darkness there, for all of his joking. And Mo! *Oh Mo—sure you were the strangest of us all, collecting your birds' skulls and amber and crystals—what Mark called your "weirdiana"!* Now that Kate knew that magic really existed, wasn't there something about her friend, Mo, that seemed to be the very essence of magic, all wrapped up within the secret world of her strange little self? *But not me*, she thought. *Not Kate Shaunessy, the doctor's daughter from Clonmel.*

When she was twelve, and in second grade with the nuns, Maire Ni Houlihan had put jam in her hair and made her cry. Her nanny, Bridey, had washed her hair and brushed out the tangles, and given her a hug. Bridey had reassured her: "Sure the quare lumpy crayture is only jealous a' ye, with yeer emerald eyes and yeer lovely red locks! Won't all the boys be fancyin' ye and none will take so much as a peek at her!"

And she had stared at herself that night in Mammy's mirror—the big glass on the bedroom dressing table—and she had blushed to look into her own green eyes and hold bunches of her thick mane of auburn hair. She hadn't believed Bridey's words. Bridey loved her and would say anything to please her. *I'm just ordinary—bog standard*, as Uncle Fergal would say about a thing that irked him. Bog standard Kate Shaunessy! Magic would never come looking for her—sure it wouldn't!

Would it?

But still there was the bag of seeds that Granny Dew had placed in her hand. And she had seen how the acorn had grown into a tree in the jaws of the Tower. And hadn't she kept hold of the same bag all the time she'd been running, the bag she now hugged against her chest, feeling its prickly grassy feel against her skin as she breathed fast and shallow, already exhausted from running. And this was different from that other time in the vegetable pit in the African mission. She couldn't hope to skulk and hide until help arrived. Help would not be forthcoming.

You're going to have to go back out there and run.

She ran on feet that were lacerated and sore through what appeared to be another ancient graveyard of rusting metal in the shape of gigantic armor, with what must once have been titanic swords and shields. She hid among skeletons—the ribcages and pelvic bones of giants. The sense of death and horror filled all her senses and oppressed her mind. She tried not to scream at the clammy feel of cobwebs on her face. Old cobwebs as thick as fishing nets, made by spiders that must have been as big as birds, judging from the husks of their discarded skins still clinging to the monstrous bones like death's own jewels.

Let me go! Get away from me!

Tearing herself free she was running again, colliding into things, tripping and falling, rising again, twisting and turning, then running again, always running, chasing the shadows among the clefts and tunnels, the breath in her lungs burning like flame. In a stinking hollow something fat as a tennis ball landed on her face, and a feeler entered her screaming mouth. She ripped it away, spat its green pussy blood off her lips, gagging at the briny taste.

Stop screaming, you idiot!

Silently now, since she didn't dare to scream, she fought off more creepy things, tearing their legs out of her hair, ripping the crawling feel of them out of her face.

Running . . . running, on and on. Ignoring the new scratches and bruises she rose again and again, stumbling, falling, rising, over and over, so many times she had long lost count, and still she was running.

"Oh, Bridey—I can't go on!"

There was such a stitch in her side, she had no option other than to stop. She fell onto her haunches, unable to take another step, then collapsed onto her hands and knees, unable even to walk, or even to creep. Cramps racked every muscle.

"Where in heaven's name am I?"

Lost was the answer. Lost amongst the tangled skeletons of trees and all manner of growths, twisted and deformed by the vapors that descended and coiled down from the Tower. Thorny tangles, leafless and tormented, that snagged and tore at her flesh, things of mildew and rot that painted foul-smelling decay all over her.

"Try to think . . . I must think!"

But no clear thought would come.

Her voice was a shaky whisper. "Granny Dew—are you there?"

No reply

"If you're there, answer me! Why won't you answer me?"

Again there was no reply, though the growling whispers amongst the thorns and tangles seemed to take heart, as if creeping closer.

A great roar, as loud as thunder, shook the ground and abruptly the tangles were aglow with a blood-red light.

"Oh no!"

In the distance, the Beast appeared to have freed its jaws. Kate could hear faint but angry shouts and shrieks that meant the succubi were pouring out of the gaping portal, hunting her. Then she heard the howling. It sounded like a wolf. And it came from much closer than the Tower.

"God help me!"

She was running again, her legs thrusting her onward with a will of their own, her terrified mind willing them on through the husks of trees and thorn bushes, her spidersweb coverings torn to shreds.

ANATHEMA AND PLOT

A DANK MIST HUNG IN THE EVENING AIR, COALESC-
ing as glistening droplets in the hair of the senior Shee
and Olhyiu who were gathering about the bonfire on the
shore. Taking his place among them Alan couldn't help
but feel humiliated. It wasn't just the recent encounter
with the young Kyra. It was everything. In spite of all his
gung-ho determination the Tyrant had easily outfoxed
him—he had so outmaneuvered Alan that the golden
robot had almost destroyed him and his mission to
rescue Kate. That was him: Alan Duval, stupidly naive!
He had refused to listen to the advice of those who
had tried to warn him—Milish, Qwenqwo, the High-
Council-in-Exile, and most particularly poor Sister
Hocht. He had allowed himself to be carried away
with his own sense of righteousness. Had it not been

for Mark—and he didn't even begin to understand how Mark had rescued him—the whole thing would have ended there, and with it any hope he might have had of saving Kate and avenging the murders of Mom and Dad.

"How could I have been so brainless?" He slapped his own brow in a mixture of frustration and humiliation.

The heavy arm of Qwenqwo Cuatzel fell around his shoulders and gripped him in a clasp of iron. "A toast—to dispel the gloom and worry."

Qwenqwo had brought a full flagon of liquor to the gathering. Alan had no idea where the dwarf mage found such a ready supply, though he suspected the Olhyiu, who revered the dwarf mage and loved his storytelling. He accepted the flagon, holding its round-bellied bulk in his two hands and raising the neck to his lips to take a measured swig. But he doubted that any simple remedy would assuage his sense of failure.

"What must Kate be suffering!"

"Then drink all the deeper. Let us curse the Great Witch together."

Even the single swig of the liquor had gone to Alan's head. Eschewing a second swig he passed the heavy flagon back. "I don't know if she can hold out any longer in that monstrous place. I've tried again and again to communicate with her through the oraculum but I can't get a response."

The dwarf mage, who looked close to being tipsy already, lifted the flagon to his own lips and took an almighty swig, dribbling droplets into his hoary red beard where they glistened like gems of amber.

"C'mon, Qwenqwo! Don't get too drunk on me. We're going to need our wits about us."

"Merry I may be already—and a good deal merrier I aspire to become this miserable night!" Qwenqwo, sitting cross-legged beside Alan, rapped a knuckle on the flask's fat belly, eliciting a fullness that demanded to sound more hollow. "To war, and the planning of it—why there's nothing more elevating to a Fir Bolg's heart! So, less of the womanish worries and drink a warrior's potion—such, if you will but share it with me, will clear those furrows from your brow. Sup—and let friendship banish woe!"

"Your heart would melt permafrost," Alan smiled wanly.

"What is this permafrost—that I might melt it all the quicker?"

"It doesn't matter." Alan took a second, larger, sip and felt it burn, like a punishing gall, at the back of his throat. At his companion's grunt of derision, he took a third swig, felt the flame expand within his chest. What would he do without the indomitable courage, and company, of Qwenqwo! But no amount of simple cheer could dispel the memory that he had failed to confront the Fáil, and with that failure his plans, and hopes for Kate, were compromised.

He needed to understand what he had experienced in that final moment, when he had been sure that his end had come.

I saw them—I saw Mom and Dad!

He recalled how they had put their arms around him. How they had pointed to something beautiful—a vision, like an ocean of stars. Were they trying to help him? But if so, what did it mean?

By Alan's side, Qwenqwo emitted an almighty belch before roaring with laughter at some private joke, his arm crushing Alan's shoulder all the more.

It seemed to Alan that even if he understood little of what had happened in the ancient city there was something important that he needed to do here and now. "Stay here, Qwenqwo. Wait for me—I'll be back." He made his way through the gathering crowds around the bonfire to discover Milish on the periphery of the meeting, in the company of Mo and Kehloke, the wife of the Olhyiu chief, Siam. Alan took Milish aside.

"I want to help the Kyra, even if she doesn't seem to want my help. But I'm just not going about it the right way."

"Be patient!" The Ambassador put a reassuring hand on his shoulder.

He suggested, on his return to the circle, that Mo and Turkeya, the son of Siam and Kehloke, sat to his left with Qwenqwo on his right. Milish, Siam and Kehloke, he placed immediately to the left of Turkeya and the right of Qwenqwo, so that they were near enough for him to talk to them in confidence, as the inner circle became the most intimate ring of several large concentric circles about the bonfire. Glancing through the mist and drifting smoke, his eyes picked out the young Kyra in close conversation with Bétaald, both standing apart from the shuffling arrangements of the various groups that made up the gathering council of war. He assumed she was telling the Shee counselor about their earlier conversation. Alan was determined to try again, and this made Qwenqwo's drinking all the more hazardous. It didn't help that the Fir Bolg and Shee shared some lingering resentment that all too easily flared into open hostility.

As if sensitive to his gaze the Kyra looked his way, and Alan found himself confronted again with that resentful glare. He turned to Milish, felt her hand touch his shoulder, and immediately she was on her feet approaching Bétaald, speaking words of confidence into the ear of the spiritual guardian of the Shee. Bétaald was looking his way, as if deeply thoughtful. Alan was relieved to see that Bétaald was now moving toward him through the smoke and babble of the gathering. He got to his feet to face a remarkable woman who, though small among the Shee, was as tall as he was, and whose skin was magnificently black, her hair sleek as the jaguar she would become in the heat of conflict. Though Bétaald moved with the same stealth and grace as the other Shee she was a good deal older, with her long hair, braided over her left shoulder, threaded with white.

"Mage Lord Duval!" She nodded. "May I wish you a speedy recovery from your recent ordeal!"

Alan acknowledged her words of comfort. He was learning, however slowly, that meanings were sometimes hidden behind words. "I'm really glad to see you, Bétaald!"

A flash of something deep in her eyes. It was only momentary, but he had not been mistaken. He needed to tread carefully.

She spoke, softly, sympathetically. "I know what you are really asking of me, but I'm afraid that the young Kyra is opposed to any such intimacy."

"Did Milish explain?"

"The ambassador did explain. You believe that you may be the repository of Kyral inheritance. You offer yourself as Seer in the exchange of the accumulated knowledge of ages, between mother-sister and daughter-sister."

"I don't pretend to be sure. All I'm suggesting is that we consider it. Oh, heck—I don't really know how to go about it. But only that it might be worth looking into—with the Kyra's willingness of course."

"Mage Lord Duval! I wonder if you understand what such an exchange, of the most intimate thoughts and memories, would mean to a Shee?"

"I guess it wouldn't be easy to accept."

"It would be more difficult than you could possibly understand. It would be a violation of the most sacred precept."

A swell of the now familiar humiliation rose in Alan. "Bétaald, you know that it isn't the first time I've violated those beliefs."

"I do not forget that, in desperate circumstances, you saved the daughter-sister of the dying Valéra. Still the new Kyra would see what you suggest as anathema."

"That was the same word the former Kyra used—anathema. And yet she still asked me to help Valéra."

Bétaald inclined her head.

Alan hesitated. "I guess I've been pretty clumsy about this. I don't know the right, or sensitive, way to go about this. Maybe if I know more of what truly worries the Kyra?"

Bétaald snorted. "Is it possible you do not realize just how powerful you are? The intrusion of such a mind into another so very different!"

Alan considered what Bétaald was saying. "She sees me as alien—and male?"

"Is that not exactly what you are?"

Alan realized he had allowed himself to be wound up by the conversation. He took a calming breath. Without his noticing it, Qwenqwo, together with Mo and Milish, had also climbed to their feet. Qwenqwo had clearly overheard Bétaald's words, and was bristling with rage. A bright alcohol-stoked flush glowered in his mist-drenched cheeks. "Will these Shee witches never change their tune!"

"Please—Qwenqwo!"

"You would have me hold my tongue. But why should I when they brook no reserve on theirs? You offer to help the graceless young Kyra—and now you hear her reply in the words of the adviser? You are not to be trusted—you, whose courage brought us safe to this harbor!"

Clapping his hand on Qwenqwo's shoulder, Alan spoke quietly, resignedly. "Please—no more arguments! Remember Kate! C'mon now—let's sit down and talk about strategies for the coming journey to the Wastelands."

Across the estuary several armed guards dragged a tall man with a steel hook for a left arm into a darkened chamber, where they threw him onto his knees on the marbled floor. Their prisoner was manacled with chains and his face was swollen and bruised. Resplendent in a long silk gown a small corpulent figure was standing with his back to the intruders, peering out of the open arrow-slit window with a spyglass on a swivel stand. He spoke to the guards in a sibilant whisper:

"There had better be good reason for disturbing my tranquillity."

"Sire, we found this harbor rat skulking in the stores, stealing food. He was no easy capture, as you will see. We would have disposed of him with pleasure but for your instructions about such vermin."

The man by the window addressed their prisoner, without troubling himself to turn and look at him. "What is your name?"

"Caleb Dour, Excellency."

"You lie. That is not your name. My nostrils tell me that you are one of them, the fish-gutters, who indulge in drunken celebration of their youthful Mage Lord on the beach opposite."

The one-armed man raised his head brazenly erect, resisting the attempts of the guards to make him bow.

"The huloima, Duval—one of four such strangers from some alien world!" He spat out a mixture of phlegm and blood with the name. "A stranger I would like to help to his grave."

The figure span around gracefully on a gilded heel, so the light reflected off his deeply scarred brow. He peered for several seconds with his coal-black eyes at the manacled prisoner. "Your real name is Snakoil Kawkaw, which, if I am not mistaken, means a thieving crow!"

"A man cannot choose the name he is born with."

"Pah! What do I care for you or your name! Do you know who I am?"

"You are Feltzvan, Excellency—adviser to the Prince, Ebrit."

Feltzvan gazed thoughtfully at the creature. His voice remained soft, little above a sibilant purr. "And you may as well know that I have been looking for one such as you, for a purpose. Disappoint me in that purpose and I shall take some small sport in killing you slowly."

"I am your servant, Excellency."

"Why such hatred of the youthful Mage Lord?"

The prisoner scratched at his chin with the hook that was his left hand. "He cost me this."

"And the fish-gutters who venerate him?"

"They cost me a good deal more." It was spoken with unmistakable venom.

"And this is why, Snakoil Kawkaw, you would help my purpose, contrary to the interests of your own kind?"

"I have my own needs."

"Needs?"

"Do we not all have needs, Excellency?"

"Do you dare to mock me, bear man?"

A smile played about the lips of the man in the silk robes, but it provoked alarm rather than comfort in the kneeling figure. A growl entered Kawkaw's voice, low pitched and urgent. "I was my people's natural leader. I had the strength and the cunning. Yet they chose Siam the stupid over me. All that should have been mine became his. Including Kehloke—the woman that became his wife."

"It would be only natural, in such circumstances, for you to feel jealousy—to desire retribution."

"Excellency—I desire blood, as well as the recovery of my rightful power. Mine was the lineage of leader. I want it all."

"You would be leader of the fish-gutters?" Feltzvan mocked him. "But if such was in my power, what would a harbor rat have to offer in return?"

"Information, Excellency."

"Information?"

"Information about the arrogant brat, Duval, and about the chief among the fish-gutters, Siam the stupid. Information also of about a female cur amongst them, she who is known as Mo. The girl is probably the strangest of all. Through such information, Excellency, you might best undermine their purpose."

"So tell me, then—what are they scheming?" He strode up and down the rug-strewn floor, his long silk gown almost tripping his dainty feet.

"I do not know, Excellency. Other than the fact that I am certain that your concerns are entirely justified."

"Don't patronize me, you vile creature."

"Only test me, then!"

"Here!" Feltzvan waved the guards to drag Kawkaw closer, his chains rattling over the marbled floor. Then he had them haul the uncouth creature to his feet so he could peer through the glass at the scene on the beach. "I am interested in the girl. Search among them. Show her to me."

Kawkaw peered at the scene, which was half obscured by smoke and fading light. "Here—this is the one, sitting by the side of Duval. She's one of the four, all claiming to have come here from another world."

Feltzvan, a nosegay applied to his face, had them drag the stinking wretch away. The adviser wiped the eyepiece with a silken handkerchief before peering for himself at the dark-haired girl. He whispered softly, in that high-pitched sibilant purr. "Four strangers, you say, from an alien world?"

"Perverse it may sound, Excellency, but there is a great deal that is strange about them, the girl in particular. I should know. Through adversity, I brought her as a gift to the Mage of Dreams in Isscan. Yet, it would appear, she readily escaped his pleasures."

"And the gangling youth—the fish-gutter that seems forever by her side?"

"An Olhyiu. Son of the excremental chief. His name is Turkeya. After the death of the shaman, Kemtuk Lapeep, this whiskerless pup took on the role of shaman."

"These primitives, so deeply embroiled in blasphemous superstitions!"

"I would not underestimate the Olhyiu, Excellency. They are renowned for their seamanship."

"Seamanship, you say?"

"The Temple Ship was their inheritance, though no more than a wreck before the coming of the huloimas reawakened it as you can see."

"Could it be that they are planning a seagoing journey? Is that what the fireside chat is all about?"

The prisoner rubbed once again at his chin with his hook. "I could discover this for you, Excellency. I could be your eyes and ears."

"I have eyes and ears enough already in that misbegotten rabble. If that were all you had to offer me, you would not leave this chamber with your own intact. I have a more practical use for you, bear-man. I want you to become my hidden weapon in any such journey they might be about to undertake."

"I will deliver Duval to you. If you will deliver those fish-gutters to me."

A flickering light entered the dark eyes of Feltzvan, where it glinted like a single mote of starlight against a sky of darkness. "Take him away. Remove his rags and hose him down. Feed him. Dress him in something less odoursome. Yet confine him while I consider how best he might serve us."

Feltzvan waited until the prisoner and guards had departed the chamber, then further until the sounds of their footsteps had receded from his hearing. It wouldn't do for them to realize the nature of his true master. Outside the open window the sun had just set and he felt the sharp breezes of the coming night on his face. Around the setting sun the sky was imbued with indigo. The adviser to Prince Ebrit opened a door onto an inner chamber, only faintly illuminated by candles made of wax infused with human blood. He paused to kneel before an altar of black marble. From a concealed recess he lifted out a dagger with a triple infinity embossed into the handle in glowing silver, above a heavy, spiraly twisted blade. His hands now trembling, he gazed down onto the blade, which was constructed of a curious matte-black metal, bringing the hilt, with its embossed sigil, to his lips, lightly kissing it, and then pressing its burning emblem against his brow.

"My beloved Lord and Master, I may be in a position to sow retribution among the Shee-witches and fish-gutters! A harbor rat has come to my attention with intimate knowledge of the Mage Lord, Duval. His mind is so delightfully clouded with hatred he may prove useful to your purpose."

NIGHTSHADE

KATE KNEW SHE WAS NO LONGER ALONE. ALL THE time she was running, she sensed her pursuer close behind her. Something big, much bigger than she was. She could hear the padding of its unhurried paws. The gully took her exhausted legs from under her, sucking her down into its marshy hollow where she massaged her hurting feet in its gloom, her eyes wide with fright, her heartbeat bursting out of her heaving ribs.

The voice, when it came in over the lip of the gully, was a deep growl. "Come out, little mouse, and let me eat you!"

Kate gasped, hunkering down into the cold wet dirt, her jerky fingers searching for the first of the grassy purses to find a tidbit, then forcing it between her chattering teeth and attempting to hold it there with her trembling tongue.

That same growl: "I have all the time in the world—but what time have you?"

She tried to find some saliva, but her throat wouldn't work. She pushed muck in between her teeth to moisten her tongue, but it only made her gag.

A great wolf head nuzzled down over the lip of the hollow. A ruff of snow-white hair stood erect in an oval around a long face that ended in enormous fangs, the slaver of its hunger dripping onto her face. Gray eyes, shining like moons, peered down into the shadows where she skulked, nostrils sniffing to right and left, puzzled to find nothing to see, yet pausing over her trembling body, as if it could smell her presence.

"A strange reward for such a delightful hunt! I know you're still here, little mouse, in spite of the fact that I can't see you. But all the while I hear this voice in my head—a voice older than the wildwoods, and instructing me to help you in the old speech. *Cha-teh-teh-teh!*"

With a start, Kate realized that she wasn't hearing the wolf through her ordinary hearing, but through her brow. And the voice in the wolf's head appeared to be that of Granny Dew—nobody other than Granny Dew had ever used the expression cha-teh-teh-teh.

Kate couldn't suppress the jitter in her voice: "Who—or what—are you?"

"Why, some know me as the wolf who hunts alone."

Her eyes were frantically searching the gully, looking for a possible escape. "I . . . I've never heard of a wolf that talks."

"If you listened to my belly you'd hear the growl of hunger. I haven't eaten in a week. Why should I heed this voice in my head rather than the hunger in my belly?"

Kate thought about trying to run . . . but every instinct told her it would be a mistake. The wolf would detect something—a sound, a scent—and those great jaws were only inches from her throat. The tidbit from the first purse had made her invisible, but it hadn't fooled the wolf's other senses. She tried to remember what Granny Dew had told her about the second purse.

A handful of life—the beginnings of things.

She didn't think that the seeds of life would make a difference to her situation. The gray eyes narrowed, the lips retracting over those enormous fangs just inches from her.

What could she do?

She recalled her crystal, which Granny Dew had only recently implanted in her brow. She had no idea what that was meant to do. *You must resist all impulse to draw on the crystal until you are far beyond the eyes and teeth of this accursed place.* She didn't know if the caution still applied. She was so hopeless with gadgets—and the thing in her brow reminded her of gadgets. She recalled how uncertain Alan had been with his ruby triangle— the Oraculum of the First Power.

Oh, lord—how do I use it?

It's an oraculum—I'm attached to an oraculum. It's become part of me—part of my brain—my body.

A rising panic consumed her. She'd have curled even further into a ball, if that had been possible. But the wolf was already contemplating eating her.

It was a waste of time trying to tell herself to calm down. There was no way she was going to calm down. But she had been familiar with the crystal when she had held it in her hand. With the exception of Mo, they were all given crystals, Alan, Mark and herself, and those crystals had enabled them to read the thoughts of others. She had grown used to her crystal—she had delighted in it. Now, as she spoke, she attempted to read the thoughts of the wolf. "Eat me, whatever, or whoever you are—Wolf-who-hunts-alone—and you are no longer hungry today. But you will be hungry again tomorrow. And what will the Witch think of that? Didn't she command you to recapture me alive? What will she have to say if she discovers you have eaten me?"

"Cunningly put—and cunning is an art I am inclined to admire. You are no mouse. Of that I am certain. So come up out of there. Let me see you. And quickly—the succubi are closer than you think, and their Garg friends are already skybound, with eyes sharp as eagles.'"

Slowly, her limbs stiff with exhaustion, Kate climbed out of the gully and stood, on tottering legs, before the wolf. He was enormous, much bigger than even she had imagined, lean as a greyhound, with shoulders higher than her own and his great long head a foot higher still.

His entire coat was white, not the gray-brown she would have expected of a wolf and, now she thought about it, his cold gray eyes, aglitter with curiosity, were not the normal amber of wolves. Though he couldn't see her he sniffed and shuffled in a circle around her, somehow—coming to size her up, she assumed. His desire to eat her was plain to see. And those jaws would surely close on flesh, however hidden from sight, if he bit. Prowling, now, in a sinewy circle around her, the wolf sniffed and slavered, yet all the while some restraint held him from attacking.

"Much is now clear, yet the more I probe you, one mystery replaces another. The Great Witch would prize your recapture, that much is true. Yet this voice, in the tongue of the ancients, bids me—hah, warns me, more like—to protect you. 'This morsel,' it proclaims, 'is not for thee!'"

"The voice you hear is my protector, Granny Dew."

The wolf snarled, a new rush of slaver oozing through the clenched trap of the great yellow fangs, as if he struggled anew to control his hunger. It seemed to overwhelm him and he roared, with jaws agape, high over Kate's head. His eyes rolled back to reveal the red-veined whites. His muscles tensed, as if ready to pounce.

Tears of fright erupted into Kate's eyes.

A thunderclap boomed immediately above them, so loud and close it shook the ground beneath Kate's feet. A voice, like a continuing low echo of that same thunder, pressed against Kate's eardrums.

THIS MORSEL IS NOT FOR THEE.

The wolf's jaws clamped shut. His eyes, cold and silvery, narrowed to slits, his great head twisting in every direction in search of the origins of the voice.

"I was told to watch out for you, Witch of Morning. The Great Witch anticipated your interference."

YOU WERE WELL WARNED.

"Yet still hunger consumes me in this famine landscape."

YOU ARE EVER NEEDFUL, FATHER OF HUNGER. THAT IS WHY YOU HUNT ALONE

With a sudden whine, as if shocked by a spasm of pain, the wolf backed a half pace away from Kate, yet still slavering. "Where are you? Why can I not see you, even when you speak like thunder?"

BE GLAD YOU DO NOT CONFRONT ME. LOOK TO THE MOUNTAIN YONDER. OR TO THE EARTH BENEATH YOUR PAWS.

The wolf spun in a circle, snarling, but finding nothing reared his head to the sky again, his fangs agape, slaver pattering over the ground like heavy drops of rain.

"Who are you to tell me what I can eat? The mountain cannot harm me, nor the earth beneath my paws. Such a feast do I sense before me—rare indeed in these famished times. I see no harm in satisfying my hunger."

A second crash of thunder shook the ground beneath Kate's feet.

DO YOU THINK I DON'T KNOW YOU, CARRION-FEEDER, WHO HAS FORGOTTEN HIS OWN NAME?

The wolf went still, tensed in every sinew. "You pretend to know me, you who dare not even show yourself?"

IT IS, AND EVER WAS, NIGHTSHADE.

The wolf's eyes widened and a moan emanated from the slavering jaws. "You have knowledge, I grant you. Yet why should I obey you? The Great Witch also harbors knowledge—and her powers grow day by day."

I WARN YOU AGAIN, AND THIS WARNING IS FINAL. STAY YOUR HUNGER OR LET IT DEVOUR YOU.

The wolf tensed again, and his eyes closed on the focus of Kate's trembling presence. "Whatever power you claim, do your worst. Yet will I live and breathe—and my hunger be sated."

But even as he leapt at Kate, there was another deafening crack of thunder, and lightning accompanied it, striking the beast in midflight and hurling him thirty yards through the air.

IF HUNGER IS YOUR NEED, FEED ON THIS!

Kate threw herself back into the hollow, peering over the rim as rivulets of green fire tore at the giant body of the wolf, invading its jaws and running down its throat. The green glow of its fire flickered and crackled inside the lean body, the white fur smoking with the intense heat of his meal of lightning until, abruptly, the light was quenched. The gaunt figure swayed and shuddered.

WILL YOU DO MY BIDDING NOW—OR WOULD YOU FEED AGAIN?

"No more, ancient mother! I have fed enough for a thousand years."

THEN CARRY THIS ORACULUM-BEARER TO SAFETY AS I HAVE BIDDEN.

"It will be done."

Even as he spoke a pack of five other wolves had arrived, much smaller, amber-eyed and gray-brown in color. Snapping and snarling they encircled Kate and the great wolf, as if cutting off any hope of escape. The great wolf howled, causing them to withdraw a pace or two, but the circle was unbroken and their leader howled back, as if calling for support from the hue and cry of the hunt in the near distance. The great wolf dropped his body low, in a crouch. "Quickly then, little mouse, climb onto my back. Take a firm grip about my neck. Hold on tight—do not allow yourself to fall."

"Aaah! Rest . . . Rest I must . . ." The wolf's voice, even through the oraculum, was a broken wheeze. "Climb down, now. You are surely safe for the moment, though it is more than I would predict for me."

Kate slid down over his heaving flank, slumping with exhaustion onto a dusty bank by the side of a stream, watching as the sweat-soaked beast, his fur matted and flattened to his hide, slunk down to the water's edge to lap. She clenched her eyes shut, recalling the huge leap that had carried them clear of the encircling pack, and then the wild, reckless race through the hideous landscape that had outdistanced their pursuers. There had been no opportunity on that nightmare ride to get a single tidbit into her mouth, though now she pressed one between her teeth at once, chewing it while she waited for her heartbeat to climb down out of her throat, then joined the wolf by the stream, kneeling on the pebbly bank and cupping her two hands to bring water up to her own parched lips.

For several minutes there was silence between them. She saw those gray eyes swivel in her direction from time to time, though the wolf's head remained bent, his long purple tongue lolling between his fangs.

When she spoke, it was in a husky whisper. "You're not an ordinary wolf—not like those others."

He made no reply, though his body tensed.

"You were consumed by lightning, but still you're alive."

The great head lifted from his chest and swiveled to face her, the icy gray eyes red-rimmed with exhaustion.

"None have I ever permitted to live, not once they knew my name."

"What's so special about your name?"

"You heard the ancient one—how cruelly she spoke it."

"She called you Nightshade?"

The wolf's lips retracted, exposing the yellow fangs.

"But why is that so important?"

Silence froze the very air between them.

"It's all right. I don't need to know. But I—I might be able to help you. In return for saving me."

"Why would you help one who would have eaten you?"

Kate turned and looked at her reflection in the stream, a broken image, but clear enough for her to see the inverted triangle in her brow—a triangle of green, flecked with moving arabesques of gold, that was now throbbing with every pulse. She stared at her reflection a little longer, blinking rapidly. "During the journey—when your mind was preoccupied with fleeing—I sensed a need deeper than your belly."

"Anger, perhaps . . ."

"I'm only discovering what this—this oraculum—means." She reached up and touched the crystal again, wincing at the sensitivity that penetrated deep within, deeper even than the bone of her brow. "I have a lot to learn."

"Why explain yourself to me?"

"Maybe because I pity you."

He snarled, averting his head.

"Perhaps the other hunger, the anger, is so deep within you, the bitterness so terrible, that you can't recall how it got there in the first place?"

The wolf lunged away from her, putting a good thirty or forty feet between them. She thought he might sprint away, abandon her altogether, so deep was his resentment. But then he turned and looked at her again. "And you—what is your purpose? What makes you so important you have such a protector?"

"I am told that my power is that of new birth—of healing."

He paused, as if to consider her words. "But what does that mean?"

"I don't know."

"Are there limits to this power?"

Kate shook her head, acknowledging her own confusion and ignorance.

"You are a mystery. Yet I cannot deny that the Great Witch appears to fear you—she fears this power you possess."

"When I look at you, when I really look—through the crystal—I see a second being inside you."

"You even talk in riddles."

"Maybe I do. But I recall Siam, the chief of the Olhyiu, who helped me and my friends escape from the ice-bound lake. He appeared to be a man but he could change into a bear, as if the bear were somehow deep inside him. It was my friend Alan who saw that in Siam. Maybe I'm seeing something like that in you? Maybe you're a wolf who has the spirit of a man inside you."

The gray eyes of the wolf stared at her and a shiver ran through the gaunt frame.

"What is it—what's the matter?"

"I felt you probe me. I sensed your power."

"I don't know what's happening to me. It frightens me."

Kate looked down at her dress of spidersweb. Where it had been torn by thorns and rock in her attempts to flee, it had repaired itself. The pockets were intact, and within them she found the second purse of grass. She peered into it, at the mixture of seeds it contained. What was she supposed to do with it? What did Granny Dew expect of her?

A pocket of life—the beginnings of things.

With a bewildered shake of her head she pressed her hand into the purse and filled her fist with the seeds. Opening it out in front of her face, she closed her eyes and searched in her mind for the eye of the oraculum. Then, with her eyes still closed, she blew on the seeds, scattering them about her with no more than her breath. She kept her eyes closed for a minute or two, staring into the void of darkness until she was alerted by the howling of the wolf.

When she opened her eyes again the desolate landscape around her was shooting up grass, bushes, flowers. The wolf was dashing through it, hopping into the air and pouncing, shrieking, in what sounded almost like human cries of glee.

"How very strange you are!" he growled.

She stared at a small bird being swallowed whole between his snapping jaws. Perhaps there had been eggs among the seeds? She felt more bewildered than ever.

Suddenly Kate sensed enormous red eyes swiveling toward her. Into her mind came dreadful sensations, visions. She became aware of a titanic figure with a great horned head as it probed the world about it, as if searching for her. She felt sick with panic.

The testing of her power had been prideful, a mistake. Granny Dew had warned her not to do so. She was still too close to the Tower of Bones. "Nightshade—if that's your true name—we're in great danger. We can't stay here a moment longer. We have to get away, right now!"

The wolf, his hunger at least partially sated, reared before her. "What is it, little mouse? What do you sense?"

"She's found me."

"Who has found you?"

"The Witch."

"But you are free of her. You have escaped the Tower."

"You're wrong. Look around you."

The wolf stared around himself to see, even in the recovered landscape, how vapors were rising and creeping in around the clefts and hollows. A hole yawned in the earth twenty feet away and purple-gray tentacles emerged to probe and destroy the tiny shoots of life.

The wolf sprang to Kate's feet and lowered his body so she could climb onto his back again. She struggled to do so through her exhaustion.

"Quickly now. And I will return a secret."

Kate blinked, trying to find the words of a reply, but her strength was gone. The great jaws of the wolf grasped her and tossed her, with a bone-jarring thump, onto his scrawny back.

"Hold on!"

Kate tried to force what strength she still had into the oraculum on her brow. Clutching at the wolf's straggly mane she held on grimly while in her inner vision she saw that sickly red glow invade the landscape and devour the life she had just sown. The

Witch's tentacles slithered and crept over everything as if sucking the spirit of memory from every stone and crevice.

"Help me, Nightshade!"

The long haunches sprang into flight with a speed that made a blur of the landscape. Kate's heart took strength from his strength.

"Tell me, Nightshade . . . tell me your story."

"You have already seen into my heart. You know that I am no ordinary wolf. I was born to rule them, but my birthright was stolen from me long ago. Yet already you have shown me your purpose. You are the healer this voice in my head proclaims you to be. One day, if you but live, you might restore the Wildwoods."

It took all of her strength to stay awake just to listen to his words, his thoughts, and take comfort from them.

On and on they wove, faster than a racehorse, into the darkening night. Kate's senses had blurred to an exhausted stupor long before they came to a great river that ran deep and wide through a barren landscape. At the shore the wolf slipped and slid over slimy rocks, before hesitating at the water's edge. Then, abruptly, he waded out into the water.

As if in a dream Kate saw an island a hundred yards away, opalescent with moonlight. She was weary beyond exhaustion. Twilight enfolded her mind, like a cloak.

"No," she murmured, "I mustn't fall asleep!"

Yeeesss, sleep now!

They had arrived at the island. She was sliding off the wolf's back, coming to rest with her exhausted head against a curl of knobbly black rock that looked like a fossilized log of driftwood. She lacked the energy to find a softer pillow.

"I can't sleep. I don't dare. I might never wake up."

Yet still she heard that comforting voice inside her mind.

Sleep!

As she struggled to keep open her eyes she saw the great wolf metamorphose into the figure of a man, a tall, ancient-looking figure, lean and bent, with sad gray eyes, but steely too, eyes that spoke of endurance and courage.

"Thank you," he mouthed, although she had no idea why he would wish to thank her.

Her eyes drifted closed—and refused to open again.

Sleep, now! Find comfort in dreams!

GHOST TALK

ALAN STOOD ALONE AT THE APEX OF THE FOREDECK of the Ship, gazing out onto a vast panorama of rolling seas and evening sky. The quiet did it—the lack of any intrusive mechanical noise. It soothed your mind, expanded your horizons both physical and mental until you could lose yourself in it. It made you deeply aware of the medley of more subtle sounds that revealed the inner workings of the Ship. He listened now to the creaking and groaning of the timbers that followed each new wave that struck the prow, the moans and shrieks of the wind in the miles of rigging. Qwenqwo's voice, when it interrupted his musing, caused him to blink with surprise.

"Do you know that my father, Urox Zel, saw the oceans as a great serpent, with the swells its coils ever-writhing."

Alan considered the extraordinary idea. "I think, Qwenqwo, that the journey is proving even more trying for you than it is for me."

Things were moving too slowly for his passionate friend. The seagoing journey of the expeditionary force, a week out of port, was making excellent, if measured, progress. Siam estimated a little under three days at most to landfall. Qwenqwo, out of boredom with the shipboard routines, had taken to spinning an inexhaustible repertoire of exceedingly bawdy tales for the off-duty sailors, who were delighted to stoke his story-telling with an equally inexhaustible supply of grog and tobacco.

"The coils of a serpent?"

"Aye!" Qwenqwo knocked the bowl of his pipe against the rail, scattering ash and sparks. "We Fir Bolg have a name for the serpent—Tunntrokka. Here, in this damnable journey, I hear it snorting, night and day."

Alan couldn't help but smile. A mist of spray washed their faces as they leaned their elbows on the rail. But Qwenqwo wasn't to be deflected from his grumbling. "We've had the good fortune of easy progress. It's tempting to underestimate Tunntrokka while she slumbers. But look yonder—beware that gentle roll of wave and current! Tunntrokka is at her most deceptive when she affects to please."

She?

Alan, still half-smiling, gazed out onto the passing ocean. "There's something I need to talk to you about."

The dwarf mage's face lit up. "Indeed?"

"It's about Mark."

Qwenqwo glanced Alan's way, his expression wary. "You have spoken to Mo about what happened on board the Ship?"

"Yes."

The dwarf mage sucked on an empty bowl. "And there's more you would ask of me?"

"Are you aware that Mark is here?"

"Your friend is here, aboard the Ship?"

"Yes—but not in the normal sense."

The Ship rolled, a slow rise and fall, as it rode a wave. Qwenqwo frowned, looking out into the ocean. "In what sense?"

"I don't know—maybe his ghost."

Qwenqwo packed away the empty pipe, sliding it into a pocket of his greatcoat, his eyes still on the sea. "You add to my confusion."

"I'm pretty confused myself. But I'm talking to him."

"You're talking to a ghost?"

"It's kind of hard to explain!"

Alan shook his head in frustration. How normal things seemed, on the surface. The Temple Ship was one with sea and elements, with the winds full in the sails and the prow cleaving through the waves. It had been restored to its present form as a great ocean-going galleon immediately after the conclusion of the war council on the beach at Carfon. Alan knew that Mark had arranged this, just as he had played a key role in the raptor transformation that had saved him from the Tyrant's robot. Right now, Alan couldn't even pretend to understand the relationship between Mark and the Ship. Other than he knew it was close—maybe very close indeed.

What's really going on?

He had no satisfactory answer to his own question. And yet soon—glancing up at the sky he judged that dusk was no more than two hours away—he would find himself talking with the ghost of his friend. Meanwhile he had other things to think about.

Qwenqwo's pipe had reminded Alan of the conference on the beach at Carfon when his eyes had followed another shower of sparks that spilled into the night air from a sudden flaring of the bonfire. Nightfall had been accompanied by icy sea breezes yet a sweat of worry had broken out over his brow. It was enough to make him shiver before he raised his voice above the murmuring. "Is there anybody here who can describe the country we'll encounter?" He gazed about him, blinking in the firelight, as if needing to clear his own mind of unease.

Siam peered across at him, frowning. He cleared his throat, reluctant to speak until Alan nodded to him in encouragement. "I do not know the land. But I have spoken to sailors in the harbor here who have described the coastline to me, with some of its dangers."

"Can you show us what you've gathered?"

The Olhyiu chief climbed to his feet and came over to squat by Alan's side, using his broad hand to smooth an expanse of sand. Using a piece of kindling as a pencil, he drew a rough sketch of the coastline of the Southern Wastelands. "There are rocky outcrops. Reefs aplenty. Strong tidal movements and currents that might trap the unwary, and with no lighthouses or guides of any sort that might alert us to danger. The climate is said to be changeable. Yet still will I guide you, if this is what the Mage Lord wishes."

"Stoutly spoken, Olhyiu warrior!" Qwenqwo shouted his words with a drunken flourish before taking another draft from the now largely empty flagon. He pulled a ceremonial dagger of Magcyn Ré, former king of the Fir Bolg, from his belt and drew a valley inland of the shores that Siam had sketched. "Here!" He finished the flagon and threw it aside. "This is where we will discover the Witch's lair."

A buzz of excitement entered the clammy night air.

"Where is that?" Alan demanded to know.

"Once," Qwenqwo hiccupped, "if legend be true, it was the land of an empire from long ago—a very great empire that rose and fell before ever the walls of Carfon, even the old city, were built. Indeed there are said to be ruins still standing that date to beyond any history of men—or witches for that matter!"

"The legendary City of the Ancients!" murmured Bétaald, with a wary glance in the direction of the young Kyra.

"Such is it called," agreed Qwenqwo. He hiccupped again, more loudly, his hand patting the sand by his side, as if searching for the now redundant flagon. "Indeed, many are the tales I could I tell you, of brutal divinities declaring war in the very heavens."

The young Kyra had laughed deprecatingly, her words addressed to the gathered company but her eyes directed at Alan. "Loath though I am to agree with the drunken dwarf, yet if the histories are to be believed the scars remain in the landscape of these terrible conflicts from long ago, with what is left of misbegotten giants in a graveyard amid brooding ruins of stone. Yet it is to this fearful landscape that this quest is now leading us."

Qwenqwo Cuatzel had struggled back onto his feet. "Do you question the wisdom, and purpose, of the Mage Lord?" He shouted the words at the young Kyra, as if to be heard about the hubbub of voices, but at that same moment the hubbub had fallen silent so his roar filled the air. He belched, then placed an apologetic hand before his mouth as if in a belated effort to suppress it.

Alan glanced across the flames to where the young Kyra was also on her feet, her face glowering with anger.

He joined them in standing. "Pay no attention to Qwenqwo," he spoke calmly to her. "When he is sober you will discover, as did your mother-sister, that he is as faithful as he is fearless."

The youthful Kyra looked from Alan to Siam, her eyes cold as winter. "Is it unreasonable that I should demand to know why so many lives will be risked, and very likely lost, for one female, no matter that she is a friend of the Mage Lord?"

"What," countered Qwenqwo, "would you know of friendship?"

"More, it would appear, than you know of sobriety and common sense."

Alan didn't want to hear any more of this. "Qwenqwo—that's enough! What do you really know of where we are headed, other than the myths and legends?"

"You ask of the Southlands? I wonder how many among this gathering have ever ventured there?"

"We have seen Nantosueta's forbidden forests—what could be worse than that?" declared Siam's son, the Shaman Turkeya.

Qwenqwo hurled the dagger of Magcyn Ré so it was buried to the hilt in Siam's rough-drawn map. "Here you will discover mires and swamps the like of which you have never seen before. Aye—and even stranger creatures."

"Creatures?"

"Gargs will be the least of your worries. Yet here-abouts is the very homeland of those creatures of night."

Alan sensed that strange feeling again: a sense of wrongness. "Nature is just nature, Qwenqwo. Can't you be more specific?"

"In the lore of the Fir Bolg it is said that the land gives forth both nourishment and punishment. And it is in the balance of such forces that the living come to be. So, in a valley of beauty, does beauty of spirit discover kinship with all that is wholesome. Yet what forces of nature might give rise to Gargs?"

"You said they'd be the least of our worries."

"Aye. Gargs are not the worst of it. Here will we discover shadow creatures, a demon people said to haunt a man's dreams. If the legends are to be believed they are a thousand times more dangerous than Gargs."

A shiver passed through the company.

"Not to forget the greatest danger of all," reminded Milish. "The Great Witch, Olc, who has made it her lair."

"A Witch," growled the Kyra, "who has made of the Mage Lord's concern for his friend the most obvious trap."

Now on board the Ship in full sail, Alan's memories of the fireside discussion were interrupted by the clanging of the midship's bell. An elderly Olhyiu pulled on the rope above the central staircase, signaling the end of one of the working shifts and calling the sailors to their evening meal. Alan was glad of the distraction.

He had never quite understood how a great ship at sea became a village of nooks and crannies, where a community went about their different businesses. Of course the Olhyiu weren't only sailors. The Children of the Sea, as Olhyiu actually meant, were ocean voyagers, and more specifically whalers. Siam looked comfortable in command when ordering men up the lines and rigging to the three enormous conglomerations of sails. Everywhere they worked in a marvelous togetherness, singing chantey songs to find a rhythm, reeling out lines, or scurrying over the three decks like ants all of a purpose, repairing lines, or tugging in chains, or spiders' webs of ropes—big men climbing with the dexterity of monkeys, seeming to exult in their work high in the rigging as if their home was truly halfway between earth and sky.

As Alan admired the shipboard world about him, an immense figure emerged from below decks. All of the Olhyiu males were tall and broad. But Larrh had the towering figure of a polar bear. His snowy white hair was braided at the back of his neck and further secured by a thong. A genial giant from all accounts, Larrh was the senior cook on board the Ship—and he ran a very efficient kitchen, preparing square meals three times a day and grog enough to fill the bellies of a small army. Now, making his ponderous way to the rail, he hung his flushed and perspiring face out to the wind, taking a breather from the sweltering ovens below. Rumor had it that his weight was so great no bunk could accommodate him, so he slept on the great slab of the galley table.

Turning back to face the ocean Alan felt the familiar anxiety flood his senses. He couldn't wait to reach the Wastelands. And yet their progress could not be hurried, given that most of these ships were not warships but merchant craft, bulk carriers for ten thousand Shee warriors, together with the weapons, food, clothing and provisioning necessary for such an army. The thought of what lay ahead was enough to make him shiver as he stared once more into the never-ending vista of waves and sky, while the Temple Ship led the small armada that sailed fanwise in its wake.

Yet it frustrated Alan to know that had the Temple Ship forged on ahead alone, it could have taken him to his destination in the blink of an eye.

All the same, he had been forced to listen to the advice of Ainé, Milish, Siam and the elders. While Kate was uppermost in his mind, common sense insisted that this would be no smash-and-grab raid. The arriving army of Shee would hit hard, if they encountered shoreline resistance, and then establish a foothold in the Southern Wastelands and wait there for the much larger army that was to follow. Alan couldn't deny the obvious consideration—that their purpose went beyond the rescue of Kate. The ultimate target was the Tyrant himself, and the destruction of his power, which was centered on the great Metropolis of Ghork Mega, at the reeking heart of the land he had made his own— the Wastelands, which occupied an entire despoiled continent.

As evening fell Alan headed for the wheel deck, a place studiously avoided at night by Siam and his sailors, who thought it haunted. Here he stood a while in contemplation of the great wheel, which was unmanned and yet appeared to move by itself.

In the gloom, surrounded by the crashing of the waves and the creaking of the taut-stretched rigging, he recalled his last memories of Mark. He saw the figures of his friend together with Nantosueta, the girl queen, now cast in stone, ten times life-sized, their bodies entwined in an embrace of love yet frozen for all eternity atop the great tower that dominated the island of Ossierel. In their brows he had witnessed the black inverted triangles that had sealed their fates.

Yet not dead . . .

Qwenqwo believed that Mark had been absorbed body and spirit into the Third Power. Alan could barely bring himself to think about what that might mean.

Something other than dead?

Mark's voice, jerking Alan back to reality, was so clear in his mind he could have been standing next to him and talking into his ear.

Thank you for coming.

I think I owe you that much!

Their conversation, as usual, took place through the oraculum. But what did that mean? What did it tell him about his friend? Just thinking about it made Alan's heart miss a beat and his throat feel dry.

Are you alone? I can't sense any other presence, but I can't be certain.

He couldn't help but catch the resentful inflection in Mark's words.

There's only you and me.

It felt so strange, talking to Mark in this way. These conversations had begun three nights ago, about half-way through the voyage. They had been very tentative—experimental, at first—as if Mark was learning how to get through to him.

Alan watched the moving wheel.

Have you figured it out yet—exactly what, or where, you are?

I think it's the place you call Dromenon.

Alan swallowed hard through his dry throat.

Sounds scary.

I'm petrified. Another of Mark's jokes.

I can't even pretend to know what it must feel like, being so alone!

I'm not alone. Nan is with me. We sense the presence of one another. But we can't feel anything. Not even to hold hands!

Nan was Nantosueta. Alan was startled to hear Mark talk about the Dark Queen in such familiar terms. He recalled the only image of the queen he knew—the fig-ure of wrath on the summit of Ossierel. But Kate had glimpsed that younger figure, a girl no older than Kate herself. She and Mark had met her . . . or sort of met her . . . in some kind of entranced vision. Mark and Nantosueta had fallen in love. But they existed only as spirits. Alan thought about that—to be able to sense thoughts and emotions, the thoughts and emotions of others as well as yourself, and yet never to feel, or to see through your own eyes, or touch, or to be touched . . .

Not even to touch or be touched by somebody you loved . . .

Are you aware that Mo keeps looking for me?

She does?

She knows I'm here. She wants to comfort me. And that's what's really strange. She has no oraculum but I can read her mind clearest of all.

Alan was startled by Mark's words. He wondered what they implied. *I'll talk to her—if you want me to.*

Yeah, thanks.

I mean it!

Talk to Mo for me. Tell her that I'm doing my best from this side. Tell her I'll never stop trying to get in touch.

Okay.

There's something else you can do for me, Alan. I want you to tell me the truth. Look at me, through the oraculum, and tell me what you can see. No bullshit. Just say what you see, or what you don't see.

Alan did as Mark asked him to do, studied the place around the wheel. *I see something. Like some ghostly outline, kinda like smoke.*

You're telling me the truth?

Would I kid you?

You want me to answer that?

I see it. You're twirling your hand around your wrist, a bit like a conductor does sometimes.

You really can see it? Like smoke?

Yes—I see you!

*What it is . . . I keep wondering if we've died. Me and
Nantosueta. What if we've really become ghosts?*

Qwenqwo doesn't think so.

But what if it's true?

These conversations were harrowing and Alan's
hands came up to brush his face, but then he allowed
them to fall by his sides.

*We looked for your body up there on the Rath. We
didn't find it.*

*I've been thinking about things. I've asked myself, if I
could return to Earth . . .*

Alan shook his head. *What's this really about, Mark?*

I've been thinking about the Temple Ship . . .

What about the Ship?

*Do you remember what it was like, how it felt, when we
all came into this world?*

How could Alan forget their arrival here through
the portal on the summit of Slievenamon! It had felt
like he was being ripped apart, reduced to the level of
molecules.

*Now tell me what it felt like when you were brought
back out of Dromenon—when the robot was about to pul-
verize your bones?*

Alan thought about it. *You could be right—could have
been something similar about how it felt . . . maybe.*

*I'm asking myself. Could we have come here from
Earth through Dromenon?*

I don't know about that.

Like maybe Dromenon is a halfway between place—a kind of Limbo?

Uh-huh?

Do you remember what Qwenqwo once told us? How in legend the Ship was the Ark of the Arinn?

Alan recalled Qwenqwo telling them a whole bunch of stories about the Ship. Stuff about the Arinn—whoever or whatever they might have been.

What I'm asking myself is whether this Ark of the Arinn was made to travel between worlds.

Alan blinked.

If so, it could take us home. Mark paused. *I mean, it's worth thinking about.*

Hey, I'm with you. I'm thinking about it. But this is just wild guesses. How in the blazes could you test that one?

That's what I want to talk to you about. After the Ship has taken you to where you're going, you won't need it then—not for a while.

Aw, c'mon! We might need to get out of there, real fast. If things go wrong . . .

The way I see it, my need is greater.

You're going to abandon us in the Wastelands? You're going to try it on nothing more than a hunch—just suck it and see if it will get you back to Earth?

We're thinking about it, Nan and I. Back to our bodies—back to life.

But your experiment could put us all at risk—including Mo!

I'm thinking of putting it to the Ship—see if the Ship agrees with me. When I figure out how to communicate the idea.

Alan exhaled hard, deeply shocked at what Mark was thinking. The loss of the Temple Ship could jeopardize their whole mission.

Couldn't you wait—at least until we rescue Kate?

I wish I could.

You're not really thinking this through.

Believe me, I am. A change came over Mark's voice, a new urgency. *We'll talk again. Meanwhile you had better look to your back. You have a problem.*

What?

Simultaneously Alan received an urgent summons, oraculum-to-oraculum, from the Kyra, who was forward at the prow.

SHINY THINGS

KATE WOKE TO SEE THAT THE SUN WAS ALREADY penetrating the mists of the horizon. She recalled the whispered warning of Granny Dew:

Cha-teh-teh-teh!

Where was she? She felt utterly bewildered and lost. Panic rose in her. She had to make a move—discover a place to hide.

But the fierce intensity of the sunlight hurt her eyes, even when she squinted through eyelids that were smarting and heavily encrusted with flaky crud. She felt exhausted already, and she hadn't even climbed to her feet.

What am I going to do?

When she lifted her head off the stony ground where she had slept her neck was excruciatingly stiff. Peering down at her body, which was still covered in a weave of cobwebs, she discovered that it was half buried in soft white sand. When she tried to move her arms, her back—even her jaw—every joint felt achingly stiff. It was as if she had slept for a hundred years . . .

Oh, heck—just how long have I been asleep?

If sleep was remotely the right word for what must have been more like a coma, brought on by exhaustion? She put all of her concentration into bracing her arms against the stony ground so she could struggle to a half sitting-up position. A premonition seized her, rendered her trembling with fright.

Faltana!

The chief succubus would be out there searching for her. The Witch would blame her for Kate's escape from the Tower. Faltana's second eye would be plucked from her head if she failed to get Kate back. She'd be frantic in her efforts to find Kate, using every power at her disposal— the succubi, the Gargs . . . the wolves!

The wolves will be coming after me . . .

When she jerked herself into a fully sitting-up position it provoked such a lancinating pain in her head that she groaned aloud. Sand blew over her face as she lifted her hands up and squeezed her head. Another throb of pain made her groan even louder. She flopped over onto her side, dragging her legs free, then inched herself over so she could haul herself onto her knees. Every small maneuver had to be carefully planned in advance.

Time for a breather—try to take stock.

Another fierce stab of pain in her head. Damn—she had forgotten the crystal embedded in her brow. With the slightest movement it felt as if the thing was boring itself into her brain.

She knelt there for several moments, holding onto her head and panting through gritted teeth.

"Shit!"

Ordinarily she didn't like to swear. It wasn't ladylike. Bridey and Uncle Fergal had taught her not to swear— although both of them were known to mutter "shit!" when it suited them.

"Shit!" Kate muttered again.

Then she swallowed, feeling guilty, while holding onto her head with both her hands and peering very carefully about herself. She could see no other living soul—no succubi, or Garg, or wolf. Her terror eased.

A step at a time. That sounded like a good idea. *Don't even bother to try to get on your feet just yet. Just think before you try to move.*

Okay—so was this really happening? Was she really here, on some island in a river, kneeling among the rocks and sand? It looked real enough—it felt excruciatingly real. How had she come to be here? A wolf, an enormous bedraggled creature who had the soul spirit of a man, had brought her here. She hadn't been in a position to give him directions at the time. It was Granny Dew who had told the wolf-man what to do. It sounded utterly crazy when you examined it like that. It made her wonder if she really was dreaming after all. But then if she was dreaming, it meant she was still back there, in that coffin-cell, with the vile creature Faltana ready to torment her . . .

Terror of Faltana made Kate attempt once more to get onto her feet. She tottered, trying for balance for a few seconds before slumping onto one knee. It wasn't just the agony in her head. With the slightest movement pain racked every joint.

Well, one thing was certain. If Faltana was nearby, with her Gargs and wolves, there was no question of Kate running. She just couldn't run anymore.

A breeze ruffled the wreck of her hair. Kate rubbed at her eyelids to try to clear them, then blinked two or three times, provoking tears of frustration.

I've just got to get out of here!

But where was here?

Panting from another spasm of pain in her brow she stared up into a sky full of wheeling birds. Dark-winged shapes, she hadn't a clue what sort they were, other than seabirds. But it meant that she must be somewhere close to the sea. Struggling to her feet, physically supporting her upper body by pressing her hands against her trembling thighs, she panted away, her teeth tightly clenched within her grimacing mouth, all the while looking around at the geography of the island. It was largely rock and sand. A craggy ellipse, one edge—the seawards side, judging from the direction of the river current—raised into a bluff about a hundred feet above the stream. It wasn't much of a sanctuary, seeming terribly exposed with little or no cover where she could hide.

Tears, the real sort this time, moistened her eyes.

The breeze gusted again, spraying sand over her exposed skin. When she sniffed back the tears there was the smell of brine, which told her that the sea was close. Her sanctuary was set in a river so big and wide it must be an estuary near the sea.

Turning through a complete circle Kate saw that the island was as barren of vegetation as it was deserted. Why had the wolf-man brought her here? Had he really been carrying out Granny Dew's instructions? And if so, why had Granny Dew directed her to this desolate place?

Slowly, stiffly, she began to search the island. After an hour or two of meandering exploration she confirmed that her first impressions had been pretty accurate. There was no sign of life here other than the creepy-crawlies that left trails in the white sand and the birds that wheeled and screeched overhead. Finding some protection from the gusting wind in the lee of some rocks, she slumped down onto her bottom and picked at the cobwebs over her knees. The shock of her situation was only slowly registering, making room for this new anxiety in a heart already congested with fears. Lifting her shaky fingers she brushed their tips against the object in her brow. A smooth, glassy surface, definitely a crystal. And the shape was without doubt a triangle.

An oraculum just like Alan's . . .

A shockwave, like electricity, made her probing fingers recoil. The thing just didn't feel natural at all.

She used the hands-on-knees trick to get back onto her tottery legs, then stumbled on, directionless, trying to persuade herself that there just had to be something special about this island, but hardly knowing what she might even be looking for. When she tripped and tumbled down the slope of a sand dune, the flare of pain in every limb and joint made her curl herself into a ball, rolling all the way down to the bottom of the slope with her eyes clenched shut. She waited for the pain to ebb before opening her eyes again to discover that she was at the entrance to a den.

It was the strangest den Kate had ever seen. The entrance was made out of a whale's jawbones. The spars supporting the roof were probably ribs. These had been rigged into the rough shape of an arch, woven with pieces of driftwood, all knotted together with sun-bleached straw. Within the gloom inside she glimpsed bright reflections. If she half closed her matted eyelids she could imagine shapes lurking inside, like hunch-backed gnomes, or the whirl of sea or wind. Creeping closer she stuck her head within the jawbones. All she could make out was a jumble, but a very sparkly jumble of shiny things, as if the owner of the den might have made a collection from what been brought up by the tide onto the nearby beach.

It was the only cover Kate had found and she crawled further in to investigate. She stared in curiosity at sharks' teeth, turtle shell-cases and the white skeletons of unknown sea creatures. A flash of memory—back in Clonmel Mo had collected things like this. Crystals, amber with insects embedded in it, the skulls of birds—stuff that Mark had called her "weirdiana." Kate gazed with curiosity at shells and carapaces the delicate colors and shades of jade or ivory, or long stringy spikes of mauve and gold that were arranged into the embroidery of what could have been a rather crude nest, and tucked in among them, like eggs, were rounded stones, their surfaces patterned by spirals and whorls or encrusted by twisty-tangled shapes. She found fragments of wood that appeared to be fossils, like the tree trunk she had slept on, or disks of cork from long-lost fishing nets, so sculpted by the sea and elements they might have been beads from the necklaces of giants. This treasure trove was piled into a heap on a bed of seaweed, the tendrils of which had been bleached to a downy blond by the sun. There was the impression the tendrils had been carefully arrayed, like the hair of a medusa.

It was pleasantly cool and sheltered here, out of the sun and wind. And the discovery of the den was so unexpected Kate just sat in the middle of it and stared around herself, open-mouthed.

She picked up a spiral shell, as crimson as a sunset. She brushed the texture of one of the rounded stones against her cheek. She brought it to her nostrils to smell the old, magical smell of the ocean. Edging deeper into the den she was shocked to discover a mound of skulls. Her heart pattering with surprise, she probed among them to see that they included what had obviously been fish or turtles, but there were others she didn't recognize at all, vaguely human-like, but with wafer thin plates of bone and higher brows—thankfully not really human at all.

The skulls intrigued her. They appeared to be deliberately arranged, fitted one into another, to make the shape of a tower.

It occurred to Kate that she should be frightened by this bizarre den, but in fact she felt curiously comfortable here, like a small bird that had fallen out of its nest and found its way into a protected nook. A nagging voice inside her head suggested that she might be deluding herself—that life didn't offer comfortable refuges for little ones lost. But she made no effort to leave the den, sitting slightly dazed amidst the bones and the treasure, her hands periodically touching her brow, uncertain what to do next.

"Yeeow!"

She held her breath at a loud clatter from outside. A globular eye the size and color of a kumquat was peering in at her from one edge of the entrance. The orange globe of the pupil was cut into two by a jagged black crescent like the eye of a crocodile. While she stared back at it, trembling with fright, it blinked. But it wasn't an ordinary blink. Some white eggshell-like thing closed over it sideways, then it opened again and the eye peered in at her once more.

Merciful mother!

Kate sat utterly still.

The eye withdrew. She heard a running clatter—it sounded horribly like claws on rock—and then there was a loud thud that shook the interior of the den and set all of the glittery things a-jingling and a-jangling. Then the eye appeared at the opposite side.

Kate clenched her eyes shut.

When she opened them again, the eye was still there—or more likely the creature's other eye, since it had clearly crossed over from one side of the entrance to the other as if needing to check her out in one eye after the other, the way a blackbird would twitch its head from side to side to get a better fix.

"Help—please go away!"

The peering eye performed that strange membranous blink she had seen in television programs about raptor birds, and she heard a perfect echo of her own words, *Help—please go away!*

"Shoo! Get lost!"

Shoo! Get lost! The echo returned, with exactly the same pitch as her quavering voice, yet also squawky.

"Shoo—*shoo!* Clear off—you kumquat-eyed parrot!"

Clear off—kumquat! Kumquat-eyed, kumquat parrot!

Was the creature mocking her? Kate wiped her sweating face with a cobwebby sleeve. She stared about herself at the den full of glittery things. Her situation was both terrifying and ridiculous at the same time. There was a renewed agony in the center of her brow. She had forgotten about the oraculum.

The copycat mockery rose to a high-pitched screech: *Shoo—shoo! Kumquat parrot!*

She clapped her hands over her ears as, all of a sudden, her fears discharged through the triangle in an almighty explosion that took the roof off the den, scattering the collection of shells and bones.

Kate sat at the epicenter of the resultant chaos, blinking her eyes back open, her coverings of cobwebs reduced to rags.

THE RED STAR

EVEN AS HE HURRIED FORWARD, TAKING THE STEPS to the foredeck two at a time, Alan noticed that the chill had worsened. It was as if all the natural warmth had been sucked out of the air to be replaced by an icy cold. Even the gentle rolling of the Ship had worsened to a disturbed heaving. He found Siam and the Ainé in a huddle of conversation before the prow. The cold was even more biting here. A dank dew had condensed over the features of the burly Olhyiu chief and the giant woman, matting their hair to their scalps.

"What's going on?"

"A storm approaches. The strangest storm you ever witnessed!" Siam's dark eyes were wide and liquidly glinting in the reflection of the nearby oil-lamp that shook and rattled on its hook on the foremast.

"Ainé?"

"It may be no more than a natural turn of the weather," the Kyra responded, shaking her head.

But Siam would have none of it. He was unable to stand still, his restless hands twisting and squeezing the battered pilgrim's hat he normally wore. Standing with his legs widely spaced for balance on a deck that had grown increasingly unsteady he growled: "Do you landlubbers imagine that I, Siam, do not know the sea? I who have sailed it even in my mother's womb. Look about you. An agitation has taken hold of the elements. But this is no nor'easterly blow such as might carry down the cold of the Whitestar Mountains. A nor'easterly is heralded by thunderheads. You witness no such portents. Look! See the sky—is it not starry and bright above us? Yet feel the very air, which harbors a different message."

Siam was right. The night sky was pellucid and calm, with starry constellations however alien to a son of Earth twinkling and visible. Alan found himself rubbing at the backs of his hands, where the tiny hairs were freezing into minuscule needles of ice.

Several Aides approached, moving noiselessly over the shadowed deck, apparently at some unseen signal from the Kyra. Ainé's order was a simple one. "Some heated grog for all. Something calculated to lift the spirits."

"It will take more than a swig of mulled ale to lift my spirits," snorted Siam. "I fear a tempest that approaches without cloud or change of wind. This is no normal storm. I fear an enchantment."

Siam's words shook Alan, reminding him of his conversation with Mark. "There's something I need to talk to you both about," Alan spoke softly, confining his words to the two leaders. He explained his conversation with Mark, going on to tell them about Mark's plans for the Temple Ship.

"This is madness heaped on madness!" Siam exclaimed. "What is to become of the sailors who presently man and serve her?"

"I didn't think to ask him. But I guess that he expects everybody to abandon ship when we move onto land." Alan blew into his cupped hands to warm them. "What do you think about this, Ainé?"

"What is the nature of this ghost you speak of?"

"I don't know what's become of Mark anymore."

"But surely you attempted to dissuade him?"

"Of course I did. And I shouldn't really call him a ghost. At the very least, his soul spirit is alive. I need to talk with Qwenqwo about this."

"Aye—that you do!"

As if responding to the mention of his name, the dwarf mage joined their company in the prow, his pupils somewhat dilated and his step a little unsteady from ale. Alan nodded in greeting to Qwenqwo. "Then you heard what I've been telling Siam and Ainé about Mark?"

The dwarf mage scowled. "I did."

"I tried to talk him out of his idea. But he wasn't of a mind to listen. He might be more prepared to listen to you."

"But I can't speak to a soul spirit—my runestone is not capable of this."

Alan shook his head. "I think I understand what he might be going through. He wants his life back."

"But what of everybody else—what of Mo, Kate?"

"We all owe him everything. Yet we live and he doesn't. We can hardly imagine what he's going through." He hesitated, thinking carefully about Mark's words. "I don't know if what he's thinking is even possible."

The Kyra took several seconds to consider the situation. "Your friend Mark brought about the transformation of the Temple Ship to the raptor form that entered Dromenon to save you. Then, once more, he brought about the transformation that made it thus." Her eyes swept over the heaving deck around them. "Whatever manner of being he has become, we know that he is immensely powerful when one with the Ship. Does he not carry the oraculum of the Third Power in his brow? Whether we agree with him or we don't, if he finds a way to leave this world there will be nothing we can do to stop him. Our best course would be one of cooperation. We should accept his offer of assistance to the point of his departure. We would still have the rest of the expeditionary fleet."

Siam slapped his hat against the rail. But like Alan, he knew the Kyra was right. There was no way any of them could oppose Mark, if he remained determined.

Alan accepted a mug of spiced ale from the returning Aides, folding his hands about its warming surface. He sipped at the refreshing drink, recalling the desperation of his friend. But desperation made for poor logic.

Turkeya's voice fell onto the decks from the crow's nest. "Harken—the mist!"

Alan peered over the rail at a rising mist that was creeping up out of the ocean. It appeared to be unnaturally drawn to the Ship. Qwenqwo's tangled eyebrows lifted. "I awoke in my bed with the premonition that an evil had fallen upon the Ship. When I looked out of my porthole it was as if the sea was writhing in agony even before I felt the first draft of icy cold on my face."

Alan glanced at the Kyra, noticing the rapid pulsation in the oraculum in her brow. "What do you make of it, Ainé?"

Ainé's leonine face wrinkled in a frown. "We must take care not to allow ourselves to be distracted by every whim of the weather."

"I don't agree," growled Qwenqwo. "I sense the presence of malice."

"What about you, Siam?"

"I agree with the dwarf mage. There is danger here. A malengin, I fear, though of a kind I do not recognize. We appear to be the focus of a powerful malice."

At the same moment Qwenqwo brought the tankard from his mouth and pointed, "Above you—in the sails!"

Alan followed the dwarf mage's gaze up into the rigging that thrummed and hissed about the three great masts with their billowing sails. Qwenqwo was right. Whatever cold and mist they were experiencing on the open deck was multiplied tenfold above them in the sails. The lines and rigging were shrouded by freezing vapor, and its chilly presence was beading the ratlines. The cold seemed to intensify from moment to moment. Alan heard crackling sounds from overhead. He stared up into the foresail, amazed to see waves of frost creeping over the canvas and rigging.

Even the sea appeared to churn with resentment, its waters violent and foaming angrily over the prow, where the spray now rose a good thirty feet into the air.

Siam growled: "Look higher—to the very sky!"

Alan followed the direction of his pointing finger to where a star he had never seen before, a red star, bigger and more lurid than all the others, pulsated amid a blood-tinged shimmering halo.

Qwenqwo shook his head. "It is no star I recognize. It is surely an eye—a monstrous red eye."

"An eye, indeed!" Siam's roar shattered the peace of the nighttime decks, waking all who slept, and alerting the Shee on board to full battle readiness. "A red eye," he murmured, "but faceted like that of a fly."

"It would appear," mused Qwenqwo, "that the Witch has found us."

Alan stared up into the mist-shrouded heavens. "Surely the Witch can't attack us from such a distance?"

"This we are about to discover."

Alan probed the giant red eye but his power discovered no focus there for attack. Instead he encountered something akin to a pocket of cold and emptiness, devoid of feeling. Then it changed and he sensed a presence, even more foul than the tormentor, the proximity of enormous power coupled with a matching malice.

Alan disconnected his oraculum from the red star. He had to lean over the icy rail to vomit back the mulled ale.

Qwenqwo was by his side, his arm supporting him. "Do not allow the Witch to work upon your will. It is but an illusion."

Alan heard the Kyra's voice, heavy with disgust. "You are allowing emotion to rule you. This friend is your weakness—and your enemies know it."

How could the Kyra be so indifferent to Kate's suffering? Alan wondered if she still resented his sacrilegious intrusion into her sacred rites of confirmation. Even though the Kyral lineages meant that the daughter-sister was a clone of the mother-sister, maybe differences could still arise. He wondered if this young and inexperienced Kyra was arriving at conclusions very different from what the former Kyra, with her greater depth of experience, would have arrived at. That worried him, causing him to shake his head to Qwenqwo. "No—the Kyra is wrong. Something is very wrong. Qwenqwo, what's going wrong? Why can't I communicate with Kate anymore?"

Qwenqwo's voice was calm, reassuring. "There could be many reasons."

"One of which being she might be dead?"

"Did you sense her death?"

Alan shook his head.

"Do you not think that, through the power of your oraculum, you would sense the death of one of the chosen?"

"I don't know what to think anymore."

"Loath as I am to agree with her, the Kyra could be right. We may be dealing with a deceit," Qwenqwo cautioned. "Do not allow despair to take control of your heart. That's what the Witch desires. Do not allow her malice to conquer your spirit even before we set foot on her accursed heartlands."

SCRAGS 'N' BONES

CLIMBING ONTO HER TOTTERING LEGS, USING THE fragments of spidersweb to cover what was left of her dignity, Kate announced somewhat redundantly: "I'm coming out now, you . . . you—whatever you are!"

She had to kick the fragments of shells and stones out of her way, stumbling barefoot over the fallen whale bones of the ruined entrance, her eyes narrowed against the full glare of the noon sun. Her tormentor was hiding behind a large black rock that protruded from the sand like a huge rotten tooth. Kate's voice was husky with fright. "I can see you—so you might as well come out and face me."

An eye was peering at her from beyond the left margin of the rock. Its crescent pupil expanded to fill the entire eye. "Fish 'n' spider!' the voice squawked. "Mmmmm! Tasty fishy!"

"What did you say?"

"Spider fishy . . . talks?"

"Of course I can talk. But surprisingly, it seems, so can you. So why don't you come out and show yourself!"

The eye contracted to the crescent slit and then expanded again. And then it did that peculiar thing, in which she heard the patter of clawed feet on the stony ground, and the eye moved to the other side of the rock, accompanied by the same enormous thud, fierce enough to judder the ground.

"Spider fishy thing—break shiny things!"

Kate hesitated. "I'm sorry I did that. I didn't mean to. It's just that you frightened me, with all that parrot talk."

The enormous thud sounded out again.

"Please stop doing that."

But of course it did exactly that.

"Well," she said, "I'm certain that you're not a parrot."

Bits and pieces of the creature appeared on either side of the rock, stretching and easing in a series of slow fanning exercises, and all covered in gossamer scales that changed from moment to moment in brilliant flashes of color.

Kate stared at the display with amazement. "You're a shiny thing yourself. Why don't you just come and let me have a proper look at you?"

But one eye merely came back to the left side of the rock and peered at her. With a start, Kate recalled the two purses that Granny Dew had given her. But only one of the purses was left. The explosion had blown away the nut-like tidbits of food. At least she still had the purse of seeds.

"I have one or two tricks up my own sleeve," she called out, grimacing at the fact that she didn't really have anything resembling sleeves. Pinching a snuff of seeds from the purse, she tapped them out into the palm of her hand and blew gently over them, scattering them like a puff of smoke over the barren ground between her and the creature's hiding place. In moments, the ground cracked open and sprouted. Tiny shoots of green appeared, filling myriad cracks and crevices, until grass and flowers and even shrubby bushes blossomed. The eyes darted with incredible rapidity from one side of the rock to another, the crescent pupils expanding and contracting, and the creature squawking.

"Spider fishy thing! Thief!"

A realization struck her with a tremendous shock:

"Oh, my—you're just a baby!"

"Not!"

"Yes you are. I'm truly sorry," she said. "I really am. I never meant to break your shiny things."

"Liar!"

"Look! I'll show you what a mess I really am." Kate walked out in front of the rock and she stood there, chewing on her lip, and pulling with one hand on the bedraggled mess of her hair.

With a tentative glide, the creature emerged from behind the stone, first the green-glinting head, which was heavy and triangular, and then the neck, which was a bright yellow, ringed by golden barbs. Her jaw dropping with surprise, Kate's eyes roamed over the elongated, sinewy body, which was covered by multicolored scales that jangled and tinkled as it moved, and then, as long again as the body, an enormous scaly crescent of tail. All the while she was sizing it up those great orange eyes were doing the same to her. And now that each was done, those huge orange spheres were fixed on Kate's green eyes, each blinking back at the other in astonishment.

There was something about the creature that reminded her of a crocodile, though the head wasn't as long as a crocodile's, being relatively wider and prism-shaped, and the teeth, what she could see of them, were much finer. There was also no doubt that it was male. Why—it was more curious than terrifying. And all the while it was looking at her with those huge intelligent eyes.

"What are you?"

"What is you?"

"My name is Kate—Kate Shaunessy. I'm a girl." She paused, struggling to recover her wits. "It's you that's the puzzle. I mean, for goodness sake—I just can't believe . . . No, I don't even dare to believe . . . Ah, forget it—you're surely not a dragon?"

"Kate Shaunessy—girl-thing!" Big circular nostrils flared open in the snout and it sniffed in her direction. "Fishy spidery girl-thing. Yum yum!"

Kate clutched at the fragments of spidersweb she had very nearly allowed to fall around her ankles. "What's that supposed to mean? Are you suggesting what I think you are? You—the most forlorn excuse for a dragon anybody could meet. Why, except for your eyes—the rest of you could pass for a spindly old piece of driftwood."

"Fishy girly spider thing—mmmmm!"

Kate ran at the creature and kicked it, barefooted, on its scaly belly. "Ow—ouch!" She hopped about the sand, holding her injured foot. The kick had hurt her a lot more than it did the dragon. His scales seemed to be cast of iron. Kate's throat was still dry with fright but she still couldn't help but laugh. "I mean, what are those stumpy bits? Are they supposed to be your wings?"

The creature stood up and opened its jaws wide, as if to roar. And Kate stood back several paces on realizing the disproportionate size of the jaws, now they were yawningly ajar, with twin rows of long, needle-sharp teeth that seemed to occupy half of its face. It made a hawking sound deep in its throat, but nothing happened.

"Don't talk about eating me again. Don't even joke about it."

With a sigh, it closed its jaws and, wriggling the stumpy things on its back, it hung its head.

"We need to sort this out."

Kate flopped down to sit in the sand, screwing up her eyes against the grit carried in the wind, and she rubbed at her bruised toes. "I can't believe it—a baby boy dragon! Oh, my—the den, the collection, it must have been your hoard. I'm so sorry about that."

It reached out a forepaw and tried to brush her wrist.

"That's it! You've got to get this through your head. There is no question of girl-thing being fish for you."

"Lovely bones!"

Suddenly the oraculum in Kate's brow flared. The dragon recoiled as its body was scorched by the emerald light. Squealing with outrage he ran under a rocky overhang, where Kate could make out his bulky shape in the shadows.

"Not fair!"

"Oh, for goodness sake!" Kate crossed to what had been the floor of the den, looking for the spot where she had been sitting when her oraculum had blown it all away. There was precious little left of the little dragon's hoard. She shoved her hands down into the soft sand and drew back something brilliantly opalescent. It was a nautilus shell, made of pure mother-of-pearl.

"Mine! Mine!"

The dragon shrieked and hurled itself into the air, performing a series of somersaults, shaking the ground whenever he landed.

"It's really beautiful."

The little dragon wheeled its head from side to side. "Gift from Momu—mine—my gift! Girl-thing please not break shiny thing!"

"I just want you to answer my questions."

"Girl-thing puts back shiny thing—or dragon will fight. Dragon will kill. Slaughter!"

"Don't exaggerate." Kate held the nautilus shell up to the sun and attempted to peer through it. "It's really lovely."

"A bargain is made. Dragon will answer questions. A bargain made! Dragon promise is not broken."

Kate was uncertain whether to feel afraid or amused. "A lopsided bargain—with a hungry dragon that wants to eat me."

His eyes never leaving the nautilus shell in her lap, the dragon uttered a sigh. He lifted up his eyes, now speckled with gold dust and ruby splinters, to plead with her. His tail thumped the sand like a drum. He did one of his somersaults, crashing back to earth with claws fully extended. Sand and chips of stone showered over Kate, settling in her bedraggled hair and her tatters of spidersweb.

"Dragon promises—gives Dragon back his shiny thing?"

"Your shiny thing is safe with me."

The dragon peered at her resentfully.

"We need to get to know one another. My name is Kate. But what do I call you?" She gazed once more at his starved and bedraggled shape, so like a piece of driftwood. "Driftwood—that's what I'm going to call you."

"Driftwood, pah!"

"What else does Driftwood have to offer Kate, as part of this bargain—besides agreeing not to eat me?"

His head fell, and his eyes could not face her. "Driftwood has nothing." With a sudden, furious stab of his forepaw, he extended a claw to within half an inch of her oraculum, causing Kate to wince. "Dragon secrets!"

"You can keep your secrets if you'll promise not to eat me."

"Scrags 'n' bones!" He ran in a circle, thrashing his tail. He howled and hopped, trumpeting through his nostrils.

"Poor Driftwood!" She laughed in spite of her returning exhaustion and hunger, watching how he had flopped down onto the rubble of his den, his weight crunching shells and stones. He was gazing out at her with reproachful eyes. "Is there nothing at all to eat in this godforsaken place—besides each other?"

"Driftwood dreams of eatings. Of swallowing um whole, squirming and wriggling in his belly!"

Kate reached out and ran her fingers over the sticking-out bones of his chest, her hand brushing his back and stopping at the stumps of what must once have been wings.

"Did you eat them? Were you so hungry you ate your own wings?"

He lowered his head and squinted back at her.

"Ah, sure I know you're miserable with hunger." Kate sighed. "I am too." She considered her situation. She recalled how Granny Dew had warned her that the tidbits would last, at most, for a few days. She shook her head. "But Granny Dew wouldn't have sent me here if there was nothing to eat."

Kate looked at what was left of the den. She laid the nautilus shell down on the sand close to where she had first scooped it out.

"Here you are—your shiny thing."

Picking it up with a delicate pinch of his claws, he curled his body around it. He licked away the adherent sand with his long blue tongue and crooned.

"Lovely . . . lovely . . . my shiny!"

"You wouldn't dare to eat a girl."

"Hundreds of girls Driftwood has gobbled up. We likes um fat. Flesh and bones crackling! Mmmmmmmmmmm-mmm!"

"You've never eaten anybody. There haven't been any live things—am I right? Not so much as a frog, or even a lizard?"

"Scrags 'n' bones girl-thing not worth the eatings of!"

"I only wish you had a taste for succubi."

"Succulent succubi! Gobble um live." He smacked his lips.

"You're so hungry you fantasize about eating anything that moves."

He smacked his lips again. "Nnnnggggrrrr!" He
emitted a purring sound, as if to indicate how he felt
when fat and contented.

Kate sighed. "You and me, we should stop this talking about food."

"Fat uns. Fat little girl-things. Fat'n juicy.
Mmmmmm-mmmmmm!"

"You're incorrigible!"

Driftwood curled his blue tongue through a bone
with elongated eyeholes and huge interlocking teeth. It
looked like the skull of a small crocodile. It was well and
truly gnawed already. He started chewing.

Kate looked down at her bare legs and feet below the
tattered rags of cobweb. She ran her hands through the
squalid wreck of her hair. Tears sprang into her eyes.
She supposed that she should search again for some
kind of a shelter. But memories of the Tower made her
glad that the sky was over her head. No more had she
forgotten Faltana, or the Gargs and the wolves. But her
weariness overwhelmed any continuing sense of caution. Curling into a ball on her side in a hollow, she
could hear the gnawing sound of the dragon's teeth in
the background, like the comforting rhythm of an old
rocking chair.

She wiped her eyes with the backs of her hands. "Oh,
Driftwood, I'm so tired I could sleep for a week. But can
I trust you to keep out of mischief while I sleep?"

There was a hesitation. Then, the munching continued.

"Don't even think about eating me." She drifted for a moment or two, came to again. "Though I don't expect you'll be able to stop fantasizing about it. We'll look for food. I promise—when I wake up—okay?" She was drifting again, her voice increasingly slurred. "We'd better . . . Or our bones will end up in someone else's hoard."

THE AMULET

AT DAYBREAK ALAN STARED UP INTO A SPINDRIFT of snow falling through the rigging of the enormous mainmast. He couldn't believe it—snow in what should be subtropical waters. He stretched out his hand to let those first tiny flakes fall into his palm, and immediately regretted it. The snowflakes scorched his skin, the freezing equivalent of sparks from a blacksmith's forge. Even as he blew into his cupped hands, the breeze that had so conveniently filled the sails for a week grew fierce, tensing the canvases to rigid bellows and stretching taut every inch of rigging.

Forced to turn his face away from a polar blast Alan headed back to his cabin to wrap the fleecy coverings of his bunk over the existing protection of his greatcoat. When he returned to Siam's side, his face now hooded against the snow, a rising storm was breaking about the pitching and rolling decks. The air was so cold it pained his nostrils just to take a breath. He shouted to Siam above the howling of the wind.

"What's going on?"

Siam lifted his face into the wind and snow to peer directly at the lurid star that appeared in the gaps of cloud, even in daylight, and which seemed to follow their every twist and turn. Even the gnarled Olhyiu chief, who must be inured to cold, had to squint his eyes under a furrowed brow already rimed with frost.

"The Witch's doing—curse her bones!"

Alan shook his head. "We're still a good two days sail from the coastline, and even further from her Tower. I can't believe the Witch can get to us here!"

Siam shrugged, turning to the Kyra, who had stayed with them in the prow. It was the Kyra who now spoke, her eyes narrowed as they peered into the worsening weather. "Olc is wily. She is second in malice to the Tyrant himself. Yet even I wonder if she can cast a malengin thus far."

"What else would explain it?"

"What advice did you receive from the ancient sister in the Council-in-Exile? Did she not speak to you of her fears?"

Alan frowned, thinking back. It wasn't altogether clear what Sister Hocht had tried to tell him. "It was when she was dying . . . consumed by the deathmaw.

She talked about some ancient prediction that mentioned a rath of bones."

Ainé's eyes turned to look into his own.

Alan shook his head in bafflement. He felt a prickling dread that erupted over his skin. If only he could fight back against the eye—but still no matter how hard he probed it with the oraculum, he could discover no substance there to attack.

Siam raised his face, as if sniffing at the star. "Is it not plain to see? The Witch's malice has invaded the blessed night."

As the hours passed the red star remained luridly brilliant, even through the falling snow, and the sense of its menace grew in his mind so that Alan could barely look at it. No other star or moon was visible. Even the ocean, heaving and breaking about the bows, was aglitter with lurid reflections as if the pounding waves were flecked with blood. High above them a spar snapped in the force of the driving wind, tearing free of the rigging. They stared up as it flapped and splintered, then came crashing down onto the decks amidships.

Siam cursed. "Nature raises its hand against us?"

"Get a hold of yourself, man. The last thing we want to do is panic." Alan was about to argue it out with the Olhyiu chief when he felt Ainé's hand grip his shoulder, heard her voice whisper closely, urgently into his ear.

"Tell me more—of when the ancient sister was dying?"

Alan thought back to those terrible moments when he had turned the power of his oraculum inwards to protect himself, yet still he had clasped the hand of Sister Hocht as she was consumed by the deathmaw. He attempted to recall her exact words:

"She talked about the Witch. How she was resurrecting the soul spirit of the titan, Fangorath."

Ainé's eyes bored into his own. "What else?"

"There were things I didn't understand. You have to realize how hurt she was . . . She became confused."

"Recount her words to me—exactly."

Alan returned in his mind to Hocht's faint whisper, her voice so low he had to move his ear over her mouth to catch her dying breath. His hand reached up to his cheek, where Hocht's dying fingers had risen to touch him as she whispered her final counsel. "She said Fangorath was half divine, 'a being of darkness'."

"A being of darkness!" Ainé's tawny head lifted to stare up into the red eye, as if assessing it anew.

"She also called him 'Dragonbane.'"

"Ah!"

"This means something to you?"

"In legend, Dragonbane was the King of the titans. He is said to have led them in a terrible war against the Dragons, in which there was no quarter given."

"She talked about that. She said that Fangorath ended the Age of Dragons."

The Kyra looked worried. "Did she say what the Witch might want of such a resurrection?"

Alan hesitated. "She talked about a Third Portal."

"Are you sure of this? You said she was confused."

Alan stared up into Kyra's eyes. "Ussha De Danaan spoke to us of three portals to the Fáil. We know that the Tyrant has control of one—and a second is located in Carfon. I wondered if the Tower of Bones marks the position of the Third Portal."

The Kyra stared at him, evidently stunned.

"You think this is what Olc is really after?" he asked.

"If so, our mission has grown a good deal more dangerous."

The Oraculum of Bree flared in the Kyra's brow and she lifted her head in a way that suggested she was communicating urgently with the Shee throughout the fleet.

"What is it?"

"I believe that we face an impending attack. The fleet is mostly merchantmen, burdened ships that have little protection. We cannot tell, as yet, what form the attack will take. But I presume that it will focus on the Temple Ship. The remainder of the fleet must pull away—find a safe distance from the attack."

Squinting through the freezing snowfall Snakoil Kawkaw, with just his head and shoulders emerging from his hidey hole, rubbed at his ears, which were already raw from the excoriating wind.

"Scheming hog's entrails!" He slid a tentative leg out of the pit that had concealed his presence from the fish-gutters—a hidey hole he had discovered just before the Ship set sail. He had discovered many such hidden places long ago as a boy, when the derelict hulk had been the children's playground. Kawkaw hadn't been able to believe his luck when the Ship had turned back to its old galleon shape. Who better than he knew every nook and cranny? Had he not played hide and seek here with Siam the stupid and the lovely Kehloke, whom he had already planned to be his future bride? Even then he had kept a sharp eye for advantages, such as this pit, where he could hide the trinkets he stole. But now his hidey hole had enabled him to conceal a present for his enemies. Emerging onto the heaving decks he exulted with a power for mischief undreamed of by the fish-gutters and the huloima brat with the bauble embedded in his head.

"Aarrgh!" He rubbed at his aching back, struggling to stretch it without fainting from the agony it brought.

The Ship that had been a secret pleasure for the boy had proved a bucket out of hell for the grown man, forcing his body into an unnatural crouch that could be pounded and shaken with every roll of the sea. His occasional emergences, to relieve himself or to trawl for scraps of food, had offered little respite. Confound the fish-gutters who had reduced him to this! And even if the anticipated success of his mischief was to be savored, his guts had been drained of puke, in common with the fish-gutters, whose stench befouled the air he was emerging into. It was almost worth the torment to revel in the fact they too were suffering.

And how much worse a fate can I promise you, and soon!

When he was only half emerged from his bolthole, his guts rose again, and despite the fact there wasn't a drop of bile or spit left in them, he retched again, before falling in a moaning crouch on the snow-covered planks.

"Suffering hogspiss!"

It had proved so miserably cramped that both his legs had gone dead below the knees and he hobbled across the mist-laden deck, stamping the life back into his feet, then hopping from one to another, cursing the pins and needles that came with the return of circulation.

Peering right and left to ensure his presence had not been noticed, he took a breather, turning his head to the sky and squinting at the bloody orb that shed its baleful light down on the Ship even through the storm.

How sweet, even in adversity, is revenge!

He savored the thought, scratching contentedly at his chin with the hook that had replaced his left arm, and hopping awkwardly from foot to foot. His narrow face split into a toothy grin. *Is not such an opportunity worth a little discomfort?* Amid the storm, and the confusion it brought aboard the Ship, the timing was perfect for a cunning strategy—one that would put an end to Siam the stupid and his huloima friends. At the same time it would bring rewards beyond dreaming to him, Snakoil Kawkaw—power to take whatever he desired, in gold or women—*including the lovely Kehloke*—as well as extracting his revenge on whoever he wanted.

He almost howled with glee at the thought. *And I, the outcast, the accursed one, will have returned in triumph!* With a stumbling but determined progress he found the stairs that led down onto the center deck. He descended stiff-leggedly step by step, hugging the rail with his one functioning hand. Yet still he tumbled, cursing aloud, onto the slippery rubble-strewn boards. The hook scrambled for purchase as, with his functioning arm, he hauled himself back onto his feet.

Rats' guts for garters!

The present—the object of desire—hung from his throat on a thong of leather. Through the week he had been cooped up like a starving rat it had gnawed a hole into his breastbone. He winced anew at the burning reminder of its presence, panting through wide-flared nostrils, then grasped the thong that suspended it in his fist, holding it away from his flesh. That traitorous turd, Feltzvan—who preened like a woman but who smelt of the charnel-house—hadn't warned him of the personal price to be paid when he had placed the amulet around Kawkaw's throat back in Carfon. Kawkaw knew he had to get rid of it soon—before it got rid of him.

He peered about himself, welcoming the gloom. Nobody had spotted his emergence from the hidey hole. The decks were exactly as he remembered them from so many boyish excursions, cluttered with bollards and rigging, with myriad crevices and shadows. Pulling his face down into his coat he hobbled forward grasping rail and rigging for support until he found the door;

then, wrenching it ajar, he descended the curl of stairs that would take him deep into the bowels of the Ship, cursing the legs that were still bent at the knees from cramp. And there in the galley, laid out fast asleep on the great slab of the chopping board, was the answer to the devil's own needs. Kawkaw plucked down the oil lamp dangling from a ceiling hook so he could inspect the figure that slept on the chopping board, fully a foot and a half thick in cleaver-scarred beech. The snoring face was so enormous with fat it enfolded the ears, and the great head was juddering with the thunderous snores that marked every exhalation of breath, followed by the slobbering sighs of every inhalation.

"Porky Larrh! As I live and breathe!"

Deep as he slumbered through the tossing and rocking of the disturbed ocean, the cook jerked awake in an instant. Two eyes sprang ajar within their buttery-yellow folds of flesh at this intrusion into his galley.

"Porky, me old pal! How in a hog's testicles did you contrive your own heaven? Lord of the kitchens!" Snakoil sneered.

"Snakoil Kawkaw—is it you? Have you come back to haunt me, like the foul breath of a thousand wasted lives?"

Kawkaw stood back as the cook heaved himself to a sitting position. Larrh's head was bent against the black oak ceiling and his two enormous thighs had fallen over the edge of the board. But Kawkaw held his ground, his teeth bared in a wary grin. "We have much to reminisce about, you and me. But first a man must eat. I have spent what feels like a year in a vomit-filled rat hole, where all to be had were the stinking flecks of leftovers stuck between my teeth."

"We have nothing to talk about." Larrh swung his body off the board and onto the floor on the opposite side to Kawkaw, who would have sworn the movement brought its own additional heave and roll of the decks above. A cleaver appeared in the cook's right hand, as he confronted Kawkaw across the board.

"Tsk, tsk! You can put down the cook's savior. You know you are no match for me. Are we not friends? Pah—I could tell you such stories of where I have been and what I have seen on my travels. Tales my old chum would give his right leg to hear."

"I never shared your taste for debauchery."

"Only one love for you, Porky, and it fair surrounds you here." Kawkaw's eyes took in the great mountains of food. "Methinks that for every morsel sent above, two have found their way between those overfed chops!"

The cook raised the cleaver above his head, as high as he was able within the low confines of the ceiling. "Get out of my galley, you scheming piece of dogshit! Or . . . or . . ."

"Or what?" Kawkaw drew a wicked-looking knife from within his greatcoat. "Are we to play king-of-the-castle again, skittering around the board, waiting to see which of us manages to stick the other before he is stuck?"

Kawkaw made a feint with the blade, causing the cook to back away. "Old friends—old pals—why do we sport?"

"You are no friend of mine."

Kawkaw heaved his narrow shoulders into a shrug, and rammed the blade into the fissured surface of the chopping board, where it hummed with a low vibration.

The cook's eyes stayed on Kawkaw's.

"Ach!" The hook rose to scratch at Kawkaw's chin, beneath his grin. "Such have been my tribulations of late that I am beyond caring. I truly have not eaten for a week. Can you, my old friend, even imagine my exhaustion?"

"Why are you really here? What devilry are you up to?"

"A morsel of food—a place to lay my head. Somewhere my poor old legs are not dead from cramp."

"I won't feed you—nor give you so much as the floor for your head."

"Such unkind sentiments! From the friend I took care of! Have you forgotten how I defended you from their taunts in childhood?"

Larrh smashed the cleaver down on the board with such vehemence it buried itself an inch deep in the wood. "And who was my main persecutor? Who declared that if I were roasted on a spit he would be the first to taste the crackling?"

"Ah, my old friend—I look back on it all now with such nostalgia. You might laugh—I see it in your face and eyes that indeed you relish my discomfort, having landed so wonderfully on your feet. Meanwhile I, the outcast, am condemned to beg for a morsel of food."

"Always the sly one—the easy lie on your lips!"

"But we are children no longer. We are men of the world, you and I. You would not be deceived by promises. Not even if I were to offer in exchange the only possession I retain. An amulet so precious it is all I have left of my wanderings."

"Another of your stolen trinkets?"

"No trinket—not this!" Kawkaw lifted the thong that had tethered the amulet from around his neck. He dropped it, with a careless toss, into the hand of the cook. "Yet so exquisite, only desperation would persuade me to part with it."

Larrh froze, gazing at the blood-red prism within his palm, a multifaceted jewel the size of his thumb. "All you ever offered me were lies."

"Such power would this treasure confer on its owner."

Larrh threw it back across the board. "Another of your tricks!"

Kawkaw lifted it up again by the thong. He held it aloft against the light. The blood crystal began to spin about its vertical axis. A black vapor materialized over the board. It solidified as a perfect pentagon, smoother than still water with a silvery triple infinity at the heart of it.

"Still think that what I offer is a trinket?"

The cook stared at the spinning amulet, dumbstruck.

Kawkaw came around the board and he hung the crystal around the cook's throat. As he did so, his voice softened to a whisper. "Judge its potential for yourself. What do you have to lose? I would gladly have it back."

The cook's left hand reached up to grasp the amulet. Larrh's voice trembled. "I know that sign. That's the Tyrant's sigil."

"And his bounty for the wearer!"

"What bounty is that?"

"You were ever the decent man, the generous and honest man, who did his job and harmed no one. But who, among the fish-gutters, responded with respect? Wear this and see how the worm has turned. And then— what further rewards!"

"Rewards?"

"All the heart might desire. Of riches—of the needs of the flesh." Kawkaw's eyelids fell, as if embarrassed at where the very thought was taking him. "Imagine it! All you have ever wanted, secretly coveted, in your wildest dreams . . ."

THE SACRIFICE OF THE DRAGONS

In Kate's dream the dragon was beside her in a night bright with moon and stars. They were accompanied by beings that appeared semi-transparent, like wisps of smoke. These diaphanous beings carried her down to the riverbank where they removed her tattered remnants of cobwebs and re-dressed her in silken underwear and a dress of emerald, as fine as gossamer. Then they melted into thin air, leaving her cocooned in the long grass and wild flowers. She was aware of time flowing about her like the steady current of a clear bright stream, and she was aware that dawn had broken, and still she lay on the riverbank, reluctant to wake from the nice dream.

A crooning voice castigated her: "Girl-thing must hold head still."

In her curiously lucid dream she conversed with the dragon, as if it were the most natural thing in the world: "I really am sorry about your lost hoard. I'm good at making a mess of things."

"Is no matter—keep head still."

"My food purse is gone altogether. I know it was half empty, but I blew that away too—all that was left of it."

"Driftwood has plan."

"What are you up to?"

The dragon was getting annoyed with her because she couldn't stop fidgeting. "Girl-thing—must keep still!"

She opened her eyes—sat upright with a start. "No—it's just a dream!"

The astonishing thing was that she really was on the bank by the river. And her spidersweb rags really were gone. Her hands darted all over to feel the same fine-spun emerald dress she had dreamed about. Underneath—she confirmed it with a wriggle of her body—she was wearing the softest, most comfortable, underwear.

"How could it possibly . . . ?"

"Mmmmm! Hold still!"

"Stop that—whatever you're doing with my hair!"

"Girl-thing—sad. Sad Kate Shaunessy—cries and cries in her sleep. Driftwood listens to cries of woe. Driftwood makes better."

"What?"

"Girl-thing not cry."

Kate tried to turn her head to look behind her, but it was clasped between his front paws in a grip of iron.

"What are you doing to me?"

"Grooming."

She upbraided herself: "Kate Shaunessy—wake up! You're losing it!"

"Driftwood grooming girl-thing, Kate Shaunessy—her hair."

"Whaaaaat!"

In a high-pitched mewling voice, the dragon whined: *"I'm Kate Shaunessy—from Clonmel town."*

Kate reached up with her hands and, tentatively, she brought some strands of her hair around to the front of her face. The auburn strands felt sleek. They ran through her fingers wonderfully glossy, lubricated with some fine oil and scented with something she had never smelled in her life before—but not unpleasant.

"What in the world. . . ."

"Girl-thing not cry! Nooooo!"

"I must be dreaming—what else could it be?"

"Momu—her gift."

"Momu?"

"Momu come."

Kate reached up and she removed his paws from her hair. "Enough. You've groomed me enough. Who is this Momu?"

"Sad girl-thing. Momu comes to see. Girl secrets—magic! Yeeeeessss!"

"Oh, I just give up!"

She shivered with cold, staring out into the early morning estuary. It all seemed so real and yet nothing made the slightest sense. How was she ever going to understand what was going on?

"Mmmm!"

Kate ran her fingers through her hair, blinking still as if to make her reluctant mind accept that this was really happening. "My hair feels lovely—so perfumed and clean." Tears erupted into her eyes again.

"Pah!"

"Somehow—I don't even pretend to understand what you did, or how—you took care of me while I was asleep."

"Kate Shaunessy—cries in sleep."

"I'm sorry about yesterday. I was frightened—and so very tired."

"Girl-thing magic—Momu say."

"Who is this Momu?"

The dragon pointed with a single claw at her brow. Then he swept his forepaw over the ground, the island, which was blooming with flowers, grasses and shrubs.

"I did that?"

She drew herself erect, all of her five and a half feet, and faced his triangular head which, since most of him trailed back close to the ground, was pretty much on the same level as her chest. His ears were small and trumpet-shaped, like a rhinoceros. And there was a distinct smell about him at close quarters, not unpleasant—like the hot smell of a turf fire. His skin was incredibly craggy, ridged and scaly from top to bottom, like some old conch shell. But those lovely kumquat eyes were truly huge in relation to his face, and his mouth—that same wide mouth he had used to comb her hair—formed a frighteningly broad grin between his relatively tiny ears, and when he opened it to pant with the long forked tongue, Kate saw two rows of razor-fine teeth. Indeed, she saw that a few auburn hairs were still trapped between those teeth. But his skin was much cleaner, faintly glowing, when compared to yesterday—if it had been truly yesterday, and not a week ago, she had fallen asleep. She guessed that he must have had a nocturnal bath in the river. Now she could see that his skin comprised a complex pattern of finely wrought scales, which had a blue-green, bronze-like sheen, a bit like the luster of a dragonfly.

The thought caused her to bark a laugh: dragonfly indeed!

"Oh, forgive me, Driftwood—I'm only getting used to the fact that you really are a dragon. Even though you're not at all what I would have expected of a dragon."

"Girl-thing knows of dragons?"

"Well, for a start, you don't really talk like I would have imagined a dragon should talk."

His chest heaved in a disgruntled sigh, sparks of silver and gold sheening over the scales. There seemed to be a weightiness about him as he moved, as if he was largely made out of metals. No wonder the ground shook when he did a somersault.

"Girl-thing knows of dragons?"

"Well . . . of course I don't. But I should have expected . . . Oh, I don't know what I should have expected."

"Pah!"

"What about the silly things you say? A dragon should be talking about . . ." The truth was, now that she thought about it, she had no idea what a dragon should be talking about. "Well, I don't know."

As he turned his back on her, she saw that the same scales, only much broader and stronger, ran over the stumps of his two wings. And, now that he was annoyed with her, there were green and yellow feathers standing to attention about his neck, rather like the Elizabethan ruffs you saw in films.

"Gosh—how would I know!" Kate bit her lip. "Of course I don't really have a clue what a dragon should talk about. I'm being an idiot."

"Food?"

Her eyes lifted to the gorgeous, if chilly, expanse of blue sky overhead. "As a matter of fact, food seems good to me right now. I'm starving."

The dragon curled his emaciated body around her, his head turned toward her on his long neck from her left, and his even longer tail curling around her, protectively, possessively. "Dragon likes Kate Shaunessy—bad girl! Clonmel town!"

"I like you too!"

Suddenly her brow pulsed. It was so unexpected, so powerful, it overwhelmed her thoughts. Kate's heartbeat rose into her throat. Her breath caught. Her hand lifted up, to brush against the hard cool crystal surface of the triangle.

"Oh, heck—I still have a lot to learn."

Kate stared at the strange, emaciated creature. "You know that the Witch is chasing me. Out there, probably not very far away, the succubi and the Gargs—and wolves too—they're all looking for me."

"Hmmmmm!"

The dragon rose onto his squat hind legs until his head was more than twice as high as Kate's. His voice fell, becoming very deep and resonant, and a cold hard glitter invaded his eyes. This was altogether more like what she would have expected of a dragon. He flattened his body in the grass and the flowers and wriggled his back from side to side. Then he reached out with his forepaw, the talon of which was pointing at Kate's brow. "Momu say—magic!"

"You're looking at me like you want something." Kate reached out and brushed his brow, sensing a peculiar tingle from the contact. "What is it?"

He wriggled his back again, rolled those magnificent eyes and, with a sweep of his talon, he indicated the island again, the fact it was blooming.

"Make better!"

Kate's heart rose into her throat. "Oh, Driftwood—you want me to heal you? You're asking me to give you back your wings?"

* * *

Standing erect, so her arms were at much the same level as the wing stubs of the dragon now squatting before her, Kate really hadn't the slightest idea of how to grow back a dragon's wings. She thought of Alan, of the difficulties he had experienced in coming to terms with the Oraculum of the First Power. She remembered how bewildered he had been at first. But there was one experience in particular that came to mind. It was the bizarre idea of blood rage, as Kemtuk, the former Olhyiu shaman, had called it. The Olhyiu and the four friends had been trapped in an ice-bound lake under the threat of attack from the Storm Wolves. Siam, the Olhyiu chief, had called for his people to remember the courage and warrior spirit of their ancestors. Then, somehow, Alan had discovered a special ability that Siam retained from his distant history—a secret that had proved both extraordinary and frightening.

The Olhyiu were descended from bears. When through the power of his oraculum, Alan had explored the subconscious mind of Siam, he had discovered the ghost of his bear ancestry. Alan had reawakened this spiritual inheritance, and this had allowed Siam to change into an enormous grizzly bear. The grizzly had fought the Storm Wolves, giving them time to escape.

Later on Alan had talked about it, in amazement, with Kate. He had explained how he hadn't fully under-stood what he was doing; he had simply allowed his own instinct, and belief in the oraculum, to do the right thing. Now, inspired by Alan's example, Kate laid her hands on the two scarred stubs of wings that protruded from Driftwood's back. She began by caressing them with her fingers, doing her best to imagine the hurt he must have felt when they were ruined. But she realized that the situation she faced was quite different from that of Alan and Siam. There was no ghost of an ancestor for her to reawaken. The dragon had always been a dragon. The inspiration she needed must lie deeper, lost in the eons of time since dragons last flew across the skies.

Kate was uncertain how to begin. Then she whispered softly into Driftwood's trumpet-shaped ear: "I think I'll have to explore your innermost feelings. I must enter your memories—maybe even the memories of your soul spirit, if soul spirits have memories. I'm worried that I'll be hopeless and clumsy about it, because I've never done anything like this before. But I won't do it if you don't want me to."

The dragon turned his head to the side and a single great orange eye regarded her, unblinkingly.

"I'll take that as a reluctant yes!"

Kate sighed, then brushed her fingertips once more over the mutilated stubs. She so deeply empathized with him, she kissed them, one by one. "Poor Driftwood. I promise you, with all my heart, that I'll respect your secrets."

The ridged and scaly head fell.

"Kate Shaunessy, destroyer of shiny things—makes solemn promise. Driftwood also makes solemn promise. Will do his best not to think about eating Kate

Shaunessy, red hair, green eyes. Bearing in mind great hunger of dragons."

"I suppose it's as good a promise as I'm likely to get!"

Slowly, patiently, Kate felt her mind open out into what appeared to be an enormous space of time . . . and longing . . . and most extraordinary of all, endurance. She felt the fall of summer rain on her face; she drifted through clouds and sunsets; she felt time begin to speed up, faster and faster, through the willowy visions of days and nights, and then years, and then centuries. She arrived back at a time when the world was young, and she could smell the blood of living things, the growing power of the soil, the sensation of oneness with the world about her as solid as stone.

"Oh, my!" she breathed. "It's so beautiful. As if you think, not in words at all, but in touches, scents, tastes, emotions . . . and . . . Oh, I don't know how to put it into words. It's like looking out into a world too rich for my experience . . . as if every color and shade was precious . . . as if every moment was too exquisite ever to allow it to pass . . ."

Gooseflesh erupted over her body.

"Oh, goodness—I'm flying!"

It felt utterly different from what she had ever imagined it might actually feel to fly. She soared between enormous trees, with trunks as thick as houses and foliage that reached thousands of feet into the blue, sunlit sky. In the foliage of a single tree, which was the size of a field, were nests of young calling to be fed in voices unlike any voices she had heard—a heady, undeniable yearning, spirit to spirit, through the communication of minds. She reveled in the intimacy of such communication, then soared again, a feral blood running through her veins, as her body was spiraling into the sun—merely to glory in its warmth and being. She felt enormously alive, one with wind and earth and sky. She was enthralled by this expansion of being. She felt so full of joy, she longed for it never to end even while her heart couldn't bear the wild glee of it, her wings and body curling and spiraling and then swooping through air that felt as thick as water because of her speed, flying far over the shimmering oceans where creatures she did not, could not possibly recognize, scurried or dived or took off into the air on tensed fins, merely at her shadow.

And then she dived, shearing through the surface waters, then coursing deeper over coral reefs full of brilliantly colored living things.

"I'm a . . . a sea dragon!"

She felt the enormous heart of the dragon contract within her own chest as she lofted into the air again; she felt the exhalation of fiery breath as she roared . . .

"Oh, Driftwood!"

Her heart sang with the exhilaration of soaring amongst mountains. But still there was more—breathtakingly more.

Within the exquisite joy of communion she felt her being drift stranger still, through veils of perception, to a time before people, a time of the beginnings . . . A time, as it now appeared, that belonged to beings resembling angels. Ethereal spirits who existed in a perfect harmony of being, devoid of ordinary mortal needs.

The Arinn!

Driftwood, you're allowing me to see them... You're letting me sense their loveliness... their gift of innocence...

Beings of magic, as she was now permitted to witness, who could not foresee the coming of evil brought into existence by their gift to the world. The arrival of creatures less perfect, corrupted by that same gift, seduced by their proximity to something approaching infinite power...

Kate saw how it was the corruption of this very legacy of the Arinn that gave rise to change. The evolution of darkness was the tragic inevitability of imperfect beings. And from this darkness came the rise of the titans. Half gods, spoiled by power, yet coveting the power that was half of their birthright, and amoral to the extent they would think nothing of the destruction of an entire world.

Kate didn't relish this new vision. She averted her face and senses from this growing lust for absolute and unreasoning power. Yet she couldn't escape this dreadful journey into the hearts and minds of beings as monstrous in evil as they were in stature. If the forces they lusted after belonged exclusively to the gods, the only beings powerful enough to oppose them, in physical strength and power of magic, were the dragons.

War was inevitable.

A terrible, pitiless war, that seemed to go on forever. The ruthlessness of the titans, their lack of empathy—no young to tend or care for, no love of life, or care for the life about them. Kate saw their glee in ripping apart mountains, or tearing open the river beds, or despoiling oceans—the furious, headlong urge to destroy, until there was little left to destroy anymore. And most dreadful of all, King of the Titans, reared Fangorath, a colossus of pride and rage.

She flinched from this glimpse of the monster whose skull had become the Tower of Bones. He so terrified her that she shrank back into her tiny normal self from the vision of his great horned head and the baleful furnaces that were his eyes.

"Fangorath!" There were sparks in the breath of the little dragon as he spat out the accursed name. "Fangorath—Dragonslayer!"

"But what happened to Fangorath? How was he beaten?"

"All dragons come together. All dragons—and all powerful allies. Together we fought Dragonslayer."

"Who were these allies?"

Driftwood panted with excitement and fear. "Old Ones! Wisdom-that-was."

"The Arinn?"

"Fight together. Old Ones and dragons. Fight greatest of battles—here! In Valley of Bones!" The dragon performed a somersault and landed, shaking the ground. "But Dragonslayer too strong. Defeat us all. Defeat wisdom-that-was. Destroy, destroy—*destroy*! All is darkness. Destroyer of Worlds!"

"Oh, Driftwood!" With a shiver, Kate recalled the gigantic skeletons and armor she had seen around the Tower of Bones.

"Fangorath cannot be beaten. Demi-god—immortal. But can be banished. Dragons beseech Dark One."

"Who was this Dark One?"

Driftwood's eyes became very large, so large that Kate could see herself in their shiny reflections. "Call down great goddess. Raven of battlefields. Make sacrifice! Great sacrifice—the joy of dragons."

"Oh, no!"

Kate had never seen Driftwood so restless or excited. He was pacing around, hopping from foot to foot and running around in circles, while growling to himself, his eyes shining like miniature suns.

"All the dragons died except you, it seems," she said gently, not wishing to excite him more, yet tremulous with sympathy.

"Died me too!"

"But . . . ?"

Then she understood. The sacrifice of the dragons, the tribute to the Great Raven—to Mórígán—had been the loss of their wings. To end the carnage, to save what still remained of the war-ravaged world, the surviving dragons had bitten off their own wings. The dragons had abandoned the source of their joy, and she saw them, all the poor dragons, as they plunged from the skies into the depths of the oceans.

Died me too . . .

Kate felt her heart breaking with anguish for her little dragon. She made no attempt to stop the flood of her tears. For a long time she just brushed her fingertips over the stumps of wings, grieving over their broken remains, feeling such a sense of loss she couldn't think at all. She hugged the small dragon, huddled into a ball with the horror of what he had allowed her to see. She clung to him, feeling the immense discharge of whatever the oraculum did to her, whatever power it gave to her, itself the gift of a goddess. She poured her grief and love into the ravaged stumps where the wings should have been, feeling the changes already beginning to take place in the scarred and deformed flesh. Withdrawing her hands she watched the proliferation of new growth, swelling first like enormous mushrooms, then further expanding amid wrinkles and folds in which the throb of arteries could clearly be seen. She sensed the ongoing proliferation of nerves and bones and muscles, the growth of new life.

Then, her emotion too overwhelming for words, she threw her arms around the long, scaly neck, squeezing his unresisting solidity.

The great wings, which must have been twenty feet in their span, opened out on either side of the dragon's back like fabulous sails, stretching taut and moving in slow fanning exercises, their surface covered in gossamer scales that flickered into color in sweeping iridescent waves.

"Ooooh!"

With the sun behind him it was like looking up through the most beautiful cathedral window, her eyes dazzled by the kaleidoscope of gorgeous colors against the light. She could see a fine filigree of gold running everywhere, like marbling under the delicate scales, thrilling her all the more to realize that she was looking at the color of his blood—that a dragon's blood was not red like her own, but golden.

The dragon roared.

Kate clapped her hands. "Ah, sure—you're magnificent!"

She tottered amid the powerful currents of air that blew back from the enormous beating wings. Wiping the tears from her face with the back of her hand, she made her way back up the slope, searching for where she had slept that first night . . . probing the rocky ground with care. There was such a crazy idea in her mind—she just had to find out—she just had to be sure . . .

And finally she found it, the place where she had fallen into an exhausted sleep when she had first arrived at the island, her head resting against the knobbly black log of fossilized driftwood . . .

The log was gone. In its place was an empty outline in the rocks.

A SPLINTER OF MALICE

A DAY AFTER THE FIRST SPINDRIFT OF SNOW HAD scorched Alan's palm the storm worsened to a blizzard. His face, though protected by a sealskin hood, felt like a frozen mask and his fingers, inside their fur-lined gloves, were numb. The wind howled about his ears as if competing with the angry roar of the ocean. At least they had managed to furl the sails and anything loose on deck had been stowed below. All the while the snow blew horizontally across the deck, hard as hail, bringing tears of irritation to his eyes and, as the cold deepened, the ice froze in his eyelashes.

This is crazy.

Crabbing across the slippery decks he clung to whatever solid structures he came across, making his labored progress to the stern rail from where he attempted to probe the sea in their wake. But it was impossible to make out whether or not the fleet had been able to follow the Kyra's order. Visibility was so reduced he could detect nothing. He could only hope that, by now, they were tacking southwards, aiming to put as many leagues as possible between them and the storm-wracked Temple Ship, haunted by the baleful red eye that leered threateningly over it.

It's downright unbelievable!

It made no sense that the Ship, which should have been their protector, had become a source of the gravest threat. Above his head the tempest tore and ripped at the masts and rigging, even as the snow was freezing and thickening, burying everything in ice as hard as concrete. The same ice was sticking to the decks and rails so that no matter how hard Siam's crew picked it away with shovels it overwhelmed their efforts, making any movement on the pitching and rolling surfaces hazardous.

Alan clapped his gloved hands together, then stuck them under his armpits. But it made no difference. There was no escaping the fact that over just one day a power of darkness had invaded the entire fabric of the Ship. And that same darkness had weakened his oraculum.

Nearby a gathering of Olhyiu sailors, their sideburns frozen to icy sculptures about their faces, murmured among themselves. He saw fear in their eyes. The sharp sound of hammering sounded overhead, where Siam had sent a party of men aloft with mallets to hammer at the ice that had encased every inch of rigging. Taking what grip he could of the rails, and just holding on during the worst of the pitching and tossing of the decks, Alan made his way back to the prow. When he got there he shouted into the ears of the captain, Siam.

"Your sailors are panicking."

"Who would blame them? The Ship is accursed." Siam's eyes fell on the oraculum in Alan's brow. "Can you not aid her?"

"I've tried. Nothing seems to make a difference."

Siam's eyes met Alan's, as if to urge him to try harder.

Alan focused on the frozen deck, his eyes almost closed against the cold. He felt the power grow in him, felt it discharge through the oraculum. But it was as if he were shining a flashlight into the night sky. The battening darkness sucked up the feeble beam and it was gone. What slight effect it had in melting the surface layer of ice proved useless, the ice reforming in moments. And it left him exhausted.

"What is it, Mage Lord? Why is it to no avail?"

Alan shook his head.

"But what could it be, out here? Three hundred leagues separate us from the Witch and her plotting!"

"The power in my oraculum feels weakened somehow. Try as I might, the response is too feeble."

As he stood by Siam the sky swelled with black storm clouds and the wind rose to a hurricane. The great Ship twisted about on itself, yawing violently from side to side as if to cast off its Arctic shackles. A groaning rose up from the timbers below their feet. The movement and the deep, sad sounds were terrifying, throwing people off their feet amid the clattering of belongings falling about the cabins and storerooms. Shouts from below decks alerted Siam to the fact that a fire was being put out in the galley.

Alan gritted his teeth. His stomach clenched with another of the monstrous yaws, seeing the starboard rail pitch so low it was several feet below the seething invasion of a great wave. He hollered into the ear of the chief. "Siam—you know the moods of the oceans. What do your instincts suggest?"

"Strangeness is imposed upon strangeness. Yet this weakening of your power arrived as one with that eye in the sky."

Alan nodded, peering up into the madness of sky, through which he glimpsed the baleful red glow.

As the Ship righted itself once more he glanced about himself in a rare moment or two of respite. He saw the breath rising from the sailors' mouths in puffs of steam. But there was something odd about the way the steam was moving, something he wouldn't have noticed amid the fury of the wind. Arcs of breath were coming from people's faces and whirling away, to join together into a vague but definite stream.

He followed the movement of the stream: *It's as if it's revolving about the fulcrum of the Ship.*

But what could that mean? He wondered if he was looking at a clue to what was going on. But if so it was a clue he hadn't yet figured.

Something resembling the eye of a storm?

Oh, man! He sensed it could be important—he sensed it strongly, instinctively. Something in the way the Ship was rocking from side to side, and how their breath was circling . . .

"O great A-kol-i, look down upon us from your leap on high! Save us, Lord of the Deep, from the red eye, and the Witch's challenge!"

The youthful shaman, Turkeya, trembled as he knelt on the bare plank floor of his cabin, his numbed fingers clasped before him and his elbows hugging the wooden bunk for support against the heaving of the decks. Though younger than many of his fellow Olhyiu on board, he was privileged to have this billet to himself. But in truth he would have been happier to share the swinging hammocks of the sailors, with their grog-inspired chantey-singing. It would have made a welcome change from his gloomy solitude amid this terrifying blizzard.

No wintry storm, not even a gale of snow, would ordinarily have worried the young shaman, who had spent his entire childhood in the Whitestar Mountains where winter reigned seven months of the year. But this was no seasonal chill or blow of winter. This was a bane of malevolence arrived out of the blue to harrow these summer waters. It had proved impossible to sleep, with the wild rolling of the Ship, and with the porthole, though battened shut against the storm, pitching below the massive swells and the wintry forces seeping in past the wooden shutter to freeze to ice inside the cabin wall. In the pallid daylight that filtered into the tiny cabin he had seen the rime of ice creep and spread. He could hear it squeaking like a horde of mice, as the living timbers heaved and groaned under the battering of wind and ocean. And with its icy presence the accompanying cold was invading the very air around him, freezing muscle and sinew, slowing the thoughts in his head as he attempted to pray.

With the new dawn a bizarre invasion of ice and rime encrusted his cabin wall, a bloom like a gigantic rose, but instead of the white of snow or the glassy reflections of ice this sinister flower was made up entirely of greys and darks, as if in its very nature it was devouring the light, and spreading in huge concentric florets around the focus of the porthole. The sight of it chilled more than mere flesh. And at the very heart of it, haunting the corners of his vision, was a shadow—a head cowled in black—in which the eyes appeared darker still, like windows into a soul of darkness.

"O—O great A-kol-i . . ." he stammered, the prayer failing on his lips, the image of the leviathan that, in the legends of the Olhyiu, was the creator of worlds, melting from his very imagination. His prayer faltered, and his courage with it.

"Turkeya!"

He was only confusedly aware that someone was calling out his name. He recognized the voice, soft in his ears, but was unsure if it might be real or a dream, his whole being still haunted by the cowled figure. He felt hands take hold of his shoulders to shake him out of his torpor, slim girlish fingers, yet surprisingly determined. "What's happening? You're like a block of ice!"

Allowing his face to be turned, he blinked slowly at the vision of his friend, Mo, who had entered the cabin on silent feet and who was standing over his still-kneeling form.

"Mo!" he whispered. "What is happening to us?"

"Here! Let me help you back onto your feet. I've had a message from Mark."

"A message?"

"Please listen to me!" Mo began to rub at his hands, his face, to try to unthaw him from the clutches of the cold.

Turkeya's eyes blinked again with a painful sluggishness. He began to blow into his numbed fingers, to stamp life back into his feet. "Mark? Your brother has spoken to you?" He shook his head, wiped his face with what felt like somebody else's awkward hands.

"He's sent me a warning."

"What?"

"A splinter of malice has somehow invaded the Ship. It will destroy us all if we don't do something."

"What can we do?"

"I don't know. All I know is that time is short. We must hurry. We have to find Alan. He'll know what to do."

Climbing the central staircase proved to be hazardous, with their feet slipping and sliding over icy timbers and rimy debris. Everywhere below the decks they encountered shivering sailors, their furry surcoats stiffened with hoar frost. Their very breaths were transformed as they exhaled, thickening to a freezing vapor that added to the deposits of rime and ice so the cabins and chambers looked like the interior of cooling stores. Even as they stumbled out into the middle deck, thick slurries of snow obscured their vision to a few yards, whirling down out of a wrack of storm, stinging and burning with the tiniest contact on exposed skin, all the while their numbed ears tormented by the shriek of the wind. Great waves pounded the Ship, coming in over the pitching sides, rushing over the decks and sweeping away everything in their path. The gaps in the ratlines were filling with thick panes of ice, like windows. Already the ice over the middle deck was a foot deep and the sheer weight of it was dragging the Ship, and all aboard, deeper into the turmoil of the ocean.

What few sailors they saw, clinging to rails or ropes on deck, stared at them with haggard faces encrusted with ice and snow. Everywhere they witnessed broken spars and fallen rigging. With every tread they had to negotiate an obstacle course of debris made treacherous by thick ice.

An almighty wave struck from starboard, and Turkeya and Mo lost their footing on the middle deck, their bodies skidding over the ice to be flung against the great pillar of the central mast.

Turkeya attempted to protect Mo but his fingers were too numb to hold her, so that she began to roll and slide away from him, at the mercy of the next great wave. Turkeya began to slide into oblivion himself, his eyes clenched shut, expecting death. Abruptly, an enormous hand took a firm grip of his hair and yanked him back to his feet. He blinked open his eyes to be confronted by the cook, Larrh. The cook's mane of white hair had broken free of its braid so it whirled about his head and face in the frenzy of wind. The giant figure took a better grip of Turkeya, pushing him up against an ice-encrusted rope where he managed to find a grip. His blurred vision searched frantically for Mo. He glimpsed her through the snow flurries, clinging onto the starboard rail.

"There!" he cried to Larrh. "The girl—save her!"

But Larrh ignored him, staring up into the wrack of sky, his arm pointing to where the lurid red light of the star was faintly visible even through the deluge of snow and storm.

"That spiteful moon!" Larrh cried, as if there was no escaping the fact that the star was directly overhead. The vortex that gripped them spun about the fulcrum of the red star. "It robs me of sleep. It invades my dreams. It fills me with foreboding."

Turkeya shouted into Larrh's distracted ear. "Listen to me! The girl will perish, unless we save her!"

Larrh's enormous head was shaking, his lips trembling. "That monstrosity—I cannot tear it from my mind. Is it possible that we are being punished?"

Turkeya reached up and slapped Larrh's face. "Will you not listen to me, Mr. Larrh? You know who I am. I am the shaman. If we lose the girl we are lost!"

Larrh's head swiveled slowly down. His brow glowered, his eyes protruding with what appeared to be uncontrollable emotions.

"Such is my torment I can neither rest nor sleep. That confounded thing—that damn eye."

"Only you have the strength to save my friend. Save her, Mr. Larrh. Save the girl and you will save us all."

The wheel was the only fragment of superstructure that resisted the ice. Shivering, holding onto it with every ounce of his strength, Alan waited for the Temple Ship to recover from the blow of another wave that had pitched the starboard rail below the waves. His breath was reduced to a desperate panting through nostrils that were encrusted with ice. Through similarly ice-grimed eyelids he surveyed the aft deck, or what little he could make of it, with visibility reduced to snatches between squalls. He was startled to see movement, a small huddle of figures breaking through the blizzard in a series of shuffles, holding on wherever they discovered a foothold, but determined, it seemed, to approach him at the wheel. With hair frozen awry on their heads and a wild, desperate look in their grime-etched faces, he recognized Turkeya and Mo—and then the giant figure that released them both from his powerful grip, before fading away into storm.

"Are you crazy?"

What could they be thinking of, coming up from below into these conditions? He shouted for Ainé.

"I see them!"

The Kyra, in some form he had never witnessed before, half woman, half tigress, with extended claws on all four limbs, hauled the two shivering figures up close to Alan, where they clutched onto the wheel on either side of him. Mo's features were luminescent with pallor. Alan extended his right arm so it encircled her, helping her cling to the wheel, then turned to Turkeya, whose eyes were closed and whose lips appeared to be praying.

"What's going on?"

It was Mo who answered, her girlish voice strong enough in his ear to penetrate the shriek of the wind.

"Mark has spoken to me." Mo explained the nature of Mark's message. A splinter of malice had invaded the Ship.

"But what does that mean? Are you talking about the red eye?"

"No. Not the eye. Something else. Something here, within the Ship itself. Mark believes that it will destroy us all if we don't do something about it."

Alan shook his head, baffled by her words. If only he could communicate directly with Mark himself. But he had been trying to do that, without success, ever since he had come back to the after deck. He turned to the Kyra, who was crouched nearby, her arms about a stanchion of iron at the base of the wheel, her talons extended and gripping. The fur of her face was solid with ice and even the pulsations in her oraculum were dulled.

"Do you sense anything more of this splinter of malice?" He addressed the young shaman.

Turkeya told Alan about the rose of ice that had invaded his cabin—and the figure of darkness he had sensed to be part of it.

"Not the Witch?"

"The Tyrant, I fear!"

The Tyrant?

A new blast of wind threatened their balance, so each held tightly to the wheel and waited for it to ebb. Alan closed his eyes, forcing himself to think. "The Tyrant is mounting some kind of attack from inside the Ship?"

"It's as if some malign force is weakening us from within. Some malaise of the spirit. But it attacks more than the Ship. It attacks us all, in heart and spirit. Do you not sense it—feel it—within yourself?"

Alan stared at the young shaman, shocked by what he was suggesting.

"Mage Lord!" He heard the Kyra's urgent call, mind-to-mind. "The Ship is heeling about!"

"Watch out, Mo, Turkeya. I'm taking the wheel."

But the Ship did not respond to the wheel. The Ship was turning by itself—spinning around its own axis—and the sensation was dizzying. Even as it did so another gigantic wave struck. Water surged over the decks, the spray from the wave foaming high into the upper masts and lines, then cascading back down onto the decks. They had to cling to the wheel, their hearts in their throats and their breaths suspended. With a sudden deafening crack the center mast snapped. There was a thunderous series of detonations as the huge timbers crashed down onto the decks, dragging rigging and fragments of the other two great masts down with it, smashing through superstructure and rails, killing sailors.

Mo cried into Alan's ear. "Talk to the Ship!"

He glanced down into her face, observing up close the beaded tracery of the ice in her eyelids that made it almost impossible for her to blink.

"Find a way, Alan!"

All of a sudden the light faded, as though the sun, already obscured by the pall of blizzard, had been eclipsed. The Ship reeled as another monstrous wave struck it broadside, and Alan lost his footing on the slippery planks, crashing heavily against the rail. Half-stunned, he felt the surging rise of the recovering deck, which hurled him forward, smashing him against the base of the wheel. It stunned him for several moments while he clung to the icy woodwork, attempting to recover his senses. He could only hope that Mo and Turkeya remained safe nearby.

The Kyra helped him struggle back onto his feet. He felt her claws penetrate his surcoat as she pressed him back against the wheel. Thank goodness, Mo and Turkeya were still alive, huddled together immediately below him.

"Mark!" he cried, staring anew at the great wheel, realizing that this too was now frozen solid, encased in ice. There was no impression of the soul spirit of his friend, no impression of Mark's presence at all.

The world about him had gone berserk.

Close to his ear he heard the Kyra roar. "The sea ahead! A monster wave. It is twenty feet above the deck."

"Tie me to the wheel!"

Wordlessly the Kyra took hold of Alan's right arm. She lashed it to the rim of the great wheel. The Ship heeled, as if anticipating the approaching horror. With an almighty heave, the Kyra was at his other side, lashing his left arm to the other side of the wheel. He heard her departing words, mind-to-mind.

"Discover the source of malice!"

The Kyra was gone, and with her, his friends Mo and Turkeya. Alan counted the seconds, hoping that they made it to safety below decks before the great wave swept over the decks. He held his breath as the monster wave struck, tearing his feet from under him and roaring through him.

Mysteries Still

Returning to the riverbank, with the morning sun warming the air about her, Kate had never felt more exhausted and yet so exhilarated. The dragon waited for her return, his tail swishing through the long grass, disturbing a swarm of brightly colored butterflies. She stared at him, as if to reassure herself that what she recalled had been real: those great wings really were there, furled like collapsed tents along his back. When she squatted back down beside him, his head and neck extended almost to her lap.

It had all been so exciting she had forgotten her hunger. But that hunger had never gone away.

She murmured, "I feel so famished my muscles feel jittery."

"Driftwood find food."

"I don't know where—but I wish you would."

She threw her arms around the long, scaly neck, squeezing his iron-like solidity. "Show me that you can fly. Let me see those wonderful wings in action. Let me see the real you—Driftwood the magnificent!"

With a swirl of his long body he turned riverwards, and then he moved with a blur of speed in those powerful hind legs that startled her. In moments he was airborne, the long slender body rising in a spiral so graceful it took her breath away. She watched as he grew smaller with distance, moving out until he hovered several hundred feet above the central stream, and then plummeted down, his body sheening blue-black as he dived vertically into the river. He was gone for something like a minute, with just the spreading ripples to show the place of his entry, and then suddenly he surfaced again in a cascade of water, and with a fish in his jaws. His great wings beat the air as he lifted slowly clear of the river, and a small rainbow shimmered within the rain of droplets falling from his wings. Kate squealed with delight. She thought a rainbow needed a peep of sunlight twinkling through it. But then she realized that Driftwood was himself the source of the light. She blinked, a slow entranced blink, only just realizing something she should have grasped before. The odd, cantankerous little dragon wasn't just some exotic animal. He was a being of magic.

Even so he couldn't resist showing off, rising in another glorious spiral, preening his brightly colored ruff so it flashed a delight of iridescent colors for her benefit, before swooping down to alight before her, his wings folding about him like a cape, and depositing a flapping salmon at her feet.

She clapped her applause.

"Kate—eat!"

"I can't just eat it like that. It's still jumping."

He bit off the head and swallowed it. "Not jumping."

"I just couldn't. It's still raw."

The dragon bit the remains of the fish into two halves. One half he swallowed whole before he picked up what remained of the fish and trapped it between his sharp teeth. Then flames rose from his throat and he grilled the fish for her, allowing the cooked meat to lie within the bowl of his lower jaw.

He looked so pelican-like, unable to speak because his mouth was full, a talon-tipped finger—or maybe it was a thumb—pointing toward his burdened jaw.

"Mmmmmm!"

Kate sniffed: it really did smell delicious.

"Mmmmmm—mmmmmmmmhhhhh!"

"I think I've found a way to stop you prattling on."

Those great eyes regarded her, fast blinking, with steam exuding from between his nostrils.

Kate's mouth slavered with hunger. She wanted to taste the fish very badly, but she quaked with fear at the thought of going anywhere near those jaws. At the same time she really was starving and her hunger got the better of her, so she dashed one hand quickly into the maw and took a fistful of fish, burning her fingers so she had to pass the hot flesh rapidly from one hand to another, blowing on it in an attempt to cool it. She was forced to drop it before dashing off and gathering several dock-like leaves and returning, arranging them into a make-shift platter before the dragon on the ground.

"Put it there."

He dropped the mouthful of fish, then snorted, blowing steam and fragments of fish all over her.

But Kate didn't care. She blew on a morsel of fish and she tasted it as hot as her mouth would bear it.

"It's lovely." She snorted through her nose, with her mouth still half full. "It's the most delicious food I have ever tasted."

"Eatings—not talks!"

She couldn't wait. She blew on some more, aware that she was slobbering saliva from the corners of her mouth.

"Just look at the state of me!"

The dragon watched her all the while, those great kumquat eyes blinking slowly, as Kate couldn't stop herself slobbering, or her poor wasted body shivering and trembling, and all the while her fingers dipped repeatedly into the mess of fish, and her mouth gobbled, reluctant even to chew properly, until her belly felt full to bursting.

Although her mind was full of wonder at all that had happened, yet still there were mysteries about the dragon, and about the island, that deeply puzzled her. For example, who was this Momu who had dressed her in the diaphanous clothes while she slept that second night? And there were mysteries that applied to Driftwood himself. If she was right, and her oraculum had somehow restored life to the dragon from what had appeared nothing more than an ancient fossil, he had come back into the world as a new-born—a child. That would explain the childish behavior and speech. But over the few days—a week at the most—he appeared to be growing, maturing at enormous speed. Granny Dew had sent her here, to this island. So there had to be a logic to her arrival here, even if she couldn't fathom any of it.

"Can I ask you a question?" It emerged more like, "Unn ahh assshhh u ehhh wesssnnn?"

The dragon merely flicked an eye in her direction. He was lying prone in the grass, peering down at the river, as if impatient to hunt again.

"I know that our meeting—even if it just seemed to happen by chance—must signify something important."

His tail whumped in the grass.

Kate sighed. Then she began to twirl a seed head of grass before her eyes, astonished in studying it that it had grown from the purse given to her by Granny Dew.

"What about this Momu? Who, or what, is the Momu?"

"Soon! Girl-thing meet—see!"

A prickle of apprehension swept over her. "I don't follow."

The dragon's tail started to swish again, but more purposefully, not the gentle, day-dreamy whumping as before. Kate looked askance at him. "I didn't know where I was running when I got free of the Tower. Any direction would do. It was just chance that I met the wolf-man."

"Ummm." The tail was still swishing gently in the grass.

"And then it was sheer chance where I fell down into an exhausted sleep. It just happened that your fossil bones were under my head. Under the oraculum all the while I was sleeping."

His voice sounded surprisingly deep. "Not chance!"

"What?"

"Fate!"

The seed head fell from Kate's loosened fingers. "What are you implying? Are you saying that Granny Dew is controlling me?"

Driftwood swiveled his lumpy head, with a knowing widening of the eyes. "Fate controlling Granny Dew."

Kate hesitated, wondering if this could possibly be true. "We need to get away. The Witch and all the others—they're out there looking for me. We need to run."

"Driftwood will not run."

Kate's heart faltered. "We have to get away. We're both too weak to fight them. We'll be slaughtered if we just sit here and wait for them to find us. We have to escape. If you won't come with me, I'll have to go on my own."

But the dragon reared to his full height and simply shook his head. "No running. Driftwood and Kate fight. We fight—no running anymore!"

THE GYRE

ALAN GASPED FOR BREATH AS ANOTHER ENOR-
mous wave struck them broadside, close to the bow this
time, the great ship plunging down at a terrifying angle
beneath the solid wall of water, then twisting and rolling as the fury of the ocean tore over the decks before
righting itself to an uncertain juddering balance again.
Soaked and frozen, his skin numbed by ice, his eyes
almost blinded, he was only dimly aware that the spars
and rigging were gone, wrenched away by the fury of
storm and waves. Of the three great masts, only splintered stumps remained. How many of her crew, and
of the guardian Shee, had also been lost? The tether-
ing of his arms to the wheel had saved him from being
washed overboard. Holding his breath, too exhausted to
do anything other than squeeze his eyes shut, he hung

on as another great wave struck, tearing him off his feet until his whole body was horizontal under the rushing tide of water. The force against his shackled arms was immense. It felt as if his shoulders were being torn from their sockets, but then after what seemed an eternity it eased again, the ocean draining away from his pain-racked body and limbs, abandoning him retching and coughing, his limbs and senses struggling to recover.

Mark—are you there? He pressed his call urgently, through the oraculum.

No response. Just the manic glee of the gale.

Mark! He roared again, with all of his force and concentration.

I . . . I hear you . . . faintly . . .

What's the hell is wrong?

. . . trying to call you . . . calling for hours . . . something attacking the Temple Ship . . . Ship's telling me . . . corruption from within . . .

What does that mean?

. . . don't know . . . getting to me too . . .

The Ship itself! The Temple Ship was communicating through Mark. But what was it trying to tell him? A corruption from within? It had to be the eye of malice— the red eye must be eating into both their soul spirits.

But his oraculum suggested the eye was empty. This didn't feel right . . .

Alan tried to recall something Turkeya had said. Something he was trying to remember, if only his numbed brain would respond . . .

Turkeya had spotted something.

It's as if some alien force is weakening us from within. Some malaise of the spirit . . . It attacks us all, in heart and spirit. It's turning our own minds and spirits against us . . . We're becoming our own worst enemies . . .

Alan retched against the ice-encrusted woodwork of the great wheel. But there was nothing left to bring up. He stared around himself at the heaving and rolling decks, which resembled a breaker's yard of spars and masts and bedraggled tatters of rigging. He didn't know how the Ship had survived such a battering. But it couldn't possibly survive much more of this. He closed his eyes and attempted the same scrutiny through the oraculum. He saw the Ship in ghostly outline, the heartbeat at the core of her weak, faltering.

It reminded him of something, a memory . . . a feeling of terrible sadness. He had felt this same communication of sadness from the Ship before—a sadness that had not come from his own heart but from outside, a feeling that had shocked him with the intensity of its communication. And now, when he scanned the Ship through his oraculum, he sensed despair. Could it be that the Temple Ship was sending him a personal message—a warning?

He poured what power he still retained through the oraculum into the structure of the Ship. But there was no response. If anything the weakness in the Ship seemed to worsen, its despair to deepen. Alan's head fell onto his chest.

A corruption from within? *A malaise of the spirit . . .* Maybe the malaise was within Alan himself—his failure to understand the warning message?

The threat, whatever it was, was capable of overpowering the oraculum. It was capable of silencing Mark, even his soul spirit in its powerful union with the Ship. What could possibly be so powerful? Alan recalled how the Tyrant had controlled him in their last confrontation. The Tyrant had overcome his oraculum. The Tyrant—not the Witch! But the Tyrant wasn't here to do that. He thought about Turkeya's warning: Mo had received a message from Mark.

A splinter of malice has entered the bowels of the Ship.

Not the red eye in the sky. Something attacking the Ship from within!

Alan clung to consciousness as a new cyclone tore through the wreck, hurling debris horizontally across the decks. About him the ocean heaved and pounded as if maddened with rage. The Temple Ship had been reduced to a shattered hulk amid the mountainous waves that pitched and tossed it with monstrous violence, its hull and decks groaning under the freezing torrents of water. The stumps of masts, a yard across at the base, were being further tormented and shattered, with dangerous fragments shattering and snapping, showering the air with potentially lethal splinters. There was no escape from the violence, no place of safety. The gunwales had been torn away and even the planks of the decks were being ripped from their moorings. Speech was impossible. The only communication was oraculum to oraculum. Desperately, Alan reached out to Mark again. "What is it? You sent Mo a message—something about a splinter of malice attacking the Ship?"

Mark's communication, at the core of his mind, sounded even weaker than before.

. . . malice . . . here . . . attacking from within . . .

Bewildered, Alan directed his oraculum to that of the Kyra, who was invisible in the snow and spray, but somewhere forward in the prow. The Kyra responded immediately, a reassuring return of communication, mind-to-mind.

Can you figure what's causing this, Ainé?

The Ship is caught in a deathmaw.

A deathmaw? Alan's vision attempted to probe the seas about him but all he could make out was one gigantic wave after another. What was Mark trying to tell him? What could be attacking the Temple Ship from within?

Alan attempted to think this through, doing his best to shake the confusion from his head, the muscles of his neck so stiff it felt like an agony of slow motion. But he could sense no inner rage—no inner madness. All he had done was to fight the storm, to press every mote of his being into an effort to fight back against the raging elements, and by doing so help the Ship.

He still poured out all of his power against the enraged elements. It felt as if all that was right and decent in him was draining away, being sucked out of him. And yet he was failing. Only then did he try to communicate again, mind-to-mind, with the Kyra.

Something has been brought on board the Ship. The eye is just a deception, causing us to focus all of our concern on the Witch. We've been looking outward when the real danger is within. There must be some sign of it. I'll stay at the wheel and try to communicate further with Mark. But you've got to organize a search below. Get Siam to help you—and Turkeya. Mo took Mark's message to Turkeya—he knows the Ship. And he has a shaman's instincts. Get Turkeya to conduct a search from top to bottom. If anybody can find what is wrong, it'll be the shaman.

An exhausted Turkeya held onto a timber in the murky corridor below decks and waited for the violent impact of another great wave to pass. A malice was at large among them, a danger at the very heart of the Ship. But what could it be? All he knew was what he'd been told. That if and when he saw anything strange he was to blow on the whistle he carried in his greatcoat pocket. It would have been helpful to know a little more of what to look for since just about everything he encountered in the confusion seemed awry, like the look of terror in the eyes of everybody he spoke to. But doggedly he stuck to his task, questioning all he met and poking into every nook and cranny.

So it was, after many hours of stumbling throughout the debris-littered lower decks of the Temple Ship, that he came across the cook staring out of a wide-open porthole in the galley kitchen. Larrh's white hair was a miniature storm in itself, wild and drenched about his head. His tall body was bent so he could press his face against the porthole and peer out into the storm. Turkeya was shocked to find any porthole opened, for the sea deluged in through the opening with every wave that struck them broadside, and the galley was already awash with brine. The cook himself appeared oblivious to the shaman's arrival. He was no longer wearing his apron. His body was enveloped in a greatcoat large as a tent that was itself dripping with spray. He was groaning and muttering to himself, his face haggard with worry.

"How fare you, Mr. Larrh?"

"How fare I?" The ponderous head of the cook turned and peered through red-rimmed eyes at the gangling youth, blinking with a weary deliberation. At first there was no recognition in Larrh's eyes, just a flatness, a distraction of distance.

"I find myself asking if there are still stars up there," he muttered, "stars that remain to guide us?"

Turkeya thought it again: the porthole open! When it should have been battened down tight against the waves. He attempted to slam it shut, but the bulk of the cook prevented him. For several tense moments they stood in a kind of exhausted confrontation with each other. No more did Turkeya know what to say in response to the cook's strange comment. His own words, when they emerged, came from something less than conviction. "I'm sure the Mage Lord will find a way."

"Would that I were sure of anything anymore."

Turkeya hesitated. Larrh had originally hailed from Turkeya's old tribe and village but he had not traveled down with them from the ice-bound lake. He had long abandoned his Olhyiu roots and found employment in the harbor at Carfon. If Turkeya recalled correctly, he had been recruited for this journey at the suggestion of Feltzvan, the adviser to the Prince, Ebrit.

"What is it, Mr. Larrh? You seem distressed. Is it something I can help with? A potion to help you sleep, perhaps?"

Larrh had inserted his right hand between the folds of his coat and he appeared to be scratching at his breastbone. His voice was low, halfway between a growl and a whisper. "Distressed, you say?"

"Is it a spasm of the heart that ails you?"

The huge man withdrew his hand, blinking again, as if seeing the young shaman more clearly. "Forgive a foolish man! Why I have a son and daughter older than you. You are precious young, for a shaman."

"I do what I can."

The man hesitated, then jerked his head violently away, consumed by some new spasm of torment. Crouching down again, his hand rubbing and scratching under the greatcoat, he pressed his head once more into the porthole, his face instantly drenched with more spray, yet his eyes blinking through it all, as if determined to discover an answer out there in the tormented ocean. All of a sudden he swiveled and took a powerful hold of Turkeya's shoulders.

"Am I not a responsible man? Am I not doing my very best, going about my duties to my fellow sailors aboard this Ship?"

"Yes—of course you are."

"Did I not save the girl, your friend?"

"You most certainly did, Mr. Larrh!"

Turkeya was more than a little frightened by the look in Larrh's eyes. The increasing pressure of the cook's heavy hands on his shoulders, which appeared entirely involuntary, was causing the young shaman's knees to buckle. Turkeya recalled the order of the Kyra that he should look for strangeness, in situations and in persons. The cook, Larrh, was behaving very strangely indeed. The young shaman tried to step back a pace of two but he could not.

"What troubles you—in the name of the Powers?"

Larrh's hands released Turkeya to move to his brow, where they clasped the tangle of his sodden hair and yanked at it. "In the name of the Powers, you say?" He rubbed at his brow, as if trying to catch hold of his thoughts. "Hasn't old Larrh been the epitome of all that is reasonable . . . all that is reputable and respectable . . . always?"

Turkeya had taken advantage of his release to withdraw closer to the galley door. Yet still, despite his fear, he felt a healer's sympathy with the cook's distress. "For pity's sake, let me help you!"

"Such things . . . such sounds in my head. Such visions! Tssssttttzzzz!"

Turkeya thought he could smell something burning, like flesh scorched in a flame. "You are troubled by dreams?"

"Troubled? Troubled, you ask? Haunted more like." He groaned aloud, smashing his head against the timbers to the side of the porthole, hard enough to rupture an eyebrow. Blood ran in a thick stream over his eyelid and down his cheek without appearing to trouble him. "How can a man—a decent and respectable man—be so ravaged? I demand of you—shaman? Nightmares that come when asleep—that I might understand. But nightmares even more terrible when I am awake . . ."

Turkeya's right hand groped in his pocket for the whistle. If he could only blow on it, it would emit a high-pitched tone, soundless to human ears. The Kyra would hear it, even through the roar of the wind and waves. He had managed to get a hold of it. His fingers curled around its angular shape, carved out of some fine-grained horn.

"Nightmares, you say?"

The cook's eyes turned up in his head as if they were looking through deck and storm in the direction of the red star. "Haunted by such terrible dreams." His eyes fell and he looked at the young shaman with a desperate pleading. "Such monsters . . ."

Turkeya had the whistle out. He was in the act of taking it to his lips. "Then let me summon help!"

"None can help me." Larrh shook his head. "I'm filled with such . . . such omens! Such evil presentiments . . ."

A great swell struck and the decks swung tumultu-ously to port. So overwhelming was the shock, it felt as if the entire Ship had turned onto its side. It was followed by an explosive boom and then a thunderous crash, as if the Ship had fallen through thin air to land on solid rock, causing them both to topple against the board where the cook worked and slept. There was a splintering of planks, a rupturing of the beams that supported the deck below them, a tearing and ripping, as of timbers being twisted beyond their endurance, then the screams of sailors. The after-effects reverberated in Turkeya's ears, even as everything about him was cast into a yawning tilt. He struck his head against the thick planks, and blood welled into his left eye. But still the young shaman man-aged to drag himself back onto his uncertain feet.

Larrh, with his face also bloodied, managed to find a sitting position on the puddled floor with his elbows on the table surface and his head between his hands. There was an intense impression of spinning, as if the entire Ship was rudderless. The whistle had been torn from Turkeya's grasp and he could only scramble over the sloping floor, feeling with his fingers through the brine and debris, in an effort at retrieving it.

What, he wondered, would cause the cook to be so tormented that he was losing his senses?

He saw Larrh's eyes open on him with a look of suspi-cion. He had to keep him distracted while his fingers yet hunted. With his left hand scrambling out of sight, Tur-keya stretched his right arm across the table to place his hand on the man's heavy shoulder, discovering tensed flesh that felt like rock. "Has something happened to you, Mr. Larrh? Have you noticed something awry? Remember that I am the shaman—as well as your friend."

A look of alarm spread over the cook's face. With one arm hooked over a beam, he was struggling back onto his feet, his head and shoulders rising across the great slab of board, his eyes protruding, as if the mind behind them was swelling with horror. "My head," he gasped. "Such agony!"

At last Turkeya's fingers closed around the familiar angular shape of the whistle, and as Larrh's huge hands reached out to grab hold of his throat the young shaman brought it to his lips and blew on it, a single blast.

Larrh yanked the whistle out of Turkeya's mouth and brought it before his bulging eyes. His other hand retained a firm hold of Turkeya's throat. His brow frowned into a wrinkled landscape of perplexity.

Turkeya tried to loosen the choking hand. He croaked, his voice a wheezy whisper. "The whistle calls the Aides. A . . . a potion for you. Something to help you sleep without nightmares."

The throttling grip eased slightly. "Sleep? You can help me sleep?" A look on the fellow's face as if begging him to help him, but then his face became a snarl. "You lie! Liar! You're another liar—another just pretending to be my friend!"

Turkeya felt the throttling hand tighten again. He could no longer speak.

"You're a pack of liars! All! You're clever with words. You torment and torment! Porky Lard, you call me!"

Turkeya was rapidly losing his senses, drifting into unconsciousness, but still he attempted to break the stranglehold.

The cook's other hand closed on the whistle, crumpling it to splinters.

"You have no intention of helping me." Larrh pushed the semiconscious Turkeya roughly away from him, so he stumbled back and sprawled into the space between the board and the wall. Then, as if the act of doing so heightened his agony, the cook moaned and pressed his head down onto his knees with his two hands. "None can help me. Not you. And no more those abominations in female shape that creep about, always in the shadow of the witches!" The cook grabbed a cleaver. He climbed to his feet, then began to slink around the long bulk of the board, one hand clenched tight around the cleaver while the other still clutched at his head.

"Did I hear you aright—did you not offer to share the torment with me?"

The cook reached down and lifted the shaman to his feet by the hair. Turkeya was dragged out of the galley, and then further to the staircase, which appeared to be distorted and twisted, with its risers pitched at that same crazy angle to port as the rest of the Ship. The shambling giant hauled him up onto the storm-lashed deck. "Well now, shaman—who would be my friend! Would you care to accompany old Porky Lard on his journey into hell?"

On what remained of the aft deck, Alan's numbed arms still tethered him to the frozen wheel. His saw how the Ship whirled about its axis. His ears were filled with the screams of others aboard. Peering out of his ice-stiffened eyelids, he tried to make out what was happening. Only then did he catch his first glimpse of the true nature of the threat—and his heart quailed. A second slow-motion blink and he saw it clearly off the port side. He was staring down into an enormous whirlpool—a gyre—that was the malignant eye of the tempest. Within its roiling circumference was a maw so gargantuan it must descend to the very floor of the ocean. The Temple Ship was no more than a speck of flotsam caught up in its rage.

A Vision of Apocalypse

ALAN STARED DOWN INTO THE WIDENING GYRE. He could feel its irresistible draw on the ocean around the Ship. Taking a gulp of icy breath into his lungs he exhaled between his chattering teeth, watching the steam of his breath being sucked away, swallowed down into the pit. He recalled a memory of when he was no more than eight or nine years old and the elderly Mother Superior at his primary school had taken a group of children into the small chapel with a stained-glass window. She had explained how, through the blood-red central pane, they could see the world as it would appear on the Day of Judgment. "The Second Coming," she said, quoting Yeats' poem, "when the Antichrist would come into the world." That terrifying prospect had been so etched into his memory that he had never forgotten it, a vision of a monstrous and rapidly widening gyre that caused the entire world to fall apart.

Alan saw that apocalypse now just as the elderly sister had predicted it.

He felt the oraculum flaring manically in his brow. There was nothing more that he could do. Only now, lifting his head from his chest, did he notice the disturbance on what was left of the central deck. Three figures were locked in some kind of a struggle. *Some kind of madness!* He recognized the tall figure of Ainé, who was attempting to free Turkeya from the grip of an enormous man. Alan recognized the white-haired cook, Larrh. He was dragging the young shaman by his hair across the icy deck, ignoring the fact that all that kept him upright was the centrifugal force of the gigantic whirlpool. All three figures were sliding toward the splintered gunwale. Suddenly the Kyra's sword flashed, severing the forearm that held Turkeya. With a sweep of her arm, the Kyra sent the young shaman sliding back up the slope of deck, to where he crashed into the stump of the great mast and held on for life.

What the heck . . .

The Kyra had taken hold of the cook's greatcoat just below his throat. She had buried her sword in the deck, like a pinion, and, with her claws extended out of her feet and into the icy deck she was attempting to save the life of the cook, who, despite the loss of his forearm, continued to struggle. All of a sudden the greatcoat tore apart over the cook's chest and Ainé reared backward.

Alan felt the unexpected force of her shock, mind-to-mind. He recoiled, as she did, seeing what was burning deep in the man's breast, so buried in the scorched flesh and bone it was almost out of sight. It was some kind of glowing pendant, with the Tyrant's symbol ablaze within it.

As if in slow motion, Alan's mouth opened to shout a warning. Even as he reacted Ainé released the cook from her clawed hand. He saw the man's body sucked overboard, drawn into the vortex of the whirlpool, turning over and over, his scream lost in the maelstrom.

Immediately Alan's senses cleared. But the gyre was still there. Exhausted beyond endurance he still opposed it, his heartbeat thready, his life force strained to breaking point. He renewed his struggle to resist the storm that surrounded him, but the gyre continued to grow.

What more can I do? I'm done—finished!

Think—you idiot!

Mark's voice—Mark was back, inside his head. And his words had cleared. Alan thought: *The Tyrant's amulet around the cook's neck—it must somehow have been responsible for the confusion in all of our minds.*

Think what? he called to Mark.

The Ship was being drawn into the gyre with increasing velocity. They were already over the lip. He was gazing at a whirlpool with walls like encircling mountains and the Ship was listing perilously. A few degrees more and it would turn right over and pitch them into the abyss. Alan's face was stretched, his lips torn back from gritted teeth, his eyes staring, full and round out of retracted lids.

The Earth Power—it's feeding off you.

Mark's words were insane.

It's feeding off your power . . . your oraculum.

Gritting his teeth still harder, his limbs feeling torn apart, he tried to make himself think it through. Could Mark be right? Could it be true? Was the gyre really driven by the First Power?

Stop feeding it! Close it down!

I hear you. But what if you're wrong?

Could he take the chance? What if he stopped resisting the gyre? If Mark was wrong they would be destroyed, ripped asunder in just a few moments.

I'm speaking for the Temple Ship!

Could the Earth Power have created the enormous force of the gyre? In probing it, he could feel it now, he could hear its deafening roar in his ears, he could see, through the eye of the oraculum, the myriad tiny lines of force, blue as cobalt, pure and precise and deadly, spiraling down at colossal speed, dragging wind and ocean with them, creating storm and vortex. But where were they originating? With a renewed effort, he followed the lines of force to their source, and with a shock, he discovered that it was him—he himself, his oraculum.

You're right—I can't believe it.

It had been so instinctive in him to fight back through the oraculum that it had never occurred to him he might be feeding the gyre. But now, seeing those lines all come back to a single source in his brow, it became obvious. The glowing pendant must have been some kind of malengin, smuggled on board the Ship. It had enabled the Tyrant to subvert Alan's own power. His oraculum hadn't been under his control. All the time it had been flaring madly it had been under the control of the Tyrant.

I have to turn it off immediately.

To do so he had to overcome his deepest instincts. He had to empty his mind completely, to ignore the fear and desperation in the hearts and minds of everybody around him, the sense of caring for his friends. He had to close himself down, emotionally and spiritually.

There was no time left to worry about being wrong. He closed himself down. He let go of the Ship. Mentally he withdrew his resistance, ignoring the overwhelming instinct that the gyre would be free to do its worst.

He closed his eyes with dread.

He felt the change. His ears rang like whistles as the thundering stopped. He saw through the abating blizzard the transformation of the Kyra to snow tigress, right there on the slanting main deck. He saw how she used her claws for purchase as she scrambled and tore her way to mount the steps onto the aft deck, where those same claws made short work of the thongs that tethered him to the wheel.

Alan fell to his knees, his body stiff with exhaustion. He was unable to lift his head to face her.

Ainé growled: "The splinter of malice—it was the cook? The amulet about his throat with the sigil?"

"Yeah—the Tyrant was behind it."

"The Tyrant—not the Witch?"

He tried to shake his head, but it still refused to move on his neck.

"The red eye was just a diversion." He coughed, struggling to get his still-frozen mouth to work. "You were right—my enemies knew my weakness. They used my concern for Kate. They were working together."

He couldn't believe that he had been outsmarted again. He had been tricked into allowing his power, the Power of the Earth, to be subverted. The thought shocked him to the core; it unnerved him.

"But the danger still threatens. You must recover yourself—use your power to save the Temple Ship."

"No!" His whole body was trembling with exhaustion. "I can't use the First Power to save her—it would be too dangerous!"

"But the Ship is wrecked. The masts are destroyed and the decks are rubble. There is neither sail nor rudder."

"The gyre was powered by my oraculum."

"What foolishness is this?"

"Ainé—you'll have to trust me!" It was an effort even to breathe. His chest wall felt solid, as if the ice had frozen right through. "Be my eyes. Look about you. Tell me what you see."

He was aware of her brooding presence close by him. He shut off all other awareness and senses, since the danger of subversion was still there. "Look about you," he insisted. "Tell me what you see of the gyre!"

The Kyra hesitated, her head swiveling on the muscular neck, those blue eyes studying the vortex for several seconds. Then she exhaled through her nostrils, causing the dying spindrift of snow to eddy about her face. "The storm abates. The gyre closes."

"Are you sure?"

"Elements and ocean—they heal."

"And the red star?"

"Gone!"

"Thank heaven."

"This is no time for thanksgiving. The Ship is lost."

Alan's body was slowly thawing, just sufficient for him to lay his exhausted head against the wheel. "The Ship will heal itself."

She studied him with that glacial stare, her eyelids still encrusted with snow and ice. "You know this?"

"I think so."

The Kyra was already directing the Aides to assist the injured aboard. One of the Aides brought healwell to Alan's lips.

Ainé watched him take a sip, and then another, deeper drink. She waited a minute or two for it to have some reviving effect.

"Help me to my feet."

Between them—awkwardly because the Aides was so small on one side while the Kyra was so enormous—they hoisted him to his feet, allowing time for his numbed legs to recover enough just to keep him standing. Around them the snow and ice were thawing. It was happening so quickly he could see the edges melting and shrinking. They helped him to step away from the wheel. Alan stretched his back, groaning aloud at the return of circulation to his limbs.

"Okay—stop!"

"What is it?"

"I sense the return of my friend. Mark is back at the wheel."

He felt a stiffening in the arm of the Kyra as she turned with some care—the melting ice was still treacherous underfoot—to witness the great wheel begin to take control over the rudder once more. Alan looked up, feeling the patter of meltwater on his head and face, dripping from the tattered remains of the superstructure. All three of them rocked backward with the sudden rush of force that expanded outward from the wheel, observing how the Ship immediately began to alter form, the glow of rebirth limning its broken decks and masts, one in spirit with the presence embracing the wheel.

Alan nodded to the Kyra: "The fleet?"

"I have already recalled it."

Alan and Ainé were joined on the afterdeck by Mo, in the protective company of Milish, and by Siam, with his

arm on Turkeya's shoulder. Others among the surviving
Shee and Olhyiu were emerging all over the wreck, eyes
wide, staring at sea and sky, and the changes of healing
amid so much ruin. Nobody was inclined to cheer. All
they could do was to observe the changes with a mixture of relief and awe. Alan sensed a great sigh, as if the
very heart of the Ship was also recovering from beyond
its limits of endurance. Then the decks trembled with
another massive jolt of change. The entire Ship was
bathed in the eerie glow he recalled from Isscan. It
seemed to bend out of shape, as if the great masts and
the massive superstructure were as pliable as putty—its
restoration so strange and certain that even when you
witnessed it happening right in front of your eyes it was
all the more magical.

The jerk of the deck rocked him on his unsteady legs
and caused him to take hold of the rail.

His eyes lifted to where the forward mast had resurrected itself from the shattered stump. Though still
grimed with snow and ice a sail was starting to billow,
catching the powerful breezes that fanned his hair.

MAKING A STAND

"I DON'T EVEN PRETEND TO BE BRAVE," KATE pleaded as the first pale wash of dawn broke over a transformed island.

"Driftwood knows . . ."

They were sitting side by side, or more accurately she was sitting with her legs crossed and the dragon was slouched, somewhat alligator-style, on top of the bluff that overlooked the wide river, as the eastern horizon came pinkly alive. Kate peered down at the water, a hundred feet below them.

"It's true. I'm a complete coward."

She blinked furiously at the thought of actually fighting with wolves and succubi; and as to the Witch herself!—if Driftwood was relying on her help to face all that, he was going to be disappointed.

"When girl-thing discovers memories inside Drift-wood's mind, Driftwood also discovers truth in girl-thing's mind."

Kate shook her head. He really didn't understand her at all. When it came to actual fighting, she really was a scaredy-cat. If she had any resilience at all, it was nothing more than obstinacy. Bridey used to tell her if there was an Olympic category of pig-headedness she would have won a gold for Ireland. And this was a situation where pig-headedness was unlikely to help. Neither dragon nor girl had managed to get a wink of sleep all night, though for patently different reasons. Kate made no pretense of the fact she was terrified. All through the hours of darkness she had heard the howling of the approaching wolves. Driftwood had been encouraging her to let loose her powers, as if his sole concern was to greet the dawn with a verdant island. And now, gazing about them from the rise of the bluff, it looked like his wish had been granted.

Shafts of sunlight glowed between the branches of trees along the eastern horizon. Washes of cream and blue and pink and orange were diffusing into the horizon, already bright enough to be uncomfortable when she stared at them unblinkingly. The previously barren landscape was now exuberant. She could smell the marshes, and the oases of tough grasses that carpeted the ground under palm trees, and right there in the distance, where she had slept on bare rock that first exhausted night, a small wood of oaks was sprouting.

Brightly colored dragonflies and damselflies fluttered between the branches of gum trees on the slopes leading to the bluff. Birds twittered in the branches, and bees and other insects buzzed and dived among the profusion of flowers. The dragon's island preened and buzzed with life.

"Kate, girl-thing, is hungry?"

Kate forgot her delight at the fecundity of the island as the fear returned, with a savage suddenness. "Stop calling me that. Just Kate."

"For Kate Driftwood catches nice fish—yum yum?"

"I couldn't eat a thing. My stomach is in knots."

And besides, she would have fainted outright if he took off on those liberating wings and left her here all alone.

"Driftwood would know secrets of Kate—Greeneyes."

"Kate—just Kate!"

"Secrets of how Kate came to island. How Kate's power came?"

"I'm too jittery to chat." Butterflies of panic fluttered in her gut. Her heart was missing beats like mad. "And it's a . . . a twisty-turny story."

"Driftwood likes twisty-turny stories."

He seemed perfectly happy just to talk even as those dreadful things were closing in around them. But she started to tell him her story anyway. It helped to take her mind off things, just prattling on, pretending to be calm in this strange company, and with monsters prowling all around her. She told him how she had met her friends, Alan—the boy she now loved—and Mark, and his adoptive sister, Mo, back in Clonmel.

"What is Clonmel?"

"My home town. The place where I was born. A place of streets and houses where people live."

"Kate's island!"

She hesitated. "I suppose so."

With a start, Kate realized something that had been slowly dawning on her for a day or two. The dragon was growing bigger from day to day. And he didn't talk about shiny things. He was maturing mentally. She shook her head, her sleep-deprived mind unable to grasp what was really going on.

"Kate will continue her story?"

Now she was talking, she didn't know how to stop. She described the murder of her parents. How she later discovered that their deaths were part of a pattern, along with the deaths of Alan's parents, and the presumed death of the parents of Mark and Mo. This reminder caused Kate's head to fall. She felt a cold contraction about her heart. She talked about the symbol Mark and Mo had seen on the twisted cross of Grimstone, Mark and Mo's adoptive father, and how Alan's grandfather, Padraig, had shown them the same vile symbol on the hilt of the sword of Feimhin, where it had lain for thousands of years in the barrow grave of the fearsome warrior-prince. Like the ordinary symbol for infinity with an extra loop—the triple infinity. A symbol they had come across once more in this world, where it turned out to be the mark of the Tyrant. She told him how they had gathered the waters of the three sister rivers, the Nore, Suir and Barrow, to pass through the gate on the summit of the mountain, Slievenamon. Through that gate they had escaped from danger on Earth to arrive into this alien world.

"Show Driftwood!"

"Show you what?"

The dragon pointed a single talon at the oraculum in her brow.

A wolf howled nearby. Kate sprang to her feet. She peered across the island at the far shore where slinky shapes had appeared at the lapping edges of the wide river channel.

"Kate—must show!"

She ignored the dragon. She couldn't think of anything other than the wolves. "Maybe they won't cross the water."

"Wolves not matter."

"Not to you, maybe! You can fly away. But I can't."

"Kate—Greeneyes!" The dragon pressed her. "Must not show fear."

"Are you kidding me?"

The dragon reached out with a claw and brushed the back of it against Kate's right cheek, under which her jaw muscles were clenched. She couldn't help but stare at the prowling, ravening shadows, searching among them for any sign of the wolf-man that had helped her. The sun was in her eyes, a nice cool sun of morning,

accompanied by the sweet scent of blossoms opening
their fists of petals to it—sights and scents that would
have been welcome in any other circumstances, but
now she had to squint under the shadow of her arched
hands to focus on a huge male, whose head moved from
side to side, sniffing the air. It wasn't her friendly wolf.
She knew that the moment his gaze found her. His jaws
gaped to show yellow fangs, slavering with anticipation.
He was staring across the water, looking right at her, eye
to eye. Kate sensed the feral cunning in those unblinking eyes. And beyond the animal spirit she also sensed
an even more frightening malice.

"The Witch is here. The wolves are her eyes."

"Kate—show Driftwood. Driftwood must know. Kate
must explain this Old One who gives her power."

"I can't think about things like that. We have to run.
We have to escape. Help me! The Witch—she'll get me.
She'll take me back to the Tower. You have no idea what
she will do to me."

The dragon took her hand in his paw. He squatted
back on his haunches, so tall that Kate's arm was upstretched. "Kate must listen to Driftwood. Kate show
Driftwood how it works, this oraculum thing."

The leader of the wolves had taken several steps
into the river. All the while its eyes held hers. Sweat had
broken out over Kate's body. She tried to break free of
Driftwood's paw so she could run. She moaned aloud,
finding it impossible to break free from him. "Are you
out of your mind? We have to run."

However pig-headed Kate might be, there was still greater stubbornness in the dragon. His enormous eyes bored into hers. "Not run. Not show fear!"

"Let me go!"

She just couldn't believe him. He glanced at the wolves as if they were no more than an inconvenience. But Kate could see how a dreadful determination drove them. More and more of them had entered the water. Half the pack were up to their bellies in the stream. And all of their eyes were on her.

The wolves began howling. Driftwood's head started up and his nostrils started twitching. "Witch comes." he growled.

On the far bank, Kate could see that something was moving. A thick, heavy vapor was running over the ground, extending tentacles before it, each tentacle aglow with a pallid, gangrenous light.

"It's my fault. I led them to your island."

Driftwood remained calm. "Witch-tentacles searching for Kate-girl-thing. Not thinking of dragon's trail. Dragon smell unfamiliar to tentacles of witch. Human's smell easy to follow."

Kate reflected that she had lost her mouse smell, and camouflage, given to her by Granny Dew, when she had run out of the tidbits. "Is that supposed to comfort me?"

She watched one of the tentacles creep over the ground to the water's edge. She knew it had detected her. An apparition seemed to rise up out of the licking tentacle, a wraith-like thing, taking on a vaguely human form. It grew rapidly, the wraith-head swiveling from side to side, as if searching.

"We've got to get away from here—away from the island."

"Kate must explain. Tell Driftwood of Old One."

Kate could sense the all-consuming instinct that drove the wolves. She doubted that they would even try to take her alive. There was such a ravenous hunger in their bellies that it would only be satisfied by a gluttony of flesh and blood and bone. It was almost impossible to drag her eyes away from the wolves' baleful presence. How the Witch must hate her, breaking out of the Tower and making this island come alive with trees and flowers and grasses. Her throat was bone dry. She had no saliva left to swallow. The dryness was causing her to retch. The dragon, squatting back on those great hind legs, was gazing down at her still. His eyes looked different. There was urgency in them that Kate had not seen before. He growled, deep in his throat.

"Kate must tell Driftwood!"

She clenched her teeth to stop them chattering and she clenched her head between trembling hands to try to gain control of her thoughts.

The dragon brought a taloned paw to her shoulder. His eyes blinked, in that strange sideways way. The paw lifted and the talon reached out again, longer, fiercer, and brushed her brow with a hard, pressing intensity. "Driftwood must know of Old One. Must know all—must know now."

Kate felt the threatening nearness of the Witch. She felt the evil of the Tower close around her. She could smell the sulfurous stink. She was no longer able to fill her lungs to breathe. She was close to fainting with terror. Haltingly, through a throat that retched even with the effort of just forming words, she explained about the cave where they had woken up, all four friends, when they had first come to this world. She did her best to explain how the old woman had snatched the three cell phones from their hands and shuffled back to squat by the fire.

"Alan, my friend, had a silver flask. The old woman took the flask from him and then she . . . she sat in front of her fire and she did something to it."

"Tell, tell—explain!"

"She did something strange. She just plunged it into the fire. The fire didn't harm her, didn't appear to burn her."

"Yes—yes?"

Kate's hand lifted to her mouth, trembled against it. "I—I think she molded the silver flask in her hands, inside the fire. Then, when she lifted it back out again, it turned into an eagle."

Kate's eyes glazed over with the memory. Her hands trembled—pallid, drenched in sweat—and held her face. From the river she heard a triumphant howling. She didn't dare to look in the wolves' direction. She breathed hard, the image hanging on in her memory for several seconds. "We realized it had to be magic of some sort."

"Tell—quickly! Who was Old One?"

"She crooned something like a name. 'Graaannneee Dewwww.'"

The dragon's voice was little above a growl: "Graaannneee Dewwww?" He pronounced it exactly as the old woman had pronounced it. That startled her so much she was silent for a moment or two, recalling the extraordinary scene.

"We thought it sounded like Granny Dew—that's what we called her after that." Her eyes were wide open, pupils dilated. "She made us all drink something—something very strange, horrible. It felt in my mouth as if there were living things, like spiders and insects alive in it. We were all really afraid of her. But she was helping us in her way. Oh, Granny Dew—I wish you were here to help me now!"

"Graaannneee Dewwww!" The dragon growled the name over, as if chewing on it, turning it over in his mind. "This what Old One call her name?"

"Yes."

"Kate—hear it here," he pointed to Kate's right ear, "or here?" He pointed to Kate's head, her brow.

"I had no oraculum. Of course I just heard it in my ears."

"Kate not understand. Words not name. Words from old language . . . Language of beginnings."

"None of us understood."

"Old One . . . Speaks language of makers."

"Makers?"

"Makers." He waved a paw to encompass the mountains, the river, the island, with its blooming magnificence.

Kate didn't know how she wasn't already dead from fright. Her throat was so paralyzed by fear it felt as if she was squeezing each word out of a fist of ice. "Like . . . Like the Earth Mother?"

The dragon's claw reached up to point to the oraculum in Kate's brow. "Old One—she gives Kate this?"

"Yes."

"What means this—this power?"

"I think it's the power of new life, of healing. But I have to learn how to use it."

A sudden instinct yanked her attention back to the river. Kate was on her feet, unable to stop herself looking. The first creeping tentacles of the Witch were running between the wolves. They were reaching out to where the entire pack now pressed deeper into the water, until they were immersed up to their spines, then all of a sudden the entire pack surged forward, swimming into the stream. Terror took her legs from under her. She would have tumbled to the ground if the dragon hadn't taken her shoulders and helped her to sit down again on the bluff.

Her voice trembled as she spoke out of lips so numb they didn't feel her own. "Oh, Driftwood, it's too late!"

"Witch sees through wolf eyes. Must blind Witch eyes."

"But how? I have no weapons—nothing that could hurt her."

"Weapons not hurt Witch. Power only does she fear."

"But—but she is much more powerful than I am."

"Kate must listen. Wolves are Witch's eyes. Here—now—Kate must blind eyes of Witch with her power."

The wolves were about halfway across the great river, their gaping jaws held up above the stream, the furious paddling creating v-shaped eddies, with the leader well in front of the others. His eyes were still on hers, rabidly determined. In just minutes he'd be scrambling up the island shore.

Panic caused her breath to judder through her teeth.

The dragon spoke with icy calm. "Great dragon philosopher, he whose words were as reefs to ocean, he say, 'In time of greatest danger, be most calm.'"

"I bet he didn't have a Witch, and a pack of wolves, around his throat!"

"Such wisdom!"

"This great philosopher wasn't called Driftwood, by any chance?"

"In philosopher's dying words . . ."

"Dying?"

"Kate must be calm—if calmly she thinks. If she looks, looks deeply in her own heart, at what oraculum has done here. Old One gives Kate gift of Life. Life in land, in air . . . in water."

"In water?"

"Power of oraculum—is not to give or to take away?"

Kate stared downhill to where the lead wolf, jaws ferociously agape, was no more than thirty feet from the near bank. He would be out of the water and bounding toward her in less than a minute.

"What are you saying?"

"Is not obvious?—what may be given may be taken away."

Kate tottered back onto her feet. She raised both her arms outright. She pressed her thoughts to the oraculum in her brow. Then she stared at the river, at the water where the current had carried the wolves maybe fifty yards downstream of the level where they had entered it on the far bank. She stared at how they thrashed their way across it, and she imagined how it might change with a dreadful thunderstorm. A burst of rain upstream? It was curiously easy to sense the mood and movement of the surface waters. She imagined how they might erupt with the instructions of her thoughts. Instantly they did so. The placid current changed to a catastrophic flood. Within the raging water there were living things, biting creatures, that seemed to share the water's rage. Soon there were howls of a different kind, screams of pain and terror, rising out of the stream. With her eyes closed and her heart beating into a rage of her own, she poured her being into the turbulent current. She was shaking with the sheer savagery of it, barely able to contain herself on juddering legs, her eyes clenched shut, when the dragon touched her cheek and bade her open her eyes again.

"Brave Kate. Girl-thing not coward. See!"

Kate opened her eyes. Tears of exhaustion, mixed with relief, flowed down her cheeks, as she saw the flood of water in which there was no trace of the wolves left. But then she also saw the Witch's tentacles. They were swarming over the stormy waters and invading the island at extraordinary speed. Then the voice, thunderous through the oraculum, found her.

Foolish Earth-spawn. With such feeble power would it challenge us?

"Driftwood!" she moaned, collapsing to her knees.

The Witch's laugh resonated within the vaults of her skull.

Its usefulness is done. The violator of our sanctuary no longer threatens the great purpose. Fangorath will rise and the portal will be ours. So there is naught to be served in keeping such meat alive. We shall punish it first— punish it mercilessly and long—and then take what is left to feed the Beast.

"Witch lies," the dragon whispered.

Kate shook her head, mute with horror.

"Witch searches—but will not find. Brave Kate—girl-thing—has won battle. Witch is blind."

What did it matter anymore whether the Witch could see her or not? The tentacles were everywhere. Soon they would sniff them out, where they were sitting around not even trying to run.

The dragon stretched his wings until they became taut as bowstrings, in great shimmering arcs above Kate's head.

"On Driftwood's back—now is time."

"I don't think I have the strength."

He lowered his hindquarters so his tail trailed on the ground. "Climb! Let victory give Kate strength!"

Somehow, though every muscle in her body was trembling, Kate climbed the long body as it were a staircase. She discovered a place to straddle amid the brightly colored ruff, her chin resting on his crest, her arms around his neck.

"Hold tight!"

With a spring the dragon cleared the cliff edge and swooped riverwards, but then, as his wings caught the breeze, he soared aloft in a great careening arc, while Kate clung on desperately, her hair streaming about her face, her eyes narrowed against the rushing wind.

"Kate Shaunessy—girl-thing!"

She slapped his crest with outrage. "You . . . You could have done this all along. You had me wetting myself."

It took several minutes for the fact to sink in—she was free. Free! It was so unbelievable, so exhilarating! Kate shrieked with joy as the great wings beat slowly, the passing desert landscape of hills and dunes giving way to a great coastal estuary. A scattering of small islands dotted the estuary as it widened out into a massive delta, its water streaming out into the ocean.

"Kate hold breath!"

"What?"

All of a sudden they were falling out of the sunlit sky. Kate's joy turned to panic as they plummeted toward the meeting of coast and ocean, her breath ripped out of her lungs, her arms locked around the scaly neck.

Preparations

ALAN AND MO STOOD TOGETHER ON THE HIGHEST point of one of the craggy bluffs above a desolate bay of black volcanic rock, gazing out to sea where the Temple Ship had laid anchor, perhaps a hundred yards from the rocky shore. A brisk shore breeze ruffled their hair. Alan noticed how Mo suddenly tensed up. He felt the sorrow rise in her and he understood the reason for it.

"Mark really is taking the Ship away?"

"I'm afraid so."

It was the evening of their second day in the Wastelands and the setting sun was igniting flames of red and gold over the deepening blue of the distant ocean. Below them, extending from the shore, the build-up of supplies was coming to an end, most of the goods and weapons already ferried from fleet to shore in smaller craft then transferred to makeshift sleds before being dragged further inland. The powdery green film that coated the pebbly beach was already heavily scored with ruts from the sleds, the underlying black of the lava exposed like a series of wounds. So arid was the landscape that it could have been a piece of Earth's moon. The small bay was encircled by volcanic calderas, the setting sun reflected on the crescents of their sharply delineated rims. Higher up the bay, stretching between the stony headlands, a palisade was being constructed from larger blocks of lava by sweating teams of Shee and Olhyiu, the first step toward a makeshift fort that would become their bridgehead. Here and there Alan could make out the distant, much smaller figures of the Aides, dutifully supervising the construction.

As one, they sensed it again: a wave of change rippling through the structure and fabric of the Temple Ship. Alan put his arm around Mo's shoulders, holding her close for several moments in silence.

It had upset Mo deeply to leave the Ship, knowing Mark was on board. "Mark is planning to return to Earth."

"But how . . . ?"

"I don't know how he's planning to do it."

"He can't be sure of anything."

"None of us is sure of anything anymore, Mo. He's afraid he will never be flesh and blood again."

"But how will this help?"

"I've been trying to figure out what he might be thinking. When he came for me—when I was trapped in Dromenon—Mark was one with the Ship. Somehow, he and the Ship combined minds. They became one in that raptor transformation."

"They became a single mind?"

"I can't think of any better way of explaining it. Don't you see what it means, Mo? By combining minds they entered Dromenon."

"I don't even pretend to understand."

"I don't fully understand myself. The way I figure it, Mark has found a way of tapping into the Ship's memories, the Ship's ancient knowledge. Dromenon, if I understand it right, is some kind of halfway place between worlds. If the Ship can travel halfway, then it might be capable of traveling the whole way."

Mo's brow wrinkled. "I know he's desperate enough to try."

Alan shrugged.

"And if he does it—if he manages to get back to Earth—what then?"

"Who knows, Mo?"

"Alan!" Mo's hand reached up to touch his where it still rested on her shoulder. "He'll take on Grimstone. I'm really frightened for him."

Alan hesitated, considering Mo's words. "Mark's pretty smart. I've been thinking about things. Like how he saved us all at Ossierel. We saw how he'd been cast into stone. And yet he got out of there, within the fabric and spirit of the Temple Ship. You talked to him. He's an oraculum-bearer now. We spoke, oraculum-to-oraculum, before I left the Ship. He'll be figuring out what he can do with that kind of power."

Mo stared out at the Ship.

Alan was still deeply worried at the idea of Mark taking the Ship. It looked fully restored from the wreck that had resulted from the gyre. That was a credit to Mark. Mark and the Ship—they had always been close. But now Alan guessed that they must be more than just close. They had really become one in spirit. In fact everything that had happened in the course of the last week or so—the red star, the gyre, the whole bizarre sequence of events—still puzzled Alan. The cook, Larrh, must have brought the amulet aboard at Carfon. How worrying, given that he was carrying such a power, that they had failed to detect it before embarkation and, even more so, in the confined circumstance of the Ship over many days' voyage!

Mo interrupted his thoughts: "Where are the Gargs?"

Alan rubbed his hands over his face as if sluicing it with a splash of ice-cold water. "They're everywhere."

"Watching us?"

"I don't doubt it."

"But they did nothing to stop us landing. And they haven't even tried to attack us since we landed."

"I know."

"Surely it must mean something."

"Yeah."

There were things going on that he didn't understand.

It wasn't just Mark and the Ship. Mo was changing. She was growing rapidly, her body maturing. Even her face was maturing. She bore less and less resemblance to the girl he had first met at his grandfather's sawmill. He was coming to realize that there was a good deal more to Mo than he would ever have thought possible, back in those early days of getting to know one another. He recalled that extraordinary moment when his own life was endangered with the Legun incarnate at the battle of Ossierel, and Mo had put herself between him and the Legun. How brave her small figure had stood there, unprotected by any oraculum, by anything at all, and how certain her girlish voice had sounded:

I am Mira, Léanov Fashakk—the Heralded One.

Her stance had appeared insanely brave in the circumstances. The Legun had switched all of its malice to her. Alan recalled how Mo's face had glowed, spectral with light. That foolhardy behavior had almost cost her her life. It had taken the healing power of the goddess Mab to save her. What had that meant? What might Mo know now that she wasn't telling him?

Alan exhaled. He probed the Wastelands north of them, sweeping far and wide with his oraculum.

"You're looking for Kate?"

"Looking, but never finding."

"Can you detect nothing of her?"

"Not a thing."

"It doesn't mean—?"

"That she's dead? I don't think so. I'm sure I'd sense that, even from the other side of the world."

Mo changed the subject. "The Gargs—do you think they're holding back because this place is a trap?"

Alan shrugged. "The Kyra chose it because it would be easy to defend. We're surrounded by mountains." He looked to landwards, regarded the surrounding landscape again. To put it more accurately, they were enclosed within a bowl of volcanic calderas. The bay itself was probably the result of some huge past volcanic explosion, the headlands and the bay in between all that was left. The only way inland was through marsh and bog. When the wind was blowing from that direction you could smell it.

"But you don't seem so sure."

"I'm far from certain about anything."

The arrival of the fleet had hardly been secret. They had coasted for a full day looking for a suitable vantage along cliff faces and hill-studded bays dense with Gargs. They had inspected their settlements, some in cliffs pock-marked with caves, others in strange conglomerations atop cliffs with jagged, stony projections.

A loud noise, like the screeching of tormented metal, sounded from the Temple Ship, a shockwave so powerful it swept out in a ripple through the surrounding ocean and buffeted Alan's and Mo's faces as it swept outward through the air. Alan hugged Mo, strongly, protectively, as they stared at the Ship with a shared alarm.

"What are you going to do, Alan?"

"I'm going to find Kate."

"When?"

"We set out tomorrow. At first light."

"Whoaaaahhh!"

Snakoil Kawkaw barely had time to yank himself out of the hidey hole before the hole itself began to disappear. He watched it melt out of existence with utter disbelief, its walls and floor lapping and whirling, as if a few liquids were being stirred into the soup of a boiling pot. He was forced to leap out of the ferment, heedless of where he might land, before it consumed him.

"Hellfire and abomination!"

He landed in a great tumble of rope at the base of what had, until seconds earlier, been the middle mast, but which was already well on its way to becoming another pool of soup. His left foot was caught up in the change. "Heeeaggghhh!" he wailed as he saw his great toenail disappear. With a shriek he snatched away the toe itself, which had barely escaped, hoisting his entire leg into the air, where he rubbed at the toe now swollen as a ripe plum, and throbbing like a boil.

What in the darkest bogs of reason was going on?

He felt as if he had spent half his life in that cramped hell-hole. What meager rations he had managed to wheedle from Porky Lard had run out by the second day and he had suffered such hunger he had sucked on rope for the rank residue of its oil. And for what? For every goat of a sailor to abandon ship as soon as it laid anchor in this miserable cove, surrounded by black rocks in the shape of shark's teeth, a reef-baited shallows mean enough to rip your guts out now you were forced to swim for your life. It was the last thing anyone would have expected, a contemptible dereliction of all that was supposedly held dear by the fish-gutters and witch warriors—indeed, judging from the slithering and squeaking companions that were abandoning ship with him, right down to the last bilge rat.

And the most embarrassing admission was that he had watched it happen—watched and done nothing about it for almost an entire day. When he should have been over the rail in the previous night. And now, while dodging the madness of the changes, he was seeing spectres—at least one for certain. He had seen clear through it, like pipe-smoke, hanging around the wheel. Though consumed by dread he had skulked nearby so as to hear the monstrous chattering of this demon, at a time when the last of the fish-gutters and Shee-witches had taken to the boats, leaving just Duval behind, the huloima scum who had waited for all others to depart the Ship so he could hold a lengthy conversation with the very demon.

What Kawkaw overheard had heightened his panic.

The fish-gutters were planning to hand over the Ship to this demon, who intended to change its form back to the raptor shape it had taken over Carfon harbor. Why the demon would want to do that, other than for devilment, was a mystery to Kawkaw. But there was no mystery as to the implications. Every chip of wood, every fiber of rope or sail, would be melted into that same infernal soup. If he continued to hide on board he would be subsumed, to be reconstituted in some twirl of feather, or some sausage of gut, or a piece of tailbone.

Why, in the way of things, should happenstance so threaten him? Poor old Snakoil Kawkaw, who, if he had been allowed to take his due place in society would, no doubt, have been the very pillar of rectitude! Anyone could be virtuous if the world rewarded you as you so righteously deserved. Yet through no fault of his own he had been robbed of every aspiration and fortune at every twist and turn.

Is it my fault, then, that the blessed gods of chance had turned out to be the most mischievous of devils?

A hundred yards away, in a world enviably tranquil to his present eyes, the huloimas, Duval and the girl, were making their way down from the black escarpment. He'd watched them preen at the top, glorying in the sunset. That excremental youth and that imp of a girl who had proved so bewitched you couldn't even land a good kick on her ass but she floated away from it like a leaf on the breeze. How had she escaped the warlock in Isscan? Ratspelts! Every last one of them! For a moment rage so possessed him that Snakoil Kawkaw forgot his predicament until, with an almighty groan, the spell-bewitched deck under his feet began to waver and soften.

"God damn it!"

He had no option but to hurl himself bodily over the rail without the opportunity to check whether it might be jagged rocks or freezing water he would encounter at the end of his tumble.

By early night, sheltered from the shore winds behind a stony horseshoe of the same black rocks, Alan and Mo joined Ainé, Milish, Siam and senior figures from the Shee and Olhyiu in dining on conserved provisions from the stores and huddling around a fire of driftwood. All were aware of Alan's intention of setting out for the Tower of Bones at first light. This first exploration couldn't possibly involve the entire army of Shee. It would have to be a much smaller expeditionary force. But just how far should they go before waiting for reinforcements?

Many thought the plan decidedly risky. Success or failure might be determined by whatever contingency they discovered on the ground. Neither would relent and so there was no agreement.

"I will head out tomorrow," Alan insisted, "even if I have to do it on my own."

"There is no question of that," the Kyra countered. "Though it contradicts every grain of common sense, you will be protected. But I must insist that the bulk of Shee stand by at the ready to follow on at any time I deem it necessary, and certainly before there is any attempt at an attack on the Tower."

"And what," asked Qwenqwo, "if we find this plan to be impractical?"

"If such proves to be the case, then our entire purpose here will be put at risk."

Alan nodded, looking the Kyra in the eyes. "I'm sorry, Ainé. I know that everything you say makes perfect sense. But I know—I sense it so strongly that I haven't any doubt about it—that Kate's life is at stake."

"Our mission in these lands is not merely to defeat the Witch, but also to destroy the Tyrant of the Wastelands. What will become of that mission if the Mage Lord is lost on a fool's errand even before we begin?"

"Can we compromise on this? Have the army of Shee make ready to follow on, by all means. In fact it would make sense to make it obvious. We know that while they don't make any move to attack us the Gargs are watching every move we make. If they realize the expeditionary force is small, they might decide to attack us long before we reach the Tower."

The Kyra sighed, clearly unhappy. "I have the feeling," she declared, "that the Gargs refrain from attacking us because they know something that we do not. Let us hope we don't pay a heavy price for an ill-prepared adventure." She climbed to her feet and, accompanied by an apprehensive looking Milish, departed the gathering.

Alan gazed over at Qwenqwo, catching the reflection of the flames in the eyes of his friend as the dwarf mage met his gaze, then shrugged his shoulders and settled down to a drink with the elders, sharing their pipe tobacco and content to wait and see what the morning brought. There would be neither criticism nor hesitation from that indomitable quarter.

Alan's attention was drawn by a glance from Mo, her eyes turning in the direction of the youthful shaman, Turkeya. She whispered, "He is desperate to go with you tomorrow. But Siam wants him to stay behind."

Siam was just as apprehensive about the plan as the Kyra. It was easy to understand Siam's concerns for his only son. Alan signaled to Turkeya and Mo to join him, heading off for a short walk along the shore. By now the moon was out, only a night or two off full, its silvery light glimmering on the cusps of the waves. Their ears were full of the hissing rapture of the surf against the black shingle.

Turkeya showed little interest in their surroundings. "The other boys would laugh at me when I was growing up. The son of Siam, yet it was obvious to everyone that I was never likely to become a warrior. I was too awkward and sensitive, better at hiding than fighting. But in my heart I recognized that I had no craving to kill things, even when hungry. I could survive without the dead rabbit or pigeon if it meant I could watch them at courtship, or at play. There was an ache in my heart that was answered by life, whether in the grasslands, or the forest—even the oceans."

"Warriors," Mo spoke softly, "aren't always the answer, even in war. There are other things besides fighting."

Turkeya lowered his head, his lips tight-pressed.

Alan nodded. He faced Turkeya, the two youths close to the same gangling height. "I guess that what Mo's trying to say is that there's more than one way of making a difference. My mom taught me that. You shouldn't be ashamed to care about life. You have a natural empathy with the world. You and Mo—you're alike in that way. Mo understands where you're coming from."

"You think of me as my father does. You see Turkeya, the idiot, whose very sister laughed at how he would hide when danger threatened."

Mo shook her head. "You have qualities more important than fighting. We have plenty of fighters. We have only one shaman."

"None respects me as shaman. They think I am too young, too clumsy."

"Oh, Turkeya, it was you who saved us from the gyre. Your people respect you," Mo insisted. "Siam is proud of you."

Alan saw the disappointment in Turkeya's eyes. He put his arm around his shoulders and directed the young shaman's attention to a cluster of figures a short distance further along the shore. Turkeya recognized the Kyra among them, her stature recognizable even in the moonlight. She was on her knees in the volcanic grit, a smaller figure held between her hands.

"What's happening?"

"The mother-sister is saying farewell to the daughter-sister."

"I don't understand."

"It's their custom—the Kyra thinks she's heading to her death. She is passing on her memories while she can."

Turkeya's eyes grew large and his head fell, as if only now did he truly understand the risks that Alan, and the expeditionary force, would face. But then, lifting his head again, he spoke softly, but insistently.

"I'm still coming. And Mo will insist on coming too." Turkeya glanced at the girl, who nodded quietly. "Tell him, Mo."

"Turkeya is right—I sense it."

"What do you sense, Mo?"

"That you will need us."

Alan's breath caught at the shriek from overhead. A Garg's cry, from a spy circling overhead even in the dark! He thought about something the Kyra had said: that perhaps the Gargs held off from attacking them because they knew something that the company did now know.

THE CILL

KATE CLENCHED HER EYES SHUT AGAINST THE intense rush of air yanking back her hair in a taut stream behind her face. Clinging for all she was worth to the dragon's neck, at any moment she expected to hit the water in a heart-stopping plunge. But then the headlong descent slowed and, with a powerful flapping of wings, they landed with the lightness of a feather. Only now did Kate dare to open her eyes to discover that Driftwood was perched on a ledge of rock a few yards above the surf. The skin of her face felt raw from friction with the briny air.

"Did you have to scare me half to death?"

"Witch has spies. Must not discover here."

Waves broke against jagged rocks close enough to splash her feet as she alighted from the dragon's body, still trembling with fright. She had to brush the hair from her eyes to take a good look at her surroundings. What, she asked herself, was so special about here? Then she noticed a narrow cleft in the rock, which led off the ledge into what appeared to be a cave. Kate bit her lips, squinting at the cleft. She edged closer, peering into the opening, but all she could see was darkness. Sniffing, she could smell nothing. She tried straining her ears as well but could hear nothing other than the sea breezes wailing like banshees through the rocks.

She tried to calm her heartbeat, which hadn't yet come down out of her throat. "What? You think I'm just going to hop in there?"

"Momu waits."

"Momu, whoever Momu is, can wait 'til she's blue in the face."

"Kate meets Momu. Time has come."

"Don't you dare abandon me!"

"Driftwood cannot come. Driftwood must prepare— dragon things. Kate—girl-thing—time is here."

"Absolutely forget it."

"Kate—close eyes!"

"You must be joking."

Those kumquat eyes regarded her, blinking with that peculiar membrane thing flitting across them. The next she knew, he was nudging her into the cleft.

"Stop it!"

"Kate meets Momu. Must beware her hunger!"

"Granny Dew warned me to beware you."

A forepaw lifted and a talon sprang out of it to point to her brow.

"What's that supposed . . . ?"

Too late. He had nudged Kate into the crevice for her to discover there was no floor. She was already sliding down a steep slope. Darkness yawned about her as she dropped, twisting and turning, like a helter-skelter—but this was a fairground ride whose walls were of ungiving stone. And strangely, though she felt shaken and dizzy, there were no projecting points or sharp corners to cut her skin or break a bone. In the few moments she had to appreciate this, Kate wondered if the tunnel walls were smoother than natural stone should be—maybe worn smooth by the descent of a great many bodies over a very long time. And her landing, though it shook the breath out of her, was cushioned by something soft and smelly, like seaweed. For a while she just sprawled there, panting for breath, with her head spinning. Then she heard noises from what sounded like a long way above that suggested Driftwood was taking off. She turned her face up into the gloom and called to him.

"Please—don't leave me!"

Her fright caused the oraculum to flare, illuminating a globular chamber with pallid green light. The tomb-like silence frightened her. She shouted back up into the gloomy tunnel: "Don't you dare!"

But he was gone. Sitting back, her legs now wobbly with panic, she heard a sniffing or a snuffling. She didn't like the sound of it at all. There was also a distinct, if strange, kind of smell.

"Who's there?"

The sound stopped. But then it started up again, coming closer. Kate clapped her hands to her mouth. Her heart had never come down out of her throat. She sat back against the wall, pulled her knees up to her chest.

"Oh, help!"

She heard rustling, like . . . like she didn't know what. It grew into a scurrying, and then there was the impression of something heavy rolling over. She felt a breeze play over the skin of her face. It was followed by a musical sound . . . as if somebody was running through notes in a scale. And then two faint lights appeared. Kate juddered with panic and she tucked her head down into her arms and knees. Yet something in her memory tugged at her. Hadn't she heard something like this before?

"Who are you?" Tentatively she lifted her head again and squinted at the lights.

In fact there were a great many more lights by now. She was confronted by a gathering of tiny lights, all of the faintest amber. And two much brighter lights, like minuscule beacons of turquoise. The amber lights were still but the turquoise lights were turning this way and that, like eyes. The musical sound came again, from their direction. There really was something familiar about the sound, although her senses were too overcome with alarm to recall what.

"I . . . I can't see you properly. Please—please, before I die of fright, will you let me see who or what you are?"

There was a glow in the air, not a flame exactly, but more like a gentle reflected light from the walls of the cave—if, in fact, it was a cave at all. It must be some sort of chamber carved out of stone. Now she could see more clearly Kate realized that the chamber was a perfect sphere, with walls as smooth as glass. Never in a million years could this have formed naturally. As she peered about herself she spotted patches of dewy wetness that glistened, like snail tracks, on the shiny surface. Just as she was wondering about those patches, one of them detached and in the twinkling of an eye it became a standing figure just feet away from her, its flesh as transparent as a ghost and the top of its head barely up to her chest.

"Sure, I know you!"

The Cill child gazed up at Kate with his large turquoise eyes, just as when she'd first met him in the Tower of Bones. She saw the corrugated rills of flesh, the folded stubs just above his ears where those delicate fan-like fronds had opened during his torment. And now, still gazing up at her, he emitted that tinkling musical sound. Then he closed his eyes in a slow, deliberate fashion, and when he opened them again Kate saw the irises slowly retract over the liquidly shining pupils, like the opening of an anemone.

She thought: *It's some kind of gesture . . . like friendship.*

"Thank you." Kate lifted her two hands, palms uppermost, and she did her best to return a jittery attempt at a smile.

He raised his own hands, as if copying her gesture. Then his hands slowly changed so the squidgy nail-less fingers extended to slim, elongated feelers that brushed her face around her eyes, and then, as if every bit as astonished with her as she was with him, his eyes performed that slow blink again, and then he reached up to comb out bits of seaweed that had become entangled in her hair.

Once again she had the impression he was trying to tell her something through a communication other than words. She did her best to talk to him through the oraculum: *I so want to understand.*

The Cill reached up again and touched her brow and the oraculum tingled, as if there had been a tiny spark of static electricity. Her mind filled with a single color.

"Green!" she exclaimed.

The Cill's eyes stared at her, unblinking, as if to highlight the turquoise color of his eyes. He emitted that musical sound again—the same communication.

Kate shook her head, stooping slightly, so as to come closer to his face. "Eyes . . . green eyes?" She laughed abruptly. "What are you telling me? Is that what you call me? You call me Greeneyes?"

The Cill blinked that slow, iris-changing blink again and he repeated that same musical sound.

Kate swallowed and her own eyes widened.

"The music—that's also me? That's what you're try-ing to tell me. The color and the music—it's your name for me in your language?" She clapped her hands. "How absolutely lovely!"

He slow-blinked again, but this time the music changed. He made a clicking sound and more music all at the same time. This time she saw a different color in her mind—the turquoise of his eyes. She stared at him and he stared back up at her.

"That's your name?"

The Cill grew excited. He started a high-pitched chit-tering. Others appeared out of the shadows, accompa-nied by a melodic chanting. It was the most beautiful sound Kate had ever heard. Tears of relief came to her eyes as she looked at them emerging out of the shadows and walls, with eyes a medley of jewel-like colors and skins sheening like rainbows.

"You're just entrancing!"

She wanted to grab hold of the child and squeeze him. But he was gesturing: some new message. With a sinewy movement of his arm he indicated a patch of wall where, with a five-note musical incantation, a circular door irised open. Moist patches on either side of the opening suggested it was guarded. The gesture, and the sudden look of alertness that had entered his eyes, told Kate that he was still anxious about some-thing, perhaps that the Witch and her minions could track and follow them even here.

"Go on," she nodded. "I'll follow you."

There was a momentary hesitation, as if he were readying himself. "Momu's people." He pointed to himself.

"I just heard you speak!"

"Shaami should not speak."

"Shaami—is that your name?"

"When Shaami speaks, all hear. Only the Momu can decide when Cill can speak with strangers."

"Who is this Momu?"

"Shaami has broken the rules."

"Will you be punished?"

"But Shaami wanted to thank Greeneyes for saving him." He hesitated as if he were translating in his mind. "This," he performed the slow blink with his eyes, "says 'Thank you.'"

She couldn't resist hugging him. But she did so gently, afraid that the diaphanous flesh might bruise.

The embrace provoked an overwhelming rush of feeling.

"What was that?"

"All felt—all shared."

"What do you mean? All of your people?"

He bowed his head with a shy smile, leading her to the guarded entrance, and through it into a twisting tunnel that cut through the walls of the chamber, leading away and downward, like a spout opening off a globular teapot. A second slide carried them further downward, and out into a new chamber. Shaami sounded another musical signal and the spout disappeared.

"Greeneyes must prepare."

"What am I preparing for?"

"The ocean."

With the word, she sensed a flood of emotions within Shaami's mind, reverence perhaps, as if the concept of ocean was deeply meaningful to him. But there was no time to wonder about it. The chamber began to fill with a cool, watery gurgling.

"Shaami—I'll drown!"

"Greeneyes must continue our journey."

Kate couldn't help but clutch at Shaami's hand as the seawater filled the chamber. "What is it? Some kind of defense?"

"Ulla Quemar must be protected. Once there were many cities open to the light, so my people woke to the sun in the morning and slept under the moon and stars. We gathered herbs in the meadows, listening to the birdsong and the hum of the bees amid the flowers. All gone—since the coming of the Great Witch."

Kate was staring at the rising level of the briny water, which by now was higher than her knees. She couldn't help shivering, it was so cold.

"Of all the cities of the Cill, only Ulla Quemar has survived. Here we became learned in the management of stone and water. Through such caution the Momu's people are the only ones left—the last of the Cill."

Kate clutched his hand with panic as the rising water reached her chin.

"Why," he questioned, with what she took to be a humorous tinkling, "does Greeneyes hug the floor when she might fly."

"Fly?" Her chattering teeth made it almost impossible to speak the words, even as a moment later she realized what he meant. She allowed her feet to detach from where she stood on tiptoes and she allowed her body to be directed to the surface by his guiding hand. "You mean swim?"

A thought cut through Kate's rising panic. If some enemy had discovered the cleft in the rock, and if that enemy had somehow managed to penetrate the hidden entrance and got this far, they would have drowned. *Here's hoping,* she thought, *it won't happen to me!* A new doorway appeared. Kate felt her body carried through into another chute. Down she spiraled, with Shaami holding her hand, in an exhilarating ride of water and spray . . .

"Welcome to Ulla Quemar!"

She emerged, dripping, into an enormous enclosure. The ceiling soared hundreds of feet overhead, exquisitely curved and smooth as marble. The floor was a proliferating garden of delight through which wove a labyrinth of avenues and pathways. Everywhere was the gleam and glitter of water. Moisture beaded the thick leaves of plants that were as brightly colored as the flowers that carpeted a wild meadow. Butterflies, bees, dragonflies and damselflies fluttered and buzzed amid an exuberance of flowers and shrubs. Birds too . . . they must have been chosen for their lovely song and plumage. The sights and sounds were so breathtaking that Kate hesitated to intrude into this world—her guide's home city of Ulla Quemar. But the city drew her into it, seducing all of her senses and filling her mind with wonder.

"It's paradise!"

A gentle spray of water was falling from somewhere high overhead, changing to mist and creating rainbows. But how could it ever rain in here? An engineering marvel it seemed, where tiny streams had been sculpted into the roof and contrived to sprinkle steadily. Everywhere she allowed herself to be led by Shaami brought new wonders of color and scent and sound. In time they emerged onto a beach opening onto an inner sea, a meeting of land and ocean united by a fine ivory sand, which became many different shades of ultramarine, turquoise and violet as it glowed under the waves. Fish and crabs and other marine life darted in glimmering shoals of movement all around her.

"My goodness—but how does it all work?"

"Ulla Quemar is one with the coral reef."

"But the light—it's just like daylight."

"Our ancestors discovered the light that glows in the hidden places deep beneath the oceans."

"But . . . but . . ." For several moments she stared about herself, lost for words. "Why doesn't the sea just flood in?"

"There are balances, of water and air, which are as one with the life you see about you. In addition we have the valves of rock we came through, and the equalizing chambers filled with ocean waters. Here in Ulla Quemar we keep open a window on our birth world, the ocean, with its delights and freedom."

All of a sudden Shaami dived into the lagoon and astonished Kate with his transformation. The radiating fronds sprang erect on either side of his head, even as he moved away with lightning speed. The ocean was his natural habitat. The fan-like fronds over the dome of his head were gills.

"You're amphibians!"

She had lost track of where he went underwater until his head broke, just yards away from where she had wandered knee-deep in the shallows. "Such delights do we maintain and cherish—but even this legacy is threatened. Only you, Greeneyes, with your power of healing, can help us."

"What do you mean?"

He smiled wanly. "Kate—girl-thing!"

A chill invaded her. "You've been watching me— me and the dragon!" She would never have seen them, even if there had been hundreds of them present. She recalled her dream-like experience on the island, when ghostly figures had taken her down onto the riverbank and removed her spidersweb rags, dressing her in the soft underwear and the silky dress.

"It was you," she whispered, "the Cill, who cared for me while I was sleeping that time. You dressed me."

"The Momu took care of her beloved Greeneyes."

Beloved!

Kate stood there, staring down into his turquoise eyes, her mouth gaping wordlessly as the gills shrank to the stubbly rills.

"But now Greeneyes must take care of the Momu!"

Into the Chasm

WITHIN A FEW HOURS OF THEIR PICKING THEIR way through a lava field, Shee scouts led them to the edge of a deep ravine. Black boulders lay scattered all about them from some past volcanic explosion. The leaders approached the edge, which fell precipitously downward, perhaps borne up by the same forces that had raised the surrounding calderas. They peered down into the enormous fissure in a thoughtful silence. Mist cloaked the valley below, gray and dense, and it rose like a lapping tide against the wall of the chasm. Gazing further out over the valley itself they glimpsed snags of rock protruding out of the rolling gray, like reefs in a perilous ocean.

"Is there no other way?" Qwenqwo growled.

"None," the Kyra replied.

Alan adjusted the straps that secured the Spear of Lug to his back. Half as long again as he was tall, the spiral blade with its cutting edges warded with Ogham reared more than three feet above his head. If they had reckoned it correctly, the Tower of Bones was no more than four days' march from here, directly north, through the mist-cloaked valley at the bottom of the ravine. He wiped his hands down over his face with the thought: *four days*! With any luck, that was all that separated him from finding Kate.

Some of the Shee carried coils of rope looped over one shoulder, while Aides bore packs of provisions and weaponry. The Kyra signaled one of her most experienced trackers—a tall, gray-haired warrior named Xeenra—to assess the drop, and she uncoiled an enormous length of rope with a heavy lance head attached to the end of it. Fixing the free end of the rope to her own waist, she cast the lance head far out into the chasm, holding her body taut against the pull of the rope, all the while observing the wide sector of its arc until the rope stopped running.

"It is very deep," she spoke calmly to the Kyra. "Almost three hundred paces!"

Alan saw how Mo squeezed the bog-oak figurine that dangled on a thong around her neck. He gave her a gentle hug. "Keep close to me—okay?"

They had set out at daybreak, the expeditionary force amounting to roughly a hundred Shee together with half as many Aides. A secondary force of Shee would set up camp here at the lip of the chasm, linking with the main force by the bay, and making preparations as if to follow. Much would depend on what the expeditionary force encountered along the way. But even if contingency decided that the expeditionary force would go it alone, this secondary force, and the main army back at the bay, were to show every sign of imminent departure. This way they would conceal their weakness of numbers right up to the moment of attacking the Tower.

"You realize," the Kyra muttered, for Alan's ear alone, "that we are heading into an obvious trap?"

Alan stared into the sky, where the Gargs were still circling while keeping their distance.

"You anticipate an attack?"

"Why bother to attack us when we are heading, with a wanton alacrity, for the Great Witch's own fastness?"

They had no need for a compass. There was no mystery as to the direction of the Tower of Bones. Alan and the Kyra could sense it through their oracula, like a baleful lighthouse at the heart of their inner visions, incandescent with dark spiritual power, lurid and moiling against a sky of darkness.

The Witch must be well aware of their presence. They could anticipate danger at every step. While Alan and the Kyra would be able to detect a deathmaw there would be additional perils, including some that might not signal themselves through any oraculum. Turkeya might yet prove helpful to them, with his unique knowledge of nature. Siam, having failed to dissuade his son from joining the expedition, had belatedly insisted that an Olhyiu warrior named Kataba—the son of his late brother-in-law, Topgal—should accompany them. Kataba was the stoutest of the warrior Olhyiu, a man in the bear-like mold of Siam himself. The Kyra didn't like it any more than Alan; Kataba looked as if he would give a brave account for himself in battle, but he was hardly suited to a mission that called for dexterity and cunning.

Siam's final warning had been addressed to Kataba: "My son is apt to fall into mischief without seeing it until it bites him. Make sure that he keeps his day-dreaming eyes and ears open."

Xeenra now led the descent, the upper end of the long rope secured by the guardian Shee and the lower end looped under her arms as she abseiled down into the pit, yard by yard, until her distant figure was lost in the mist. The wait seemed interminable before she signaled the bottom with three pulls on the rope.

Qwenqwo whispered into Alan's ear, "Difficult as this descent may prove, any retreat will be ten times so."

"There will be no retreat," hissed the Kyra, whose heightened hearing had easily overhead the whisper.

Strong arms cast more ropes into the void. The Kyra was the next to go, disappearing into the abyss with impressive agility.

"Me next," declared Turkeya.

"No—you follow me!" Alan was mindful of Siam's concerns about his son. "I'll follow the Kyra, with Mo close behind me. Then you, Turkeya!" So saying, Alan nodded toward the watchful Qwenqwo, to suggest he keep an eye on the shaman.

Kataba insisted on following after Turkeya, to make certain of the young shaman's safety. Alan exchanged a look with Qwenqwo. Then Ainé's voice called back up from somewhere in the mists below: "We must hurry. We cannot allow the descent to take up the entire morning."

Alan fixed a loop around Mo's chest, tested it under her arms, then fixed the end of the rope to his own waist. He took a firm grasp of the rope and headed on down, with Mo only yards behind him. They got into a rhythm of allowing their body weights to slip down the rope, pausing at ledges strong enough to bear their weight before finally coming to rest on the shale-strewn floor at the bottom. Here, as Turkeya arrived to join them, they freed themselves and assessed their surroundings. A dank, humid mist congealed over their skins. In the crevices strange plants captured Turkeya's attention. But the young shaman's inspection was interrupted by the clumsy arrival of Kataba, who had managed the entire descent without problem but then slipped on scree at the bottom and twisted his right ankle.

The Kyra's gaze met Alan's. They hadn't progressed a yard into the valley and yet here was Kataba already groaning with pain. The sensible solution was to leave him here to be rescued by the cliff-top guardians. But the brawny young Olhyiu wouldn't hear of it. He shrugged off any advice and refused any offer of attention from the Aides. Alan could only exhale with annoyance.

All around them streams of bodies were arriving along the various ropes, before forming ranks about the Kyra, and peering into the mist. The valley led away from them, rock-strewn and mist-drenched, with shrubby trees forming coppices where the volcanic rock gave way to a meager, cindery soil.

"Let us waste no time," called Ainé. "We should make the most of the daylight, murky as it appears to be."

"Agreed," said Qwenqwo, with a protective arm around Mo.

The Kyra flashed an alert to the Shee through her oraculum. "Visibility is poor. We march single file, but stay constantly within sight of the one in front. It would not do to get separated."

Although the Kyra spoke to the company in general it was obvious that her warning was directed in partic-ular at Kataba, who was now limping over the uneven ground. Progress was difficult enough through the treach-erous rocks and the obscuring mist but then, after no more than a few miles of difficult progress, the heavens opened. A relentless downpour inundated the company, rain so heavy they could see no more than a dozen yards ahead. There was no sheltering from such a torrent. They had no desire to huddle in the gloom of the twisted trees, not knowing what lurked in their shadows. Alan, with the Spear of Lug now serving as a staff, kept within close touch of Qwenqwo, Mo and Turkeya.

The downpour stopped as quickly as it had begun. As they pressed on through a stretch of boggy mud it became clear that they were descending into a swampy abyss, with visibility dangerously obscured by the mist. Indeed the mist appeared to be drawn to them, creeping up out of the shadows, coiling and twisting and sliding over the rocks before brushing against them like giant tongues. The humidity was oppressive. Alan could see droplets of moisture in his eyelashes and he felt it clogging up his lungs. All about them was a continuous rush of water, hissing in the streams, rushing in the torrents, roaring in cataracts over the broken rocky surfaces, a sound that, in other circumstances, might have provoked more pleasant emotions but here seemed only to threaten.

"Hsst!"

Qwenqwo's whisper shook him out of his ruminations. The dwarf mage nodded to a spot nearby where, highlighted in the foggy light, twisted boughs and leafless twigs were petrified, as if frozen in the agony that had killed them. Alan was about to move on but Qwenqwo shook his head. There was something alive in there, skulking in the shadows—something big as a crocodile, yet slippery and dark, that was creeping over the surface nearby, following their progress while keeping silent as a snake.

"They're everywhere," Qwenqwo whispered. "The entire landscape is infested with similar creatures. And they look hungry."

A sudden scream from further back in the single-file column chilled Alan's heart. It had sounded so full of pain and terror.

"Keep moving!" the Kyra barked.

"What's happened?"

"We have lost the Aides, Éineas."

Alan glanced at the Kyra, wondering if she could sense individual injury or loss among the Shee or the Aides through her oraculum. "Weapons ready," she barked. "Close ranks to within arm's length of those in front and behind."

Immediately ahead Alan saw Xeenra put her arm under the limping Kataba, to take some of his weight. They pressed on through gushing rapids, then a muddy stream, their legs immersed to midthigh.

When forced to stop for the night Alan approached the Kyra, who had elected to mount guard while others sat or lay down among the wet rocks. "I'm sorry about losing Éineas. It must have been a tough decision for you to just abandon her, without any ceremony."

The Kyra's eyes gazed evenly into his own. "Like we Shee, the Aides are born for war. They accept sacrifice—it is their being. You come from a different world. In so far as I have been able to determine, you were not born to fight. No more do you have a land, or a people, to die for here. Yet you risk your life in fighting our battles."

"The Tyrant murdered my parents."

The Kyra nodded before turning to address the company. "Take what opportunity you can to rest. Two hours—no more!"

From inside an emptied slatted crate a bedraggled Snakoil Kawkaw searched for a refuge within the Olhyiu section of the hastily erected camp. His swollen toe throbbed as if it had been scorched by a flame, his stomach contracted on several days of near starvation, his hair stuck to his body with malodorous algae from his swim ashore, and his red-rimmed eyes were so gummy with the same vile vermin of the oceans he could barely squint. "Tried to drown me, you did. Tried to finish me off!" His surviving hand was clenched in rage at the devilry that was consuming the Ship.

He had watched the camp for two nights and a day. And now a single target had become the focus of his spying. He recognized a small, miserable-looking woman who had been press-ganged back at the docks of Carfon, and hauled aboard one of Ebrit's escorts for the rough pleasure of the sailors—a doughty face, with its ring of matted black hair, meaner in the eye than a tinker's cur. They had found a second task for her here, that of stirring up a great cauldron of soup with a ladle half as big as herself, and with this she fed all and sundry within the camp, which she did with a baleful rancor. He took the measure of her as one after another demanded the free bounty of her ladle, with not one of them looking her in the eye or uttering a word of thanks, and the lady herself no recourse but to counter with oaths and a flow of fine arcs of spittle directed at every departing back. In his studied assessment, here was a slow-witted receptacle of fermenting malice, ready for a companion with whom she could share her misfortune.

He tested the greeting: "Ah, we meet again—my lovely!"

So miserable and angry was he still that he struggled to find suitable words of commiseration, suppressing the impulse to just step out and hug the bag of bones, whispering the imprecations those piggy ears had longed for all her life, meanwhile kissing those injured eyes shut.

Ach! Many a plan had been spoiled by hastiness.

"Better a name first," he whispered to himself, "a little time spent in discovering me darling's name!"

An hour and a half of such patience and he had it from a boy of perhaps ten or eleven years, screeching it at the top of his voice in the poor lady's face after she had no more than reprimanded him, judging the coast to be clear to do so, with a hefty wallop of the ladle over his head.

"Yah—Soup Scully Oops!"

Soup Scully Oops indeed!

It was time for Snakoil Kawkaw to clamber out of the crate, spitting aside the hard marbles of corn he had been swilling around his mouth, and venture a bold and upright step in the direction of this maligned fellow victim. His stretched himself fully erect, then marched forward until he loomed tall and soldierly before her.

"My dear lady," he shook his head before her cauldron, "I saw and heard for myself—such disrespect from a kick-deserving urchin! Would it be presumptuous of an old soldier to share a modicum of sympathy with one the world treats with such disdain—a lady, as I see, who has devoted her life, as did I, to its undeserving care?"

Her eyes narrowed and he witnessed, with a certain chagrin, how she ground what remained of her teeth.

"What d'yer want, yer old tramp?"

"Since the loss of my arm in the battle for Ossierel, serving these fish-gutters as you serve them daily, I have witnessed how their very bones are filled not with red marrow but with black ingratitude."

"Appears yer wants ter know if I agree," she hissed, "with wot little as ye be utterin' as was true."

"Mmmm!" he inhaled the aroma of the soup, then patted the dirt-engrained hand that draped over the ladle. "Did you brew it yerself, Scully?"

"It be soup, not mare's piss."

He laughed, with his good hand on his right hip. "How droll! I declare—if you were but to add a kiss to that ladle, it'd taste ten times as good."

She spat into the soup before giving it a half-hearted stir. "How 'bout that then? Ur goin' about tastin' me in that bowl a soup?"

"Make it a double portion!"

She doled out two ladles into a bowl and handed it to him, her eyes gleaming. "Next thing ur be a butterin' ole Scully up."

"Mmmm! Delicious!" The honest truth is, Kawkaw was so starving, he couldn't give a rat's ass damn about the spit. "Scully—Scully, my darling! This old soldier would be willing to bet that if it was love and not soup you were doling out here, why the ocean's own cauldron would not contain it."

"Maybe ur like a baked roll, ur useless rogue, if 'is one arm is even capable a handlin' 'is soup 'n 's sandwich 'n not a droppin' um both."

"If only if I could have you, lovely lady, as the main ingredient in my sandwich."

"Arrr, go button yer leery mouth."

"Comely lady, I might have a pretty something for you. Surely there's a tent where such banter might be shared with this war-weary soldier?"

Her eyes turned to flint and her voice lost its patois. "D'you think I don't know who you are, Snakoil Kawkaw? I've been watching you from the corner of my eye all the time you've been spying on me from that crate."

"Then you're not half as stupid as you appear."

His erect posture remolded itself to the more comfortable stoop and his eyes scanned the vicinity, ensuring that there were no witnesses, while reaching for the knife beneath his shirt.

"Don't even think of it," she muttered, producing a dagger with a spiral blade from the folds of her apron.

She kissed the triple infinity emblazoned in silver on its handle, her lips drawn back into a sneer.

"A Preceptress," he groaned.

"My master is not pleased—the brat still lives."

"I don't give a bitch-bat's teat. Do you imagine I would have taken his trinket on board had I known he intended to sink me along with the fish-gutters!"

"Your miserable existence is of no matter."

"It matters to me."

She observed him coldly. "I will be sure to communicate your devotion to my blessed Lord and Master, who, no doubt, will suitably reward you."

Plague-rotted fate of a whorehound!

They hurried on through a maze of plants that sprouted large, ugly-looking thorns. From the moment they had arrived in the swamps they had been beset with biting insects, from the whines of mosquitoes buzzing about their heads to swamp flies and horseflies as big as bumble bees, inflicting bites that turned into blisters. Now these thorns appeared more hazardous still. Turkeya led them into the shade of a lengthy face of cliff where the thorns were less threatening, but even here, to judge from the ground about them, they faced the alternative danger of falling rocks. You couldn't drop your guard, not for an instant, amid the perils of falling rock, biting insects, poisonous thorns or the hungry shadows.

Turkeya found balm leaves they could squeeze and rub over their smarting skins, while gazing about themselves at the mist that was rolling through the fangs of rock. At this deeper point in the valley the plants were more twisted still, deformed beyond anything recognizable, as if this were the price they had paid for survival in such a poisonous environment. The plants, and the animal life that battened on them and on one another, appeared perfectly attuned with a landscape that was unremittingly hostile, an omnipresent menace.

While hurrying over rocky ground Kataba stumbled again—even with the help of Xeenra, his progress had been hampered by falls—but this time his ankle completely gave way under him, sending him sprawling.

"Ainé—we've got to stop. See if the Aides can help him."

Kataba was helped to a ledge of rock, where Turkeya rubbed liniment into the swollen flesh, then he stood back to allow the Aides to strap the badly sprained ankle joint. As if encouraged by their halt, growls of hunger crept closer amid the shadows. When he had the chance to have a word with Alan, Turkeya admitted that the landscape increasingly dismayed him.

"Never have I witnessed such plants before. All appears to be primitive, the forms, as I would imagine, from the time of beginnings. A great many are parasitic on others, yet so dense and entangled that it is impossible to pick out the parasites from the fruitful. I dread to think that perhaps none are truly fruitful—which would mean they are all parasitic upon one another." His eyes widened under a lined brow, then he drew close to Alan so as to whisper out of Mo's earshot. "I think that some of the bigger plants—the ones with the gigantic flowers—might be man-eaters."

They moved on into a narrow defile where walls of granite leaned in toward them, evoking an overwhelming claustrophobia. Emerging from it the Shee were obliged to carry Kataba across wide slabs of the slippery rock, like treacherous stepping stones, while a drop of a hundred feet yawned below them into which a great river fell in a roaring cataract. It took something like an hour to inch their way across, only to discover that the ground on the other side had reverted to bog. A yellow slime oozed all around them and a family of overgrown slug-like creatures, banded in bright green, halted its slow slithering movements across their path to watch them.

"Shaman!" the Kyra's voice called out.

Turkeya hurried forward to see what troubled her. Ainé pointed to the way ahead. Inching forward, yard by yard, Turkeya peered into the gloom. Alan and Mo came forward to join him. The Kyra was wary about a dense proliferation of the giant plants Turkeya had warned Alan about earlier, extensive growths with enormous flowers made up of wide rings of misshapen petals, the flowers alone some twenty feet in diameter. Tendrils, as thick and ridged as the bore of a small palm tree, snaked out in a low curve from the base of the plants to end in fat bulbous organs.

"What are they?"

Turkeya picked up a piece of rock as big as a man's head and rubbed it with a little of the smoked meat they carried in their back packs, then cast it onto one of the giant flowers. With lightning speed the central tendril snapped around and the bulb at the end of it opened out on pink jaws lined by rows of teeth, like the gaping mouth of a shark. The jaws snapped shut on the rock and the fronds of the giant flower closed over it, enclosing the captured prey. The tendril withdrew to hunt again. Meanwhile the gaps between the closed petals began to ooze copious amounts of a rank-smelling liquid, which hissed like acid.

"They really are man-eaters!" Turkeya sighed.

Alan shook his head, hardly daring to imagine what it would mean to be a victim caught in that trap and digested alive.

Qwenqwo nodded. "I have heard of such, but never have I encountered the like."

Even as they stared in amazement at the feeding plant a tendril of another appeared out of the mist and moved, with a swaying, searching motion, close to Turkeya.

"Beware!" the Kyra roared, hauling him backward.

They probed the land about them with even more care. Everywhere they encountered man-eaters in a variety of different kinds. Some had long narrow tendrils that hunted thirty or forty yards away from the ground-based flowers. Others had black creepers, spiked with dagger-like thorns, that burrowed under the soil and lay in wait.

They struggled chest deep across a vile swamp whose vapors attacked their nostrils and throats, leaving them choking. Pressing onward, the Kyra refused to rest in such perilous surroundings. By degrees the noise of water became louder. They had entered a water-laden basin, where the streams and rivers fed by the mountains emptied into a morass of lakes. Thick bulbous forms dominated the plants, with nothing that could be recognizably described as leaves, yet crawling with vines and creepers, rank-smelling and fleshy, with hives of insects in wait above, ready to swarm down and attack the intruders. Suddenly, huge globular pods burst in the branches over the company, showering them with thick, musky clouds of pollen, provoking panic.

"Turkeya?"

"The pollen may be poisonous. We must wash it off our skins—anywhere we come into contact with it."

Alan splashed stream water all over his face, his hands, his arms, with his sleeves pulled up to his elbows. There was a livid scar running up his left shin, from ankle to knee, where he had been scratched by one of the thorns. Many of the company were coughing, as if their lungs were inflamed from inhaling the pollen.

"I don't understand it," Turkeya exclaimed. "There is little nourishment in the soil. Yet these plants grow so thick and strong!"

Hearing a screech from overhead they turned their bug-bitten faces up to glimpse Gargs, wheeling and spiraling in an updraught. Alan heard another anguished cry in the near distance, followed by thrashing sounds, and then, heart-stopping silence.

The Kyra spoke without pausing. "Another Aides! And the Shee, Llediana, who tried to save her!"

At the next rest stop Ainé, looking grim, took Alan to one side. "We need to talk in private—you and I—and perhaps the Fir Bolg too!"

Alan exchanged glances with Qwenqwo, wondering what to expect.

When they were alone Ainé announced that she had come to a decision. "This landscape is too dangerous to risk the following army of Shee."

Alan dropped his head. They would have to face the Tower on their own.

He recalled the scene on the beach when the Kyra had thought it necessary to pass on her learning to her daughter-sister, who was no more than a child. The Shee were very secretive. He realized that he knew next to nothing about them, or their homeland in the Guhttan Mountains. How old were they when the mother-sisters bore their cloned daughter-sisters? He had no idea. The new Kyra looked perhaps twenty years old and the daughter he had glimpsed in the ceremony on the beach no more than six. It suggested that they bore their daughters as soon as possible after puberty. An early birth made sense when you realized that the immortality of their lineage depended on it. They were warriors who anticipated death. The realization shocked him into silence.

Qwenqwo spoke softly. "It's unfortunate, but may prove less than a catastrophe."

"How so?" the Kyra asked.

The dwarf mage plucked at his red beard, as if gathering his thoughts. "We know that at journey's end there will be no conventional battle of sword or javelin. The enemy will be the Great Witch herself. I have given thought to this, as no doubt you have. The might of a conventional army would serve little purpose in such a confrontation, which will be determined not by military force but by a battle of powers—that of the Witch against the Mage Lord's oraculum."

The Kyra's voice was icy. "But first we need to survive the journey there. Do you imagine that the approaches to her fastness will be unprotected? And what of the Gargs who have no need to tramp through such perils on foot? Will they attack us when they realize that this small force is all they face?"

THE MOMU

KATE STOOD AT THE END OF ONE OF MANY PROM-
ontories that led from the main city square and marveled at the city of Ulla Quemar. Once—a very long time
ago—there must have been an enormous natural cave
beneath the ocean. It would have been as deep as direct
sunlight could penetrate from the surface waters above,
with an entrance, perhaps a quarter of a mile in diameter, opening onto the cave. Somehow the Cill had made a
world out of it. They had built a gargantuan curtain wall
of transparent quartz that swept down from the roof
and extended out in a great semicircle into the ocean.
This formed a partial seal, which, complemented by the
pressure of air within the cave, enabled the city to hold
onto its atmosphere, and in turn allowed the tide that
flowed into the cavern. Like a prism, the quartz bent the

sunlight so it illuminated the entire city with daylight, making the city one with a coral reef.

Here, in the softness of evening, the beauty of the city was so intoxicating that Kate just wanted to breathe it in. The Cill were truly amphibian. That was what made Ulla Quemar so unique. They had constructed a meeting of worlds that flowed seamlessly and naturally into one another, an astonishing symbiosis of land and sea.

Snuggling down in the sand at the very edge of the tide she let her fingers be washed over by the waves, marveling at the turquoise luminescence beneath the ocean, and the life that darted and wheeled within it. The reef literally flowed past and around her deep into the city, the brilliantly colored fish at home in the floral gardens of corals, anemones and flower-like creatures that seemed curiously intermediate between animals and plants, with so many bizarre and enchanting forms she couldn't even begin to identify them. What a wonder it must be to live amid such an exuberance of beauty! Kate couldn't help but be entranced.

She felt refreshed by a restful sleep in a bed of eiderdown in a spacious chamber shaped like a sea urchin. Its inner walls seemed to be real mother-of-pearl, so she had woken into what felt a dream, bedazzled by glittering reflections. She was ravenously hungry when Shaami appeared with tiny plates of shellfish, two hot cakes of roasted seaweed, potato-like vegetables and nice fruits sweetened with honey. The breakfast was curiously light, as if designed to stave off the worst of her hunger while not fully assuaging it. Even so, as she dined out of doors with the coral reef sweeping around her feet, the waning daylight told her that evening must be falling on the surface waters above, extinguishing the daylight filtering down through this great natural window.

"How long have I slept?" she asked Shaami, who kept her company across a table constructed out of a single piece of red coral.

"You were very tired."

"A whole night and a day?" She watched how the artificial lights had begun to twinkle and glow in the streets around her.

Just how old might Ulla Quemar be? The interwoven labyrinths of land and reef couldn't have been constructed in years and probably not even in centuries. This complex ecosystem must have evolved over thousands of years. The Cill were exquisitely sensitive to beauty and harmony. The construction, the evolution, of Ulla Quemar wouldn't have been hurried. But there was more, much more, to wonder at.

Oh, my!

Her heart beat so in her breast as she paused to reflect on the nature of the Cill themselves. So powerful were the emotions this place evoked, and these beings in particular! Kate had marveled at how delicate the Cill appeared on land. Watching a group of them swim by underwater, with their undulating limbs and streaming fins, she was all the more impressed by their

exquisite natural grace, their streamlined bodies gliding like sylphs between the corals. They appeared so
gentle, their world so well ordered, she couldn't imagine a Cill wanting to hurt anyone. It made it all the more
monstrous that such gentle beings should be exposed to
the cruelties of the Witch. All her life, Kate had loathed
fighting, aggression, war and the grief it caused to ordinary people. It was the stupidity of war that had killed
her parents. She had always believed, deep in her heart,
that their deaths had served nothing, no purpose at all.

"Greeneyes is feeling better?"

"In more ways than one. Your world is so lovely—and
the air seems so clean, so pure, it's a pleasure just to
breathe it."

"Evening is restful, when the day closes its eyes. Yet
look—see the large leaves, with bubbles rising from the
water beneath."

Kate looked at the surface waters around her, assuming that Shaami was referring to plants that looked like
water lilies. But now she looked more closely there were
no flower heads, just broad leaves of a dappled green.

"You see the opening at the center of the pad? This is
the nostril for a sunstealer tethered to the coral below."

"A sunstealer?"

Kate had to leave her seat by the table and lie flat on
the sand with her eyes only an inch or two from the surface water to peer into the shadowed depths. "What am I
looking for? Is it that enormous greeny-yellow balloon?"

"You can follow the bubbles?"

"Yes—I see them. They're rising from its surface."

"This is the sunstealer."

"That's an odd name."

"It isn't really a plant—or even a single creature— but many plant-animals that join together to make the hollow balloon. A single balloon can grow to the size of a small house. It must hold onto the coral to prevent it from rising up and floating away. Through their green leaves, sunstealers consume the daylight falling onto the sunlit waters—in doing so they also clean the air."

Kate clapped her hands. "Back home—on Earth—we have green plants, and the algae in the oceans, which do the same thing. They capture sunlight and make the oxygen we breathe."

"Are there witches also in your world?"

"Well . . . No. Not like the one you're thinking of."

"How fortunate you are. I would love to hear more of your world. But for now the Momu waits . . . If Greeneyes is sufficiently refreshed?"

With a start Kate recalled something Driftwood had said, when he was desperate about his nautilus shell, his shiny thing. *Gift from Momu—mine—my gift!* The dragon had known all along about the Cill. He must have watched them dress her on the island as she slept. And he had brought her here, to the landward entrance to the city.

She sighed: "I suppose I'm as ready as I'll ever be!"

Turning around to face the square she walked, bare-foot, to where he was waiting for her. "Come," he said, with another of those strange expressions of his irises. "Long has the Momu dreamed of this meeting."

"She knew that I was coming?"

"The Momu is knowing. She has cared for her people even from the ancient times, when Ulla Quemar was first created."

"Gosh—she must be very old."

His eyes performed the movements, a slow close followed by a rapid opening, that Kate now recognized as "Yes."

In the falling dusk she was reminded of how Shaami's eyes actually glowed. And now she saw that everything about her was also glowing in a variety of soft pastel shades and colors.

Shaami led her through the city, where none of the buildings took the boring rectangular forms she was used to back home. Here every house, temple or garden followed exquisitely naturalistic shapes. Oyster-shells the size of a three-story building gaped ajar. Periwinkle shapes clustered in diminishing sizes into a spiral. Gigantic five-limbed starfish rose out of floral gardens, or the whorled organic loveliness of the shapes of nautilus shells, or the ears of conchs. And even now in the quiet of evening she saw the abundance of plants, fluttering birds, the flight of butterflies, bees and other insects. Her fingers brushed against the velvety surface of toadstool-like growths, pungently fragrant, that must be cultivated foods. There was a sense of oneness with life, its needs and balances respected in a way she would have loved to have seen back home. She wasn't sure where the boundary lay between architecture and what was natural anymore, such was the weave and flow of one into the other.

Shaami showed her inscriptions on walls that she would have passed by without noticing had he not reached out and brushed them into awareness. Hieroglyphs of their history, or murals, or simply artwork for its own sake—it was all so exhilarating Kate just let the wonder of it flow around her, and through her. A door irised open with the flat of a hand pressed against a hieroglyph and a chant—Shaami was allowing her to catch a little of what he must be hearing within his mind, the melody of interacting voices—so delightful when two or more were communicating with each other, a language far more complex than her own, one in which subtleties of insight and emotion were conveyed in music as much as in the words. Sometimes she noticed, and thought it must be significant, that many Cill voices chanted in unison, as if fusing into a single melodic symphony. And she realized what should have been immediately obvious, yet was so alien to her human perspective and senses, that she had probably resisted the notion. The city was a hive. A living, thinking, overwhelmingly interactive hive, in which the Momu . . .

Oh, lord . . . Can it really be true?

Kate hardly dared to think this through, it so startled her. Yet there was only one logical conclusion. The Momu was the hive queen.

And now, as Shaami took her deeper into the city, she began to notice more. None of the buildings was new. Looking more closely, she saw signs of decay. Some of the streets were collapsing in on themselves. Even amid the decorous shapes there were places where the rainbow glitter over the dome of a shell-home had moldered to lifeless gray, as if the gorgeous structures were withering and perishing.

Then she saw armed figures. Cill who were half as tall again as Shaami and much more warlike. Although their bodies had the same streamlined contours, these were heavily muscled. Their eyes were cold, a steely gray, and their heads were elongated front to back, with bulging brows and heavy jaws, curiously ugly in the faces of Cills, with large overlapping canines. Their armor was shell-like—like the carapace of a lobster—and lobster-like claws had replaced their right forearms and hands. The blades on the claws were curved and overlapping, perhaps nine inches long, and fearsomely sharp. They would sever a limb, or a neck, with a single snip.

Kate couldn't help but imagine such warriors in combat, combining implacable ferocity with the Cill potential to become invisible.

Shaami's voice seemed incongruously gentle in comparison. "It is not by accident that Ulla Quemar has survived where all other cities have fallen."

"You believe that, sooner or later, the Witch will find you?"

"She has discovered every other city. One by one, she has destroyed them all. No matter how well we conceal it, she will discover Ulla Quemar."

Kate was still staring at the warriors, alarmed by what Shaami had told her, when he sang open a new entrance. From out of the entrance two Cill appeared, each taking one of Kate's hands and leading her in. Although they too were devoid of breasts, Kate wondered if they might be the equivalent of female—though she was no longer sure that the Cill had anything like the male and female sexuality of humans. They so closely resembled each other they could have been twins.

Shaami's eyes did the courtesy blink of his eyes again before he left her.

"Won't you stay?"

"Shaami cannot enter here."

The handmaidens—if she interpreted them right—began to remove Kate's dress.

"What are you doing?"

Their eyes irised, as one, in what Kate now recognized as an apology. "All must be natural in the Momu's presence."

"Then I'll undress myself." Kate removed her dress and underwear and handed it to the maidens, who bowed. With exactly synchronous waves of their sinewy arms, carrying through to the slim, nail-less webbed fingers, they ushered Kate toward an inner wall where another door morphed open, and, tentatively, she stepped through.

Immediately her body was bathed in a warm mist of brine. The maidens, moving with a languid ease, washed her body and anointed her with a scented oil. A more powerful, echoing voice addressed her:

"Come! The Momu would see you!"

Kate stepped further into a large, softly illuminated chamber, flushing with embarrassment at her own nakedness. The chamber appeared to be a natural cavern within the much larger cave that housed the city. There were clusters of stalagmites, sparkling with embedded crystals, and high overhead she saw that the corresponding stalactites sprouted from the roof. The light rose from a broad, deep pool of faintly luminescent water behind which, only vaguely outlined within the shadows, stood a tree. The tree astonished Kate, who had seen no other within the plants and flowers that decorated the city. As her eyes became accustomed to the half-light, she realized that it was enormous, with boughs and branches that ramified all over the roof of the cave. She sensed even more extensive roots—roots that spread, perhaps, more widely throughout all of Ulla Quemar. And the leaves were not what one would expect of a tree. They were pink—and distinctly fleshy. She knew of no tree that could grow within a cavern in the absence of sunlight. Immediately in front of the tree, within the throne of its roots, a figure was reclining, a woman as naked as any other Cill, but considerably taller. Her face was a foot higher than Kate's even though she was half-reclining and Kate was standing erect.

A movement in the misty air caused Kate to spin around. The chamber was scented with a floral sweetness, and its surfaces, which were as complex as the reef she had seen earlier, were pierced with water-filled hollows so that sea creatures, like crabs, sea urchins and starfish, could make their homes within them.

"Come closer, child. Cross through the waters of the birthing pool. Only in the mind of Shaami has the Momu witnessed the life-giving gift in your brow. Come—let me see you in the flesh."

The birthing pool! Kate hesitated, shrinking into herself.

"Please—do not be afraid."

The voice, deep and musical, was soothing to her mind, yet behind the gentleness Kate sensed great determination and, very likely, power.

Kate waded into the cool, still water and then swam across, blinking as she emerged before the Momu. She sat where the Momu indicated with a wave of her hand, within the intimate tangle of roots.

"Are you comfortable?"

"Yes." Indeed she was perfectly comfortable. The temperature of the humid air was exactly right for her naked body.

"I know you will have many questions."

Kate's eyes lifted to gaze into a face many times the size of an adult human face, and much longer again from brow to chin; a slender and perfectly regal face with the longest ears that Kate had ever witnessed. The skin of the Momu had that strangely ethereal look, like all of the Cill, but there was some additional greenish-bronze hue. The lobes of her ears were greatly elongated and widened to take spools, like those that wrapped cotton, but these were artworks in ivory, a full six inches in diameter, dangling down on either side of her cheeks. With a slow blink, the enormous eyes sprang open, and with jaw-dropping shock Kate saw that the irises, performing that beautiful slow movement of welcome, were a silvery mother-of-pearl.

"Come—sit close beside me."

Kate hesitated before moving closer to the Momu, who was surrounded by platters of berries, nuts, tiny confections of sushi-like raw fish, a salad of fruits on a bed of three different-colored seaweeds—and more—such a variety of tidbits she couldn't even begin to identify them.

"Would you care to taste?"

Although it had only been an hour or so since her evening breakfast, Kate couldn't help but stare at the extraordinary feast that had been laid out before her. She understood now why that breakfast had been so light. Shaami knew that there would be a more substantial feast to follow. Her fingers shaking with nervousness, Kate picked up a tiny morsel of what looked like caviar on a biscuit. The caviar was probably exactly that—Kate had never actually tasted caviar in her life—and the biscuit tasted of roasted nuts.

"You like it?"

"It's delicious."

"Ah—I see now that you are more radiant in the flesh than even I had imagined. I weep a hundred thousand tears of gratitude for your courage and kindness in saving the life of my child."

"Shaami is your child?"

"My last-born—and most precious."

"All the Cill, they're all your children, aren't they?"

"Of course."

The long, webbed fingers of the Momu extended, with a languid grace, to stroke Kate's cheek. Though the hive mother, she too was devoid of breasts. It was a reminder, if Kate needed any such reminder, that the Cill were not human. A crystal of power, pellucid but tinted a greenish blue, hung on a gold filigree chain around the Momu's neck. Flickering sparks pulsated and metamorphosed in its depths.

"Well now—you may ask me your questions."

Kate nodded. "If it's not impolite, can I ask how old you are?"

"In your terms, child, I am very old indeed."

"Do you mean, centuries old?"

"A good deal older still."

Kate's eyes widened. "And throughout all that time have you been obliged to stay here—in this chamber?"

"Oh, I can leave the birthing chamber as I please. But at my age I prefer to travel through water."

"You can swim out there, into the ocean?"

The Momu's pupils performed a series of rapid oscillations, accompanied by a musical sound that might have been laughter. "Surely, the ocean is my world."

Kate clapped her hands together with delight. "There are lots of questions I want to ask you. But I don't want to be selfish. I expect that you have some questions for me?"

"Indeed I do. I have altogether too many such questions—and I can hardly restrain my own impatience. I would know everything. Who, and what, are you? Where have you come from? I would know everything of how you came to be the bearer of the great power you carry in your brow."

Kate felt surprisingly comfortable in the presence of the Momu. And she was only too glad to be able to talk about all that had happened to her in this bewildering world. Once she began she thought she would never end talking to the Momu, who sat and listened to every word, largely in silence, the strange webbed hand about her slender shoulders, and the extraordinary eyes all the while appraising Kate. When she had finished telling her story the Momu took Kate's hands between her own and kissed them with great tenderness. "So young and fair in all that you have witnessed, and suffered, and still admirable in your faith and trust. Greeneyes—you are a True Believer."

Tears rose into Kate's eyes, tears of release and uncertainty at one and the same time. "But what does it all mean? Why was I chosen? Was it just fate . . . the fact that four of us became friends? That we just happened to come together in Clonmel that day?"

"You must not talk of fate thus, as if it were random, or unimportant. Fate is a very great power—and mystery is its very essence."

Kate dropped her head and sighed. "I don't even pretend to understand. Alan has become obsessed with this thing called the Fáil. Is this another word for fate?"

"Hush! I would advise you not to speak openly of this. Yet there is a quality inborn to all True Believers, some for good, and some for evil."

"But what does that mean?"

"Ah—such questions! Perhaps a quality that comes into its own in that most mysterious of domains, the between-world we know as Dromenon. And yet, without understanding of the mysteries, or what power resides within you, have you not resurrected a being of magic? Surely there is a miraculous potency in you."

"A being of magic—you mean, Driftwood?"

"Even asleep, you willed it into being. And it became so."

"But how did I do that? How could I give life to a fossil?"

"A very great power, indeed, have you. The gift of life, of rebirth."

Kate looked up into the enormous, gentle face, astonished at what the Momu was telling her.

"This gift, will you show me how I'm supposed to use it?"

The crystal dangling from the Momu's neck took fire. The explosion of light, alive with a multi-hued matrix, filled the chamber. It was as if with an effort of will that the voice of the Momu stayed gentle. "Greeneyes—child! Your very naivety leads you to flaunt such a temptation before the Momu."

"But it's a power I don't understand. I don't know what's expected of me."

Those huge eyes came to within inches of Kate's own, as if to gaze into her mind. Then, the Momu burrowed, with one webbed hand, at the base of the tree, returning with her palm uppermost before Kate's startled gaze and nostrils. Kate saw, and smelled, decay. The heart of the great tree was rotten.

"Beloved Greeneyes, do you understand?"

"I . . . I saw the same decay in some of the houses, the streets . . ."

The Momu's pearly eyes performed that slow blink, and she put her arm around Kate's shoulders again. "Nidhoggr, the serpent, who gnawed at the roots of the world, fertilized a seed of the Tree of Life. That seed grew into the One Tree in whose roots we converse, a chimera of magic and being. The One Tree is dying, and with it my beautiful Ulla Quemar. I, the first born of that chimera— who am almost as old as the One Tree itself—am dying with her. There will be no more Shaamis."

"Please stop! You're frightening me."

The Momu's eyes were unblinking in their appraisal of Kate, now held so very close to her. "You talked of fate. And I told you that mystery was its essence. Yet was it not Fate that brought you here to me?"

"I don't know what you mean."

"Will you not stay here? Will you not help me?"

"What you're thinking . . ."

"You know my mind?"

The mind of the Momu, as Kate read it through her oraculum, was many-stranded, like a gargantuan spider's web. Her thoughts, now invading Kate's own, were a symphony of beautiful tones, yet behind the serenity Kate sensed despair. It was like drowning in an ocean of rotting silken threads.

Terror grew in Kate at what she was sensing in the mind of the Momu. "You know it would be wrong to keep me here."

"Oh, my darling Greeneyes! You must try to understand how perilous the situation has become. Even though she failed to locate and destroy my beautiful Ulla Quemar, the Great Witch has succeeded in isolating it, and in doing so, destroying the harmony it needed to survive. Yet you—so innocent and fair—you have the potential to change this. You have the power to refresh and renew."

"You want to make me a prisoner, just like the Witch. So you can use me, as she tried to use me."

"How cold are your words, now cruelly directed to me! Yet I would not use you for evil, like the Witch. On the contrary, I would cherish you, keep you safe in hope and love, with my purpose only to do good. I beg you. Grant me this respite? A year. A few years! A mote in the great cycle of time, yet together we might cure the One Tree and make Ulla Quemar whole again."

Kate pitied the Momu even though she was now very much afraid of her.

She spoke, softly, "Granny Dew sent me to Drift-wood, and he brought me to you. He didn't bring me here so you could use me. He brought me to you so I could stop running. Can't you see that you can't go on hiding? There's only one way to save you and your people. We have to beat her. We have to destroy the Witch."

"You imagine you can confront the epitome of evil and win? You will fail. Your purpose would be hopeless, even if you were to face her on her own. But you have seen for yourself that Olc is not alone. She has subverted the Eyrie People, though I know they have long balked against it."

Kate's head was spinning with these revelations. "The Eyrie People?"

"Those you call the Gargs."

"What are you saying? You know about those . . . those horrible beings?"

"Once we were allies and not enemies, the Eyrie People, and the Cill."

"You were friends with the Gargs?"

But the Momu was no longer listening to Kate. Her voice was distant, lost in memories and despair. "Long ago, these were bountiful and prosperous lands with room and plenitude. We lived in a harmony of differences that respected all. We worshipped knowledge as much as we traded the fruits of our hunting and our skills. There were powerful covenants of fire and blessings between our peoples. This world was kind to all before the coming of the Witch . . .

"But I must look beyond mere nostalgia for what was lost. Putting all that aside, more monstrous than all of the suffering she has inflicted on both the Cill and the Eyrie People, is the coming peril of her growing insanity. You, O, beloved Greeneyes—please be warned! Olc is plotting to recruit another to her cause. A demigod of immense power and malice. Can you not see that what you propose is worse than naive? It is madness to think you can confront and then destroy the Witch."

Kate looked deep into the Momu's sad and beautiful eyes, and beyond them, her tormented mind.

"Listen to me, Momu. Please think about what I'm telling you. This power, in my brow—through it I can sense things that are sick—things that are capable of confusing your thinking so you see only darkness everywhere. The sickness that is weakening the One Tree is the same despair that is eating at your heart. Sure, it wouldn't matter how long I stayed with you, I couldn't cure your world any more than I could cure you. Not while the Witch remains a threat. I hear your warning about her—I know it will be horribly risky to take her on. But still I know that there will be no hope for you, or for lovely Ulla Quemar, unless we do. My friend, Alan, is coming. He promised he would and I know he'll keep that promise. He too is an oraculum-bearer. But his oraculum is very different from mine. I won't be alone when I confront the Witch."

An Unlikely Capture

ALAN STARED DOWN WITH DISMAY INTO A TUMBLE of razor-sharp rocks and cascading water. Next to him Turkeya was pleading with Kataba, who was sitting on the waterlogged ground, his back against a lichen-encrusted cliff face. Kataba's injured leg was stretched out stiffly in front of him.

"My ankle is useless. I can't go on. I'm sorry, Turkeya. Just leave me here with a little food." The burly Olhyiu laughed, gazing about himself into the mist. "There'll be no shortage of water."

"You know we won't be coming back."

"Who knows what will be."

"It's out of the question."

The Aides helped Kataba to his feet, then rigged crutches from thick creepers so he could take the weight off his bad ankle. The contents of his pack were shared out among the others, reducing his load. They moved on again, picking their way with care down the treacherous escarpment. By midday they were confronted by a fast-rushing river channel, about sixty feet wide, that had cut through the skirts of the mountains, creating a waterfall above a drop of sixty feet or more.

"Be sensible—it's hopeless!" Kataba stood, keeping a somewhat unsteady balance on one foot with his crutches planted on solid ground, contemplating the swell of water that ran as fast as a herd of leaping bucks between stepping stones slippery with moss. "You know I'm a liability to this mission."

"It would take half a day to go around this pass. You must try," the Kyra pressed him. "Xeenra will assist you."

Alan caught the questioning glance of the gray-haired Shee, which was directed toward the Kyra. Kataba was at least as tall and three times as broad as the Shee. But Ainé was insistent. "We'll fashion a chain, holding hands, so that any who falter will be supported by the others."

Kataba threw down his crutches and appealed to Turkeya. "Stop this foolishness now. From the very beginning I've been a burden."

Turkeya sighed. He examined the swollen flesh surrounding Kataba's damaged ankle. The hard journey had made things worse. Livid trails of inflammation ran up his shin almost to the knee. Even Turkeya's examination caused Kataba to groan aloud. The poor man's face was awash with sweat. Kataba reached out and grasped Turkeya's wrist, as if attempting to squeeze sense into him. His hand trembled, yet the muscles and tendons stuck out like iron bands, so fierce was his plea.

He whispered: "Make them see."

Turkeya could not keep the worry from his voice. "Kataba is right. This ankle isn't just sprained. There's poison in the wound. It's no good. The poison is traveling into his blood. He'll die if we can't stop it."

"But what can we do?"

"I'm the shaman," Turkeya murmured, as much to himself as those gathered around him. "I'll find a way to help him!"

The senior Aides, Layheas, intervened. "I have heal-well, which will reduce the inflammation and pain. But it will not cure the poison."

Alan nodded: "Go ahead, Layheas. Do what you can for him."

Turkeya whispered into Alan's ear. "I have an idea. Something I've been thinking about through the night. A herbal plant that might subdue the poison. The queen of night as some call it—others know it as venom balm. I've no experience in using it, but Kemtuk described its benefits and the form of its leaf to me. It's said to be capable of curing most poisons if made into a brew. I'd better go and look for it."

"Not on your own!"

"I won't go far. None but I would recognize it. I'll be back before anybody knows I'm gone."

Alan turned, ready to call Qwenqwo, but a groan from Kataba distracted him. Layheas was looking up at him for assistance as she attempted to administer another sip of healwell. Alan took the cloth from her hand to dab the sweat from the man's brow.

Turkeya had pretended to be confident when speaking to Alan, but immediately he entered the encircling swamps he felt less sure about his search. The humidity among the clinging tendrils and creepers took his breath away. Still, he must strive to keep his wits about him. There were dangers here at every step. No matter how carefully he tried to avoid them, the hair-wicks of the man-eaters brushed the skin of his face, and the smell of their digestive acids grew stronger. The danger would be no more terrifying if he heard the nearby growl of a predator. And while there were no growls he could hear those horrible slithering sounds, and in the trees, hisses and panting that seemed to cluster about him in the encircling gloom. With his sword unsheathed and his eyes darting from side to side, he tiptoed over the marshy ground, searching for the herb, all the while doing his best to keep a sense of direction.

"Precious little good will it serve Kataba if I end up lost!"

He had left his water with his injured cousin and already he was thirsty from the heat and dehydration.

Following the sound of a stream he came to a pool. Peering in, he withdrew in shock from the shadows darting beneath the brackish surface. He dare not drink the water.

Increasingly thirsty, Turkeya flopped onto an island of solid ground under the shade of a rocky overhang. There was no sign of the herb. Had it been a delusion that had convinced him that venom balm was to be found here? He was coming to realize that this search was the most stupid idea imaginable. He had broken his word to his father and wandered off on a hopeless mission. And to make matters worse he might have lost his way. Despairingly, he reflected that if he truly were lost, it was unlikely he would ever find his way back. His head muzzy with worry, he hadn't noticed how the forest, previously noisy with slithering and hissing, had become so hushed he could hear his own heartbeat. There was nothing to see, yet he sensed danger nearby. And he thought perhaps that he smelt it too, a sickly smell, as of meat going putrid. Pulling back further into the shadows, his eyes searched frantically amid the gloom.

There—something moved!

He glimpsed a creature with a gargoyle's head and a huge sucker-like mouth—a mouth ringed by teeth as sharp as a snake's fangs. He didn't know what it was. An impression at the side of his vision, over to his left. But suddenly—another! There—just to the right! His heartbeat was racing and his back was pressed so hard against a jutting stone that it was burrowing into his flesh.

Something moved again . . . another shadow. But when he looked more closely there appeared to be nothing there.

"What was that?"

One of the shadows, over to his right, crept several feet closer, rippling over the ground like an advancing edge of liquid. It was faintly glistening about its manifold advancing edges, as if it they were reflecting a glimmer of moonlight. Only there was something rancid too about that light as much as the shadow itself. Something greenish, glimmeringly so, the putrid rainbows you saw on rotting fish, or floating over the surface of stagnant water.

"Oh, by the power of great A-kol-i!"

A shape was rising out of the pool of shadow. It was as if the shadow itself had taken substance. The shape had a roiling impression within it, as if vapors of that same darkling thing were twisting and turning in a tormented captivity, as it rose by degrees to something more than seven feet tall. A head, with two huge glowing eyes! Eyes of a pallid yellow, veined with red, and split from top to bottom, like the eyes of a serpent. Turkeya watched in dread as those eyes veered from side to side until they found him.

"Aaaaaah!"

Turkeya's legs had turned to jelly, yet he was flailing those very legs and running for his life. There was no rational thought in his head. He just ran in the opposite direction to the eyes, hurtling through clinging foliage and stumbling through boggy pools, pelting headlong through the very dangers he had negotiated earlier with such elaborate care.

Feelers tugged at the skin on the back of his neck. Turkeya knew it was his own voice in his ears, shrieking.

Even from a distance of several hundred yards Alan's oraculum-enhanced senses heard Turkeya's cries, followed by a gurgling hiss, as if some unfortunate creature had been taken by one of the man-eaters. Ainé heard it too. She lifted a hand for silence, attempting to locate the commotion. Then Alan heard what sounded like a husky voice call out: "Humanshhh!"

With weapons drawn, Alan, Qwenqwo and the Kyra hurried deep into the darkness. "Turkeya! Turkeya!" They called out, peering and probing amongst the tangles of plants and dense undergrowth.

"I'm here—praise the powers!"

Turkeya fled out of the jungle, then whirled back to stare in the direction of frantic struggle.

"What is it?"

Turkeya shook his head. "I don't know. Some poor creature trapped by one of the man-eaters."

"Humanshhh!" They heard the husky cry again, from very close. They moved cautiously toward the source, where something large and gray and extremely angular was trapped in a huge bell-shaped circle of fronds, its body already coated with a gummy kind of glue that was in the process of plastering down its limbs. Alan stared at the ugliest face he had ever seen, the creature three-quarters freed by its own efforts, but still tethered where the jaws of the tendril were clamped onto one wing.

"It's a Garg!"

Qwenqwo laughed. "Looks like the man-eater has done our work for us!"

The creature's head was tossing frantically from side to side, those yellow eyes wildly staring. A ratchet-like sound, like the warning of a rattlesnake, came from its throat, followed by a series of clicks. It took Alan several moments to realize that it was trying to communicate. Its eyes turned slowly toward him.

"Killhhh!"

"What did it say?"

The Garg emitted that ratchet sound again, its eyes wide with desperation. "Humanshhh—killhhh!"

The voice didn't come from vocal cords, as normal speech. It came out of a throat perforated with a series of openings, like gills.

Turkeya held Alan's arm and tried to haul him back a pace. "What's the thing asking of us? Is it asking us to kill it?"

"Humanshhh . . . Humanshhh—killhhh."

"Must have been one of those who were spying on us," muttered the Kyra, who stood next to Alan, observing the struggle with disgust.

"Must have flown too close to the canopy," Qwenqwo agreed.

But it was making such a racket, it was sure to attract other Gargs, and the company was in no position for a pitched battle. Turkeya surprised them all by stepping up close to inspect the trapped enemy. "Maybe we should try to rescue it. Even a Garg deserves better than to be eaten alive by a plant."

Alan's nostrils were overwhelmed with a sour odor, like sweaty armpits. The smell of fear.

"What's that?" Turkeya exclaimed. "It's holding something in one of its feet."

"A rat!" Qwenqwo howled with laughter.

Alan frowned. "But that makes no sense—not if it was spying on us from above."

"Not unless it spotted a meal and risked a pounce." Qwenqwo was still chortling, while holding his nose against the stink.

Alan stared at the Garg, undecided. But the look on the Garg's face was one that even a human could understand. It was utter panic. He said, "Ainé—maybe we can interrogate it. Get useful information about the way through?"

The Kyra looked doubtfully back at him, but then she darted close to the man-eater and with a slash of her green-bladed sword struck the bulbous head from the tendril, then sprang back. The Garg, with the plant head still attached to its wing, was thrown clear of the violently thrashing tendril, which was as thick as the bough of a tree. A group of a dozen or so Shee had now arrived, bringing firebrands, and they burned what remained of the tendril head off the Garg's wing, little caring if the flames singed the wing in the process. Several Shee formed a circle around the Garg, with javelins directed against its throat, even as it moaned, tearing itself free of the flaming shards, then beating out a flame or two before attempting to stretch its wings out full, as if to take to the air. The sight would have been pathetic, like dealing with a huge injured bird, had it not been for the fact they were dealing with a Garg that was more than seven feet tall and equipped with fangs and claws. It was still soaked in the digestive juices of the man-eater and its injured left wing dripped a green liquid that must be Garg blood.

Alan noticed a new smell, and he observed an oily secretion exude from the Garg's skin before it tried flapping its enormous wings again. And then the Garg made a mewling noise through its dilated nostrils and more of the ratchet-like rattle in its throat.

"Well," grinned Turkeya, "at least we know that Gargs experience fear."

The young Garg stood on one splayed foot, then used the other to spread the oil over the parts of its skin that had been gummed up by the gluey secretions of the plant, and over the joint in his left wing where the bleeding had now stopped. Still hemmed in by the lances of the Shee it tried expanding its wings again, this time more successfully, each opening fully to the size of a small tent.

Then, after expanding and closing them several times, the Garg folded back its wings and then threw itself onto its knees before Alan, pulling back its head to an extreme degree so the grotesquely gilled throat was at his mercy.

"What's it up to now?" Alan exclaimed.

Qwenqwo was beside himself with laughter. "My guess is he's inviting you to cut his throat."

Alan was bewildered by the creature's behavior, the closed eyes, the neck so tensed by the craven posture that he could see the scales parting, as if making it easier for him to slice through it with a blade. "Maybe your life is all you have to offer. But we didn't save you from the man-eater just so we could do the job ourselves."

The Garg held its posture, if anything further tensing the blue-green skin of its throat, so the scales positively gaped.

Alan waved to the Shee to put their javelins down. "Hey—why don't you get the hell out of here? You're free! Don't you understand?"

Suddenly the Garg stood erect on its powerful legs, looming over him, and those wings, even though still folded, swept round, complete with inch-long talons, to either side of Turkeya's temples.

The Shee tensed javelins again, but the Kyra lifted a finger to observe what was happening. "I believe it wishes to communicate with the shaman."

"Well, I'm not sure I welcome the conversation," Turkeya muttered, "with an overgrown bat who talks in rattles and hisses."

"Arrhhhkkkuuusss!"

"Now that's a new rattle and hiss for us to puzzle over."

"Aarrhhkkkuusss!" It was not a sound that could have been faithfully reproduced by human vocal chords. Yet it carried a meaning that was clearly important to the Garg, who swept its left wing fully around so the talon finger could touch its breast and then laid it gently against Turkeya's breast.

"What?" Turkeya sneered. "Are we now exchanging hearts?"

"Iyezzz . . ." The Garg tapped his bony chest, then held out the rat. "Iyezzzz—aarrhhkkkuusss!"

"Iyezzz—if that's your name. Thank you for the generosity, which is no doubt very becoming, for a Garg. But you can keep your heart to yourself, and the same goes for the rat."

"Aarrhhkkkuusss!"

"You stupid Garg! Don't you understand what the oraculum-bearer has told you! You're free. Go fly back to your cave, or roost, or wherever you want to go."

"Iyezzz!" he touched Turkeya's chest again with that dangerous looking talon.

"Iyezzz, my foot?" Turkeya, tiring of this hopeless attempt at communication, drew his sword and he pressed the point against the scaly chest of the Garg. "Well, maybe you had a better idea when you offered us your throat."

Alan stepped forward. "Calm down, Turkeya. Here, let me see if I can communicate. There's a whole bunch of questions I'd like to ask it."

Alan placed himself between Turkeya and the Garg. He pointed to the oraculum in his brow. The Garg stared at the oraculum, then brought his gaze around to Alan's eyes. "I'm speaking to you through this crystal. My name is Alan Duval. The shaman, Turkeya, thinks that your name is Iyezzz. Is that true—is Iyezzz your name?"

The Garg looked at him with saucer eyes.

Alan attempted the same explanation all over again.

The Garg stared back at him. Then he blinked several times.

"Perhaps," murmured the Kyra, "no communication is possible."

"No!" It was Mo who contradicted her. "I saw something in him change. I think he understood Alan. It must be scary to hear somebody you think of as utterly alien suddenly talk to you inside your head."

"Okay, Mo. Then I'll try a different approach." Alan pointed to his brow. Then he made a gesture, as if to demonstrate how he was addressing his words through it. "Do you know who I am?"

The young Garg fell onto his knees once more. Reaching down with a wing talon, he pried free a cylinder of ivory out of a scaly pouch in the skin of an ankle and placed it, with a reverential bow, on the ground at Alan's feet.

"You are Duval—bearer of the Oraculum of the First Power. My prayers are answered. I thank the gods of ocean and air for this opportunity of meeting with you."

The clarity of the communication took Alan by surprise. He made no attempt to pick up the cylinder of bone.

"We're communicating. But I don't really understand what you're saying. Let's try a different tack. Is your name Iyezzz?"

"I am Iyezzz."

"Okay—Iyezzz. So can you explain to me again? What does this word, Aarrhhkkkuusss, mean?"

"It means 'sacred.' This valley, which you desecrate with your presence, is sacred to the Eyrie People. Our Valley of the Spirits."

"Heck! Are you saying that this is some kind of graveyard—where you Gargs bury your dead?"

"Our dead—yeshhh! But not to bury."

Alan stared at the kneeling Garg, his mind racing. It suggested a very different reason for Gargs to be wheeling overhead. He also recalled what Turkeya had pointed out. The strange finding of the huge proliferation of the man-eaters in this place, where there was so little food . . .

"These plants—and the shadow creatures? They dispose of your dead?"

"They consume the flesh so the spirit may be freed."

"Yet you're here? You're trespassing in this place of the dead?"

"Iyezzz comes to the Valley of the Spirits to find Duvalhhh the slayer."

Alan needed a moment or two to digest that. "What are you saying? You came here just to find me?"

"I bring the sacred scroll."

Alan stared at the cylinder of ivory still lying on the ground.

"There is little time for explanation. Greeneyes has broken free of the Witch's Tower. The Great Witch hunts far and wide for her."

"Greeneyes? Are you talking about my friend, Kate?"

"Greeneyes—also oraculum-bearer. Oraculum of life, of rebirth. Greeneyes flees the Tower of Bones. She has healed the lands where there was no life."

Alan blinked, unable to credit what he was hearing. "Now, hold on a minute! That's the real reason you're here? It's because of Kate? You're telling me that Kate has escaped from the Witch?"

The Garg exhaled, then retracted his eyelids so his eyes appeared to protrude from his head, as if to indicate incredulity. "Duvalhhh sees. Our people do not attack. I, Iyezzz-I-Noor, son of Zelnesakkk, King of the Eyrie People, have come here to help you save Greeneyes."

"What? You're saying you want to help us?"

"I speak the truth. I have risked all to find new hope in the Valley of the Spirits. Will you not accept the scroll—make treaty?"

Alan picked up the cylinder of ivory off the mossy ground, then unrolled it into a small, rectangular plaque. He gazed, bewildered, at what turned out to be carvings and hieroglyphs that looked exceedingly old.

"What is it?"

"A blessed promise—sacred to our people. It was carved long ago from the tooth of a god, a fire-breather who sailed the wind."

Alan let Ainé and Qwenqwo see the unrolled plaque. None of them could read the hieroglyphs but all could readily see the winged shape that occupied the central area of the sheaved panel.

"It looks like a dragon."

The young Garg bowed, intoning a name, singing rather than speaking it aloud: "'Qwenuncqweqwatenzian-Phaetentiatzen.' Great god—ruler of air and water. One who is venerated above all by the Eyrie People."

Alan looked from the Kyra to Qwenqwo, as if hoping one or other of them could enlighten him. But neither did. "Tell me about Kate—Greeneyes! It was you, the Gargs, who took her prisoner."

"The Great Witch ordered us to do so. We did not know the importance of Greeneyes—she with hair of flame. We brought her here, to the Tower of Bones. We bear the responsibility of her capture, of her becoming a prisoner of the Great Witch. Only now, when she has broken free of the Witch's Tower, do we understand her purpose."

"You're sure about this? You're really talking about Kate?"

"Truly, she had fled the Tower. The Witch is hunting for her, with all of her wraiths and wolves."

"Do you know where she is? Can you take me to her?"

"I know not where she is. Only that she has escaped and now she greens the wasted lands. Such power does she bear, she has challenged the Great Witch in her Tower of Bones."

"What do you mean?"

"Why do you think the Gargs do not attack you? Why will you not listen to me? Am I not here to help you?"

Alan looked from Qwenqwo to Ainé in bewilderment. "How far are we from the Tower of Bones?"

"One day, perhaps two, as I might travel. But you cannot enter the valley of the Tower from this place. Go there unprepared and you will surely be destroyed."

"But I have to confront the Witch—that's why I'm here."

"I have come here to help you."

Alan shook his head. How could he trust a Garg?

"There is no time. The wolves are combing every sanctuary and crevice. If they find Greeneyes, they will killhhh her."

"Then what are we to do?"

"My father, King Zelnesakkk, has been summoned by the Momu. Greeneyes is under the protection of the Cill, who conceal her whereabouts from the Witch. The Momu has wisdom-that-was from ancient times. She calls for a meeting with my father. I must take you there—to the meeting of the Momu and the King, in the City of the Ancients."

Alan's heartbeat had risen into his throat. The air in his lungs had thickened so he could hardly breathe.

"This meeting—Kate will be there?"

"Greeneyes is the purpose of the meeting. The Cill and the Gargs, once allies, have long been mortal enemies. Only Greeneyes—she who restores life to the tormented lands—makes possible such a reconciliation."

"You're telling me you'll take me to meet Kate?"

Iyezzz reared to his full height and averted his head to an awkward angle, retracting his eyelids, with that eye-protruding gesture, but this time it appeared more a parody of honor rather than anything else.

"I will lead you there."

RESURRECTION

You think you understand pain and then you are made to think again. Physical pain, the pain of a blow—that was easy. Psychological pain was worse. To be cast down into a dark basement as a child, to be made to withstand the cold and the dark, was more hurtful than a blow. Still it was bearable. But spiritual pain, the pain that came from non-being—the pain of being excluded from the real world—that was unbearable. Yet you had no choice other than to bear it. Spiritual pain was what Mark Grimstone had been struggling with. That unbearable pain was what he had been forced to come to terms with, and through understanding to try to overcome, but in spite of every effort on his part it triumphed.

I want to be whole again. I want to live in this world—
any world.

The other voice said: *Be, then!*

What you say is mere words.

No, my love, words are a part of being.

In his frustration he wanted to put his face into his hands and weep. But he had neither face nor hands to weep into.

Shit!

Fight back against it!

I don't know how to.

I believe in you.

Easy to say!

I am Nantosueta—Queen of Ossierel.

I know who you are. But I'm beginning to think that you too are just words—words I'm conjuring up inside my head.

I'm real. You are not alone.

But was it true?

He recalled climbing to the top of the Rath on Ossierel, entering the ruined buildings at the very summit. It had been Kate who had sensed the true meaning of the final chamber with the stellate window. Kate had climbed up to the window and held her crystal against it, causing images to take life within the sparkle of light. That was when Mark had first seen her, fallen in love with her, the dark-haired girl who laughed as she pirouetted among the slender trunks of sapling trees. She had seemed so full of life—of gaiety—as she danced forward to take his hand.

Nan!

Then, as now, powerful feelings coursed through him.

Whether he was dead or not he was capable of feeling. He was altogether capable of rage, despair. Maybe he should be able to find strength in that, but it was incredibly hard to do so. There was a sense, a hope, that something might come from those feelings, if only he knew how to bring it about. He was prepared to try anything. But the problem was, nothing worked.

I've been reduced to nothing. And yet I can kid myself that I really exist. One thing's for sure—if I exist it's in a place that's the opposite of reality. What if I'm a non-being in a world of nowhere?

He couldn't stop himself from asking the vile question that had haunted him since Ossierel: *Nan! Don't you wonder if we're both dead?*

If so, what then is death?

What do you mean?

Are we not holding a conversation?

Maybe the dead can talk to one another?

My question remains. What then is the difference between life and death?

He thought about that. *Maybe there's no absolute difference? Maybe there's existence beyond life? Maybe non-being is a kind of bloody punishment?*

Only the irony is that there is no blood to shed!

He laughed—or at least he imagined he laughed, in his mind. He felt angry. Didn't that mean that he could feel as well as think? Shit—what did he know? He was just kidding himself with wishful thinking.

So it was that things went around and around in Mark's mind. The lessons of Dromenon were very hard lessons and it had taken him quite a while to learn them. He still thought himself dead. He had experienced the moment of death when he was subsumed by the Third Power. Yet Nan didn't agree. Maybe she was right. How could he still think as clearly as this if he were dead? For your mind to think your brain had to be alive. Or at least so he always had believed. How could his mind function if his brain was dead? Thinking like this was driving him out of his mind—whatever mind he had to relinquish. And yet he seemed perfectly able to think. *I think—therefore I am!* The French philosopher, Descartes, had said that. *Well, here I am, thinking some pretty crazy thoughts. So I am—I exist. And existence was another word for being alive.* But of course this just took him back to the circular argument about words and being.

What if you're right, Nan? Where do we go from here?

First there is faith. You discover a way to believe. And then you think through the next step from belief to confirmation.

It sounded like some religious mantra. But still he thought about her words. Somehow—logically—he wanted to believe her. He so desperately wanted to be alive. Even if he was a bit flaky on faith he so wanted to move in the direction of confirmation. How could he find substance out of the nothing that was his existence, out of the world he now inhabited—a no-place in which there was no solid form, no sense of time or of substance—a great empty nothingness?

Hey—I'm so glad you're here with me. I don't think I could bear it alone.

I was compelled to bear it alone for a very long time.

Only two thousand years!

Yours is a cruel wit.

But you like me for it.

Hmmm!

But though he joked about it, it was comforting to him just to know that Nan was with him, sharing the nothingness. And the strange thing was that he had sensed her from time to time, a feeling of something beyond words, like the feathery touch of a butterfly's wings against his skin. Two thousand years of solitary confinement in the white nothingness! He didn't know how she had remained sane. There was great strength in her. Great courage—a will of iron. Just like Qwenqwo thought he had a heart of iron. He thought about what she had said . . .

Faith first—then confirmation.

And the strangest thing, the most extraordinary thing, was the fact that an idea had just come into his head. An idea that was probably foolish. It was a very simple idea once he had time to think it through.

The whiteness was a blank page on which he must construct his own world, the materialization of his ideas—a world he must assemble, piece by piece, using nothing more than the power of his imagination.

It seemed utterly insane. But still he thought about it. And the next step—an idea that came and went, but kept on popping up in his desperate mind—was to imagine that he was standing on a beach of fine, white sand. It hardly seemed anything clever or difficult to imagine. But once he got the hang of it, he clung to it. Then he began to add to it, step by step. He could easily imagine himself standing on that beach, turning about himself, observing the fine white sand disappearing into the distance. That was the first construction—the beginning of his brave new world. And now he found he could let it go and yet find his way back to it without a problem. He could make it appear or disappear at his whim.

Like a dream, he thought.

Only this was a perfectly controllable dream.

Then he dreamed some more. He imagined how it would feel to stand there in the middle of the white beach. He felt the sandiness under his feet. He took a few steps, walking along the beach and, looking back, he saw the trail of his own footprints appear. He had imagined the footprints into being. From then on, with every step, his footprints automatically came into being behind him.

A step at a time, he thought, triumphantly.

Now he had to explain it to Nan. To explain that she had to do the same. She had to imagine herself standing on, and then walking over, the same white sandy beach.

She did so. *What now?*

I'm going to imagine you here, beside me, on the beach.

How will you do this?

I'll remember you, how you looked when I first met you.

He imagined her in his mind, and then he dreamed her into being. Nantosueta, the girl-queen of Ossierel. He had no difficulty in dreaming her up because he remembered her with a perfect clarity. And immediately she was there, standing beside him exactly as he remembered her, dressed in a white linen gown and sandals, her chocolate-brown eyes, her hair a gleaming cataract of blue-black, vivacious, playful—lovely.

Now, he said, *you have to remember me too. You have to feel the beach under your feet. And then you have to see me here, standing beside you.*

I see you.

I want us to walk, together, over the white sand.

Almost immediately, as if the thought excited her as much as it did him, they were together, a shared imagination, their figures side by side, trailing two pairs of footprints, Nan's smaller than his own . . . And then, as if equally playful, they were running together, spinning around in gleeful circles, Nan's footprints clearly visible in the white sand in their wake, entwining with his own.

Are we real?

Her voice sounded slightly breathless, but still uncertain.

We're as real as we can imagine.

Nan—the image he held of her in his mind—began to probe his image more closely in her memory. He helped her: *I'm touching the skin of your face, your left cheek, with my right hand—the back of my fingers.*

She reached up as if to discover his hand against her face. *I . . . I almost feel your touch. Mark, I almost feel you!*

I've had another thought. How we could make it more real.

Tell me!

Our oracula—we should be able to link them together. We should be able to read one another's thoughts even as we think them.

If only it were possible.

It has to be possible. We did it once—at Ossierel. When you brought us into some kind of mental, and physical, union.

Her face had turned to look into his own. He gazed down into her brown eyes, knowing that she must be looking back up into his blue eyes—and deeper, much deeper, into his mind. He felt it happen, as she must be feeling it. Their minds were coming together again, in the deepest, most intimate, consummation. He should be frightened. In real life, when it actually happened, he had been dying. At the same time his heart had been beating too fast, thready and pattering, missing beats . . . And now he felt his heart doing exactly that again. He felt his head go light, his mouth go dry.

Next to her loveliness he felt angular and awkward. She was soft and rounded, delicate, vulnerable, the opposite of how he saw himself. She was gazing up at him, her brown eyes filling up with tears.

Nan, he murmured, as if savoring her name on his tongue.

We just have to imagine it—whatever we want to happen.

And through the union of the oracula we make it so, together.

He was wearing his black leather jacket over the clumsy Olhyiu furs. She sniffed at his leather jacket, as if savoring the smell of it. *What do the girls of my age wear in your world—the girls who are free of mind and spirit?*

Wow! Now there's a question.

He took Kate as his example. Blue jeans, sneakers, a turquoise sweater. *Can you see what I am seeing?*

Within moments she was wearing Kate's clothes.

It feels strange—such alien clothes—yet they look so comfortable! Do you like the appearance of such pantaloons on me?

He chuckled. *We call them jeans. And besides—you weren't so bad wearing the skin-hugging gown.*

Wicked boy!

I wish!

They laughed in unison.

Then she ran through the sand and he ran after her. Their tracks followed them, without either of them having to think about it. When he caught her, he imagined hugging her, causing her to overbalance, so they tumbled down onto the sand.

He kissed her, gently, on the lips. *A present, fit for a queen!*

Her voice was suspicious. *What is it?*

I give you the ocean.

They gazed, enraptured, out at the sea, at the thundering of breakers against the white sand, feeling the incoming breeze on their faces, smelling the brine in their nostrils.

Their imaginations were working together in a creative symbiosis. She whispered, against his shoulder: *It's so lovely. Could this possibly become real?*

It's as real as we imagine it to be.

I want it to be real. To feel you close, against me.

I want that too.

But we're not here. We cannot be.

He saw the desperation, the need for him, in her eyes. She whispered her longing: *If only our imaginations were but powerful enough.*

If only.

In his mind he squeezed her tight as they gazed out into the ocean.

Snakoil Kawkaw had been out and about. He was returning with interesting news. But for the moment he kept it to himself, watching the Preceptress in her daily veneration of the sigil. Although he knew little about the inner workings of the Tyrant's religious cult, he knew enough to know that Preceptresses were exceedingly rare among the Tyrant's followers. He also knew that they were considered even more malicious and dangerous than Preceptors. And that made his position here tenuous, to say the least. She would think nothing of slicing a blade through his throat while he slept. And even in a straight fight, knife for knife, he wouldn't bet on his own survival against that dagger with the twisted blade and the Tyrant's sigil aglitter in the hilt. What momentous service, he wondered, could she have performed for such a demanding master to be elevated to the rank of fanatical spiritual adviser? When he had been bold enough to ask her what happened to the real soup ladler, she had gazed down lovingly, touched the sharp tip of the poisoned blade. "Craves their blood, don't you, my lovely!"

He decided it was time he made himself seem useful. "At last, formidable lady, we have intelligence."

Her red-veined eyes shook themselves free of their obsequious veneration to fix on his.

"This army, which we are bound to subvert, will not be following their masters and mistresses into the swamps."

"What nonsense is this?"

"A message has been conveyed, through what agency, I don't know or care—perhaps the wind from the Kyra's own backside—but conveyed it was. Her forces, gathered here in their tens of thousands, are playacting at following the expeditionary force. They have no intention of advancing through the swamplands."

"But the expeditionary band, even with the brat and his oraculum, wouldn't dare to confront the Witch on their own!"

"Why knows what folly they are capable of."

"The brat alone, even with his power, would hardly be a match for Olc. And there is more—a rising power—that would scatter a hundred thousand of the witch-warriors, aye, and ten times more."

"What power is that?"

"A power that is not for your hairy ears, bear-man!"

Spit rose in his throat at the insult. But he was prudent enough to hide it. "I but serve. Yet none can deceive a deceiver. Certainly not Siam the Stupid and his fish-gutters. And it is evident from my spying that there is a deception in the air."

"How can you be sure?"

"Because I marked the food."

"Explain yourself."

"The food they appear to be ferrying to the chasm above the swamps. I noticed that the bearers looked as exhausted on their return as when they set out for the chasm. So I marked some of the haunches of beef and the sacks of flour."

"And?"

"As it went out, so has it come back. The marked haunches and full sacks are returned, untouched, in the quartermaster's stores."

"Which tells you?"

"They are merely circulating the food, forward and back. Thus do they give the impression of an army about to march."

"When in fact they have been commanded to stand down?"

"Indeed."

Her eyes narrowed, savoring the thought. "If so, their mission is surely lost. The brat will die." She hesitated. "You could be mistaken?"

"I'm certain."

Kawkaw wondered if somehow, in a way as yet not altogether clear to him, he could take advantage of such happenstance.

"We cannot risk a second failure. You must test it again."

"I have already tested it twice. I assure you that the witch warriors are standing down. The expeditionary band is on its own."

The Preceptress's eyes were suddenly aglitter. She was pushing him toward the entrance flap of the tent, hissing between her teeth: "Get out!"

"At once, noble lady!"

He saved his ear-to-ear grin until he was out of her sight. Had he not seen how the dagger was already clutched in her hands? And had he not read in that look in her eyes that she was about to use it to impart this new, and valuable, information? What a precious discovery was this, which he had made through the intimacy of sharing the single tiny tent with the Preceptress—that through the dagger with its sigil-embossed handle and its black, pitted, spiral blade, she had a line of communication direct to the foulness that was her Master!

Such knowledge might prove useful.

FEARS AND SUSPICIONS

AN EXHAUSTED TURKEYA HID IN THE CANOPY OF one of the twisted trees and wept for his cousin and childhood friend Kataba, who had died in the night, killed by his own hand because he knew he was slowing their progress. Turkeya blamed himself. Had he not insisted on joining the expeditionary force, in spite of his father's reservations, and had that not resulted in his father insisting that Kataba should protect him—loyal Kataba, a born warrior, with a heart of oak—his cousin would still be alive. Turkeya grieved for Kataba, up here, where no one could witness his weeping. And he wept just a little for himself also, for the fact that his role as guide had been supplanted by the Garg, who claimed to be the son of the King, and whose posturing and arrogance should have warned Alan that he was not to be trusted.

Iyezzz, he called himself, which sounded if not rat-like, then surely serpent-like, and one very sly and overgrown serpent he was in spite of the fact he had helped Turkeya find the venom balm that had enabled him to treat Kataba, and at the very least lessen the inflammation that was consuming his leg. It was of small comfort that this treatment had enabled the Shee to construct a bier and carry Kataba this far, although this blessing had further delayed their progress and eventually provoked Kataba to take his own life in the dark of night.

Turkeya was feeling guilty, and on more than one account. He blamed himself for the death of Kataba. He also suspected that he was being overly suspicious about the Garg, but he couldn't help the way he felt about him. He didn't want to come down out of the tree into a camp that was rife with fear and paranoia. Through eyes dimmed by tears he stared around himself at the place the Garg led them to, a sheer cliff face within the foothills of a lofty range of mountains. What really awaited them here? The Garg had mentioned a City of the Ancients. But who in his right mind would trust such a creature? Turkeya had no faith in a giant bat that, whenever he grew frightened, covered his skin with an oil that stank. He couldn't get used to the fact that the Garg's eyes glowed—truly glowed like a forest wisp—in the dark. He would find himself squinting at

Iyezzz when he wasn't aware of it, taking a good look at those vicious-looking talons on his feet and the overlapping canine teeth poking out of his gaping maw. Whatever the truth of it, the Garg was excited by the prospect of what lay ahead, and that was enough to make Turkeya even more suspicious.

Turkeya wiped his eyes with the backs of his hands, matting the fur with his tears. The truth was he no longer knew what to think up here in the canopy, high above the ground. Was he being unfair to the Garg? Was he being overly mistrustful—he, the shaman, who was supposed to empathize with all manner of creatures? But this place, and the beings that populated it, so oppressed him in heart and spirit that he was in danger of losing his faith in nature.

He was familiar with forests, of winter greens or leaffall. He knew the names of most of the plants and trees in his homeland, the times of their budding and flowering in the spring, and the bounty of leaf, nut and fruit. But these plants and trees were not bountiful at all. These were alien to sight and scent and to the shaman's deepest instinct. The boughs were purplish or deep blue, with limey spatters of spots—colors and patterns Turkeya associated more with toadstools than trees. And they did not narrow to a fine lace of twigs, carrying leaves of green, but twisted and turned in amongst themselves, forming a labyrinth in which one expected danger at every step. There was a heavy smell too, a cloying pungency that thickened in the night, so that when the Kyra allowed them a few hours of sleep they breathed in a darkness of toxic aromas.

He empathized with nothing here.

The fact that he—it—the Garg—seems comfortable here, why it's all the more ominous and perfidious!

On occasion, Turkeya had caught him sucking at stubby protrusions of a pinkish color on certain of the trees. Turkeya had been disgusted to see him licking the traces of the sticky juice that stained his muzzle-like mouth. All of this sucking and licking he went about with a relish that made Turkeya think back to the rat clenched in the Garg's foot when they had found him trapped by the man-eater. And it had made Turkeya feel physically sick when Iyezzz had opened his eyes wide and, with that serpent-like sinewy movement of his long thin body, indicated that Turkeya should copy him and suck at the nipple-like things.

"Ugh!" Even now, with the memory, Turkeya couldn't help but grimace.

"Hsst—shaman!" The Kyra's voice was calling him down out of the canopy, her cat-like face peering up at him through the twisted boughs.

When Turkeya descended he found the company was examining strange carvings in upstanding rocks standing on either side of the entrance to a tunnel. The carvings were of ungodly figures, with staring eyes and bared fangs.

"Surely," the Kyra murmured, "these are intended as a warning."

Alan called up the young Garg, asking the meaning of these totems.

"Kwatekkk!"

"What does this mean?"

"Kwatekkk—it means entrance is forbidden. By order of Mahteman—high shaman to the King."

"Forbidden? Like under pain of death?"

"Yeshhh."

When Alan translated for the others, there was a disquieted murmuring, even among the Shee.

"Yet this is where you're leading us?"

"Aarrhhkkkuusss!"

Alan recognized the expression from when they had first met the Garg. "What? The way is forbidden—because it's sacred?"

"Aarrhhkkkuusss—yeshhh!"

"But it is the only way that will take us to the meeting—to Kate?"

"To the Sacred Pool—the City of the Ancients!"

"So, if we enter the tunnel, our lives will be in danger! But we have no option if we are to meet the Momu—and Kate?"

"Yeshhh!"

Alan shook his head. He paused to talk it over with Ainé and Qwenqwo. Turkeya studied the Garg for the slightest suggestion of treachery. If the shaman was no longer their guide, he still felt responsible for the safety of his friends. He muttered: "Does he think we're just going to believe everything he tells us? I don't trust him one bit. I sense that he has ideas of his own, things he is failing to tell us."

All of a sudden there was a distant howling in the forest. It was followed by gong-like sounds that sounded like drums.

"Gargs!" the Kyra hissed.

"Gargs on the ground," Turkeya cautioned, with no pretense of being friendly.

Alan confronted Iyezzz. "What does that mean? You told us the Gargs were withholding attack."

"They have assumed that we threaten the King."

"Our shaman thinks you're leading us into a trap."

Turkeya looked up into those yellow eyes and saw there a mixture of cunning and deceit. He snorted with disbelief when the Garg insisted, "Iyezzz does not lead you into a trap."

Alan pressed him: "Have you ever been to this meeting place before?"

"Never!" The ugly head of the Garg was shaking solemnly from side to side, and the solemnity was also there in the low sort of purring rattle behind his voice. "Iyezzz would not normally enter here!"

Alan glanced at Qwenqwo, whose brow was deeply furrowed, not knowing what to make of the situation. They were all exhausted from lack of sleep. And the deaths of Llediana and the two Aides had made them jumpy and suspicious.

"So why would you dare to go there now?"

"Because it is where the Momu will be. She has called the meeting with my father at the Sacred Pool in the City of the Ancients. No meeting such as this has happened in a thousand years. Forbidden or not, I must be there."

Qwenqwo squeezed forward, forcing himself between Alan and the Garg. "I trust the creature no more than the shaman. Have a care, Mage Lord!"

The drumming had started up again, causing the Garg's ears to tense, their membranes veined like spiders' webs. His face turned skywards and his eyes grew even wider, his wing-talon directed upward. "The drums say that the spywings have your scent. You cannot hide from them. We must go."

"Mo?"

"I believe him. But you must decide for yourself, Alan. You must trust to your own instincts."

Alan hesitated, looking assessingly into the mouth of the tunnel, then back into the eyes of the young Garg. "There's something else—some reason of your own why you want to be there?"

The young Garg sniffed through those gaping nostrils, as if he had perhaps said more than he had intended. "The King and the high shaman, Mahteman, will be there." There was a change in the Garg's tone, a grimace about his mouth, when he used the name, Mahteman, that suggested a background anxiety or distaste. "They, alone, will hear the counsel of the Momu."

"Why would this worry you?"

Iyezzz stood erect, his nostrils twitching, and in speaking he spread open his wings, as if to embrace the entire company. "My father is old—and Mahteman older still. Their views will be conservative. Service to the Great Witch is deeply ingrained in that generation. Such subservience must be brought to an end. I, Prince Iyezzz-I-Noor, must be present—must be allowed to speak."

"Why is this meeting so important to you?"

"The Momu will be accompanied by your friend, Greeneyes. She has the power to heal the wounded land."

Alan nodded, swallowing against a dry throat. He was beginning to understand what was really going on. This was some kind of rebellion. If so, Iyezzz was playing a dangerous game. But if Iyezzz meant what he said about ending the Garg's alliance with the Great Witch, it was a game that might also suit their purpose.

"You know that I'll be watching you. If you betray us, I'll kill you."

The young Garg stood haughtily erect, towering over all but the Shee. "If I fail on my mission my father, the King himself will killhhh me."

Ainé, assuming a threat to Alan, pressed her tall frame between Alan and the Garg, as tall as each other, each too proud to be afraid. The Kyra had her hand poised on the hilt of her sword.

"In my world we have legends that speak not of the City of the Ancients but of the City of the Dead. How do we know that you are not leading us into a trap?"

"Killhhh me then, if you will not trust me!"

But even as the Garg and the Shee faced one another in an edgy confrontation, a renewed howling sounded from all around them in the forest.

"Quickly! Before it is too late! The warriors will not follow us into the forbidden labyrinths."

AN IMPORTANT JOURNEY

A NOISY TRUMPETING ROUSED KATE FROM A REST-
ful sleep. She was surprised to find herself back in the
sea-urchin chamber, with its walls glowing with light.
Pulling the bedcovers over her face, she willed herself
back into the dream-like state she had woken from, her
mind serene in . . . a kind of revelation. She had spent
many hours in the company of the Momu, during which
she had been introduced to mysteries of being that were
deeper than mere images, or words, or even feelings. She
had experienced a transcendent level of communication, something deeply intimate, enabled by that wonderful language . . . and oneness . . . that thrilling level of
communication that seemed to derive from music. Even
now the memory of it was already fading and she didn't
want to lose it by waking. Was this what Granny Dew

had intended? Had she directed her not only to meeting with the dragon, Driftwood, but also—maybe even primarily—to the Momu?

You will discover one both ancient and wise enough to understand your need . . . But now she asked herself: *But what does that mean?*

Was it possible that through this crystal in her brow, she had acquired an ability to communicate on a more complex level? Kate wasn't altogether sure. She had no memory of being brought back to her chamber from the cave of the Momu and yet it felt as if her mind had expanded to embrace some important knowledge. As if she had, during the time they had communicated, absorbed a new level of understanding of the burden and power that had been placed on her shoulders.

It was at once exhilarating and terrifying.

She had also realized something vital to the survival of the Cill and their lovely underwater city. The Momu was dying. It was clear that her time was very limited. And this presented Kate with a dilemma.

A new Momu, young and vigorous, must be born. But before ever the Momu could give birth to her successor, she herself had to rise from her despair. And to do this she must have the blessing of hope. Hope for the future of her people so that her successor could bring the joy of new life into the world.

All of this Kate recalled before she drifted away again into a doze of contentment only to be woken for a second time by the trumpeting of conch shells. But this time she knew what it signified—an alarm sounding out throughout the whole of Ulla Quemar. Then she heard many voices answer the call, a cacophony of cries, musical, as would be expected of the Cill, but also strident and alien, like an orchestra tuning up for some grand performance in this wonderful city of beauty and peace. Even as she sat up in her bed the handmaidens arrived into her chamber, all of a bustle. They brought food, which they placed on a table before the window. But Kate was too excited even to think of eating it.

They showed her some strange new clothes. They clearly intended to dress Kate in what looked like a body-hugging material of a glistening, emerald sheen.

She was still attempting to shake the sluggishness of sleep from her mind. "What's happening?"

"The Momu waits. Greeneyes must make ready. She will accompany the Momu on her historic journey."

"What journey?"

"Why—to counsel the Garg King, Zelnesakkk, in the City of the Ancients!"

Kate was too astonished to do anything other than to allow the handmaidens to wash her down from head to foot and then dress her, but all the while a thrill of alarm coursed through her. And with it, the oraculum flared in her brow, the most powerful flare she had felt since Granny Dew had implanted the crystal, suffusing her with an overwhelming wave of power that made her feel giddy. The chamber glowed with a crackling green lightning that coursed, like static electricity, over the walls and ceiling. The handmaidens stepped back a pace, astonished.

"It's all right! It won't harm you," Kate attempted to calm them. But deep down she felt something changing within her. Somehow, as a result of her meeting with the Momu, her control over her oraculum appeared to be growing.

But there was no time to think about it. The handmaidens were hurrying her out of the chamber to where Shaami was waiting with an honor guard of six warriors. He took Kate's hands in his, his turquoise eyes wide with excitement.

"Shaami—what's happening?"

"For the first time in a thousand years the Momu is leaving Ulla Quemar. She has signaled her need for communion with the Garg King. There will be a Grand Council. You must accompany the Momu to the City of the Ancients."

As they made their way down the gentle slope toward the waterfront, it seemed that the entire population was heading in the same direction. And more warriors. Kate saw the fearsome shapes of the Cill fighters everywhere. They were marshaling the crowds lining the streets, their strange medley of weapons glinting in the morning light.

"Are the Cill going to war?"

"I hope not. But the Momu, and Greeneyes too, must be protected on their important journey."

"But how? You can't let the Gargs know about Ulla Quemar. And the Momu told me she can only travel in water."

"Yes."

"I don't understand."

"All will be revealed."

Thousands of Cill crowded the waterfront. Where Kate had never known the Cill to wear clothes of any sort, today they were dressed in diaphanous hooded gowns—silk, like the clothes they had manufactured for Kate, and dyed in a wide variety of pastel colors. Given her conversation with the Momu, Kate couldn't help but notice the absence of children. The Momu arrived at the waterfront only minutes after Kate herself, carried in a palanquin by four burly warriors, her elegant head towering above even the tallest warrior as she alighted, then turning to bestow a blessing on the population.

The warriors formed into ranks. A column of conch-trumpeters sounded out another salute. The army, as one, came to attention before the majesty of the Momu. Even as Kate's eyes scanned the waterfront, searching for any means of transport for the coming journey, the crowds began to chant a farewell in that spine-tingling counterpoint, as if it were a melodious harmony under the control of a master conductor. When it was finished the Momu stood erect, the crystal around her neck pulsating brightly, her right hand gesturing an elegant acknowledgment of their deference and love for her. Then she inclined her head to speak softly to Kate as the bustle recommenced about them. "I thank the powers I lived to see this day."

Kate sensed the importance of what the Momu was intimating.

"I hope our meeting was more blessing than confrontation?"

Kate nodded. "I . . . I learned something important from you. I feel more confident in what's expected of me."

The Momu bowed her head. "My dearest Greeneyes, we both know the dangers you will face when you confront the Tower of Bones. You will need that confidence if you are to have any chance of succeeding."

At the mention of the Tower, Kate's fears resurfaced, though she tried to hold them back. "I'm not used to confrontation—to fighting."

"Yet will you promise me that you will not allow your understandable fear of the Great Witch to deter you?"

"No—I promise you that I won't."

"It is your strength that by nature you are gentle. But gentleness alone will not prevail against the enemy you face. Even war, in all of its horror, is an inadequate term for the nature of the confrontation that is imminent."

Kate took a deep breath.

The Momu reached out and held Kate's shoulders. "Remember that you bear the Oraculum of the Second

Power of the Holy Trídédana. A goddess empowers you. Be not afraid to invoke her help."

"I wish I could say that I'm not afraid. But I'll still fight the Witch. I'll fight her with all the power that I possess."

"Well said!"

"But I don't understand what's happening here. Why is it so important—this meeting with the Gargs?"

The Momu performed one of those rapid oscillations of her silver pupils, as if the change of subject evoked her own fears.

"It is important that we meet with Zelnesakkk, King of the Eyrie People."

Kate hesitated for a moment. It seemed so odd to hear the Gargs referred to as people. "But they're your enemies. Why would you risk leaving Ulla Quemar to talk with your enemies?"

"None, not even the King, would break the covenant of a Grand Council. Even through war, and the horrors of all that has afflicted these wasted lands, there are places that yet hold the sacred promises of history. Meet we must. Wars are won by the considerations and preparations that are made in advance. The Gargs have allied themselves to the Great Witch for many thousands of years. Yet precious little have they received in return, other than craven survival. They can but resent her enslavement. And who better than they will know her defenses."

"You think the Gargs will help us?"

"I will appeal to our common legacy of suffering as well as to their pride—and, it must be said, to their brave hearts in battle."

The Momu was interrupted by a loud splashing coming from the water behind them. The crowds cheered. Kate turned around to see something enormous, a gigantic greenish-yellow cylinder, rising out of the surf. She glanced toward Shaami, who was watching her, eyes agape, from outside the immediate protection of a ring of warriors.

Kate cried out in astonishment: "A sunstealer!"

She looked down in realization at her clothes, guessing that they were water resistant and heat conserving, like a finely woven wet suit. She was to be ferried to meet the King of the Gargs inside a giant plant-animal.

"It is natural," said the Momu, "for a land-born to fear the mother ocean. Even for my ancient heart it will be a testing experience to journey far from my beloved Ulla Quemar. Yet be assured that the globe of the sunstealer is resilient and the ocean its element. You will be protected within by our stoutest warriors."

The Momu allowed herself to be lifted aloft by four of the warriors and then carried into the sweeping tide. Kate was still dumbstruck with shock as the warriors waded out until the surf was up to their waists, then laid the Momu down with a perfect coordination into the gentle tide.

"Come, now!"

Kate's eyes widened as the arrays of feather-like gills became upstanding on the head of the Momu, and her long streamlined shape slid into the ocean, leaving scarcely a ripple on the surface.

THE CITY OF THE ANCIENTS

As far as Alan could see the tunnel was entirely natural, lined with stone and earth. Leggy spiders with speckled bodies hesitated, as if considering whether the intruders represented food or danger, often holding their ground up to the last minute, as if they were the rightful owners here and intent on denying them passage, before scuttling into the many deep cracks and crevices. A hoary dust coated everything and their nostrils were filled with the smell of decay.

They were walking down a steep slope. After half an hour of continuous descent he was convinced that they must be back to the level of the forest floor, or more likely the roots of the mountain.

They emerged into a vast chamber in which their feet left impressions in what seemed to be the undisturbed dust of ages. Exploring the chamber in the rubicund light of his oraculum, Alan could see no limits to its distant extents, though its walls and high ceiling were lumpy and distorted, with gigantic knobs and protrusions breaking up the space into a semblance of streets and squares, yet too organic in shape and too enormous in size to be ancestral to any population of Tír today.

Iyezzz was gazing about himself, gibbering with excitement, his eyes reflecting the light like torches.

From the floor immense needle-shaped stalagmites formed a crescent, like some triumphal arcade they were obliged to pass through. Alan sensed power or energy about the guardian stones, and so did Ainé. When Iyezzz reached out, as if to touch one of them, the Kyra leaped forward and restrained the Garg's wrist. Her green-glowing sword blade was suddenly pressed up tight against Iyezzz's throat.

"Easy!" Alan put his hand to restrain her. But Qwenqwo had also stepped forward and his dagger was also pressed against the Garg's ribs.

"Hey—I don't think he plans to betray us."

"Betray? Nooo!"

There was such a jumble of thoughts invading the Garg's mind that Alan struggled to pick up the thread of it. "He's excited about something. But I don't sense betrayal. More like reverence—wonder!"

"We cannot trust this creature!"

"I think there's something odd about the needles." Alan hesitated, considering what he was still sensing in the mind of the Garg. "I'm going to test one of them through the oraculum."

His probing easily penetrated the layers of encrusted dirt and limestone, but then he received a shock.

"It isn't rock."

"What then?"

"The core is too smooth to be stone. The texture is all wrong."

As Alan probed deeper it didn't feel right for stone at all. Its texture was strangely familiar . . .

"Wow!" he breathed. "I think it's ivory—or bone."

"What does this mean?" the Kyra demanded.

"I don't know. But I suspect that Iyezzz is venerating some kind of deity." Alan gazed at the Garg's face for several moments, probing his mind through the oraculum. "Maybe we should turn him loose. See what happens when he touches it."

"The Mage Lord has lost his senses."

But the Kyra's blade withdrew from the Garg's throat and she released her hold on his wrist. With equal reluctance, Qwenqwo put away his dagger.

Iyezzz was still gibbering with excitement, his eyes switching from the Kyra to Alan, not daring initially to move.

"Go ahead!"

Everybody took a step backward, allowing space for the Garg to approach a needle that towered more than twice his height. As the clawed wing-hand came to grasp the center of the structure Alan thought Iyezzz was humming. But then he realized that the sound came from the structure itself, to be echoed by the walls of the chamber, growing progressively louder until it ended with three pure tones, as if coming from the pipes of a cathedral organ. A feeble greenish light began to glow throughout the giant chamber.

"Wow!"

The Garg scraped away some of the engrained dirt and encrustation, revealing the original surface of the needle. It glowed a bright actinic green. Iyezzz used both his wing talons with the delicacy of a surgeon's scalpels to expose a foot or so of the smooth green surface. They no longer had need of Alan's oraculum to illuminate the chamber. With growing amazement the company looked about themselves, observing the pulsating ripples of light that ran away from the exposed needle, deep within the substance of the rocky walls.

"Surely the rock is alive with magic," breathed Qwenqwo.

Alan shook his head. He probed deeper into the chamber, inspecting its surfaces and structures through the oraculum. That same greenish matrix, of the consistency of ivory, extended everywhere. It felt like a membrane—like living tissue.

Alan spun on his heel and gazed about himself into the dimly lit cavern. "I'm getting the same feeling as when I entered the bowels of the Temple Ship."

The sense of numinous power was everywhere.

"Iyezzz! What do you know about this place?"

"I know very little. Other than it has always been thus, as you see and sense it. The City of the Ancients."

"But who were these Ancients?"

"There are legends that claim it was here that the first peoples were born. Breathed into life through the will of the gods of rock and air and oceans."

Alan shook his head, wandering around, casting his oraculum far and wide. Was the chamber really alive? A living system, in some alien way? Rather like the Temple Ship appeared to be alive—appeared to be sentient?

It was a shocking thought.

Inside the Temple Ship he had found organic-like protrusions running around the inner walls of an enormous tunnel, as if he were looking at the cartilaginous rings of a gigantic breathing tube, a trachea leading down into living lungs. Then he had discovered what he had interpreted as the organic heart of the Temple Ship, a hidden chamber at the very core, with walls of a liquid golden material that was as shiny and heavy as metal. He had touched the golden heart, he had pressed his bleeding hands against those walls, and sensed . . . sensed what? Empathy? He had hardly understood what he was sensing. He really didn't understand it any better now. Granny Dew had warned him of his own failings when it came to understanding this strange world of Tír. She had instructed him to trust his heart, his instincts, to suspend his natural human logic. There were things in this world that went beyond rational explanation. And that, for sure, was how it had felt when he had touched the golden heart of the Temple Ship. The exalting sense of oneness with another heart, another spirit—a living, sentient being—that was aware of you, that was one with your purpose, that was sensitive to what you felt in your own heart and spirit.

Alan wondered if that was what Iyezzz was feeling right now, if it was why the Garg was so overwhelmed by the chamber, his throat visibly vibrating, emitting a kind of hymnal rhythmic cadence.

The Garg fell to his knees. "Behold, Duvalhhh—the wisdom-that-was!"

"What are you talking about?"

"Arrrhhh—humanshhh! You demand explanations where none exist. The City of the Ancients is said to contain the bones of the Old Ones, travelers, if the legends are to be believed, who explored neither land nor the deeps of the oceans, but the very arch of the heavens."

Turkeya, who was sitting inches deep in dust with his back to one of the soaring needles, stiffened with fright as he woke from sleep. He felt his arm yanked hard, only to discover it was Mo who was trying to attract his attention.

"You have to come with me," she whispered.

Alan had been worried that there might be danger ahead, so he, Qwenqwo, Ainé and the main body of Shee had explored further, led by the Garg, and leaving

Mo and Turkeya in the protection of Xeenra and half a dozen Shee.

"Look after one another," he had cautioned them, with a departing wave. "We'll be back as soon as we can."

Now Turkeya climbed reluctantly to his feet, turning his startled eyes on Mo, who was tugging impatiently at his sleeve. "What's going on?"

"Not so loud. I'm hearing voices inside my head—voices that seem to come from all around me."

"You're hearing voices?"

"Turkeya, haven't you sensed it? This is a magical place. It makes you anticipate the possibility of amazing things."

Turkeya didn't feel anything of the sort. The chamber, with its green-glowing walls, oppressed his spirit. This whole journey through swamps and caves had exhausted rather than enchanted him. Here the air felt unclean in his lungs, tainted with mildew.

In fact, with the departure of the two oraculum-bearers, the glow had fallen to a faint glimmering of green. Xeenra had erected an additional soft light nearby, the dull moon-like glow of a wyre-stone, placed close to the ground. In this pallid light Turkeya's eyes had to strain even to make out the tiny figurine Mo wore on a cord around her neck, a piece of bog oak crafted by nature into a figure with three heads, which she had tugged from concealment below the neckline of her jerkin and was now twirling between thumb and forefinger.

He whispered: "Tell me about the voices."

"I sense that they're really here in the chamber, among us. But there's one voice that rises above the others."

"There is?"

Turkeya shook his head. Mo had infected him with her spooky talk. And now Turkeya's eyes peered in the direction of the nearby Shee, who stood guard amid the shadows, camouflaged by her cloak among the arcade of needle-shaped stones. He resisted being pulled another inch away from that comfort and security.

"Don't you sense it? Can't you feel their presence all around us? There's something really weird going on."

"Weird?" Turkeya's eyes were growing larger and larger in the dark.

"I think they want us to do some exploring," Mo murmured, her lips so close to his left ear he felt them brush against the fur.

"They?"

"The voices!" Her own voice had a jittery quality, as if she were frightening herself through putting her thoughts into words—and her words certainly frightened him. "I think I'm getting a message. They want us to look for something."

Turkeya glanced about at the now vague shapes of lowering shadows and strange shapes of stone. "I'm not sure it would be safe to become separated from the others."

"Look at the Shee! Look closely—look at their faces, their eyes."

"What about them?"

"Just do it! Get closer to Xeenra and take a peep."

Mo—this new Mo—could be very demanding when she set her mind to it. Turkeya moved closer to the gray-haired warrior who was deputizing for Ainé. She didn't seem to notice him. Her eyes, even this close to the soft light, appeared to be staring into darkness, unblinking.

"Now do you see?"

"She's entranced?"

"They're all the same—all of the Shee!"

"The Powers preserve us!"

A constellation of stars materialized in the air before them. They moved with a fluid motion, forming a stream of light above their heads, then moving slowly away, as if illuminating a path through the warren of needles and the myriad other shapes that littered the floor of the giant cavern.

"It's fine. I don't think we're in any danger."

Turkeya stared overhead at the stream of stars, wishing he had Mo's confidence.

"Turkeya—we have to follow where they lead us! I sense that time is short and our mission is important."

Turkeya whispered a prayer under his breath while allowing this strangest of girls to lead him away through the dark. "Mo—these lights. How can you trust these terrifying stars to be friendly?"

She tugged him on, resolutely. "Because I think I know who they are."

He stopped her dead. "You do?"

"They call themselves True Believers."

"True Believers?"

"Don't you remember? Alan told us about his experience at the time the young Shee, Valéra, was dying."

"I remember no Shee called Valéra."

"We never met her. It was after Alan left the Temple Ship at the rapids on the Snowmelt River. There was a struggle with a Preceptor. She took the poisoned wound intended for Alan. She was pregnant with her daughter-sister."

A Shee—pregnant! Turkeya felt his eyes widen. But Mo hauled him on again, following the twinkling stream of stars that led them deeper into the chamber's labyrinth.

"Alan got lost for a while in the snowy wilderness. But then he had a vision. He saw lights just like these stars."

"I wish Alan was here, right now."

"One of the lights spoke to him. It warned him about the Fáil."

"Mercy! Say no more!"

"I think we may be there."

"Where?"

A single star stood before them, rapidly increasing in brilliance. They were standing on an infinite plane of the purest white.

Turkeya was trembling with such fear he could hardly speak. "Where, in the name of blessed A-kol-i, is this place?"

It is all places and all times and therefore nowhere and timeless. To some it does not exist while to others it is the only reason for existing.

This time he heard the voice that replied to his question, and he realized, instinctively, that this was a conversation that had absolutely nothing to do with him but everything to do with his companion, Mo.

Mo spoke with a calmness that surprised herself: "Why have you brought us here?"

The seeds that have long been dormant are now blossoming, for good or for evil.

"What can we do about that?"

We would have wished for more time, for the courtesy of explanation. But time is no longer our luxury. Your birth mother was one of us.

She felt Turkeya's arm encircle her shoulders, as if he sensed how her mind was reeling with the strange revelations. Her strength evaporated, and her slender body wilted as she almost fainted.

"Mo!"

She wrestled herself free. "What are you saying?"

The being—she who you call your birth mother— bequeathed you a legacy. The time has come for your inheritance.

Mo was suddenly racked with grief. "What are you saying? What are telling me about my mother?"

She understood that this object was special. That it had to be kept safe for you, hidden where it was least expected to be found.

"You talk in the past?"

Child—you know she is dead!

"She abandoned me."

She would never have done so had it not been to grant you safety.

"What does that mean?"

She died so that you should live.

"Oh, no!"

Turkeya wrapped both his arms around his friend, who, sagging with shock, this time accepted his comforting.

"But Granny Dew described my mother as a lost soul. I was told she died of sorrow, before I was even a year old."

Once blessed with you within her womb, it was inevitable that she would be hunted remorselessly. So frail and yet her courage was boundless.

Mo's voice was interrupted by sobs. "What am I, then, that would have . . . have cursed her life even when I was in her womb?"

The answering voice was gentle: *You were—you are—precious.*

"If you know me, you must know my true name?"

You are Mira—the Heralded One.

Mo's head fell. She reached up and held the protective arm of Turkeya, though she struggled to speak.

"What am I looking for?"

I place in your hand your mother's legacy to you.

Mo felt something enter her right hand, something rounded in shape that filled her palm. "Is it so very important?"

Indeed so. The Torus is a portal of sorts—but also a means of communication. If you accept it, you will become one with us.

Mo stared down into her hand, where a doughnut shaped disk of something gray, like stone, rested. It glittered as she turned it from side to side. Its surface was patterned with minuscule flowers of many colors, like lichens. She frowned at the tiny flowers, which appeared to change as if constantly fashioning alien hieroglyphs against the misty gray background.

"My mother died for this?"

She understood that the Torus was of the greatest importance. But tell me—does it weigh heavy in your hand?

"It seems to weigh nothing at all."

There was a lengthy pause before the bright star twinkled and the voice entered her mind once more.

For Mira it will be a different kind of burden—if you will bear it.

"If it comes from my mother, I will treasure it. But tell me, please! What did you mean when you said I will become one with you?"

Silence.

"Please—if you pretend to care about me at all—at the very least tell me more about my birth mother. There's so much I want to know."

The voice remained cool, detached.

To any other than you, the Torus would weigh as the burden of Aaiksi, who carried the world on his shoulders. In time, through the sharing of the same burden, you will discover more of your birth mother.

Mo couldn't pretend to be strong anymore. Her face was streaked with tears. It took all of her resolve to reply at all.

"I'm frightened. I want to believe what you're telling me. But already it's really scaring me."

The Torus is capable of sensing you as different from all others—of responding in kind, spirit to spirit. For you it poses no danger. Rather, the time will come, and soon enough, when you will have need of its protection.

There was so much to consider, so much to take in, that Mo felt breathless, her heart pattering uncomfortably in her breast.

"But Turkeya . . ."

Your companion is now caught in the enchantment. He will accompany your return, but he already imagines it a dream. A dream it will remain to his senses even when he wakes. Close your eyes, Mira, Léanov Fashakk. Still your understandable fears so that the extraordinary may blossom.

Mo closed her eyes. She saw, as if in her mind's eye, a moonlit landscape in which a path weaved around islands of dark silhouettes, limned inside by the barest hints of colors. The path, which was so narrow as to allow just a single passage, was silvery, like a pebbled walk, illuminated by moonlight.

Can you feel it? Can you sense it guiding your return?

"Yes."

Now please attach the Torus to the leather thong about your throat.

Mo did so, feeling it jostle against the bog-oak figurine.

Thus shall you be true to your birthright and your burden. Do not call upon it needlessly. Only when you have grave need of it.

"But how will I know when that time has come?"

You will know.

A Historic Meeting

As Alan and the main party moved deeper into the gloom of the cave, illuminated by the smoky flame of firebrands, they saw fragments of walls and buildings emerging out of the rock. Alan was reminded of the pictures he had once seen of Pompeii, the Roman town buried under a flow of lava and ash from the eruption of Vesuvius. But the rock here wasn't like volcanic ash or lava. It was limestone, the kind of rock laid down on the floor of the ocean by the dying shells and skeletons of marine creatures. The Ancient City appeared to be itself a gigantic fossil, its buildings unlike any he had ever seen, comprising sweeping curves and ellipses cut by rising needles and towers, in a mixture of different-colored marble. If so it must have been laid down long before the present-day volcanic landscape. It might well be incredibly old.

"I see light up ahead!" the Kyra called.

"Daylight?"

"I don't know," she said. "The quality of the light is strange."

"It is said that there is a light that comes from the Sacred Pool," Iyezzz whispered in a voice of reverence.

Alan could certainly hear what sounded like falling water up ahead.

The young Garg was all the while sniffing and snuffling, clearly excited, his huge eyes glowing like yellow pumpkins. He went down onto his knees again as they came to a stone circle. It took Alan a minute or two of exploration to realize that they were looking at tree stumps, each five or six feet in diameter, the wood long ago fossilized to stone. In the center of the circle stood a single enormous tree that still retained its organic shape, but the more closely he studied it the stranger it looked. Then he realized why, with a startled widening of his eyes. The tree, which seemed less ancient than the circle in which it had been buried, was upside-down. What appeared to be a tangle of branches reaching into the air were roots, some eighty or ninety feet high and perhaps a hundred and twenty feet in width.

Alan stood peering up at the curious canopy.

Iyezzz answered his unspoken thoughts. "It pays homage."

"What do you mean? Are you saying that this place might mark a burial? Like the tomb of some chief, or king?"

Iyezzz shook his head. "It is an Altar—to Death."

Alan looked at the Garg prince, stunned.

"Long ago, or so the legends say, the ancestors of the Eyrie People made such an altar. At a time of apocalyptic threat. They sent out scouts to discover the king of trees within the forests that were commonplace then. The roots were dug out of the earth and the tree brought here, where the underworld was strong. Life was buried within the earth and Death was freed to enter the world."

Death was freed?

Alan stared up anew into the extraordinary symbol. "What crisis could have been so terrible?"

"I think Duvalhhh knows."

The young Garg prostrated himself before the upended tree, his skin turning a pallid gray, a musky new scent emanating from his pores. His whole being was consumed by grief, accompanied by a mewling hymn that came from the slits now visibly vibrating on the sides of his neck.

"The coming of the Witch?"

"The wisdom-that-was became lost. Long have we endured a world of anguish, where the lessons of history went unheeded."

After several more minutes of abasement and prayer Iyezzz climbed back onto his feet, his face and bearing still deeply affected as he led them further, through half a mile of ruins and underground artifacts, to enter a chamber flooded with light. The sound of water was much louder here. And the source of the light became clear as Alan and the others approached it, the roof opening to the skies overhead where an incoming river had eroded a massive cleft. That river now cascaded through hundreds of feet of jagged cliffs, to fall, in a never-ending filmy cataract, into a mist-shrouded pool in the floor. It was the pool that gave a greenish tinge to the light, itself glowing with pearly phosphorescence.

Alan's eyes, accustomed to the previous gloom, were dazzled by the brilliance of the light in the chamber. But as he became accustomed to it he saw that the natural cavern had been molded to a new purpose, perhaps by the same civilization that had built the ancient city. Rock-hewn tiers made an amphitheater of the sloping ledges on two sides of the pool. And half of the amphitheater was already occupied by hundreds of seated figures—Gargs!

"Iyezzz—you said your father would be alone!"

"It does not matter. I will protect you here."

The Garg led them around the periphery of the amphitheater, keeping to the shadows. He was heading toward a position at the top of a flight of steps hewn into the rock. All of a sudden Alan's oraculum detected a powerful new presence.

"Kate!" He shouted it aloud.

"Hush—it is not permitted to interrupt the ceremony."

Alan didn't give a damn about their ceremony. "I sense Kate's presence. I know that she's somewhere close."

His shout alerted the Garg sentries, a provocation that might have led to a battle had Iyezzz not been there to talk to them. The sentries refused to allow the Shee guards passage, allowing only Alan, Qwenqwo and Ainé to proceed, and forbidding any sort of weapon. Iyezzz had insisted he travel on ahead to talk with his father, and he was still engaged in furious argument with an elderly looking Garg wearing a gold regalia around his throat when Alan and the others were ushered into their presence.

This close the Sacred Pool looked wider and deeper than Alan had realized. It seemed enchantingly ethereal, bathed in mist from the waterfall. Enormous pillars of rock soared into the sunlit heights above. Alan made sure that the fifty or so Gargs seated on one side of the pool were unarmed, though they hardly needed conventional weaponry, given their fangs and claws. And now, descending the worn path that sloped down between the tiers, he allowed himself to be detached from the fretfully suspicious Qwenqwo to approach Iyezzz and the elderly Garg. They waited for him in silence, standing at the pool's edge before a seated figure whose aging skin was marred by a patchwork of blotches and wrinkles, and whose only adornment was a simple torc of gold.

The seated figure waited for Alan to come before him, staring at him with heavy-lidded eyes in evident rancor.

With his voice trembling with emotion, Iyezzz confirmed that this was his father, Zelnesakkk, King of the Gargs, and that the Garg wearing the regalia was Mahteman—the high shaman. Alan stopped before the trio, his eyes moving from face to face. His attention was arrested by the shaman, who regarded Alan with the same hatred as the King, the slits in his throat visibly vibrating as the bass tones of his voice carried far and wide throughout the bowl of the sacred pool.

"We have before us Duvalhhh the Slayer! Why should we be surprised that he profanes this sacred chamber?"

Alan felt a flush of anger color his face. But before he could think of a reply, Iyezzz held his hand aloft, taking it upon himself to counter the shaman's rage. "These are desperate times—times when, no matter what the history of bloodshed between us, the Eyrie People should make compact with former foes."

"No matter the history!" The shaman stamped a clawed foot on the resounding floor, causing the metalwork over his breast to jangle. "You bring to this meeting a foe that cost us half an army at Ossierel. He who has grievously wounded the pride of the Eyrie Nation. This is who you would commend to your father!"

Iyezzz went down on one knee before the King. "My Father—and my liege! Once, before the coming of the Great Witch, we were hunters of the oceans. We caught

the silver salmon on the wing. Now we inhabit a wasteland in which hunger and subjugation are the inheritance a father bestows upon his son."

Hunters of the oceans? Only now did Alan realize that
the Garg's clawed feet closely resembled the talons of
sea eagles. It certainly made him see them differently—
magnificent creatures skimming the surface waters,
catching their food and bringing it back to those lofty
eyries. The sheening camouflage of their scales, the
ability to change color, would have helped them blend
with the light so they became invisible in the meeting of
ocean and air as they skimmed and swooped.

The Garg King spoke, his voice more solemn than
hateful when compared to that of the shaman. "My
son—we all hunger for what we have lost. But these are
times of crisis."

"Perhaps the world that was is not entirely lost?"

The King shook his head, as if sadly. "What provokes
you to bring this humanhhh into our presence?"

"Duvalhhh is not the only oraculum-bearer here."

"Blasphemy!" hissed the shaman. He swept a wing
talon to within inches of Alan's brow, his skin turning
plum purple with anger, his body exuding a sulfurous
stink. "This portal is abomination!"

Iyezzz's skin rippled with bands of color, as if consumed
by an equal and opposite anger. "Thanks to generations
of shamans and their superstitions, we have prostrated
ourselves to the Witch. And what did it profit us?"

In spite of his age, the shaman reared to his full height, the wings expanding from his shoulders, wing talons dripping venom. "Who else survived, in the entire realm of the Southlands? Servitude was preferable to extermination."

Iyezzz confronted him, stretching even taller than the shaman, his wings beating slowly and threateningly at the air. "Survival is not preferable to honorable death. Are we not the Eyrie Nation, whose domain was the skies and oceans?"

The King intervened. "Come, now! We acknowledge that loss. But survive we must—and so are bound to be practical. This humanhhh—he destroyed the cream of a generation of warriors. My eldest son, and your brother, Gndirrexa, at their helm! Is it any wonder I, like Mahteman, am outraged at his presence. And should I not, in all prudence, be concerned as to why he is here? What manner of folly caused you, my son, to bring this foe to this holy of holies, and on this most delicate of occasions?"

At that moment the chamber shook to a faint earthquake, which caused the floor and walls to tremble, and ripples to wash over the pool.

Mahteman fell to his knees. "The Witch's warning!"

"A prognostication," Iyezzz said, "based no doubt on the fanciful interpretation of the movements of the sun and moon and the planets, and driven, as ever, by fear of the unknown."

"As opposed to the prognostication of my son, who is no shaman, yet assumes himself superior on matters spiritual!"

A second quake shook the ground under their feet. Alan stared into the water, which seemed to be lit from below. He was startled by a rise of bubbles, then a more diffuse disturbance in the water, followed by a sustained explosion of ripples and currents, as if something monstrous were making its way to the surface. The lake seethed. There was a sound too, gathering in the echoing chamber, a harmonic musical sound, and all the time the explosion in the lake deepened and spread until—suddenly—two silvery eyes appeared, as big as saucers. Alan stared with astonishment as the eyes contracted in a slow, sensuous deliberation before expanding again. It was some kind of signal or greeting from the extraordinary being that was surfacing in the Sacred Pool.

The being's head was decorated by enormous frills that reared backward, in three tall rows, over the crown. The face, distinctly female, was bronze-skinned and finely scaled: it was enormously long if vaguely triangular, wide across the enormous eyes and tapering down to a generously lipped mouth. The elongated lobes of her ears bore ivory inserts that resembled minuscule drums. A crescent-shaped crystal hung about her neck, in which a matrix of power throbbed and changed. Her voice was addressing him, mind-to-mind, cool and musical, yet behind the courtesy he sensed great power.

"Duval! Oraculum-bearer of the First Power."

"Who are you?"

"I am the Momu."

The reply puzzled him before he recalled that Iyezzz had mentioned the Momu; she was the leader of a people called the Cill.

"Kate? You've brought her?"

"I must beg your patience."

The Momu appeared to float out of the water, as if weightless, gliding ashore with a boneless fluidity to take a seat on the opposite side of the pool to the Garg King. The surface of the pond was now a writhing mass of new movement as strange creatures, tall and lean and armored in mother-of-pearl carapaces, rose out of the pool. Carrying no weapons that Alan could see, other than vicious-looking lobster claws in place of one of their hands, they gathered in a defensive formation about the Momu where she sat, smiling benignly at the gathering, as if enthroned.

"Greetings to you, Zelnesakkk, King of the Eyrie Nation. Long has it been since our peoples conferred. The times are in a dangerous flux. I bring a visitor whose safety must be assured at all costs. Will you, in formal covenant, give sanctuary? Your word, my Lord, and your blessing—in welcome of Greeneyes! She who—as your spies will, no doubt, have reported—has been returning life to the blighted lands."

Alan saw how the Garg King's eyes widened, already turning to his shaman whose eyes were wider still.

"Your surety, if you please—King Zelnesakkk?"

The Garg King lifted a wing talon and spoke: "The guest of the Momu has my blessing—the Eyrie Nation offers surety of her safety and protection."

The shaman wheeled, a mixture of rage and bewilderment transfixing his features. He shambled over to slump down in a position at some remove from the King. As he did so there was another watery explosion in the center of the pool. More of the Cill warriors materialized from thin air at the far edge of the pool, causing the Gargs on this side to rise from their seats. They watched the Cill lift an enormous green sphere, dripping a rain of phosphorescent droplets, out of the water. Alan stared in amazement. Its filigreed surface looked like an enormous dandelion clock, some twenty feet in diameter. The Cill warriors slit open its roof and lifted a figure from its interior, a slim, elegant female, barefoot, with a body-hugging silken dress of emerald green, whom they led into a seat by the side of the Momu. Although the face and head of the figure were covered in gossamer, Alan caught a glimpse of auburn through the veil.

"Kate!" His throat was suddenly dry with emotion, his voice struggling to emerge from his lips. "Kate!" he roared through his oraculum, the sudden eruption of its rubicund light startling everyone in the chamber.

In his mind there was an impression, like a tiny candle of light opening on darkness—then the candle exploded into an emerald sun. As Alan stumbled around the periphery of the pool the figure reached out to him, climbing tremblingly to her feet.

"Kate!" He couldn't believe that he was actually holding her, that Kate was in his arms.

"You said you would come for me—and you came!"

He kissed her—he never wanted the kiss to end. They only broke the kiss when they were forced to separate their lips just to breathe.

"There's so much I want to tell you."

"Me too."

Webbed hands on the ends of willowy arms enfolded both their shoulders and the voice of the Momu sounded gently in their minds. "Come—come—young bearers of hope, on whose shoulders so much now rests. You have not arrived at this meeting by chance. The Fates, praise them, have brought you amongst two wronged peoples, their histories corrupted by a monstrous tyranny. Come now! Be seated here beside me. Be one with me in this communion."

"I love you!" Alan whispered, still clinging to Kate's hand.

"Tonight!" Kate whispered as they parted and took their seats to the right and the left of the Momu.

Tonight! He folded the whisper into the depths of his being.

As the two sides, arranged in their opposing semicircles, made ready to parley, another rumble of thunder provoked a hail of grit and stones from the cavern roof. The Momu waited for it to subside before taking to her feet and bowing ceremoniously before the King and his ministers, addressing them through her gentle, melodious voice.

"We have no time for the platitudes of civilized greeting. Our peoples have not communed in eons, time in which our cities were reduced to dust and your people were reduced to slavery."

The King's neck slits contracted, as if one with the Momu in profound emotion, and he glanced at his son before he replied. "Momu—Queen of the Shadow People, whose world is the changing of the tides—would you speak to me in the same vein of rebellion as my son, Iyezzz-I-Noor? If my welcome is guarded, it reflects my fearful heart. Though the high shaman might augur otherwise, I am too salted by experience not to recognize truth, even when doom-laden. I am in receipt of grave tidings from the honor guard that has recently fled the Tower."

"Grave tidings, my Lord?"

The King ignored the stare of the shaman to look toward his son, his eyes filled with emotion. "Likely what you, Iyezzz, have augured for some years. The Great Witch has taken leave of her senses—whatever senses she might ever be presumed to have possessed. She sacrifices all to this demon she is resurrecting. She sings to it, night and day, as it thunders and roars and causes the very mountains to shake."

"My Lord, the Great Witch is close to resurrecting the soul spirit of Fangorath."

"You perhaps understand more of her purpose than I do."

"She seeks consummation. Union of spirit with one a thousand times more dreadful than she. A being half divine and wholly of darkness. But even this, terrible as it might appear, is only the first step in her ambition. Olc seeks to reopen the Third Portal of the Fáil. What then, if she succeeds? What do you think will become of the proud Eyrie Nation—or indeed the sole surviving city of the Cill?"

The King rose to join her on his feet. "How then do we confound her?"

Iyezzz stood and roared: "We fight. At least if we die fighting, we die with honor."

The Momu spoke gravely, lifting Alan and Kate to their feet. "Though the situation is grave, not one but two oraculum-bearers have come among us, bearing a mission of hope from an alien world. Is this not the omen we have long prayed for?"

"A stripling boy and a girl of little more than skin and bone. You think these will defeat the Witch, who is resurrecting a demigod?"

"I have come to know just one of these. Let me introduce Greeneyes. I weep a thousand tears of gratitude for this girl whose courage and kindness saved the life of my child under the very nose of the Witch."

The hoary old head was shaking. He stared at Kate in meditative silence. "This is not the Léanov Fashakk!"

"Yet still the Great Witch fears her."

Alan stared from the King to the Momu. *The Léanov Fashakk!* He had heard this expression before. It was Mo—Mo had pressed herself between him and the Legun incarnate at the battle of Ossierel.

The King's hand appeared stiff as he raised it into the air, as if he were struggling to prevent it from trembling. "We clutch at straws. Must we, in this time of apocalypse, place all of our hope in children?"

His words brought a powerful sense of déjà vu to Alan, causing gooseflesh to spring up over his entire skin. They echoed the words of the High Architect, Ussha De Danaan, when she had addressed all four friends as chosen. But Ossierel, with all that it had held dear, had fallen.

A Penitence of Blood

From her Tower of Bones the Great Witch crooned her hymn of triumph, even as her many tentacles, thick as pythons, slithered and scraped homeward from the marshes and caves and sewer-like ravines in which the last vestiges of life in her blasted landscape still attempted to skulk and hide. Another thunderous eruption from the pit caused the Tower to judder, and in its wake a craquelure of splintering ran over its bony walls. Even the surrounding packs of wolves were cowed into silence for a while before they howled anew their chorus of anticipation over the ravished landscape, gathering close around the Tower as if sensing that the time for change was drawing near.

A new age dawns, pretty ones!

Faltana, whose own heart quailed with the colossal violence that was invading her beloved Tower from the thing that brooded within the pit, gathered what little courage she had left to encourage the others to come deeper into the great chamber and bow before their mistress.

"Your deliverance, beloved one!"

But her mistress was so consumed with gloating she appeared not to notice.

"Hsst!" Faltana waved to the succubi. All within the Tower had been summoned to gather by the pit, from which the thunderous roars shook the floor and walls and ceiling about them, as if a volcano readied itself to explode. The fury never abated now, night or day, invoking such a terrifying prospect that the sentinel Gargs had taken to the skies and abandoned them to their fate.

"Sing!" she hissed. "Children of Olc, celebrate your joy!"

The eyes of the succubi stared back at her, unable to hide their terror.

"Sing!" she commanded, moving among them with the Garg-tail whip. "Sing! Hail the glorious day!"

Without realizing it Faltana had drifted to the very edge of the pit, with the rumbles and roars ascending through her naked feet. "Oh, sing!" she shrieked, her own voice faltering as a crackling boom almost pitched her headlong. It was followed by an incandescent torrent of energy, seething to the very rim of the pit. Faltana had come to recognize the baleful nature of the rumbles. It was a voice of a kind. A roar so rage-filled it had no need of words. The succubi were creeping backward, many pressing against the outermost walls of the chamber, fighting with one another to be nearer the exit. Faltana wished that, like the Gargs, she had wings that would carry her away. The walls around her were deeply split and fissured as if, with just a final terrible eruption, the entire Tower would disintegrate and the thing below would consume all within its blazing red furnace.

"Sing!" she screamed.

Too loud—she realized her mistake as the multifaceted eyes blinked awake, the pulsating furnace coming alive in their depths.

What is the meaning of this shrieking? How dare you profane our thoughts at the very imminence of our communion?

"My love—my adored one! This thing—the fury below! Forgive my saying so, but you have such immense courage—courage enough for all of us. We, whose days are so filled with the mundane, while yours are consumed by the divine. Forgive our faltering hearts, too easily overwhelmed with fear."

What nonsense is this?

"You are so bounteous in your wisdom—so immense in your comprehension of what we cannot even begin to fathom. Forgive the timidity of your children, who cannot sleep with worry."

Worry?

"It's just that—my beloved Mistress! To such timid hearts and minds as ours—why, it seems so dreadful it may not be controlled."

The insectile eyes of the Witch shifted focus to take in the terrified sea of faces that filled the chamber. Showers of splintered stone and ash were falling from the ceiling, matting the already bedraggled hair of the succubi. Glowing splinters were spiraling through the air, causing the foul smell of singeing hair. The Witch's voice, now sounding in every mind, was deceptively soft, with just the faintest of sibilant purrs.

What need have we of control? Is it not the point of such union that Fangorath cannot be controlled?

"Majesty—manifold joys fill my heart to be thus reassured. Come—let us sing—let us celebrate the imminence of consummation!"

Be quiet! Are we alone in this desert of stupidity? Are you so visionless you cannot grasp the wonder? Fangorath the Almighty, Destroyer of Worlds—did he not confront the very Goddesses, complacent in their thrones? Surely he must be reborn in all of his strength and power. Why else would we become one?

"Of course—forgive my limitations, beloved Mistress—in such . . . such a great and numinous presence . . ."

A numinous presence indeed!

"In . . . in truly a godly presence . . . the very proximity to such a being . . ."

Another growl thundered from below, shaking the floor under Faltana's feet and ascending through her bones from her ankles to her skull. The charnel stench arising from the pit clogged her nostrils. But even in attempting to put a few more feet between herself and the lip, it brought her into closer proximity to those terrible red-pulsating eyes, while from behind, her back was burning from the rising maelstrom. The succubi were whining, crushing one another in their attempts to pull back against the walls, as far back from the caldera as they could get, but the fury was so intense it was blistering their exposed skin and igniting their hair.

The voice in Faltana's mind had risen from a whisper to a harsh hiss. *You cannot sleep, you say, fearful of what will become of us? Or is it what will become of you?*

"Mistress—so deserving of our love—our caring!"

Is it possible that all of you, our misbegotten children, care only for your miserable mortal selves?

"Oh, no—my dearest, dearest love. It is you, you alone, we care for."

Why then, have no fear. You all will share the blessing of union with us—you who so love us, you couldn't possibly desire otherwise.

Faltana could not conceal the crackle of terror from her voice. "Such joy—my beloved majesty!"

A pity you, personally, will not witness our glory.

A tentacle, as slender as a whip, stroked the empty eye socket of the chief succubus as Faltana prostrated herself before the glowering eyes, perilously close to the lip of the red-glowing pit.

You allowed our captive to escape.

"My fault . . . My most grievous fault!"

Desist from this spineless caterwauling.

"As you wish . . . muh-muh, my beloved Mistress."

As we wish?

"Absolutely—your very desire is my heart."

We do have such a desire—and you will fulfill it.

"Merely name it, muh-muh my heart."

The tentacle stroked Faltana's cheek. *Fangorath—does he not hunger? And his coming so imminent. He requires feeding. Be good enough to see to it.*

"Gladly—gladly will I do so! I—I will command your servants—thuh-thuh they will find suitable meat."

A momentary exhilaration glowed in the Witch's eyes, and they blinked, slowly and purposefully, as she registered the ruin that had once been her chief succubus. The ground trembled, as if in anticipation.

His hunger is best satisfied with live meat.

Faltana shrank back, as if she wished that the cracked and fissured bone might swallow her. Her flesh trembled like jelly with every floor-jarring thunder from below. Deep in the great multi-faceted eyes of Olc she saw the red glow come vigorously alive, become truly one with the fiery furnace that crackled and roared at the very lip of the pit.

"Live meat, my Mistress? Then—then live meat shall it be. I—I will command it. It will be forthcoming in an instant."

We think you will provide a sufficiency—for the moment.

"I—I, Excellency?"

What use have we for a chief succubus who has lost her wits? Did you not offer to satisfy our every desire?

Faltana felt the Garg-tail whip torn from her grasp, and tossed toward the cowering herd of succubi. "But—but you would not—you could not . . ."

Your successor has been chosen. Hashiri!

Faltana's eye wheeled to where a tall, bony-faced succubus, vigorous and youthful, detached from the cowering mob. A recent scar already disfigured Hashiri's left arm, extending all the way from her elbow into her hand—the same hand that now picked up the Garg-tail whip. A warning against future disappointment of her Mistress's expectations.

Inform this piece of meat of our instruction. It is our desire that it takes the necessary steps, backwards—bowing obediently as it does so.

Hashiri picked up the Garg-tail whip. She flexed it, staring at the former chief succubus, who was trembling against the blazing furnace of the pit.

"My beloved, my heart—you surely would not ask this of me? Have I not served you with every mote of my being?"

You have served none but yourself—but we shall not waste another moment in useless debate. You cannot imagine the immortal glory of what is to come. Yet even the dirt-born such as you may redeem yourself. You may offer the sacrifice of your living flesh and blood to our transubstantiation.

"Brave heart—ask and I will do it for love of you."

We do ask it. Only thus shall we forgive you your venal weaknesses—and your excruciating stupidity. Be so penitent as to offer yourself to the pit.

The Witch's eyes turned to Hashiri. The Garg-tail whip arced, then struck Faltana's left thigh above the knee, raising a livid welt. Faltana screamed.

"Please—say you but jest with me."

But we do.

A last spark of defiance rose in Faltana's outraged throat. "I will not do this—I deserve better."

The Garg whip arced again, discovering the same welt, this time drawing blood. As Faltana screamed it arced again, and again.

The Witch tentacle stroked, with exquisite sensitivity, the tormented flesh where the whip had scourged.

"Stop this—desist, my beloved Mistress. Or . . ."

Or what? Do you so quail with each stroke of the Garg tail? You, who were so profligate with its infliction upon others?

"You—you spied on me?"

Observing your weakness was delicious, moment by moment.

"You've been cruel—taken out my beautiful eye. And for what? For no transgression. I was ever dutiful. How dare you use me like this—how dare you abuse me."

The whip cracked, finding the target of her calf. It cracked, again and again.

Sing, pretty ones. Sing to the glory of the rising power!

The succubi, scorched and blistered, shrieked their song, relieved that the fury of their mistress was turned on somebody other than themselves. The chamber reverberated with the rising chorus of their chanting, eliciting a sympathetic roaring from the pit.

"Feed the beast! Feed the beast!"

Faltana had fallen onto her knees, but still she clawed with her nails at the cinder-filled floor. She was consumed by her own rage, the rage, even in the face of hopelessness, of a servant abused.

Several larger tentacles approached her, thick and muscular, nudging and pushing at her, ignoring the slaps of her hands. They tugged at her arms, ripping the fingernails from where they were attempting to find purchase. Then, rising between the mounds of her breasts, they encircled her throat, slyly embracing it. Then they began to squeeze, so the veins of Faltana's throat stood out like bloated cords.

"Oh—be-lov-ed. Plee-eea-se!"

There was a murderous thrashing of several thick tentacles before the screaming wreck of the chief suc- cubus was consigned to the flaming maw.

THE FOREST OF HARROW

AT FIRST LIGHT IYEZZZ DREW A PICTURE OF THE valley ahead in the mud by the side of a rank-smelling stream. At its center was the Tower of Bones, where they were now headed. It was the day after the meeting by the Sacred Lake, and the expeditionary force, which now included Kate, had rejoined Turkeya, Mo and the others to be led out of the subterranean chambers of the Ancient City by their Garg guide. Dusk had fallen by the time they emerged so they were forced to rest, allowing time for stories to be told and friendships to be renewed. All night long the sky had flashed and glowed a lurid red, and the distant thunderous detonations had reverberated in the ground beneath them as they attempted to sleep.

For Alan and Kate, just being able to hold one another, to kiss, and to lie in each other's arms, was heaven—even if they had to put up with the gentle banter of their friends. On awakening, Alan had found Kate's head still resting on his shoulder and her sleeping body still cradled in his own. He just couldn't believe that his Kate was by his side again. Looking down into her sleeping face he was reminded of how beautiful she was, though the girlish roundness of her cheeks had been replaced by hollows of hunger. He kissed her brow, careful not to wake her, covering her over again with the blanket they had shared. But light as it was, his kiss caused her eyes to flutter and his whispered name to come from her dreaming lips—lips he couldn't stop himself kissing with a butterfly gentleness before rising quietly to join the others.

Squatting by Iyezzz as he sketched in the dirt by the morning campfire, Alan couldn't help but reflect on those hollowed cheeks. It was a reminder of what she must have gone through, and it made him all the more determined that the Witch would pay for it, and soon.

"How long before we reach the Tower?"

"For me—half a day's flight. For humanshhh," the Garg lifted his yellow eyes to gaze into Alan's own, "three days, perhaps, of hard and dangerous march."

Alan nodded to himself. This really was a menacing place. Up to now he had thought of nothing but freeing Kate from the Witch's clutches. But now that Kate was free, the enormity of the continuing danger loomed larger in his mind. He was also aware of Kate's vulnerability in accompanying them in their attack on the

Tower. She would be returning to the place of nightmare and torment.

How brave you are—my Kate!

His eyes returned to her sleeping form, and in particular to the green triangle in her brow. At that moment he deeply resented it—not because he saw it as a rival to his own power but rather because of the weight of responsibility it placed on her emaciated shoulders.

Qwenqwo spoke to Alan. "Ask him to describe the actual stronghold."

The young Garg hissed, "It takes the form of an almighty skull—vast and up-reared as a Tower designed for war. If rumor be true, the skull is that of Fangorath himself, at the very place where he fell."

"How did he fall?"

"In a disastrous war fought long ago, in the most distant mists of time. Older by far than the histories of the Eyrie People. Perhaps as old as the City of the Ancients. If legend is to be believed, the war was fought between titans and dragons."

"Titans and dragons?" Alan pursed his lips in a skeptical smile.

"Titans, Duvalhhh. Demigods! Born of the union of gods, or goddesses—and worldly beings."

"And Fangorath was one of these titans?"

"In legend he was King of the titans."

"And Fangorath destroyed the dragons?"

"Alan—don't mock Iyezzz." Kate had woken and had come over to join them, the blanket still wrapped around her shoulders against the morning chill. "This dreadful war—it isn't just a legend. It's true."

Alan wrapped his arm around Kate's shoulders and squeezed her, but he was still shaking his head and smiling.

"I told you last night that I met one—a real dragon!"

"In your dreams, maybe."

"It wasn't a dream. I resurrected it—from a fossil in the rocks. We became friends. He helped me escape from the Witch."

"I thought you were just kidding me."

"I wasn't kidding."

"And he confirmed this—your dragon? He told you about this war—and this titan, Fangorath."

"He let me see it, in his memories—his dreams."

"If legend be true," the Garg continued, "the war between titans and dragons was the most terrible war in the history of Tír. The beings that fought were gods in themselves. The war tore the world apart."

"The dragon, Driftwood, told me the same story. He said that his people couldn't bear the terrible destruction, so they ended it by biting off their own wings and drowning in the oceans."

Alan shook his head, his arm still wrapped around Kate's shoulders. "It sounds like a fairy tale—and it hardly makes any sense."

"I saw Driftwood's scars—the stumps of his wings. I healed him so that he could become whole again. So he could fly."

Alan smiled again. He just couldn't help his skepticism. "Hey, Kate—you've been through a terrible time. Dreams can seem real."

"I didn't dream it, Alan."

"So how come the titan died? How come he's buried here, in this valley? How come the Tower is his skull?"

Qwenqwo interrupted Kate's reply. "Mage Lord—we should listen to what Kate is telling us. It may be important in what we are facing."

"What—the Tower really is the skull of Fangorath?"

"What if the titans were punished by the gods? Since it would appear that in their arrogance, they challenged the world that was itself the creation of the gods?"

"The goddesses, more like," added Kate. "Granny Dew is close to the Trídédana. She sent me to the island where I resurrected the dragon."

Alan shook his head. "You mean—like, one goddess in particular? One that might well have had the power to destroy Fangorath?"

"Yes—I'm talking about Mórígán! Do you recall what your grandfather, Padraig, told us? She's the . . . the raven of the battlefield. And Driftwood talked about her—how the loss of the dragons' wings had been a last desperate sacrifice to Mórígán."

"But if Mórígán destroyed Fangorath, how could the Witch resurrect him?"

Qwenqwo answered that question: "A demigod is immortal. He could not die. But he could be banished."

"Banished to where?" Kate pressed.

"I think I might have an idea," Alan replied. "When the Tyrant tried to destroy me, he said I would be condemned to haunt the wastes of Dromenon. Like some kind of ghost." He squeezed Kate tighter, then returned his attentions to the sketches the Garg had been making in the dirt. "Iyezzz, can you tell us more of the dangers we will face in the approach to the Tower?"

Iyezzz inhaled, as if astonished by what he had been hearing, then blew a sigh-like vibration through the slits in his throat. "It can be no accident, then, that the Witch chose the Tower as her lair, for the spirit of darkness may linger there. To get to it, you must cross a wasted land— truly a wound on the face of the world." The Garg's eyes closed to slits, as if he were choosing his words carefully. "A river valley once lush and fertile, yet now utterly desolate, and baited with traps for the unwary."

They set out soon after a snatched breakfast of fish soup and rock-hard bread, with Iyezzz to the fore and the Shee mounting guard on all sides. After several hours of marching through rock and scrub their progress was blocked by a withered forest, with skeletal trees as gray as ash and barbed with thorns, some a foot long and sharp as blades. It looked impenetrable.

They called a halt, asking Iyezzz for his advice.

"You face the Forest of Harrow. Its trees are unlike any you know as such—they do not grow, nor do they bear leaves, only the thorns that you can see. Yet you must pass through it in a single march. Rest, or attempt to sleep within the forest, and it will encircle and destroy you, for the trees can move, ensnaring the unwary, as a spider weaves."

The Kyra pressed him: "Then we have no recourse other than to hack our way through this bane of thorns?"

"It is the only way for those who travel on foot. But have a care as you do so, for the prick of these thorns is poisonous."

Iyezzz took flight, holding his position above them; in this tangle of forest his wings would be too great an encumbrance, but from the air he could guide them through where the tangles appeared less dense. And so, yard by yard, they began to hack and slash a narrow course through branches that were as tough as bones and whose thorns were daggers that would penetrate deep and poison the flesh. They saw no evidence of life here, not even the pests of biting insects. By midday there was nobody among them who wasn't tormented by festering scratches, so they were forced to call a temporary rest to allow the Aides to busy themselves with tending wounds and administering sips of healwell.

Mo and Turkeya followed the beckoning Kyra to where three severely injured Shee were being treated. All three were comatose. Mo watched as Turkeya knelt by the injured warriors, examining forearms and calves that bore livid puncture wounds.

"Come—see!" The shaman pointed to the flares of inflammation around the punctures, tracing the red lines that ran from there and ascended the limbs.

"What does it mean?"

"The poison has entered the deeper flesh to become blood-borne." His look told her what that would mean.

"Can't you do something?"

"I can try."

Mo watched intently as Turkeya heated a very sharp knife in a torch flame and then, with a sizzling slash, lanced open a septic puncture wounds so the stinking pus spurted out. The stricken warriors moaned and writhed with pain. Then the Aides attempted to pour a sip of healwell into their troubled mouths before packing the gaping wounds with herbal balms that would nullify the poison and soothe the hurt.

"Well done, Turkeya! Can you save them—will they survive?"

"I don't think so, Mo."

"But some might. And you've eased their pain. You're helping people." Mo spoke softly, reassuringly. "Your coming along wasn't a mistake. You've been blaming yourself ever since Kataba died. But you're needed here."

The young shaman nodded, grateful for her words. "I was wrong to distrust the Garg. Iyezzz has proved to be a friend. And he spoke truly of this place," he whispered. "We journey through a tormented land."

Kate's voice interrupted their whispering as she joined them in the tiny makeshift hospital: "The Witch's doing!"

Mo threw her arms around Kate and hugged her, so glad of the return of her friend. "We can't just let her win."

Turkeya agreed. "Iyezzz warned us not to rest within the wood. But what can we do? There are so many wounded."

Kate shook her head. "I don't know. But we have to think of something."

He insisted: "Can't you use your power?"

"My power is intended as the power of healing— and rebirth. But up to now I've only ever tried turning it on the land. I have no experience of using it to heal wounds."

"Didn't you use it to restore the dragon's wings?"

"Oh, yes—I did. Of course I'll try. But Turkeya will have to help me. You must explain to me about wounds, and poisons, and thorn trees."

They soldiered on. It seemed almost miraculous that, sweating and exhausted, they managed to hack their way further until late afternoon. They had been encouraged by messages from Iyezzz, who signaled that they were halfway through the woods. But then, abruptly, they heard him cry out.

"Beware! The trees are moving."

The Kyra halted their progress, and ordered the Shee to hack out a clearing that could be defended. The warriors made a wall of swords about Alan, Kate, Turkeya and Mo. Through his oraculum, Alan attempted to read the mind of the Garg. "Iyezzz—I need to see what's happening. Let me look out through your eyes."

Through Iyezzz's mind he saw a wave-like movement, such as one might see from a stone thrown into a pond. The pond was the forest of ash-pale branches and leafless crowns, but the ripples were moving in the opposite direction, arising from without and building toward a crescendo at a single focus. His heartbeat rose into his throat when he realized that the company was that focus.

"What is it?" the Kyra demanded.

"The trees are coming toward us—from everywhere."

"How can this be?"

"They're tearing themselves out of the ground." Alan pointed to the forest immediately surrounding them, where the thorn trees were swaying, backward and forward, as if determined to rip out their roots. The swaying became more and more extreme until, with an audible tearing, one of the trees completely uprooted itself. But then the movement did not halt. The uprooted tree rolled itself into a tangled ball. And the enormous ball, covered with dagger-like thorns, began to roll determinedly toward them. Other trees were doing the same. There was a thunder of loosening roots. All about them a wall of thorn trees was advancing in a deadly embrace.

Ainé went down on one knee, murmuring a prayer with closed eyes, and then, one by one, she pressed the

blades of her warrior sisters against the pulsating Oraculum of Bree in her brow. The Shee immediately moved
out to hack at the trunks of the trees that surrounded
them. Sparks of green rained down from the clash of
blade against the resisting trunks. But it was close to
suicidal for the Shee. Branches moved, lashing back and
then forward, sweeping the giant warriors off their feet
and inflicting terrible wounds with their thorns. The
dwarf mage, Qwenqwo, joined the Shee, slashing at
trunks with his rune-glowing battleaxe, chopping back
tree after tree.

"Help us," the Kyra flashed Alan, mind-to-mind.

Alan waded in with the Spear of Lug, his oraculum
blazing with power, and runes flaring over the long
spiral blade, so it cut through the advancing wall like
white-hot steel. He destroyed one thorn tree, then
another, but for every tree he destroyed several more
tore themselves loose and curled into giant balls of malice, hurling themselves against the protective wall with
poisoned daggers. Only yards from him a Shee hacked
an enormous branch from a tree only to see the remaining branches explode, deluging the warrior in a rain of
thorns that ripped her body to shreds.

Many Shee were already dead. Yet their sacrifice had
hacked out a ring of broken trees as a protective barrier
around their company, and against this a cannonade of
newly arriving trees crashed and disintegrated, showering them with splinters of wood and thorns. The thorn
trees were building up, layer upon layer, in concentric

rings about them, until the barrier, at its inner perime-
ter, was several trees high. Through the terrible destruction of trees tearing against one another, Alan heard a
wailing—as if the forest were screaming in agony, maddened beyond reason.

He probed the avalanche of violence that attacked
them from every direction. Wave after wave of incoming
trees crashed against the barrier, the violence of which
threw huge fragments into the air, and already some
of the attacks were breaking through. The despairing
company huddled under the massed shields of the Shee.
They gazed out onto the mania of destruction, watching
it contract with deadly certainty, and expecting annihilation at any moment.

Kate wailed: "Do something, Alan. Use the First
Power!"

Alan stared out at the crumbling barrier. He heard
the tremendous ripping and tearing, saw the breach
in the protective circle, where a lava-like flow of those
enormous spiked balls was coming through. The memory of the gyre haunted him—the knowledge that if he
called up the power in his oraculum it might be out of
his control. The First Power might destroy them all.

"Do it now—or we're done for!"

Rage flowed through Alan, spreading to become an
incandescent lightning, erupting out of the oraculum
and down through his arm into the extended spear.
The lightning crackled and spread, in an instant forming a dome of incandescence over the shield wall, then

roaring outward in an all-devouring wave, burning whole trees to ash with its touch, then sweeping through the forest until not a single tree survived its fury. Gasping for breath and with his heart still pounding in his throat, he became aware that Kate was signaling to him. She was begging him to stop. In those charged moments, when he was still emerging from the rage that had consumed him, he saw how Kate's eyes were wide with fear.

Wiping his sweat-soaked face down with hands blackened with ash, he hugged her fleetingly, then headed off in search of the Kyra. He found her covered with wounds, yet still alive.

"Aides!" he roared.

Kate gazed out into the ruins of trunks and branches that extended for mile after mile. Her legs were buried up to midcalf in ashes. Alan had done that—through the awesome power of the oraculum in his brow. Now that the obscuring forest was gone she saw, however distantly, the blood-red light of the Tower of Bones, which was invading the sky from the north. And high overhead, black shapes, limned by the glow of the sky, which must be Gargs—Garg spies—who had been observing it all, and who would report back to the King.

Her mind numbed with shock, she turned to face the two Aides, themselves injured, who came to the assistance of Shee on the ground nearby. Everywhere she looked, she saw wounds that were deep and festering with poison. She had been hurt herself, over her arms, her back and legs. She held her arms out in front of her and stared at her own cuts and slashes, which were livid and pus-filled, in places penetrating to the bone. She began to tremble.

"Granny Dew!"

Kate felt the impulse to separate herself from the company, to wade out into the sea of ash and stand alone. She discovered a small hillock standing a little higher than the wasteland of ash and whirling smoke. She recalled the words of the Momu: *A goddess empowers you. Be not afraid to invoke her help.*

Holding the purse before her lips she blew on it while turning slowly in a circle, addressing the wounded land, which had known nothing but torment for thousands of years. As she rotated her body, dispersing the seeds, the green light of her oraculum pulsated with the rhythm of her heartbeat, its light falling over the charred limbs, the ashes gamboling in the rising wind. Her lips were pressed tight together, her words expressed exclusively through the oraculum. She had no idea if a blighted land would understand her attempts at comforting, but she tried anyway.

"How terrible your suffering must have been. Once you lived in beauty and harmony with all of life. But the coming of the Great Witch changed you. She ravaged your spirit, and with it all hope, so you came to know only despair. You have endured that despair. But now, through the power given to me by Granny Dew,

I return the spirit of life to you. I return the joy of the seasons, the hope of the seed in spring, the life-giving sunlight in your leaves, the healing rain, the flight of pollinating insects among your flowers, the song of the birds among your branches."

Alan had arrived to stand beside her, his arm about her shoulders, staring out with her at the rain that was now pattering over the smoking ashes. As the first large drops struck their faces they saw the rising green begin to sprout everywhere, the tiny shoots penetrating the ash before throwing apart their embryonic leaves.

With a noisy flapping of wings, Iyezzz alighted before them. He knelt before Kate, kissing the rain-soaked ash so the white of it coated his gargoyle face like a mask. Qwenqwo, Mo and Turkeya had come to join them, their faces lifted to the rain, speechless with shock, yet their feelings altogether clear from their tear-filled eyes. The wounds that had cut their arms to the bone were closing.

"The Kyra—the others?" Alan hardly dared to ask.

"All healing!"

Alan threw his arms about Kate and hugged her. "Oh, wow! Kate! How we've needed you!"

GOLDEN HEART

"I'M NOT MR. NICE GUY!" MARK ADDRESSED THE silence in which he basically didn't exist, except in spirit, needing to communicate with the being that was the Temple Ship, which was unable to communicate in words.

"No, you are not."

He imagined Nan, and within a second he saw her. In his mind she was standing beside him on the white beach, wearing Kate's clothes. He assumed she was imagining him also, standing beside her, wearing jeans and leather jacket.

"I'm Mr. Angry."

He saw, mind-to-mind, that she was reaching out as if to touch his cheek. By now she was sufficiently practiced to know the feel of his cheek. He even felt the touch of her fingers on it.

They could do this more easily now. It was comforting—helped to keep him sane. But he needed more. They both did.

"I'm not Mr. Romeo."

"No—you are Mark Grimstone."

He laughed, making a little snort through his nose, a nose that in reality did not exist. "That's right!"

"Good!"

"Good?"

"If you are Mr. Angry, I am Queen Angry!"

She was a fast learner. He laughed again. "If only we were together, really together. If I could touch you, I'd kiss you now."

"Kiss me, then!"

They kissed, as best they could. There was something thrilling about it, but it was a long way from a real kiss.

"It's no good, Nan. I can't rest—I can't focus on anything else but the thought of getting out of here."

It was a bad idea to think too much about it. You could become overwhelmed by it, frantic. He couldn't rest until he attempted the crossing between worlds, even if the risks—and he had a suspicion that there were almighty risks involved—might cost them the spiritual life that was all they had. "Okay. The thing to do is to get it crystal clear in our minds. There must be a first step?"

"Which is to grasp the impossible nature of our dilemma."

He chuckled, again. "You're really good for me."

"To visualize our extraordinary need."

"Keep on talking—I like it!"

"You mock me?"

"What—Her Royal Majesty, Queen Angry?"

"If I had flesh, I would slap your cheek for your impudence."

"Ow!"

They laughed together.

He was silent again for a while, thinking deeply. In spirit he knew that he and the Ship were one. But that didn't seem to be enough.

"To be born again." He whispered it slowly, musingly, finding words to best express what he was now thinking.

"To be born again." Her answering concord.

"I don't fully understand what it involves, how it happens. But I sense, even if it's only vaguely, that it involves something like that . . . When the Ship changes. When it metamorphoses."

"The Ship is born again?"

"I think so."

"How glorious!"

"Yeah! But the question is—what does that really mean?"

"But you did it—you brought about the raptor change."

"My friend's life was threatened."

"So?"

Somehow that threat, in Mark's heart and mind, had become a visceral fear. Mark's desperate need to save Alan had communicated itself to the Ship. But this situation—this present need—was too subtle, perhaps.

"There's something missing. Something I've been racking my brains to think through. Like back then, when we were stuck in the ice-bound lake . . ."

"Think back."

"We all sensed the Ship. I sensed it deeper than the others. A feeling of desolation, of sadness."

"Like loneliness?"

"Yeah! Maybe. The Olhyiu were about to set the Ship on fire."

He was aware that she was looking at him. He showed her the image of himself blinking. *We're becoming more subtly aware of each other.*

"They had to melt the ice to escape."

"So you felt it—you felt the Ship's sadness?"

"It was more than that. I knew that was what they were planning to do—and I felt strongly about it. It was similar in Isscan."

He knew that she was lifting her fingers to touch his lips. He imagined that he was feeling her touch.

"How similar?"

"Kind of empathic. As if the Ship understood our need. Nan—it needs to know how desperately we feel it."

"Think harder."

"I'm so wound up. I can't remember."

"Let the memories come. Do not force them. This experience, the feelings you shared with the Ship. It must have been frightening—terrifying."

"We connected . . . Somehow."

In spirit, in his mind, Mark recalled the feeling, how overwhelming it had felt. Strange—so terribly sad. And then . . .

"That's what we did—we connected!"

"What do you mean?"

"The union felt close, physical."

"Mark! Don't you see?"

"What?"

"This union with the Ship—you became one."

"Yeah. But I'm not sure what that means."

"Can't you see what is abundantly clear to me? We are becoming one. I see what you are thinking. I feel what you are feeling."

"It was different with the Ship . . ."

"How different?"

"I'm still not sure . . ."

"If only I could slap your face!"

He laughed. "I'd slap you right back."

In his mind, he blinked again. He tried putting it into words: *I need your help. I'm desperate. I need to return to my world—to Earth. I need to get away from the control of the Third Power. I need to feel my body again—Nan and I both need to. If it involves risk, we are prepared to take it. Because if we can't feel our bodies again, if we can't reach out and touch one another, we might as well be dead.*

He stopped, nauseated by his own words, his rising desperation. *It's all a waste of time. No damn good!*

He felt weighted down, as if his body and mind were trapped in lead. This would never change. There would be no escape.

Despair overwhelmed him . . .

He stood within a pentagonal chamber whose walls were liquidly golden. He had no memory of how he had arrived here. When he looked down at himself—when he held his hands before his face—he appeared to be real. He paused, finding it difficult to fill his lungs with breath, for several seconds.

Fill my lungs . . .

It had to be some new kind of virtual reality. Nevertheless he felt strangely at ease with the impression of a presence that went deeper than the sheen of the golden walls about him, a presence he felt even more strongly as he reached out to touch the golden walls with the tips of his fingers, and then the flats of his hands. The walls felt heavy and soft like mercury, and yet they were curiously devoid of reflection. They were pulsating. Not expanding and contracting, but pulsating with energy, in liquid-sheening waves.

"Hey!"

He hardly dared to think of where he might be. It was the strangest feeling—the sensation that came back to him through fingertips, passing through his arms, like pins and needles, to arrive like a tranquil whisper in his mind.

"My God!"

He was flooded by a new sensation. It was exhilarating, like . . . rapture. The depression, the sense of desolation, was gone from his mind. These walls, the entire chamber, were as sensitive as living tissue. They were alive in the sense that he himself was alive.

He laughed, abruptly, nervously, bringing his fingertips to his lips. He felt himself breathing again, even though there surely wasn't any air, and he was breathing through nonexistent lungs.

He knew, without pretending to understand the mystery, that he was confronting the heart of the Temple Ship.

Mark closed his eyes for a moment, and when he reopened them Nantosueta appeared, as if the thought of her was all it needed to make her real. Her eyes were very dark against the downy milkiness of her skin. Her hair was the gorgeous blue-black that he remembered. He felt the compulsion to touch it. He reached out, softly, with his left hand, and ran his fingers through it.

"I can really feel your hair!"

He heard her whisper in his mind.

"I feel your touch!"

His breath caught in his throat. He held her face with his splayed fingers, felt the firm roundness of the bone beneath, brushed with the backs of his fingers the

features of her face, feeling the silken brush of her eyelashes as she blinked.

She lightly slapped his face.

He laughed. He couldn't stop himself laughing. He
could feel the tears that were rolling down his cheeks.

"You said you would slap me back."

He kissed her instead. The feel of her lips, kissing him
back, was extraordinary.

"Hold me!"

He held her. There was some awkwardness still in
the tentative flow of their limbs, her arms now enfolding
his neck, drawing him to her, and his embracing her in
turn, each unable to quite believe how they had become
so much more real in the soft, golden light, each needing to confirm the delight of the other, face to face, eye
to eye.

He kissed her again, with a strange, delightful awkwardness, as if to confirm the most intimate touch of
her, lips on lips.

She kissed him back, more certain of him, and this
time he felt the soft, heavy brush of her lips without the
need of communication, mind-to-mind.

He hugged her fiercely to him, even as he was aware
that the world about them was changing.

"The Ship," he whispered against her ear, "something's happening."

The golden glow of the Ship's heart seemed to
invade them, so they became one with the pulse of its
heartbeat.

Their eyes met—a fierceness shared—before the golden aura receded back into the walls and their bodies began to melt away again. Instinctively reaching out, Mark pressed his splayed hands against the yielding pulsation of two adjacent walls, yearningly, longingly, while he still could.

It was late evening, close to pitch dark, when Snakoil Kawkaw escaped the nosy attentions of the Preceptress, whose evening abasement before the foulness of her master would consume her for an hour or so.

Oh, my beloved Master! Punish me—make me deserving.

Such an obsequious litany, accompanied by the burning touch of the sigil against adoring flesh, such self-mutilations and floggings—might she inflict many more hours of it! He gloated at the thought of it.

The Shee guards were patrolling the waterfront so he had to be resourceful, moving quickly from rock to rock, and then biding patience.

He spotted the dark-haired one—the one they kowtowed to as their spiritual guardian. She stood in a triangle of figures that included that buffoon, Siam, and the lovely Kehloke, outside a tent erected for their meetings and war preparations. They were staring out into the ocean, in the direction of the Temple Ship.

Something's going on—something has become the focus of their attentions!

Intrigued, Kawkaw crept closer to the rocks at one end of the bay, from where he observed that the Ship appeared to be changing again. How strange that he should have grown up in its shadow without knowing anything of its secret nature. And what interesting secrets it had so deftly concealed! He peered out at it through a gap in the stones. He knew this was important. With a suppressed oath, he realized that he had allowed his enthusiasm to get the better of him, leaning too far forward, his boots slipping on the black volcanic pebbles as rounded as berries. He lost his footing, ending up with a sorely bruised ass on the rocks. But nobody noticed.

Indeed, he thought, returning his attention to the Ship, *it changes so very rapidly this very instant.*

As far as he could see there was no one on board, other than ghosts. He had heard their voices. *Ghosts who appear to have plans of their own.*

He recalled the huloima called Mark. He had been one of the four brats who had appeared out of a snowstorm back at the ice-bound lake. Thanks to Snakoil Kawkaw's insistence they had been called to account in front of the council of the Olhyiu. They had described killings back in their home world. Killings of parents, for the most part. Those killings had enraged the brats. They had linked those killings, and their coming here, to the Tyrant himself. And curiously, the Tyrant, and latterly the Witch, had behaved as if threatened by them. That made them all the more interesting. And this one, this huloima called Mark, had some curious link with the Ship. Anything to do with the Ship—any tidbit of news—would be of interest to certain ears. And this, in turn, made these changes in the Ship mightily important.

Yes! Yes, my beauty! I see you, I watch you as closely as the snake watches the mouse. And you are changing still, changing moment by moment, and all in utter silence and secrecy.

He stared at it from his perch among the rocks, his eyes protruding with fascination, as its shape went through a temporary amorphousness, resembling a storm cloud, to emerge somewhat like the raptor but more streamlined, like a diving cormorant perhaps. A shape intended for very rapid fall—or flight.

A bright glow permeated the thing even as it lifted, with hardly a ripple from the ocean, turning in a seemingly weightless fashion as if searching for its bearings. The prow directed itself heavenwards.

"Serpent's-tongued hogsturd!"

Snakoil Kawkaw stared, his mouth fallen open, as the streamlined shape rose into the night air like an upwardly directed bolt of lightning. It was gone in a trice, diminishing to a point in less time than it took him to blink. And then there was nothing. It had winked out, as if lost amid the stars.

SOUL STEALERS

THINGS GREW ASKEW HERE, PERVERTED IN THEIR desire for light and form. The most beautiful flower was a trap. The water was putrescent. Slime moved. It changed patterns, played tricks with you when you weren't looking. Then, when you noticed, those patterns had evolved some primal intelligence, so they were gathering and thickening, creeping toward you. The insects were vicious and stinging—they laid eggs that hatched into monstrous parasites inside your body . . .

A hand was shaking Alan's shoulder. Ainé's voice in his ear: "Wake up! You cry out in your dreams."

"Was it a dream?" He sat up and rubbed his hands over his face. The events of yesterday had been so terrible, this place so threatening, he had lain awake for most of the night, assuming he would spend a second night without a wink—and then . . .

"A dream of darkness, perhaps?"

"Yes!" He had been confronting the Tyrant again. But it had been here, in this haunted landscape rather than Dromenon. And yet the buzzing words of malice still echoed within his skull as he climbed to his feet, shaking his head fully awake in the cool of the early dawn.

"Kate—where is she?"

"She tends the wounded land."

"What—on her own?"

"She's not alone. She is accompanied by the shaman. And the dwarf mage watches over both." The Kyra paused, as if deep in thought. Then she added: "I understand now—why you insisted on saving her. And perhaps more."

Alan looked up at the Kyra in the murky light. Was she reconsidering his offer to help her with her mother-sister's memories?

He climbed to his feet, brushing ash and the wrinkles of sleep from his clothes. He had to remind himself of where he was. They had rested here when they had reached the furthermost limits of what had been the Forest of Harrow.

He said, "You were right, too—about the risks."

"There are times when risks must be taken."

He scanned the figures among the ashes of the thorn trees, glimpsing Kate and Turkeya at perhaps fifty yards distance. They were hard to discern in the drifting mists.

They were huddled over the sprouting shoots that were
the new growth, brought into being by Kate's power of
healing. For a little while he watched Kate, as if needing
to reassure himself that this was real, and not merely
another dream, feeling almost dizzy with the warmth
of his love for her. He could just about hear the chat-
ter of her voice, the soft Irish accent, even at this distance sounding curiously relaxed amid the devastation.
Then, stretching limbs that ached with stiffness from a
night on the ungiving ground, he accepted a dampened
cloth from an Aides and used it to rub the sleep from his
eyes. He knew that many Aides, as well as Shee, had died
from wounds, but her face was impassive. He couldn't
help but reflect how brave they all were, Aides, Shee—
Qwenqwo too.

He breathed in deeply, feeling ravenously hungry.
"And you, Ainé—is your sleep tormented by this place?"

"Normally I sleep without dreams—but here . . ."

Alan was silent, sensing she was of a mind to say
more.

"I awoke to memories of my grandmother-sister."

He had to reflect a moment or two on that. Then he
recalled a memory. "Once, at a time of great danger
in another forest, your mother talked to me about her
mother-sister. How she died in the Great Arena in Ghork
Mega."

"My mother-sister, when still a child, was captured
with her mother-sister at the fall of Ossierel. They were
taken prisoner to the Tyrant's city. There, in the arena,

my grandmother-sister was made to fight in protection of her daughter. She fought a Legun—the one they call the Captain."

Alan coughed ash from his throat. "It was this same Legun that killed your mother-sister."

He saw the Kyra look at him askance, those glacial blue eyes that so easily could turn to a terrifying glare. How little Alan understood the Shee, or for that matter their Kyras. All that stuff about ancient lineages and the sharing of memories across those lineages! He knew, for example, that the Kyras were related by blood to the martyred high Architect of Ossierel, Ussha De Danaan, who had refused to use her oracular powers in defense of the ancient capital.

Then the Kyra surprised him, her eyes gazing away into the distance to where in the north sky the red glow emanating from the Tower of Bones was unmistakable, even in the early light. Her oraculum ignited to a gentle background glow in which whorls and arabesques of silvery light metamorphosed and pulsated. "If I were to dream, it would be to see myself kill that one. I would kill him a thousand times, in a thousand different ways, in a thousand different dreams."

"Huh!" Alan dropped his head. It was the closest thing he had ever come to an intimate discussion with a Shee.

Once more gazing toward Kate in the distance, he couldn't help but reflect on the strangeness of his situation. He wouldn't have described himself as imaginative.

And yet to be faced with Leguns! Witches! Immortals! How could an ordinary guy come to terms with this place? There were times when he felt such a desperate yearning for his ordinary world, for Earth with its easy logic, its respect for what was demonstrable, measurable, comprehensible . . .

"Have you thought about what I suggested—the return of your mother-sister's memories?"

The Kyra's reply was pitched low as a growl. "I'll admit that I have considered it. I will speak of it with Bétaald . . ."

She hesitated, as if uncertain whether to elaborate further. Indeed Ainé had fallen into a silence so deep he wondered if she was any longer aware that he was present. Then he realized she was listening. The Kyra was instantly alert, and the mood of alertness moved, like a contagion, throughout the Shee.

Alan climbed to his feet, probing their surroundings as he did so. The warming air appeared stiller than ever, without even the rustle of the wind.

"The Garg returns!"

Even following the direction of her gaze it was several seconds before he saw the swooping figure appear out of the mists, then Iyezzz alighting, with the flapping of those enormous leathery wings, onto the ground just feet away.

"How far are we from the Tower?" the Kyra demanded.

"A day's march!"

"And a night's rest," Qwenqwo had joined them. "If rest is possible."

The Kyra growled: "What new perils can we anticipate?"

"The wolves—we call them 'witch's teeth'—will hold back until you are closer to the Tower. More immediately you will enter a landscape permanently cloaked in mist. I know not what malice to expect there." The Garg's face looked pensive. "Though there are stories . . ."

Alan turned to Qwenqwo. "You talked about this—back on the beach, when we had the counsel. You mentioned shadow creatures—a thousand times more dangerous than Gargs?"

"Hah!" Qwenqwo laughed. "Well might a warrior regret his battle-talk, born of the flagon around the campfire. Now sober, I will admit that they may be nothing more than yarns to frighten children."

"Not so, Fir Bolg!" Iyezzz dropped his eyes, speaking softly, his neck gills purring with a high-pitched vibration that Alan interpreted as awe. "The Witch took pleasure in punishing succubi, according to her whim. One would be selected and forced to endure a night outside the Tower." The young Garg's skin color paled and his eyes performed a prolonged blink.

The Kyra intervened. "It would appear, then, that we need to be wary of new dangers in these mist-shrouded approaches. But what manner of dangers?"

"You will arrive at the valley of the Tower by nightfall. But thereafter, whatever sleep you might need in anticipation of a dawn attack on the Tower will be at your peril."

The Kyra stared at the young Garg, the glare now full in those terrible eyes. "Up to now, the last defense before the Tower has been the guardian Gargs. Can we anticipate an attack by your people as we sleep?"

"There will be no threat from the Eyrie People."

The Kyra's glare was unrelenting. "These perils ahead—their threat in sleep must be graver than bad dreams?"

"Among my people there are rumors of mist wraiths—creatures of the night that feed on the soul spirits of the living as vultures feed on the dead. Rumor or fact, I know not. But if the rumors are true, any attempt at sleep in such close proximity to the Tower of Bones may be more dangerous than what you have encountered in the swamps or the forest of the thorn trees."

The Kyra remained pensive. "I must know more. The Great Witch herself—what of her designs?"

The young Garg's eyes met those of the Kyra without flinching. "Olc has sacrificed all to resurrecting the soul spirit of the titan, Fangorath."

"What does this resurrection mean?"

The Garg opened wide his wings in what might be the equivalent of an expression of uncertainty or even awe. "Stay clear of the Tower itself. Such is the conflagration that consumes it, the very bones are splintering, as if about to explode."

More and more of the company were gathering about Iyezzz, while a breeze blew rain-matted ash into their faces and clothes. People were staring up at the Garg with eyes agog but the Kyra remained practical.

"I must press you. In your judgment, has the Witch succeeded in reawakening the soul spirit of the titan?"

"I know not—how would one judge such a thing? If I were to hazard a guess I would imagine that while the Tower yet stands, she has not succeeded. But that moment surely approaches."

Ainé stood stiffly erect, her oraculum pulsating strongly, and confronted both Alan and Kate. "Are you still set on this?"

They nodded—Alan first and then Kate.

"Then there is no time to be lost in further discussion. We must make what progress we can by daylight." The Kyra signaled the Shee to make haste to break camp. What nourishment they needed would have to be taken on the move. They would keep to a steady pace, with no possibility of rest before nightfall. The surviving Shee formed a trapezoid about Alan and Kate, and without further preamble all headed out into the thickening mists under the bloodied sky.

What was the matter with him? Iyezzz had warned them not to fall sleep so close to the Tower and yet Alan found himself, for the second night running, being woken from a nightmare by a hand shaking his shoulder. This time it wasn't the Kyra but the older Shee, Xeenra, who was rousing him. Attempting to blink the heavy sleep from his eyes he found that his mind was unusually clouded, as if the torpor of sleep was one with the dense mist into which he had awakened. Seduction, he thought—the idea trying to break through into his consciousness. *Seduction—such as the Witch employed through her succubi!* He struggled to his feet, alarmed to find that even the Shee guardians were sluggish with that same torpor. Many appeared to have fallen asleep, with only a scattering of alert warriors protecting the fireless encampment. Xeenra, with a finger to her lips, was urging him to silence.

What now?

The Kyra! She mouthed the words without speaking them, sweeping an arm wide, as if to indicate that the Kyra was somewhere out there, in the mists.

"Where is she?"

Between thumb and forefinger, she waggled the lobe of her left ear.

Silence!

Alan was still, feeling the chill of the condensing mist on his skin. His own breathing sounded loud in his ears.

Xeenra raised a finger. *Something comes!*

Damn it—I let this happen! I couldn't resist the drowsiness. Iyezzz was right in his warning. There's something in the mist—something that must be attacking us in some subtle kind of way.

Alan peered around the camp but saw nothing. There was no intimation of movement. Sniffing at the still air, there wasn't even a scent. Yet through the oraculum he sensed something terribly wrong, an ominous presence all around them.

He grabbed the spear of Lug. Suddenly he had an idea his stupefied mind had been slow to think of. He turned the oraculum to the mind of the Shee. It shocked him—terrified him—to discover the fear that proliferated there.

In Xeenra's mind he found himself sharing a memory. Like many of her sister-warriors Xeenra had been unable to stay awake. She had drowsed fitfully in this blighted land and, in brief snatches of sleep, had witnessed dreams she now saw as omens. Her mother-sister, also called Xeenra, had witnessed similar omens immediately prior to her death. In Xeenra's dreams a darkness had fallen on her from the sky, entered her being and stolen her soul-memories. It was the worst fate that could possibly befall a Shee, for the soul-memories were the most precious inheritance the mother-sister bequeathed to her daughter-sister. A Shee devoid of her soul-memories was bereft of meaning, no more than a husk. Neavrhashvahar, the sacred union with life, was ended.

My God!

Alan wheeled about, the spear of Lug erupting into flame, searching in all directions. A fury of power danced in the runes running over the edges of its spiral blade. But still nothing was visible, there was no sound, no scent, but the ominous presence was closer now. He kept an eye on Xeenra, stayed connected with her mind as, ever watchful, she unsheathed her sword and brought its green-glowing blade to her brow. He heard the plea for absolution she sent to the Kyra of Kyras, the late High Architect and Shee, Ussha De Danaan.

I, Xeenra, of the matrilineal line of Desuccorr, embrace my death. Let me be one with the communion of mother-sisters. Let my daughter-sister be the future and hope of the unbroken circle.

Alan's eyes followed those of the Shee as they swiveled up to the darker patch within the mist overhead. He saw the first rancid drop of the spittle as it fell, a pearly gray gobbet that struck Xeenra's brow even as her sword sprang up to pierce the spectral tentacles that were descending over her amid a deluge of slimy malice. Alan thrust the spear into the vile thing that hovered in the air above the Shee. But as he did so Xeenra shoved him forcefully away from the trap even as she screamed with pain, while the spittle, like the most powerful acid, bored through the skin of her brow and invaded the bone. In seconds it had reached her brain, where it fed on her mind, gorging on the memories it found there, stealing her hopes and dreams in the moments before death.

Ainé arrived in time to see the horror of what enveloped and consumed the body of the dead warrior.

A vaporous thing, jelly-like and phosphorescent with putridity, enveloped the Shee like a shroud. Then it slid off the white-glowing bones, like an insect shedding its skin. There was a shape of sorts, vaguely humanoid, with sheening pinpoints of light where the eyes should be. Keeping Alan behind her, the Kyra ran her sword through the vileness, but it had no effect. She might as well be running the blade through water. A sound rose from the thing, a wrenching sigh, as if sated. Even when the Kyra tried again, touching the blade against her oraculum until it shone with green fire, the blade simply went through the ghost-like wraith, which ascended like smoke into the misty shadows overhead.

Ainé stared after it, horrified.

Alan rushed among the sleepers, waking them, warning them to wake all the others. Everybody seemed unusually bleary, unnaturally disorientated, as if their minds were as fogged as his had been.

"What is it?" a drowsy Qwenqwo demanded. "Are we under attack?"

"Yes—but by what, I don't know." Alan could only do his best to describe the horror of what he had seen. Even as he spoke there was another heart-wrenching scream, quickly followed by several others: more Shee, or Aides, dead. Alan's oraculum burst into brilliant red flame.

But the dwarf mage held his arm, restraining him from running in the direction of the scream. "Shadow spawn!" he hissed.

As more and more screams erupted in the mists, Qwenqwo's roar sounded out throughout the camp. "These beings are stealers of souls. Hear me—if you would survive this terrible place! There is nothing to gain through concealment. Our enemy knows where we are. Make noises. Light fires—and a firebrand to every hand. These ghouls are said to prosper in the dark of night, and in the silence. Above all they fear the flame."

In the time it took to get several fires blazing, and sufficient torches to fill every waking hand, many more died. And so it was, clustering together for protection about the fires, and in the light of the firebrands, they saw a terrifying sight, with shadow spawn appearing out of the dark in hundreds, perhaps thousands—their sickly forms floating through the mists, as if weightless. The more they searched in all directions, the more numerous the shadow spawn appeared to be. Yet at the slightest touch of a firebrand, the seemingly indestructible creatures, whose diaphanous bodies had felt no sting from sword or spear, were consumed to smoke. Moaning horribly, as if they couldn't bear to deny themselves this feast of life, they still descended to attack again and again, often in dozens at once, in spite of the fact that the flames consumed them. Only with the first light of dawn did the exhausted company see them retreat into the mists, their wretched eyes sheening like balefire.

"Qwenqwo—you saved us!"

"We were fortunate, those of us who survived the horror," Qwenqwo said, as the sky lightened over the guttering bonfires, "that we had such a ready supply of dry tinder from the ruins of the thorn trees."

"But why," asked Kate, "would the Witch attempt to kill us before ever we get to the Tower when she wants to draw Alan into her trap?"

"Maybe she doesn't intend to kill me—or you, Kate." Alan's head had fallen, but now he lifted it to look at her, dawn's glimmer reflecting in his eyes.

"The Mage Lord is right," Qwenqwo nodded. "The power of your oracula might very well have saved you from thorn trees and shadow spawn. But not us—your protectors and guardians."

Qwenqwo paused, lifting his head to listen to the sound that cut through the early morning air. Now that they were so much closer to the Tower, they heard the first howling of its guardian wolves. It was an unpleasant welcome for the new day for a company with no option but to trudge on northwards, under an increasingly livid sky, its blood-red light penetrating the mists with thunderous detonations of awakening power.

They moved on cautiously, on the lookout for any new traps that might await them. In the daylight it was sobering to witness how reduced was their company; no more than half the original Shee now guarded them. And despite their fabled reserves of strength, the Shee were obviously exhausted, physically and mentally. The Kyra, reassured that the sun was now well above the horizon, called for a brief rest, during which the surviving Aides allowed a single sip of healwell to aid the flagging spirits of the warriors. Although the Kyra denied herself.

Alan rested in the company of Kate, Turkeya, Qwenqwo and Mo, the exhausted friends flopping down
in the arid dirt, their backs resting against the trunk
of a long-dead tree that had grown within the fossilized ribs of some monstrous beast. Too tired to make
conversation, Alan held Kate's hand, each only too
aware of the fears and uncertainties that must be rising in the heart of the other and wondering where they
would find the courage to face what they must face
very soon.

The landscape here was reduced to lifeless dirt and
rock, its surface pitted with irregular craters—traps
filled with stagnant water to drown the unfortunates
who might take a wrong step. The wolf howls sounded
closer now, and Iyezzz frequently sniffed at the air, his
head twisting in an arc, as if searching for any new
manifestation of the enemy.

"Can you see it, from here?" Kate's voice was a husky
whisper addressing the tall, winged figure, who alone
stood erect with his wings folded across his back, their
tips extending from high above his head to his scaly feet.

"Indeed. The Tower of Bones is all too visible from
the air, even as a shadow upthrust against the sky."

"Then, she—the Witch—can also see us."

It was a statement, and not a question. The Garg
acknowledged this, retracting his eyelids in a respectful silence.

There was no point holding it off any longer. Alan
hauled himself back onto his feet. He wondered if the

circle of destruction provoked by his own power had reached even as far as here. Cinders and ash blew against his face, stinging his eyes, causing him to hold the sleeve of his coat against his face.

"Okay! It's not much of a plan. But I guess that from now on we save every ounce of strength for what's to come."

A new smell, the acrid stench of sulfur, penetrated through the sleeve; he thought he could taste it on his tongue. He didn't think it came from the thorn trees. It had to come from the Tower. Turning the oraculum inwards, he felt the First Power invade his being. He allowed it to grow to the point of pain, coursing through the tired muscles and sinews, feeling its charge invade his heart, until he could feel the pulsations of its chambers swell the arteries in his throat.

The Kyra spoke: "What do you perceive of the land ahead?"

Through the oraculum Alan could penetrate the mists and see that they had reached the edge of a great plateau, a blighted landscape certainly, but underneath the desolate surface were shapes and ruins. "Looks like some kind of a graveyard—from the size of the bones, I guess a graveyard of giants."

The Kyra exhaled. "Were there no mist, we should see the Tower itself."

Alan stared ahead, forcing his concentration to increase, sensing the Tower's looming presence, the horror of it so very close.

The Kyra interrupted his thoughts, springing to alertness and roaring out a warning: "Shee beware! Something comes!"

The Shee formed a barrier between their charges and the direction from which the red-pulsating menace colored the sky.

With a limping gait, a gigantic wolf appeared out of the mists, white hair soaked with sweat and clotted with the blood of many wounds. Its jaws were parted on enormous fangs. Its gray eyes, bloodshot yet defiant, stared at the company, nostrils snuffling in their direction. With a growl that caused every hackle to rise, it moved with limping strides in their direction until it stood before them, its muzzle slavering blood. Its emaciated chest was spasming in great wincing drafts, as if it were panting its last breaths.

Several among the Shee lofted javelins, but Kate pushed through the defensive line to throw her arms about the creature's neck.

"No! Please don't harm him." She almost blurted out his secret name, but held her tongue. "This is my friend. He ignored his own hunger and saved my life when I was running from the Tower. He risked his life to protect me from the other wolves."

Kate's oraculum burst into flame, covering the trembling figure in its soft green light. Before their astonished gazes the wolf changed into a tall, emaciated man, a very old man, also terribly wounded.

"Let us help you."

"This is no time to concern yourself about me. I have come to warn you, little healer. You should immediately turn about—and run!"

"We can't do that." Alan joined Kate in standing before the wolf-man, who had fallen onto his knees, struggling for breath.

"The entire pack, the Witch's teeth, they come in their hundreds. They outnumber you by more than ten to one. You must flee—or die."

FANGORATH

KATE'S LIPS WERE COMPRESSED WITH WORRY AS she knelt by the injured Nightshade, whose pain was being treated with healwell while his wounds were being dressed by several Aides. There was no guarantee he would survive—and even if he did he would face the very attack he had risked his life to warn them about. Kate closed her eyes and directed whatever healing powers her oraculum possessed onto his ravaged body.

She felt Alan put his arm around her shoulders. He spoke softly: "Maybe I'd better go ahead on my own!"

"No!" Kate climbed back onto her feet and hugged him tight. She couldn't stop herself trembling, even though she knew he could feel it.

He kissed her brow. "You heard what the wolf-man said. Maybe you should all retreat—find a safer place. Leave me to go on alone?"

"Not without me!"

He insisted gently. "We both know that Ainé thinks it's suicidal."

"I don't care. I keep thinking—Granny Dew—when she gave me this power, she told me something. She told me to trust my heart alone."

They could hear the howling of the wolves, rapidly closing. Looking up into Alan's face, Kate saw the same stubborn look she recalled from the day she had first met him on the bank of the River Suir, when the swans were beating though the air, heading straight at him, and he refused to duck down.

"I'm not waiting for them to attack. I'm going to take the fight to them."

With the small gathering of surviving Shee singing their battle hymn around them Alan pressed forward, Kate next to him, leading the company into a mist so dense it could have been a cloud.

"What is it?" she asked him. "You're scowling."

"The Witch—I sense her watching us."

Feeling Kate's grip tightening about his arm, Alan recalled what Sister Hocht in her dying moments had told him about this place in answer to his question: "What is it about the Tower of Bones?"

Her words had been slurred. But he had read her meaning on her destroyed lips . . .

The Third Portal!

"Oh, man!"

"What is it?"

Should he add to her terror by explaining what he knew?

There was no longer time for him to think about it. They had broken through the bank of mists to be confronted by an extraordinary sight. Up ahead, so monstrous it made them hesitate, the Tower had been subsumed in a furnace of baleful red, erupting over the landscape and into the sky in pulsating waves. It was as if the magma at the core of the world had burst through the surface and was clawing at the sky. Dark shapes flickered within it, like two beings of enormous power at war with one another.

"What's that noise?" Alan's voice was husky with disbelief.

"The Witch's song—Olc exultant!"

"Hey, don't allow her to frighten you, Kate"

"I can't help it. She terrifies me."

A cloud of dust was approaching. It came from the pounding feet of wolves, a multitude of them, with fangs agape and tongues slavering. The small defensive wall of Shee tensed, javelins raised.

The oraculum in Alan's brow burst into flame, directed at the ground immediately in front of the wolves. Lightning struck in a series of incandescent arcs, descending out of the darkening sky and ripping at the land. A gigantic rent appeared directly across the path of the wolves. They continued their charge, despite many of them plummeting into the chasm. But most of them made it, sweeping around the edges of the chasm, some leaping across seemingly impossible distances as if their frenzy had given them wings. Hundreds survived and continued their attack. By now these were close enough for the Shee javelins to take out their leaders. But it made little difference.

The approaching wolves were close enough now for Alan and Kate to smell them, the rabid breath mixed with the sweat-soaked pelts. They could see the bloodlust that burned in their eyes. At a signal from the Kyra the Shee metamorphosed into great cats, and they closed, in a snarling arc, in front of the company. Alan caught sight of Qwenqwo Cuatzel, his lips moving in a chant of prayer, the runes over the edges of his battleaxe glowing in his upraised arm. But the odds were still hopeless.

Then Alan heard Iyezzz's screech—and he followed the direction of the pointed wing-claw, to where a dark cloud was blotting out the daylight. Gargs! A vast horde of them. He could even make out the extended claws that glittered over the extended feet. Where was he to turn the power of his oraculum, to the wall of slavering fangs on the ground or against the Gargs falling out of the sky?

Kate was tugging at his arm, her trembling hand gesticulating . . .

Alan shook his head, assuming that she was trying to tell him what he already knew. But she yanked at him still harder, pointing to where the Gargs were descending, claws extended, fangs bared.

He heard Iyezzz's roar. "The King—my father—has kept his word."

The Gargs weren't attacking them. They were swooping on the wolves, the animals massing about the protective wall of Shee. Confused by the attack falling on them from out of the sky, many of the wolves were turning their rage on one another. He felt Kate's arm hug his own, both watching in amazement as the Eyrie Gargs snatched wolves bodily off the ground and, ignoring their howling and snapping, bore them high into the air—only to hurl them to their deaths on the rocky ground.

Thank you, Momu!

Even as he sensed Kate's words of gratitude, he felt a hand on his shoulder and he turned around to gaze into the eyes of Nightshade. The wolf-man was less stooped, his wounds healing. But still it was his species who were being destroyed.

"I'm sorry!"

"A thousand generations were lost to the Witch's purpose. But there will be a new generation—if you can but defeat her this day."

Acrid smoke poured into the sky from the furnace of the Tower, consuming the daylight so it appeared like dusk in the early afternoon. Fierce gusts of wind erupted outward in waves, tearing at their faces so they were forced to squint, and ripping at their hair. Kate's dress was flattened against her body. Oh, lord! Now she had arrived at the moment of confrontation, her courage was failing her.

"You don't know her," she pleaded with Alan. "I don't know if I dare to take another step out there. Look at it!"

"I have to go now, Kate. While the Witch is preoccupied with getting close and comfortable with the titan."

"Not without me!"

"Qwenqwo! Please tell her?"

"The Mage Lord is right. Now is the time for him to face the Witch. He must destroy her or be destroyed."

The ground quaked beneath them as another thunderous detonation emanated from the furnace.

Kate whispered: "I'm frightened for him, Qwenqwo."

"Only a fool would not be frightened. Yet if the Witch achieves full consummation with the titan the emerging being will be powerful beyond belief. Its malice will be far more dangerous than the sum of each individually."

Alan nodded to Qwenqwo. "Please make it clear to Kate what will happen if we fail—the Cill, the Gargs?"

"They will perish."

"And us—Kate and me?"

"You will be seen as rivals in power. Whatever emerges from that consummation will destroy you both."

Alan gently pried himself free of Kate. Gazing into his eyes she was looking at the reflection of the horrible pulsating furnace that was the Tower. "You know in your heart that there's no time left. If the Witch wins, everything I came here to do will be over. It was always going to be her or me."

"I'm coming with you."

Another thunderous detonation pitched even the Shee off-balance. Within seconds a storm of gray ash descended over the company, whirling among them like snow caught up in a gale.

"No, Kate!"

"I'll get over my terror."

"She knows you. She knows your weaknesses. If you're there with me, I'll be worrying all the time about protecting you instead of killing her." He kissed her softly, then held her at arms' length.

Qwenqwo, one burly arm around Mo, reached out his other arm and embraced the trembling Kate. "The Mage Lord is right. You will not help him by accompanying him out there. But there is a way in which you might truly help him undermine the Witch. It is through your gift, Kate. If you can counter the evil of her purpose here, it will injure her at the fulcrum of her malice."

In Qwenqwo's embrace, Kate wept, through closed eyelids.

Another way . . .

Kate nodded, understanding now, and she opened her tear-filled eyes and took a reluctant step away from Alan. Placing the seed pouch in the bowl of her hands, with lips and mind as one, she blew life out into the valley of the Tower of Bones.

Qwenqwo released Kate and Mo to take a fierce grip of Alan's shoulders. "Before you face such a foe, a word of advice. Back there, on the lip of the maelstrom, the Tyrant used your power against you."

"You're right. I've thought about that." Alan wiped the coating of ash from his lips, which was making it difficult even to speak. "I won't fall for it a second time."

The dwarf mage, his red hair and beard, even his very eyebrows, turned gray with the same ash, looked him fiercely in the eyes. "You cannot go there alone. I will accompany you—aye, and the Kyra also!"

"No, Qwenqwo. There's nothing your battleaxe, or the Kyra's sword or javelin, can do there."

"Even so, we can stand shoulder to shoulder with you. We can give you the comfort of our presence."

"If I fail, you'll have to try to save Kate and Mo." Alan hugged the burly Fir Bolg warrior. But then, as he turned to leave them, the Kyra strode forward, and to his surprise she offered the twining of arms that was the Shee mark of respect in battle. Their eyes met for a moment before he broke the contact, turning to Iyezzz. "I need to get over the chasm I created with the First Power. I don't have time to go around it. Can your people help me to get as close as possible to the Witch without being blown apart?"

Kate stared, her exhausted arms fallen to her sides, as two of the biggest Gargs took an arm each, their wings beating slowly and powerfully, lofting Alan in seconds and then sweeping out in the direction of the Tower. She felt Mo's embrace close around her as they watched him become diminished with distance until he appeared vulnerably tiny, dwarfed by the spuming monstrosity.

"I can't believe I let him go. Mo—if he dies, I will too!"

"If he dies, we'll all die with him."

Alan's attack was immediate. Lightning erupted from the tiny figure and struck the Tower, causing an ear-crackling thunder, and in its wake an earthquake shook the ground under their feet.

Kate struggled against her fears to try to remember more of what the Momu had taught her. *Olc . . . dependent for her sustenance on cruelty, exulting in the agony suffered by the Momu as city after city was hunted down and discovered, then annihilated, spiritually sucked dry.* She poured out her own attack upon the Witch, delivering a great wave of healing, of rebirth, feeling it deluge from the oraculum in her brow and spread the force of life far and wide throughout the valley. Even as she did so she heard the scream of outrage from the incandescent monstrosity that had replaced the Tower, sensing the shudder of pain that came from the depraved soul at the very heart of it. For a fleeting moment, they faced one another in open confrontation, two minds, two wills, two soul spirits— and she felt the weakening of her enemy.

The lightning still poured relentlessly out of the Alan's brow, tearing through and around the roiling furnace, erupting skywards where it struck, flattening overhead against the black mountains of clouds that had grown into a gigantic mushroom of darkness, and then cascading back down again in a cataract of twisting, spiraling devastation that extinguished the raging furnace of the Tower. And still the First Power continued to pour out of Alan as if his rage was limitless.

How brave he was! Surely there was nothing left to fight in the great ball of lightning that had replaced the pulsating red. Kate's heart flooded with admiration for him. She poured out her love for him through the oraculum in her brow, only wanting the terrible vision to stop. But it didn't stop.

Her voice was little above a whisper. "Mo, I don't think he can stop. I don't think he's in control of it anymore."

Mo's face appeared to glow. There was something going on with Mo but Kate was too stressed to take it in. Her friend spoke urgently, "The Witch is defeated."

"I—I don't understand."

Kate stared uncomprehendingly at the new apocalyptic shape that was rising out of the ruin of the Tower. She watched as the colossus swelled and expanded, rising until it seemed to bury its head in the clouds, high above the dwarfed figure of Alan in the field of ash, then threw back its great horned head and bared its fangs, roaring with triumph into the maelstrom of clouds.

Mo fell silent, staring with Kate at the distant figure of Alan, and toying with the amulet she wore about her neck. She looked so very different from when Kate had seen her before being carried off to the Tower; this new Mo was hardly recognizable. How tall she had grown, her face longer, hauntingly beautiful. Kate blinked, realizing that there was also something different about the amulet she was holding onto. It wasn't the bog-oak figurine she had expected. It was something circular, and pulsating with light. Kate caught a glimpse of a crystalline disk in which flickering motes and arabesques formed and reformed in a perpetual metamorphosis. The light of the disk was illuminating Mo's face from below, highlighting the rapt expression of this rapidly maturing young woman.

Kate thought, *I'm not sure I know Mo anymore.*

She grabbed hold of Mo's hand, staring into the eyes of her friend, and trying to understand what was going on. "Mo—you know something I don't. What is it? What's happening?"

"It's the Witch, not Alan, who has lost control."

Staring skywards at the monstrous figure, Kate was stunned. She found herself falling back onto the oraculum in her brow, examining the scene as if through a third eye. Her gaze found Alan, his distant figure looking so tiny and brave before the towering inferno that was the titan. Suddenly he looked more vulnerable still. With a cry of anguish, Kate saw that he had switched off the attack, the oraculum in his brow now spent.

THE DRAGON KING

THE VOICE THAT SPOKE TO MO—THAT HAD BEEN
speaking to her from the moment Alan had first attacked
the Tower—came through the Torus. It was the same
voice that had spoken to her in the cave of the City of
the Ancients. Now it was telling her what had become
of the Great Witch.

Gone—destroyed.

"Alan won?"

*Through the First Power, the Mage Lord, Duval, has
initiated the fate that was preordained here, at the Tower
of Bones. He was assisted by the weakening of her purpose
wrought by your companion, in restoring life to the land
through the Power of Mab. Through both their courage
and endurance a great wrong may yet be righted. That
wrong led to the wasting of these lands. It began long*

ago—before ever the Great Witch came to the Tower. So it was that even as the Witch imagined that she was fulfilling her own destiny, it was a much greater power and destiny that lurked and conspired beyond the veil of reality.

"Then, in destroying the Witch, Alan may have completed the resurrection of the titan?"

This was ever Fangorath's purpose. Knowing so, we gave you the Torus in anticipation of this moment. Now that he has been resurrected he will look to complete his original aim. He will attempt to open the portal that was sealed on his original destruction. In this he must not succeed. To prevent that from happening, a terrible battle, fought out long ago in this very place, must be fought anew.

"What do you mean?"

What ended that eons-old conflict was an error of judgment. It was expedient, for the danger that ensued would have been too terrible to contemplate. Mórígán was implored to intercede. But in answering such a desperate prayer the Third Power contravened the laws of Fate. So you glimpse a trajectory that was set in motion long ago. However indirectly, it was this error that led to your coming here. The laws of Fate cannot be broken again. Those earlier consequences must be redressed.

"But what can we possibly do, if Fangorath is so powerful?"

Unknowingly, your companion, with her gift of the Second Power, has set a course in motion. Look to the south, to the life-giving oceans!

* * *

Kate blinked in recognition of Mo's hand on her shoulder, this new Mo, curiously calm and purposive, encouraging her to turn around and gaze back in the direction they had come. Kate saw, through the clogging ash in her eyelashes, the strangeness that was invading the lowering sky. And then it appeared to come alive. The entire southern horizon twinkled in the gloom, and something at the very center of it began to swell and to advance, as if the air was transformed by the magic in its passing, cascading every color of the rainbow over the enormous spread of what looked like wings. They stiffened in astonishment to hear it thunder, words too deep and strange to recognize as any familiar language, the challenge trembling through the ground under their feet as it swept forward and found its focus.

The titan roared.

"Oh, Mo! It must be Driftwood."

All around her, Kate saw the Gargs and Cill warriors fall to their knees. She heard their communal cries:

"Omdorrréilliuc—Omdorrréilliuc!"

They were prostrating themselves, as if before a god.

The thunder erupted again, juddering through the rocks under their feet as if they were standing on lumbering tectonic plates. Driftwood, if it truly was Driftwood, had grown enormous, and the swirling waves of power iridescing from his wings made him appear ten times larger. Kate could make out the sinewy bend of the great neck as the long, serpent-like body undulated in a powerful rhythm, advancing through the resisting air.

In what seemed little more than a few leviathan beats of his wings, his head, as large as a house, was directly over her. The huge eyes were slitted, as if streamlined for speed, the orange sparkle within them like the inner heat of an iron-smelting furnace. This time she sensed the words speeding over her like the rattle of a passing train:

Dragon secrets—Kate—Greeneyes—girl-thing!

As if he had read her mind.

It was hard to concentrate, to think back about things, with her mind racing. *What was he, really?* Her eyes moved from Mo, holding onto her arm, to the figure of Alan in the distance, standing perfectly still though he appeared to be surrounded by a whirling hurricane of energy.

Dragon secrets!

She made herself think, recall the history she had discovered when she had entered Driftwood's mind. The dreadful war between the dragons and the titans and how, in order to bring an end to the destruction, the surviving dragons had chewed off their own wings and drowned in the oceans.

But there was more . . . There had always been more. What?

Driftwood had warned her that he was the bearer of secrets. And now she understood something that had puzzled her on their very first meeting. How the ground had shaken with the impact when he had performed those somersaults. There had been something immense about him even then, when he was a very small dragon fawning over his shiny thing.

The titan turned to face the approaching dragon, one hand outstretched, every finger capped by an enormous black claw. From the tips of the claws lightning poured in a crackling deluge to erupt over the head of the dragon. Kate saw that the dragon's flight slowed. Then, with eyes ablaze and fangs agape, the titan issued a command that sounded like the same thunderous rumble of the dragon's own tongue. Lightning exploded again, with multiple arcs attacking the dragon from head to tail. Fangorath reared against the sky, thunderbolts clenched in either hand. Dragon and titan circled one another like mountains, roaring challenges that crackled and echoed through ground and sky. The atmosphere flooded with oceans of red, as if the world were drowning in blood.

Then something exploded into a colossal turquoise brilliance, like the birth of a sun, at the center of the conflict. The landscape about Kate shuddered. Cracks appeared through the rocks under her feet, through which clouds of incandescent vapor billowed high into the sky, with vast secondary trails and movements within them, amid which explosions took place from moment to moment.

Kate and Mo clung to one another, seeing the world dissolve around them. They were free-falling into nothingness. Kate heard Mo's whisper as if it were addressed to somebody else. Mo was still clinging to her arm. With her other hand Mo was holding tight to the amulet strung around her neck. Her whisper was: *"Dromenon!"*

"What's happening?"

Kate couldn't imagine that this was the Dromenon Alan had described to her. He had talked in awe about an endless white plain. This was like falling into a nebula in space. Gargantuan clouds of light and dark wheeled about some unknown center of gravity, moving cataracts of mauve and gold, rapidly changing shape and substance as they formed, and all so vast as to overwhelm her senses.

Mo whispered again—strange words, repeating some realization that had crept into her mind: *Battle has entered Dromenon.*

Kate's jaws ached from clenching them. She was screwing shut her eyes. "Mo—if you know we're not already dead, or worse, will you explain to me what in the world is happening?"

Mo's reply was strangely calm: "I don't know any more than you do. But I suspect that Dromenon, or at least this version of it, is bottomless."

Thunderous explosions rippled through the darkness, evidence of the ongoing battle between the dragon and the titan.

"Have you any idea what's going on?"

"Fangorath is searching for the Third Portal."

"Oh, lord!"

"It's what it was all about, all along."

"Do you think . . . I mean, this portal, is it close?"

"I don't know, Kate."

"What are you implying? He's trying to break through into the Fáil? While we're still here?"

"I think that's the idea."

Kate shook her head. She would have screamed if screaming did any good. "Mo—I sense that Alan is near. He's really close."

"Where?"

"I'm not sure."

As Kate turned, searching for Alan, there was another enormous explosion. It felt as if an atomic bomb had gone off somewhere close—not that Kate had ever been near an atomic bomb, but she'd seen films and she could altogether imagine it. In a gap in the whirling vapors of red, turquoise and black she glimpsed the reclining hill of scaly flesh that was Driftwood. He looked stunned. His eyes were half closed, his expression bewildered. His gargantuan frame was floating slowly away from the site of the explosion. Yet, as far as she could see, he was physically undamaged.

And then Kate heard Fangorath roar again. She made him out some distance away, arms windmilling as if clawing his way through the maelstrom, following one of the black arms of a spiral of matter or energy or whatever it really was, to approach an ovoid shape.

Kate blinked. Or at least she imagined she blinked—she was no longer sure how substantial anything, or anyone, was here. The ovoid was gleaming and semitransparent. It might have been a gargantuan crystal.

Drifting closer, there was something a little too perfect about it—something mathematical. Its axes were delineated, as if its creator had left the original drawings in space after its construction, so it was cut through by sectors like the slices of an orange, which, as it slowly rotated, proved to be glowing. It must mean something but it was beyond Kate's ability to understand. As the titan neared the ovoid she saw that it was truly colossal, dwarfing the demigod like a bat against the moon. It seemed, perhaps, like some gigantic oraculum of power in which mysteries came into being and dissolved into unbeing, second by second—and from which radiating arcs of power, like luminescent smoke, billowed out into the surrounding chaos.

The Third Portal to the Fáil!

Kate gazed on it, stupefied with awe.

She could make out a ghostly outline within it, as if it contained an individual being. She sensed that the being was aware of her presence.

Kate found no comfort in that awareness. The being was cold, observing yet devoid of reaction, even as Fangorath began to batter against the shell of the ovoid with his claws and fangs. That coldness worried her. She flailed her legs and arms, every instinct telling her to swim away from it, her whole being overwhelmed by the sense of numinous power coming from the ovoid.

At last she found her voice: "Mo—help!"

Mo was fingering the glowing amulet around her neck. "I know, Kate. I sense it too. We have to get away from here—as quickly as possible."

But how could they escape? They were lost and powerless, free-floating, as if trapped within a dream. And then, as one, they saw Alan. He was clutched in the left hand of the titan. It was impossible to see whether he was still conscious or not. The titan must still be attempting to draw on the First Power, but Alan seemed to be resisting any manipulation. The oraculum in his brow looked dead. Mo was whispering to herself . . .

"True believers—if you can hear me . . . ?"

We hear you, child.

"What can we do to help Alan?"

The situation is fraught with peril, not only for your friend but for all that is blessed in this world. Escape is not possible through deliberate machination.

"There must be something we can do."

You must trust to Fate.

"Fate?"

Was it not Fate that brought you to this world? And allowed your companion to resurrect the King of Dragons? Is the Fáil not another word for this same almighty power?

"I don't understand."

Think you the Fáil will take kindly to such violent attempts at forced entry? Let Fate decide what it will.

Meanwhile, you are threatened merely by proximity to what will be. You are within the threshold of the gods.

Mo's eyes drifted to the stars within the vast metamorphosing clouds. There was an idea that was close to consciousness, but she couldn't quite grasp it. Her heart palpitated with a new fear. The stars appeared to be moving. She watched them, sensing that there must be something deeper, more important, that she was failing to grasp.

She whispered, urgently: "Kate—you must call the dragon."

"But how?"

How could she wake Driftwood out of his stupor?

"Use your oraculum."

Kate summoned up every fiber of what courage she had left: "Driftwood—if you can hear me—you have to wake up!"

Her eyes followed Mo's to the stars. They were aligning themselves into patterns.

The movement of the stars worried her. They couldn't be real stars, not suns out in the far reaches of space. Perhaps what she was seeing were images created by her own mind, symbols that represented something else entirely. And now the massive cloud formations were also changing. They were aligning about the focus of the ovoid. There was something about the patterns of the clouds, and the stars within them, that seemed frighteningly purposive.

The dragon groaned, as if waking up.

"Wake up, Driftwood—please."

Kate's frightened eyes returned to the portal. She didn't dare to attempt to make contact with the mind, or intelligence, that was harbored there.

She heard a rumbling incantation. Driftwood's eyes were blinking open—that sideways movement of the membrane she recalled.

If only she understood what was happening!

The danger, she sensed, was enormous and imminent.

Kate—girl-thing . . .

"Driftwood—thank God! There are frightening things going on all around us. I sense that it's important that I understand. But I don't understand a thing."

Girl-thing must flee!

"I can't. Alan is trapped by the titan—and Mo is here too."

Beside her, Kate saw that Mo's eyes were closed. There was a brilliance clutched between her fingers. Something pulsating, like . . . like the stars! The stars were pulsating in synchrony with what was glowing between Mo's fingers. And the movement of those stars was speeding up. Kate couldn't stop her jaw trembling as she spoke. "Mo—talk to me. Tell me what's going on!"

Mo whispered: "The True Believers are following the lines of Fate."

Oh, God!

Kate knew that she was going to die here, in this terrible and incomprehensible landscape, along with her friends.

Mo whispered again: "I think they're joining up in a kind of communion."

Then everything was moving in a frantic whirl around her. The stars were raining down on the figure of the titan, whose battering movements were faltering, slowing to a halt. It was all the more terrifying that it was happening in utter silence, as if the titan's screams were also being consumed. The stars were flowing along the arcs of force emerging from the portal. These were passing through the radiant substance of Fangorath— and in passing through him they were consuming him. His being, his soul being, was disintegrating.

Something long and sinewy lashed itself around Kate and Mo. They were spiraling through the air. Kate's heart faltered. In the silent pandemonium, overwhelmed by the violence that engulfed her, she was vaguely aware that another being was being pinned down close by them.

I so hope and pray it's Alan!

Then a dizzying sense of movement, movement so rapid she felt physically sick. She was blacking out. She welcomed the fading of her senses. The terror of what was happening was too much to bear.

A Painful Goodbye

Kate gazed about herself, bewildered by the valley that was already greened with wild grasses to midcalf. *Am I really responsible for that?* It seemed impossible to believe that this was the valley of the Tower of Bones. She had awoken in the dark, bewildered and alarmed, next to the sleeping forms of Alan and Mo. In her nostrils was the scent of wild flowers. She had sensed that Driftwood was nearby, though it had been pitch dark and impossible to see. The continuing messages of her senses had confused her. Her memories had confused her even more. She had lifted Alan's unconscious head onto her lap and . . . and had dozed off again. And now she had woken with a start to realize that dawn was breaking and Mo had disappeared. Meanwhile the world about her had turned to pandemonium.

Gargs! Thousands of them—maybe tens of thousands!

They were everywhere, in the air, alighting and taking off again. She hadn't noticed how they made a sound when flying. A flapping noise like swans, and sometimes a loud knocking sound like pigeons, when their wings, or maybe it was the claws on their wings, struck together with a particularly strong beat. Perhaps it was some kind of signal? Clusters of them were busy in the grass, doing things she failed to grasp, and making deep-throated humming sounds amongst themselves. She could even smell them, some secretion of all those thousands of bodies, but it wasn't an unpleasant smell. It was a . . . a vaguely homely smell, like the musky sweat of horses after a hard ride, or maybe the hot smell of Darkie, when she had hugged her dog after one of their walks by the river.

Oh, Darkie—how I miss you and Bridey!

Iyezzz was somewhere out there among them. He had brought her a drink in a brown-and-cream-colored nautilus shell—a fermentation that smelt briny and sweet at the same time, probably a mixture of things she didn't want to know about from the depths of the oceans, sweetened with honey. Was it possible that the Gargs were getting merry on it? It hardly seemed to fit with the images of Gargs she recalled from their duty at the Tower. But then nothing seemed to fit anymore.

Her eyes searched for Mo and Turkeya, finding them wandering through the grass in the distance, looking no doubt for herbs to collect. Briefly, surreptitiously, she gazed back over her shoulder, as if to confirm the dragon was still there. Though perhaps fifty yards distant there was no doubting his presence. He was so huge he seemed to press against all of her senses, even when she wasn't directly looking at him. His proximity stirred her but it also provoked a sense of guilt, knowing why such a strange and monstrous creature was waiting patiently in the meadow of grasses and wild flowers.

Alan woke, sitting up beside her. Kate put her arm about his shoulders, her eyes blinking slowly, still clearing themselves of what felt like the deepest sleep. A breeze blew about them, scattering pollen. She had another, longer, look around her. Nearby Qwenqwo and Ainé were keeping a close watch on the activity of the Gargs. In the distance, in his human form, Nightshade lifted his head and their eyes met. He must have been waiting for her to wake. Now he held her gaze for several moments before transforming into the shape of the wolf and loping wordlessly away.

"Is it really over, Kate?"

Alan was rubbing the sleep from his eyes. She laid her head against his shoulder, relieved to hear his voice. "Don't you remember what happened?"

"I remember some of it—I remember the attack."

"You did it, Alan. You destroyed the Witch."

Climbing to her knees, Kate compressed her lips while running her fingers through his ash-grimed hair.

He said: "I remember that much. But then . . ."

She held his face, gazing into his eyes. "It was the titan, Fangorath, all along. He was controlling her. He tried to feed off you."

Alan looked down at the grasses sprouting between his outstretched feet. He pulled out a grass-head and stuck the stalk between his teeth. Kate was startled at the passion of recall his action elicited—a memory of their climb to the top of the Comeragh Mountains, that day when they sensed the calling for the first time . . . But here and now Alan had just spotted Driftwood. He was staring at the recumbent figure of the dragon, the grass stalk tumbling from his open mouth.

"That what I think it is?"

Kate nodded.

"Fangorath was too powerful to be destroyed by the First Power. You must have put two and two together—realized that he was feeding off you. We saw how you stopped the oraculum." She couldn't keep the jitter of nervousness out of her voice. He knew her too well not to notice. And the same tension had entered her hand now as she brushed his upturned stubbly cheek.

Alan frowned. "But the Witch was destroyed by then?"

"Yes."

"So—the titan was controlling her, and not the other way round?"

"Fangorath planned to take over the Fáil."

"What?" Alan was dumbfounded. He climbed, a little shakily, to his feet and gazed down at her.

Kate nodded. "Mo and I, we saw what happened."

"You saw the portal?"

"Yes. You were unconscious." Kate spoke softly, anxious not to distress him. "Fangorath tried to break into it."

"Heck—and I don't recall a thing!"

"It's probably as well." Kate wished that she had no memory of those terrifying events. Mo had talked about Dromenon but to Kate it had seemed more like hell. "If Fangorath had succeeded he'd have taken you through with him." She kissed him on the lips. "Thank goodness he didn't."

Alan was silent for several moments, shocked. "Why would Fangorath—a demigod—want to take over the Fáil?"

"I don't know."

He shook his head. "What stopped him?"

Kate shook her head. "It became really strange. Fate intervened. Or so Mo said."

"Mo?"

"Mo is changing, Alan. She has some new amulet— she calls it the Torus. She hears voices coming out of it. They told her it was something to do with Mórígán, how she broke the rules to stop Fangorath a long time ago."

Alan stared about himself, utterly bemused.

Kate kissed him, holding him close. She recalled the extraordinary scene again, the impression of vastness—of dangerous, implacable power. It was only natural that they were all feeling somewhat overwhelmed by things. She lifted her head to gaze into the near distance, as if to reassure herself that the Tower really was gone. Where it had stood was nothing more than an ash-covered hole in the ground.

Alan was staring up into her eyes. He needed more explanation. She said, "If it will help, it all happened in Dromenon. There were beings that looked like stars."

He nodded slowly. "True believers!"

"That's what Mo called them. Their voices were coming to her though the Torus." Kate hugged him tight again. "You encountered them earlier yourself. You told me about it."

"Yes, I did. When Valéra was dying." He sat erect, looked at her, brushed her blustering hair from her eyes. "It was kind of frustrating. They talked in riddles."

Kate laughed. He managed a wan smile. It was so nice to see him smile again. "From what Mo was telling me, they haven't changed."

Kate so wanted to hold onto this moment.

All of a sudden there were cries of excitement from the Gargs. Glancing over, she saw that the Garg king, Zelnesakkk, had arrived, alighting among the milling throng of his subjects. Iyezzz strode forward to greet him, going down onto one knee before his father. The King reached out and brushed his son's brow. Kate saw Iyezzz point with a wing talon in their direction, then indicate with a widespread flourish of wings the landscape with its profusion of life.

Alan sighed, climbing to his feet, brushing ash from his hair and clothing. He extended an arm to help Kate to her feet. "I'm going to have to talk to them."

"There's something I need to do as well."

"Is that why the dragon is waiting?"

"Perhaps."

"You're going to leave me already?"

"The Cill helped save me from the Witch. But the Momu is dying. The Witch all but destroyed her people."

"And you think you can cure her?"

"I might be able to help."

"How?"

"I'm not sure. I just know I must try." She hugged him again, tightly, fiercely. "I hope I won't have to leave you for long." She hesitated. "You could come with me?"

"I wish I could. But the Tyrant is still out there." His head fell and he looked deeply thoughtful. "And there's some unfinished business with the Kyra."

Kate looked into his eyes and sighed.

"Hey, I know." He brushed the back of his hand against her face. "We're going to need the help of the Gargs. Will you help me—come speak to the King with me? He's more likely to listen if we do it together."

"Of course I will. Just give me a few minutes."

Kate stared at the great shape, laid down in a bed of long grass in the shade of a feathery leafed tree, with those enormous orange eyes patiently watching her. The others, Qwenqwo, Mo, the Shee, and most especially the Gargs, were keeping a respectful distance from the dragon. She went onto tiptoe to kiss Alan's lips, before walking through the field of ash, leaving footprints as if in virgin snow.

* * *

When the time came, Kate couldn't bear to hug Alan again before turning to face the dragon. She left Alan preoccupied in conversation with the King and Iyezzz, and she hugged Mo and Turkeya instead, and said good-bye to the Kyra, Ainé, and of course, the dwarf mage, Qwenqwo, whose emerald eyes bristled with tears. Iyezzz had assured Alan that the Gargs would assist the party in getting back to the beach head. They would also help the main army find a new route out of the bridgehead and into the main landmass of the Southern Wastelands, from where Alan and Ainé would begin the coming campaign of all-out war against the Tyrant and his armies. And so, with all the loose ends tied up here, Kate finally approached the dragon, who waited patiently for her in the long grass, observing her every move.

He lowered his head to the ground in acknowledgment as she drew near. Yellow pollen from the proliferating young trees gusted in the breeze.

Kate hesitated a short distance away, keeping enough distance so she could comfortably look up into his eyes. They appeared to be the same eyes she recalled, bulging orbs of a brilliant orange, but now they were as big as tractor wheels. The crescents of pupils yawned, lustrous mirrors in which she saw her own reflection. When she spoke, she couldn't stop her voice from quavering:

"Are you really my Driftwood?"

His answering whisper vibrated in the rocky ground beneath her feet. "You know that is not my name."

"Even so, it's how I want to remember you."

"Then Driftwood it shall be."

"Thank you—for saving us!"

The great eyes blinked, that strange membrane flitting sideways over them.

"I returned what you so generously gave me."

"I . . . I didn't know—when we met earlier—that you were some kind of a god."

"I had forgotten myself."

She hesitated, a wan smile drifting over her face. "It's pathetic, I know, but I want to remember you as my friend. But now you're not little anymore. You're not pining for your shiny things."

"I recall the pleasure of grooming your hair."

There was a new commotion among the Gargs. A great flock of them appeared in the sky, bearing some huge burden. Kate stared in astonishment at the gigantic leafless tree they were carrying into the valley. They had dug up the upended tree from the cavern of the City of the Ancients. Hundreds of Gargs milled about in the air and on the ground, maneuvering the enormous structure into the precise position where the Tower had stood. She watched as they rotated it around, so the roots were once more facing the ground and the branches returned to the original crown.

"What are they up to?"

"They are constructing a new altar."

"An altar to what?"

"To life—what you have returned to them!"

There was a whispered discussion, and then the masses of Gargs spread out, forming a triangle, its apex directed to where Kate was standing. The stubborn old shaman, Mahteman, appeared before them, casting pollen onto the breeze. The Gargs went down onto their knees, spreading their wings flat on the ground in homage.

"What do they want?"

"Your blessing."

The Gargs were intoning some kind of hymn. Kate wiped the tears from her eyes with the back of her forearm. She couldn't even pretend to understand the monumental events that were taking place here, in the valley of the Tower of Bones.

Bending down, she picked up a handful of the pollen that covered the ground at her feet. She held it in her open palm, facing the Gargs, and she blew on the pollen, gazing out at them and at the altar they had constructed of the fossil tree. She had no need even to think of what they wanted of her. Her oraculum flared.

She watched as the tree sprouted buds and, within moments, fresh green leaves. The old shaman fell onto his knees in front of her and chanted again—two names, it now seemed. One of them was Omdorrréilliuc, and the second, sounding utterly alien to Kate's ears, must be her own: Greeneyes, the life-giver!

The dragon rumbled: "I think it is time."

Kate turned away from the chanting Gargs. She smiled up at the dragon. "You're so restless. You can't wait to leave?"

"A sea dragon hungers for the deep."

She closed the small distance between them, then reached out to touch him, the lowest edge of one nostril, which was as high as she could reach. She brushed her fingers against the scaly flesh, as hard as iron.

"Will you take me back—to Ulla Quemar?"

"Yes."

"Then you understand . . . ?"

"A new Momu must be born."

He made a staircase of one wing so she could climb to the natural seat at the back of his neck, between the mountainous shoulder-blades, amid the brilliant green and yellow feathers of his ruff. Even climbing onto his neck, ascending the valley between his wings, the ground already seemed so far below it was like sitting on the top of a tall building. Kate discovered a secure-looking perch. She lashed herself to him, using some of the finest feather-hairs, which were as tough to manipulate as cables. She became aware of the extraordinary silence that had taken hold of the multitude below, the gathering of the Gargs, now on their feet. Her eyes found Alan, leaning on his spear, in the company of Mo, Turkeya, Qwenqwo and the towering figure of Ainé. They were all watching her. Tears sprang into her eyes. As she lifted her hand to wave the great wings were already starting to beat.

"The ocean is in your eyes again."

"I know."

Already they were rising. The power in each massive wing-beat simply took her breath away.

"Driftwood dreams of eatings."

"Stop it!"

"Ummmm! Of swallowing um whole, squirming and wriggling!"

"Please don't."

Her eyes still wept, but her tears had turned to laughter. She shrieked with the mad, careening pleasure of winged flight, clinging on to whatever came to hand in the nest of dragon feathers as they soared into the sky.

"Juicy bones—crunchy!"

At Feimhin's Grave

Mark kissed Nan in the grass down by the river, ignoring the rain bucketing down on them out of a cloud-wracked sky. She was wearing the familiar white linen gown edged with silver he remembered from the vision through the stellate window. The material was so gossamer-fine it clung to her skin with the rain. She must have worn the same gown two thousand years before at the very moment when she had been subsumed by the Third Power. The very thought of it caused him to laugh with disbelief before taking a shuddering breath.

We're alive! We made it!

He took a deeper, gulping breath. His limbs felt jittery, as if unsure of themselves, but they also felt healthy. His heart was pounding but it was through excitement—sheer exhilaration!

She whispered, "Do you love me still?"

He kissed her again. They kissed one another with their eyes wide open. Neither could get enough of just looking at the other—of staring into each other's eyes—of touching, holding, hugging, kissing.

"I damn-well adore you."

He too was wearing the same clothes as when he had been subsumed, the leather jacket over the Olhyiu seal skins. But now the jacket felt too small. That puzzled him until he realized that he must have grown. The oracula were still present in both their brows. He could see Nan's and he could feel his own, pulsating strongly. He brought his left hand back over his shoulder to confirm that the battleaxe was also there, suspended in the leather harness. He got to his knees so he could shed the harness. Then he removed the jacket, wrapping it about her shivering body.

He reckoned that it was the closing hour of daylight in what, judging from the yellowing of the leaves, must be early autumn.

The doctor's house. Clonmel—Earth!

Just the thought of it was enough to make him want to shout out with triumph. He felt giddy. When he staggered onto uncertain feet, it provoked a roaring in his ears. In restrapping the battleaxe to his rain-soaked back, rivulets of static electricity, like minuscule bolts of lightning, ran over his body before discharging through his feet into the earth. He helped Nan onto her feet in the sodden grass, supporting her unsteady legs.

Even as he struggled to comprehend what was happening, a blue-black flame burst out of his brow. The clouds became transparent, so he could see beyond them to something else: a streamlined raptor shape, shimmering against the fading blue of evening. It had been the oraculum that had erupted into blue-black fire. Maybe it was the same power that had burned the poisons out of his blood?

She whispered, "You're growing a boyish beard."

He felt at his chin and confirmed it. So much appeared to have changed! He hugged her, supported her with his arm around her shoulders, kissed her blue-black hair, flattened to her brow.

Their muscles were still jittery as they walked up the garden through the mud and puddles. The Doctor's House looked every bit as strange as he remembered it from when he and Mo had occasionally met up here with Kate and Alan. He looked up at the Georgian paned windows, standing proud of the walls with their bases and porticos, and the pentagonal tower on the corner with its dilapidated flagpole, bearing the drooping tricolor. They made their way to the heavy front door, where he knocked hard enough to be heard in the cavernous old building, his teeth chattering and his fingers trembling.

"Hello, Bridey! I'm Kate's friend, Mark."

The stout woman who came out of the door in response to his knocking narrowed her eyes against the downpour. A small black and white sheepdog—Mark recognized Kate's beloved Darkie—scampered about her ankles, her feet wrapped in worn-out slippers on the worn stone step. She stared at him, and then at Nan.

"And who's she?"

"Nan—Nantosueta! Queen of Ossierel!"

Bridey exclaimed: "Glory be!"

An attack of the shivers ran through Mark's body. "Sorry if we've startled you, Bridey. But we're freezing out here."

"Ye better come in, then, young Mark—ye and yeer Queen. Sure ye look like a couple of drownded rats!"

"Are ye ghosts?"

"No. But I can imagine we might look like it."

Their arrival had been a considerable shock to her. And it wasn't likely to get any easier. But there was also something disturbing about Bridey's appearance. She looked bleary-eyed and disheveled. They were sitting on either side of the big square table in the kitchen, on which Mark had placed the Fir Bolg battleaxe. Upstairs he had discovered some jeans and a denim shirt belonging to Kate's uncle, Fergal, that went close enough to fitting him, and Nan was wearing jeans and a knitted sweater of Kate's. She looked remarkably close to how he had imagined her in Dromenon. Upstairs he had also found the bathroom, with its sink-top mirror. The face that gazed back at him from the glass looked like somebody else's. A grown-up man's face with a sprinkle of gingery blond beard. He had shaved off that beard with

Fergal's razor. And he had stared at the clean-shaven face that remained, stared at the black triangle, with its metamorphosing arabesques of silver pulsating in time with his heartbeat.

Nothing is the same . . .

He had to force the memory out of his mind as he now sipped at a mug of strong coffee by the big square table. "Bridey—Kate's alive."

Bridey's face paled. But still there was a dogged look in her eyes. "Alive . . . ?"

She was sitting in a chair across from him, her elbows resting on the table, rubbing work-reddened hands one over the other. Her eyes stared fixedly at the rune-glowing blades of the battleaxe. Darkie whined, twining itself around her feet. Nan, a glass of water clutched in her hand, stood in the doorway and stared about the kitchen, with its pots and pans, and the turf fire blazing in the cast-iron range.

Bridey exhaled. "Are ye goin' to tell me what happened to Kate?"

"I'm afraid that you'll find it hard to believe." Mark took a breath. "And I need to know if you're on your own here."

"Fergal doesn't spend much time here any more—not now . . ." Her eyes grew moist, but she shook it off. "Sure I can't wait all day. Why, ye're making me dizzy just looking at the pair a ye. There are rainbows running over yeer skin."

Mark nodded, then began to tell her their story. It took him quite a while. Darkie seemed to lift up its eyes every time he mentioned Kate's name. When he got to the part where Kate was injured, Bridey poured herself a large whiskey. Mark had the impression this was nothing unusual for Bridey these days. She grabbed the dog by the scruff of the neck and hauled it up onto her lap, fondling it distractedly, squashing its ears flat onto its head as she listened and, when she needed to, she asked questions. She seemed unable to keep eye-to-eye contact with Mark. Her gaze kept wandering back to the battleaxe, with its glowing blades.

"Sure it's the strangest story I've ever heard."

"I suppose it must be."

"You say that Kate's lost? She's a prisoner of a . . . a witch?"

"So Alan told me. By the time that happened I was . . . Well I was out of the picture."

"And that's why I haven't heard a word from her in two years?"

Mark thought: *Two years! In Tír it had seemed no more than one.*

"She's a prisoner—but alive, as far as I know. Alan has gone to rescue her, with the help of the army of the Shee."

"Dear lord!" Bridey's hands loosened on the dog, which took the opportunity of scrambling out of her lap. But it only moved a foot or two away from her, staring up at her bewildered face. "Sure none of it makes a bit of sense!"

Mark hesitated, uncertain how to convince Bridey of what he was telling her. "Look at me, Bridey. Look at my face!"

Bridey's gaze lifted to Mark's face, her eyes fastening on the black triangle in his brow. She could hardly miss the silver motes and arabesques that were pulsating within it in time with his heartbeat.

"Look at Nan—at her face."

Bridey gazed from one to the other.

"They're not birthmarks." Mark's own eyes wandered over the central portion of the table surface, which was covered by an accumulation of newspapers. Everywhere he saw pictures of a world in turmoil. Buildings, whole streets, in flames.

"There's something going on here. I didn't guide the Temple Ship to you, Bridey. I had the image of the sawmill in my mind."

Bridey sighed, looking down at the dog.

"You know, just to look at us, that we haven't come from anywhere normal or nice. But things seem to be wrong here too. What's going on?"

Bridey murmured, barely audibly, but clearly expecting him to hear. "Could be that madman of a father sent ye?"

The triangle pulsated violently in Mark's brow. It brought a rush of sweat to his face.

"What has Grimstone got to do with it?"

"Don't pretend ye don't know."

"What am I supposed to know?"

"What he did to Padraig!"

"What did he do, Bridey?"

"Them eejits burned his sawmill to the ground."

Mark stared once again at the pile of newspapers—at the mayhem in the pictures all over the pages. *Has Bridey been gathering newspapers—hoarding them for some particular reason?*

"Padraig was hurt?"

"Dead—so the guards have assumed. Though such was the intensity of the heat there was nothing left of him."

Mark slumped in his chair. "When did this happen?"

"Barely a month ago."

"And Grimstone was behind it—you're sure?"

"His eejit sect."

"Bridey, could you possibly find us some boots for our feet? We need to go to Padraig's mill. See what happened for ourselves."

Bridey stared back at him, a hard glint entering her eyes. "Then ye should look harder at them papers."

Mark began searching through the newspapers, page by page. There was a pile of them, going back several months. With a snort of impatience, Bridey grabbed one of them, a Dublin-based broadsheet. She opened it out onto two central pages. She tapped with her finger at the single picture that took up two-thirds of the pages. It showed hooded figures running from a chasing pack of uniformed men wearing riot gear. They were silhouetted against the flames. The headline read: NEW OUTBREAK OF RIOTS IN LONDON.

Mark felt the triangle pulsate in his brow.

"Nan!" He spoke quietly. "Come look at this!"

She came and stood beside him, gazing down at the shields of the uniformed figures, which displayed a silvery logo. It looked like a very familiar triple infinity.

Bridey watched them, her eyes filled with suspicion. Mark took hold of her unresisting hand. "You recognized the symbol, didn't you?"

"It's the same as Grimstone's eejit sect."

Mark looked more closely at the newspaper picture. "These people dealing with the riots—they don't look like ordinary police."

Bridey's glare was unrelenting. "Paramilitaries, they call themselves."

Mark was silent for several minutes, working his way more carefully through the mass of newspapers, which detailed riots going on for months in London as well as several other major cities in Britain.

He heard the gurgle of Bridey pouring herself a second whiskey, the swig of her downing half of it in one.

The following morning Mark hesitated in the area that had formerly been the sawmill yard, swiveling the battleaxe around in his left hand. The best Bridey could find for him were some ancient forestry boots that had belonged to Kate's grandfather. They laced to just below his knees, their uppers now coated in ash. Nan wore one of Kate's hooded cagoules over the thick-knit sweater and blue jeans, with the yellow calf-length Wellingtons Bridey had found for her. Around them there was nothing left standing of the great sheds that had stored the lumber. The redbrick house was gutted and roofless. Tatters of rugs and remnants of furniture had been hauled out of the wreckage and lay scattered over the yard. Mark's gaze picked out some framed photographs, trodden into the dirt.

Is Padraig really dead?

Mark thought about what Bridey had said. No remains had been found in the ruins. The authorities had naturally assumed the worst, putting the lack of a body down to the intensity of the fire.

Their den was wrecked, the door hanging askew from a single contorted hinge. He looked down at the stump of the old pear tree, where the four friends had sat out of the sun and listened to Padraig's fables. The tree had been sawed off close to ground level, used maybe to fuel the flames. He walked over to the smithy, with its blackened iron chimney, peering into the trashed inside. The anvil still stood, half hidden in the debris of the roof. Here, in the blistering heat of the furnace, with sparks flying, Mark had helped Padraig to forge the Spear of Lug.

He mused aloud: "Bridey's right. Grimstone couldn't have done this on his own."

Nan sniffed at the air, like a cat. "There were many."

What was it Bridey had called them? *His eejit sect.* Local people, Mark assumed. Local idiots who had been brainwashed by Grimstone. Mark looked across to Nan, who stood twenty yards away, her jeans and sweater almost luminescent against the black of the ash. It was strangely comforting to see her wearing Kate's old clothes. She had also washed her blue-black hair in Bridey's sink, before gathering it up in a purple scrunchie. He watched her throw her head back, eyes closed, sniffing further at the air.

"I cannot sense death!"

"You think you'd be able to smell it—even after such a furnace?"

"I would sense it."

Mark fell silent a moment, just looking at her and feeling the wave of love that swept over him. But there was something else missing here. Padraig had brought down the ancient bronze Fir Bolg battleaxe that had decorated a lintel over the barrow grave. Mark wondered if the historic battleaxe was still here, lost in the tumbled walls and fire-ravaged ruins.

"You really think Padraig escaped?" she interrupted his musing.

"Or they took him away."

Grimstone liked to possess people. He had kept Mark and Mo alive when he could easily have killed them. He liked to possess people even when he hated them. It allowed him to torment them. There was no mystery as to where "the eejits" had gone after they had razed the sawmill. The trail led upland—into the rain-swept trees.

The last time Mark was here, Padraig had led the way with a machete. Today Mark led with his own Fir Bolg battleaxe, hacking at the nettles and brambles at the edges of Padraig's woods, then climbing higher within the deciduous forest that grew thick and shady over the foothills of the Comeraghs. Their jeans were soaked from brush and brambles, and their hair plastered to their heads from droplets falling from the disturbed foliage overhead, before they arrived at the coppice of oaks that Mark remembered, trees hoary with age, with gaps where branches had been torn from them by winter storms. The mound was there, at least what was left of it after Grimstone's fanatics had torn away its roof with picks and shovels. With the loss of the roof the octagonal stone-lined chamber had been exposed to the weather. The stones of the upper walls lay broken and scattered amid the white fragments of bone.

Nan asked him: "What is this place?"

"It's a barrow—the Grave of Feimhin." Mark stared about himself in sorrow. "Padraig was its guardian. Alan's mother was an O'Brien—Padraig's daughter. She ran away to America to escape the burden."

Nan nodded—who better to understand that sense of burden. For two thousand lonely years her soul spirit had protected her island fortress in the Vale of Tazan.

Mark climbed down into the open wound of the grave. He ran his fingers over some of the broken lines of Ogham. He recalled Padraig's words, when he had attempted to explain things that had seemed too preposterous to be taken seriously. Now those words seemed altogether prophetic.

"What did the writing say?"

"It described a history of terrible things from long ago."

Mark pointed to the flat oblong of stone in the center of the chamber. "There was a skeleton laid out here—a warrior, dressed in armor. Padraig said his name was Feimhin—a prince from the Bronze Age—maybe four thousand years ago."

His eyes searched the debris-strewn floor, poking and probing with the blade of the battleaxe, until he found a piece of the green-tarnished armor, what looked like a cheek-plate.

"The sword is gone."

"The sword? This is what they came for?"

"Padraig treated it with great respect. There were warnings all over the walls. He told us the sword was dangerous."

"How dangerous?"

"It had the triple infinity symbol on the hilt. Padraig showed us what it meant. Even after thousands of years the blade was ominous with magic—loaded with some kind of killing frenzy."

Mark climbed back out, the Fir Bolg battleaxe strapped across his back. He couldn't suppress an involuntary shiver. "The Ogham inscriptions talked about war—never-ending war."

"Like Tír?"

"Exactly like Tír. So long as Prince Feimhin lived, and he had possession of the sword."

Frank P. Ryan

"And now Grimstone has it?"

Mark nodded. He was reflecting back on those pictures in Bridey's newspapers. Riots. The streets of London in flames.

"Oh, Mark—what does this mean?"

"I'm not sure. But I wonder if it could have been the sword that really brought Grimstone here to Clonmel."

"To what purpose?"

"He already had his twisted cross. At least it looked like a cross, forged out of some blackish metal. But it wasn't a cross. It was what remained of a dagger. Like the dagger of the Preceptor that Alan fought by the river."

"Grimstone—he's a Preceptor?"

"I don't know what he is. With the sword I dread to think what he might become."

Nan came over to hold him.

Mark took a deep breath. Leaning back against the rain-soaked trunk of an ancient oak tree, he stared down into the valley of the Suir, the road junction by the ruined sawmill far below them, and the little Irish town of Clonmel, with its smoking chimneys, stretching out in the distance around the silvery stream of the river.

He thought: *Riots in London—and Grimstone has the Sword!*

ACKNOWLEDGMENTS

I SHOULD BEGIN WITH A "HUNDRED THOUSAND thanks" to my agent Leslie Gardner for her encouragement and guidance over several years. It was Leslie's influence that led to what promises to be an exciting and creative symbiosis with my publisher, Jo Fletcher, of Jo Fletcher Books. My thanks also to David V Barrett, who was tough with me when I needed it, and to my copy editor Seán Costello, who was perceptive and sensitive as a good copy editor must be. It is a special pleasure to acknowledge Brendan Murphy, whose practical support was helpful from the outset, and Mark Salwowski, whose artistry has been much appreciated over the years. Finally, I am indebted to my wife, Barbara, for her enduring patience and indefatigable support.

www.frankpryan.com

About the Type

Text set in Utopia Regular at 10/14.25pt.

Utopia is a multifunctional typeface designed by Robert Slimbach in 1989. It is solidly based on types of the eighteenth-century, with the addition of contemporary type innovations.

Typeset by Scribe Inc., Philadelphia, Pennsylvania